fourpla~~y~~

Jane Moore is a columnist for the *Sun* and writes articles for the *Sunday Times*. She regularly presents documentaries, including the hugely successful 'Supermarket Secrets' for Channel 4's *Dispatches*, *The Beckhams* for Sky One, and *Spoilt Kids*, also for Channel 4. She is also the author of the bestsellers *Fourplay*, *The Ex-Files*, *Dot.Homme* and *The Second Wives Club*. She lives in London.

'Moore's endearing exuberance and sense of humour are seductive' *The Times*

'An hilarious and assured modern-day Jane Austen romp' *GQ*

'A feel-good read, which sparkles with her trademark funny one-liners' *Elle*

'Delicious, duplicitous fun' *heat*

'Moore's slickly plotted, sassy tale takes a look at the highs and lows of being newly single' *Cosmopolitan*

'A terrific read . . . great characters, great plot and great writing . . . Deserves to be a big fat hit, and I can't wait for more from Moore' Jonathan Ross

'Fancy an extended gossip session with mates? Well, that's exactly what Jane Moore's novel feels like . . . Hilarious cynicism about relationships will appeal to anyone who's ever lost in love. As therapeutic for heartbreak as a voodoo doll!' *Glamour*

Also by Jane Moore

The Ex-Files
Dot.Homme
The Second Wives Club

JaneMoore
fourplay

arrow books

Published by Arrow Books in 2006

5 7 9 10 8 6

First published in the United Kingdom in 2001 by Orion Books Ltd

Arrow Books
The Random House Group Limited
20 Vauxhall Bridge Road, London, SW1V 2SA

www.rbooks.co.uk

Addresses for companies within The Random House Group Limited
can be found at:
www.randomhouse.co.uk/offices.htm

The Random House Group Limited Reg. No. 954009

A CIP catalogue record for this book
is available from the British Library

ISBN 9780099498445

The Random House Group Limited makes every effort to ensure that the
papers used in its books are made from trees that have been legally
sourced from well-managed and credibly certified forests. Our paper
procurement policy can be found at: www.randomhouse.co.uk/paper.htm

Typeset by Palimpsest Book Production Limited,
Polmont, Stirlingshire
Printed and bound in the United Kingdom by
Cox & Wyman Ltd, Reading, Berkshire

For Mum and Ellie

'All this divorce – when I meet a man now, the first thing I think about is: is this the sort of man I want my children to spend their weekends with?'

RITA RUDNER

Part One

1

To this day, she doesn't know what made her do it. Feminine intuition perhaps.

The day started the same as any other. Jo was rushing around getting the kids ready for school; Jeff was rushing around thinking only of himself. As usual, he had already asked several moronic questions as if he were merely a guest in the house in which they'd lived for four years. 'Where are the clean towels? Is there any milk? How does the central heating timer work? We're running out of loo roll.' And so on. It was a never-ending assault on Jo's senses, like having a third child.

Trouble was, Jeff was one of those men who had grown up with a mother who did everything for him. All his life, he had been accustomed to just dropping an item of clothing on the floor and not seeing it again until it miraculously reappeared in his wardrobe, washed, ironed, and hung neatly on a padded hanger. Jo suspected Jeff's mother prided herself on being there to catch her son's discarded clothing before it touched the floor. There was little doubt she had been disappointed by her son's choice of such a shambolic, dishevelled wife.

This morning, the Planet Hollywood T-shirt Jo had worn in bed the night before was tucked into a pair of baggy-bummed, black tracksuit bottoms, and her dark blond hair was scraped back into a messy ponytail. On her feet were a pair of those flat, airline socks designed for people with no ankle, heel or arch.

Thomas and Sophie were sitting at the breakfast table. Thomas, who was eight, wore only the bottoms of his Batman pyjamas; the top was tied around his head like a pint-size commando. His shock of blond hair was in its early morning Woody Woodpecker style, and he was spilling cornflakes over the floor as he turned to watch the TV set flickering in the corner.

Like most six-year-old girls, Sophie was in her pink phase. Barbie pink phase to be more precise, with Barbie nightdress and slippers, and a Barbie hairslide wedged on one side of her head, giving her hair the attractive swept-over look favoured by Arthur Scargill. She was drawing a misshapen heart on a piece of scrap paper with one hand and eating a jam-covered bagel with the other.

Jo was frantically buttering two rounds of Marmite sandwiches for their lunchboxes when Jeff burst into the kitchen adjusting his tie. He had two pieces of tissue stuck to his face where he'd cut himself shaving.

'Have you been using my razor on your legs again? It's blunt.'

'No.' Jo wiped a buttery finger on her trouser leg. Well, it wasn't strictly a lie. She *had* used the razor – but on her bikini line.

Jeff looked businesslike in a dark blue Jasper Conran suit and royal-blue shirt. His hair was still damp from the shower and combed back in the Gordon Gecko 'lunch-is-for-wimps' look favoured by the eighties yuppie. As soon as it dried it fell forward into a more attractive flop, making him look less like a solicitor, Jo thought. Jeff was a partner in a local practice that relied heavily on conveyancing work, divorces and legal aid cases. It wasn't exactly Kavanagh QC but it paid the bills.

'Where's my—'

'Behind the door.' Jo answered him before he could complete the question he asked every morning.

Grabbing his briefcase, he rushed up to each of the children and kissed the top of their heads.

'Be good, you two,' Jo mouthed to herself.

'Be good, you two.' Jeff's voice was in perfect sync with her mime.

'Daddy, look!' said Sophie excitedly, waving a scrap of paper at him as he headed out of the kitchen door. 'This is for you.'

Clearly irritated by this delay, Jeff stopped in his tracks and came back to the cluttered table where Sophie was brandishing her little drawing of a heart. 'To Daddy, lots of love, Sophie' was scribbled on it.

'That's a lovely apple, darling,' he said, glancing at it

then leaving it on the table. Jo's heart lurched as she saw the disappointment on her daughter's face.

'Silly Daddy, it's a heart, isn't it, sweetie?' she said, picking up the drawing and holding it out to Jeff. 'Here, take it to work and pin it on your wall.'

With an ostentatious I'm-a-terribly-busy-person sigh, he threw his briefcase on to the table and flipped open the lid. Inside was a packet of photographs. 'Oh here, I forgot. I got that film developed. There are some nice snaps of you and the kids from that weekend at your mum and dad's.' He threw the packet on the table.

'Thanks. What time will you be home tonight?' Jo tried desperately to sound casual. It was her greatest fear in life that she might turn into a nagging wife, but life with Mr Slippery sometimes made this hard to avoid.

'Not sure. Got a late meeting I think. Call you later.' And he was gone.

She stood and stared down the hallway as the front door closed behind him, and wondered at what point they had stopped communicating with each other. He had stopped kissing her goodbye in the mornings some months ago, and it now seemed their lives were linked by little other than the children and a hefty mortgage.

She sent the children upstairs for their morning ritual of washing faces and cleaning teeth, then wandered down the hallway to the large, sunny room at the front of their Victorian semi in leafy West London.

She stood in the bay window and let other people's

6

lives wash over her for a moment. The block of flats oppo-site was always a good source of amusement, whether it was the gay couple in 4c having a loud row with all the windows open, or Mrs Hobbs, the eighty-year-old woman who lived on the ground floor. Jo had made quite an effort to get to know her when they had first moved in, know-ing she would be useful for keeping a curtain-twitching eye on the house whenever they were out. Then, one day, when they were chatting about the other residents in the block, Mrs Hobbs had brought the subject round to the poetically suited Derek and Eric in 4c.

'They're homosapiens you know,' she whispered conspiratorially, screwing up her deeply wrinkled face in disapproval.

Jo laughed, and replied, 'So am I.' Mrs Hobbs had given her a wide berth ever since.

This morning, a smartly dressed young couple came out of the communal doorway, both clutching briefcases and umbrellas. It was starting to drizzle slightly, and he took her umbrella from her, opened it out, and handed it back. It was a simple act of consideration, but one that reminded Jo of how detached her and Jeff's lives had become. Those little gestures were so important. Someone pouring you a drink before you'd got round to asking for one, running you a bath because you looked tired, or opening your umbrella before you even thought of doing it yourself. The last time Jeff had done anything for her had been about six months ago when she was struck down by food poisoning. And that was only because he had to, she thought ruefully. The young couple shared a tender kiss and went their separate ways.

With a sigh, Jo walked back through to the kitchen, pausing briefly at the foot of the stairs. 'Get a move on you two, your uniforms are on your beds.' She picked up the photographs from where they lay on the kitchen table, half covering Sophie's heart drawing which, after all that, Jeff had forgotten to take.

The first two pictures were of her dad, Jim, peering round the door of his potting shed at her parents' Oxford home, where he did more pottering than potting. It was his bolt-hole from Jo's mother Pam, and he would spend his time reading old crime novels or trying to have a crafty fag without being nagged to death. Jo often wondered why they were still together as they seemed to have so little in common. A couple of years earlier she had asked her father that exact question and he'd replied, rather bitterly she thought, 'Saves spoiling another couple.'

The next few photographs showed her mother, pinched and uptight, standing with the children on the small patio area at the back of the house. She was not a naturally affectionate woman and obviously found it difficult having them to stay. Thomas hated going there because his grandparents' television was too old to accommodate his PlayStation – a blessed relief as far as Jo was concerned. The thought of her mother catching sight of 'Mortal Kombat' was right up there with another Status Quo comeback concert on the list of things you don't want to see.

And as for Sophie, Jo lived in constant fear of her breaking one of the hideous but plentiful ornaments that adorned the neat little bungalow with its ruched lace curtains and latticed windows.

Adding to the stress of staying with her parents was the fact that Jo worked as an interior designer, and had been itching to get her hands on their dreadful decor for years.

'Don't come here with your fancy ideas,' her mother said sharply when Jo once dared to suggest redecorating. 'We like it this way.'

The rest of the photographs were taken up with Sophie's sixth birthday party at the house, a couple of weeks after their Oxford visit.

Jo and Jeff had invited fifteen of Sophie's friends along and booked a children's entertainer to keep them occupied. But on the morning of the party 'Jolly Jake' had rung to say he had flu and couldn't make it, so Jeff got out his old guitar and tried to amuse the children with his appalling rendition of 'Smoke on the Water'. Within seconds of one of Sophie's more forward friends declaring, 'Your dad's crap,' he had resorted to putting on the Spice Girls CD and took several photographs of all the children high-kicking their way round the room to the torturous strains of 'Wannabe'.

Jo's brow furrowed as she patted the photographs into a neat pile to place back in the packet. There didn't seem to be enough. She counted them. Nineteen prints out of a possible twenty-four. Strange, she thought. The film had been developed digitally so there were no negatives, just a small plastic cassette. The contact sheet that usually came with them was nowhere to be seen.

'Can I see, Mum?' Thomas had come back downstairs and was looking over her shoulder. Sophie stood in the doorway picking her nose, with her school skirt tucked into the back of her knickers.

'No, we haven't got time now. You can both see them when you get back from school. Come on.' Jo stuffed the photographs into her overflowing handbag and they all headed out of the door.

It was still niggling her as she walked to the local shops after dropping off the children. Only nineteen prints and no contact sheet. Maybe the shop had cocked up the developing and were trying to pull a fast one. Most people would have let it go, but Jo could be obsessive about detail. Her best friend Rosie called her an anal retentive.

So, fifteen minutes later, she walked through Boots to the photographic counter at the back. The place was quiet except for a confused pensioner with a problem she couldn't quite get to grips with. The assistant was speaking in loud, deliberate tones.

'You've used the same film twice, madam,' she bellowed, showing the woman a picture of herself in ghostly form standing over some bougainvillea.

A bored second assistant came out from a back room. Silently, she extended a hand in Jo's direction.

'Hello, could I have another set of prints and a contact sheet off this please?' Jo handed over the little cassette.

'When d'ya want 'em for?' She had six gold studs in one ear and a necklace which spelt out the name 'Cheyenne'.

'Um, is one hour OK?'

'Cost ya.'

'That's fine. I'll be back at about ten-thirty then.'

She headed for a little French café just down the road, stopping briefly to buy a copy of the *Sun*. Heaven was a child-free time slot in which to read a newspaper from cover to cover.

Before Thomas and Sophie came along, she and Jeff had always enjoyed the same Sunday routine. They would sleep in late, then one or other would go downstairs and make a breakfast of fresh coffee, warm croissants, and scrambled eggs with smoked salmon. Then they would sit and eat in silence, each reading a different section of the *Sunday Times* and only conversing when a particular article prompted discussion.

Last Sunday, Thomas and Sophie had come into their room at 7 a.m., bickering about the ownership of a Cyberpet. Jo confiscated it from both of them and left Jeff to have a lie-in while she went downstairs and threw cereal into two bowls. As the children wolfed it down, she tried to read a three-day-old paper which had been left lying on the sideboard, but gave up after the fifth interruption from Sophie whinging about her brother's teasing.

11

Ordering a caffe latte, she settled down in a quiet corner of the café and lost herself in the day's news.

By the time she lifted her head and checked the time, it was 10.20. Leaving payment and a generous tip, she left and crossed the road to Marks & Spencer to stock up on food for the next couple of days.

It was the rule rather than the exception these days that she never knew when Jeff would walk in the door each night, so she'd pretty much given up any attempt at home-cooking. Instead she would buy a variety of precooked meals, and when she heard the key in the lock she'd take one out of the freezer, peel off the plastic film and stick it in the microwave. Frozen meal, frozen relationship.

It was 10.45 by the time she found herself back at Boots's photographic counter. Handing over the paper slip, she decided she'd look at the pictures there and then so she could point out any discrepancies immediately. Ripping open the packet, which definitely felt chunkier than the first one, she started sifting through the photos. Dad and his potting shed, Mum and the kids, Sophie dancing to the Spice Girls. Nestling halfway through the pile, between the Oxford visit and Sophie's birthday party, were the five missing photographs.

She looked in her early twenties, with hazel eyes and blonde curly hair down to her shoulders. In the first three pictures, she was lying on a brass bed that was covered in a thick white cotton throw. On the wall behind her head was a framed print of a Degas nude. Propped up by her

12

elbow on two square white pillowcases, the girl was wearing a thin-strapped, green, floral dress, her long legs outstretched. There was nothing on her feet but pastel-pink varnish, and her laughing face reached out towards the camera. By the fourth picture, one of the straps had fallen down her arm, revealing the firm, round top of a young breast. Her eyes were fixed on the lens, her mouth slightly open in a provocative fashion. This picture was at a slightly different angle and her bedside table was visible. Lying on it was the Tag Heuer watch Jo had bought Jeff for his thirtieth birthday. In the final shot she was naked, her legs modestly tucked to one side. Her arms were stretched above her head, making her full breasts look perfectly shaped, and her eyes were full of mischief. A small area of pubic hair was just visible – enough to register she was not a natural blonde.

She had absolutely no idea who the woman was, but Jo was sure of one thing. This picture was taken just seconds before she had passionate sex with whoever was behind the camera.

She knew she had stumbled across something she shouldn't have but, clutching at straws, she toyed with the idea that there had been some kind of mistake. It was what she needed to believe. She would go back to the counter and Cheyenne would tell her there had been a terrible mix-up.

'Don't worry, madam. Someone else's pictures have been muddled up with your own,' she'd say, 'so your husband hasn't been having sex with someone else after all. Have a nice day.'

Then she remembered the contact sheet that had been missing from the first packet Jeff had given her. Her fingers fumbling with nerves, she re-opened the new batch and pulled out the small contact sheet tucked inside. Taking a deep breath, her eyes ran along the tiny images in front of her. The five pictures were there, right in the middle.

Jo closed her eyes and started to sway unsteadily on her feet.

'You alright?' The assistant's voice startled her and she opened her eyes to find a concerned Cheyenne and her colleague staring at her.

'F-f-fine thanks.' She had to get out of here.

Tucking the pictures under her arm, she ran from the shop and didn't stop until she reached the busy junction at the end of the main street.

She had no idea how long she stood on the corner with cars speeding past her. It was as though the world had suddenly become a place she was no longer part of. Other shoppers looked curious as they walked past her, standing frozen, a carrier bag in each hand. Jo hardly registered them.

God knows, she tried to come up with an explanation, but there was no doubt about it.

Jeff was having an affair.

She got through the next few hours on automatic

pilot. The children were picked up from school, given tea, bathed, and finally – at 8.30 – they were asleep.

There was no sign of Jeff. He hadn't even called. He used to call up and bluster about some 'damn late meeting', but now he'd stopped bothering. It was taken as read that he'd be late home most nights, and she was generally too exhausted to care. There was a repetitive pattern to their evenings that made one completely indistinguishable from another. The only variant was the TV schedules. If Jeff got home before Jo had collapsed, exhausted, into bed, they would exchange a cursory, 'Hello, how was your day?' 'Fine thanks,' conversation, then sit in silence watching the television. Inevitably, about an hour after getting home, Jeff would fall asleep on the sofa, his mouth open, emitting loud snores. Jo would sigh, turn down the volume on the TV, then go upstairs and leave him to it. Most of the time he would wake up in the early hours and creep in beside her. Some mornings she came down to find him still scrunched up on the sofa.

It hadn't always been that way. When they first met they couldn't keep their hands off each other, even rushing home on the occasional lunch hour for a passionate session. Then the children were born. Now their sex life was more endangered than the Giant Panda.

On the rare occasions he showed an interest, Jeff would roll over and whisper, 'How about a quickie?'

As opposed to what? she thought to herself as he made the cursory attempt at foreplay by twiddling her nipple as if he were fine-tuning Radio Five.

'I think I'm hermetically sealed it's been so long,' Jo had said wistfully to her friend Rosie a few weeks earlier.

Now Jeff's lack of interest made perfect sense.

Jo watched *News At Ten*, but absorbed none of it. Bong! Jo Miles discovers photos. Bong! It has to be her husband's girlfriend. Bong! She castrates him.

All her thoughts centred on the moment when Jeff finally bothered to come home.

When the programme had finished she walked down their dark hallway and flicked on the kitchen light. The long wooden table in the centre of the room was cluttered with colouring books, papers, and unread newsletters from the children's school. Jo used her arm to sweep the lot onto the floor. She wanted a clean surface for what she was about to do. One by one, she placed the five photographs in a line across the centre of the table, in order of undress. Then she sat down in the large wicker chair at the far end and waited.

For half an hour, there was only the sound of the clock ticking and Jo's breathing. Then finally she heard a key in the lock. It was 11 p.m.

She heard Jeff's footsteps coming down the hallway before he peered round the kitchen door, surprise registering on his face. He had assumed she would be in bed by now. His dark brown hair looked mussed and his cheeks were bright red. His tie had been loosened and his suit looked like it had been trampled by a herd of wildebeest.

Crumpled of the Bailey. I wonder if he's been with her, thought Jo. She felt completely numb.

'Hello. I thought you'd probably have gone for an early night. What are you—' He stopped mid-sentence as he caught sight of the photographs. 'What are these?' He had gone deathly white and his pupils had expanded to the size of dinner plates.

Jo stared at him impassively, knowing it was important for her to stay calm at this point. She had to admit she was relishing his obvious discomfort. She glanced at the photographs again, before looking him straight in the eye.

'I was hoping you'd be able to tell me that.'

2

He stared at her like a rabbit caught in headlights. She could see he was desperate to come up with a simple explanation, but clearly knew there wasn't one. Running a hand through his hair, he sat down at the other end of the table and made an attempt to worm his way out of the situation.

'She's nobody, Jo, honest.' He looked beseechingly at her.

'Try again.' Her voice was clipped.

Jeff looked down at his feet. He was a solicitor and Jo knew he could recognise conclusive evidence when he saw it. There was no point lying. With no dramatic pause or build-up, he came out with it in a matter-of-fact, could-you-pass-the-salt kind of way.

'I've been seeing her for about six months.' He looked pathetically sheepish.

Six months. Six, deceitful, conniving, duplicitous bloody months, thought Jo as she struggled to take it in. Was this really happening? To her, Jo Miles? Right now she felt she was in the middle of someone else's nightmare or cruel joke.

'Are you in love with her?' The knot of emotion at the

back of her throat made it difficult to speak. She hoped – prayed even – that the answer would be no.

He said nothing for a moment, then slowly began to nod his head. 'I am, yes.'

The unmistakable feeling of cold fear began to creep along Jo's arms. Every major argument they had ever had became insignificant. People have arguments because they still care. This was different. She felt she was facing her emotional Armageddon. A million questions raced through her mind, but the raw need to know what she was up against won through.

'Who is she?'

She was fascinated by how calm she sounded. Fear of what was coming next had paralysed her senses. She waited for an answer from the man who now seemed like a complete stranger to her. Behind his head on the kitchen wall was a collage of family holiday snaps from over the years. Jeff holding Sophie as a baby, playing football on the beach with Thomas, the four of them tucking into a huge paella. In every picture they were all glowing with happiness.

'I said, who is she?'

She watched him shuffle uncomfortably and start picking at a piece of loose wickerwork on the arm of the chair. He didn't want to have this conversation. Jo knew he'd rather run out of the front door and put it all in a detailed letter. But there was no way she would let him get away with that.

'She's one of the secretaries at work.'

His voice was barely audible as he fixed his gaze on one of the Italian ceramic floor tiles they had spent a fortune on. The same tiles they had uncharacteristically made love on after a drunken night out two weeks earlier. It took a lot of alcohol these days. Jo burst into bitter laughter. For a second, she thought he must be joking, that this whole laughable scenario was his idea of fun and Noel Edmonds was going to walk through the door at any second clutching a 'Gotcha' trophy. But there was no tell-tale twinkle in Jeff's eyes nor even the faintest trace of a smirk.

'Oh God, the bloody boss-shags-secretary cliché,' she spat, close to hysteria now. 'No doubt you've told her your wife doesn't understand you or that I'm paralysed from the waist down.'

Sarcasm suited her mood right now. Other men were pathetic enough to go off with their secretaries, but not her husband. Not the man she had respected and trusted enough to marry and have children by.

Jeff's face was pinched. 'She's not a shag, Jo. I'm in love with her. Believe me, I've tried not to be, but I just can't stop it and I can't carry on pretending any more – it's not fair on you and the kids.'

The kids. The words snapped into her consciousness.

'Are we having this conversation because you're going to leave us?' Her voice sounded cracked and distant. She was beginning to feel *really* scared.

Jeff stood up and walked towards her. He knelt down in front of her chair and took her hands in his.

'I have to leave, Jo. Believe me, I would stay and sort things out if I could, but the whole thing is completely out of my control now and I can't contemplate life without her.'

He was looking up at her, waiting for a reaction. But Jo was completely numbed by what she'd just heard. She was bright, funny and self-motivated – she had to be. But when she stood at that altar, 'she' became a 'we'. They were a unit. Now she was terrified by the prospect of it ending.

'The last thing I wanted to do was hurt you,' he said softly, laying his head in her lap.

She sat staring down at the back of his head as the enormity of the situation began to sink in. 'But I know you'll be able to cope because you're so strong. She would fall to pieces if I left her. She's so vulnerable.'

Jo felt it slowly at first, a dull sensation that began in her chest and rose in a tidal wave through the rest of her body. A violent, unstoppable surge of pure anger.

Grabbing her half-empty coffee cup from the table, she used all the force she could muster to bring it smashing down on the back of his head.

'Jesus fucking Christ,' he cursed, his hand shooting to where a small trickle of blood was now mingling with the cold coffee. 'What the fuck did you do that for?'

But Jo didn't answer. She grabbed Jeff's head and pushed him to the floor with a strength that surprised even her, then leapt to her feet. As he scrambled around trying to stand up, she stood over him, her face twisting with rage and searing pain. At that moment, her loathing of him was absolute. Suddenly, he was standing in front of her.

'Jo, please . . .' He raised his arms as if he were about to embrace her, but her response was swift.

The first blow struck him across the right side of his face and he fell back against the oven door, gasping in pain as his lower back struck the handle. Jo couldn't have cared less. She flew at him, pummelling his chest with clenched fists until he managed to grab one of her arms and restrain her. Sobbing, she sank to the floor in front of him.

'Bastard . . . bastard,' she whispered, shaking her head in disbelief.

Jeff didn't move. Jo knew her extreme behaviour had stunned him because she'd never been the emotional sort. She hadn't even cried on their wedding day, but her mother had made up for that.

'Why *do* mothers always cry at their daughters' weddings?' Jeff had whispered in her ear as they walked back down the aisle to the sounds of her mother's loud nose-blowing.

'Because they know girls always marry a man like their father,' she'd laughed.

Now here she was crumpled at her husband's feet.

Bending down, Jeff gently placed a hand under her arm and helped her up. 'Sit down. I'll get you a drink.'

He walked over to the cupboard above the sink and got out the bottle of whisky they kept there. She watched as he poured a generous measure and placed it in front her. Amazing, isn't it? she marvelled to herself. Men spend their lives making decisions and cut-throat deals, planning wars, erecting buildings – or whatever it is they damn well do. Yet throw a bit of young totty in a short skirt into the mix and they all lose ability to take control of their lives. Here was the man she loved suddenly throwing everything away on the 'love' of someone he'd known five minutes. Another suspicion crept in. She had to ask.

'How old is she?'

'Is that relevant?'

'For fuck's sake, Jeff, we're not in court. Just answer the question.'

'Twenty-three.'

Her chair made a loud scraping noise as Jo pushed it backwards and stood up. Jeff flinched, expecting another blow to the head. But her desire to get away from him was all-consuming. She ran down the hallway and into the sitting room where she sat in darkness on one of the two faded floral sofas. Jeff followed her, as she knew he would, and switched on the lights. She winced at the brightness.

'Twenty-three? Jesus Christ. Are you seriously going to walk out on me and the kids because you want to shack up with some love-struck bimbo?' She hissed the words at him, mindful that Sophie's room was at the top of the stairs.

He stood there, fiddling with the corner of a framed stick-drawing Thomas had done at nursery school. A small amount of blood had now soaked into the back of his shirt collar. When he finally spoke, his voice was chillingly measured.

'She's not a bimbo, Jo. She's actually very bright and she knows what hurt all this will cause, but she feels the same way as me. It's unavoidable.'

Unavoidable. Un-bloody-avoidable. God, her husband could be a pompous prick when he wanted to be.

'No, Jeff. Paying tax is fucking unavoidable. Old age is unavoidable. But throwing away your marriage simply because some teenager bats her eyelids at you is entirely avoidable.'

For every crass remark he made, a thousand sarcastic retorts sprang into her mind. But she knew that whatever she said wouldn't be taken as common sense, simply the words of a bitter woman whose husband was about to leave her. It was no longer her and him against the world. It was him and the other woman against her. He had defended her when Jo called her a bimbo. No doubt they had been having cosy dinners and discussing the marriage. Mulling over how he would tell her, wondering how she would react, contemplating the effect on the children. How bloody noble of them.

'And as for her knowing what hurt this will cause, how the fuck can she? Does she have two kids she has to tell that their dad's walking out on them?'

She had no idea what was going through Jeff's mind at that precise moment, but she'd hazard a guess at, 'Beam me up Scotty.' He was rocking on his heels, his eyes fixed on the ceiling. His hands were tucked behind his back like Prince Charles when meeting the great unwashed. The emotional distance between them yawned, and Jo's anger subsided as she became overwhelmed by a sense of hopelessness and total incomprehension.

'I thought affairs were supposed to be a symptom of an unhappy marriage. I had no idea you were unhappy,' she faltered.

'I kept thinking things would get better, I really did. But we never seemed to talk about it.'

'You never brought it up.'

'No, but I shouldn't have to, should I? Isn't marriage all about reading each other's moods and looking out for each other?'

'Maybe . . .' Jo shrugged her shoulders.

'Well, we seemed to stop doing that. We've just been existing under the same roof and never really communicating. So I found myself turning to someone else for conversation, support, and . . . understanding, I suppose.'

'And sex, Jeff? What about sex? Have you slept with her?'

'I'm not going to answer that question.'

'I'll take that as a "yes" then.'

He ignored her and carried on. 'After a while I lost the urge to sort things out with you. You were so wrapped up in your work, the kids, the house. There didn't seem to be a great deal of room in your life for me.'

The anger was back. Years of pent-up frustration bubbled to the surface and she leapt to her feet. 'You've just fucking said it, haven't you? Because I'm the woman in this relationship I'm expected to come home and get the kids into bed, make sure there's food on the table, wash Thomas's football kit for the morning, iron Sophie's uniform, blah blah fucking blah. I don't have time for myself, Jeff, let alone you. And all you have to do is look after Number One in the mornings, then swan off to work where a secretary makes you a cup of coffee and probably gives you a fucking blow job.'

Pausing for breath, she looked across at Jeff, who was saying absolutely nothing. He must know the sentiment of what she'd said was true.

She freelanced as an interior designer, something Jeff always thought of as a 'hobby'. He had once made the mistake of saying, 'Anyone can throw a few colours on a wall and add some pictures.' So Jo challenged him to mastermind the decor of the spare bedroom. It was still there as visible testament to Jeff's complete lack of imagination.

During the two weeks that he spent working on it, disappearing up there most evenings with the door closed, Jo and the kids weren't allowed to see a thing. Every night he would lock the door and take the key to work with him.

On the night of the grand unveiling, he made Jo close her eyes until she was inside. She opened them and thought she'd passed on to another spiritual plane. It had cream walls, cream curtains, a cream carpet.

'It's . . . er . . . very cream,' she said, as Jeff beamed with pride.

Of course, several years on, it was no longer cream, particularly after several of the children's friends had stayed in it. Shades of grubby grey would be a more accurate description.

But at least the little exercise had forced Jeff to admit that Jo's choice of career did require creativity and talent. He had also to concede that it was lucrative, particularly in the middle-class neighbourhood where they lived. Most of the working couples there had no qualms about forking out a few grand to Jo for a *Homes & Gardens*-style decor.

The room they were standing in now glowed in the rich, warm colours of red and gold. Jo had spent weeks poring over plans and swatches, keen to make sure that the room they spent the most time in was cosy and welcoming for their evenings at home together. Fat lot of good it was now.

'Do you love me?' He raised his eyebrows and looked at her quizzically.

'What do you mean?' The question had taken her completely by surprise.

'It's not a hard question is it, hon?' he said softly. Hon. He hadn't called her that for months, maybe even years.

'Of course I love you. You're the father of my children.' She was annoyed that the focus had suddenly been put onto her when *he* was the one about to walk out.

His eyes dulled and he started scraping his foot backwards and forwards along one side of the kilim rug at his feet. 'It's not enough, Jo,' he said, shaking his head. 'I don't want you to be with me because we have children. Just remove them from the equation for the moment. Would you still love me enough to be with me?'

Did their future together depend on her answer? She could lie and say yes, or she could tell the truth.

'I don't know.'

'Well, maybe that goes some way to explain why we're in this situation now. At least I know she loves me.'

'Oh, for Christ's sake don't be so pathetic! She wants you *now*, but what happens when some twenty-four-year-old bloke makes a pass at her? She'll take one look at you with your bald patch and emotional baggage and decide her brief flirtation with older men is over. Then you'll be left wondering why you gave up on your marriage and kids for something so shallow.'

Jeff sat down on the sofa opposite her and shook his head. 'Candy's not like that. She gives me time and makes me feel wanted.'

There were so many serious observations to be made on the drama unfolding in their sitting room, but Jo couldn't help herself.

'Candy? Is that her name? Christ, she sounds like a porn star.'

'It's short for Candida,' said Jeff sullenly, traces of a red flush creeping up his face.

Jo laughed long and hard. 'Oh God, I've heard everything now. My husband is leaving me for a woman named after a vaginal infection. Appropriate though, because she sure as hell irritates the fuck out of me.'

Jeff scowled. 'Can we just try and have a conversation for once, without you taking the piss? That's another problem with you, you're so cynical about everything.'

She ignored his criticism and decided to have one more go at making him see sense. This was no time to give up, she was fighting for her marriage.

Consciously softening her expression, she walked across and sat next to him on the sofa. She spoke evenly, trying to sound as rational and reasonable as possible.

'Look, of course this girl has time to give you. She's twenty-three with no kids. She can watch a film uninterrupted to the end, read a book, go down the pub at a moment's notice – all the things we could do when we first met. But the minute she has kids that will all change and she'll be as knackered as I am most of the time. Being with her won't be better, it will just be different. I know that seems appealing, but it's not enough to walk out on your kids for.'

She looked at him pleadingly, but the leaden feeling in her heart told her it was hopeless. There were tears in his eyes, but his body language was screaming, 'Let me out of here.'

'I understand everything you're saying Jo, but it's totally out of my control. I have never felt this way before and I hate myself for it, but I *have* to be with her. I lie in bed at night thinking about her, I lie in the bath thinking about her until the water goes cold around me, and—'

'And you lie to me,' Jo interrupted before he said any more. Her mind was furiously rewinding through all the occasions she had thought he was working late but was probably with *her*.

She was absolutely convinced Jeff's new relationship wouldn't last – the inevitability of it depressed her. But most of all she felt anger and humiliation. She had trusted this marriage, this man. She had always felt that whatever life threw at them, they would weather it. And she had always been absolutely certain they would be together for ever. Why? Because she had two ace cards – the children he adored. She had been so convinced he would never leave them, she had barely given any thought to what was going on between him and her. Then The Cliché comes along and he walks, simple as that. How wrong could she be?

She studied him as he sat next to her, wiping his tear-stained face with the back of his hand. Tears of self-pity, tears of guilt.

Too tired to feel any more anger, all she felt was an overwhelming sadness that the man she loved could be so bloody stupid. He suddenly looked old, defeated almost, and Jo realised it was a long time since she'd actually sat down and taken a long hard look at the man she married.

Her mind drifted back to the first time she'd met him. Tall with broad shoulders and a washboard stomach, he had a nose that was slightly too big for his face, but in some strange way it suited him.

And those eyes. They were electrifyingly sexy and she had known immediately they were about to embark on a passionate relationship. He had 'rogue' written all over his face. Jo had fully expected to wake up one morning and find an 'It's been nice' note on the pillow next to her. But he just kept on coming back.

They'd been quite the golden couple for a while. Attractive, healthy, pretty well-off, flitting from one party to another or taking last-minute flights to somewhere hot. Then they had Thomas and their wings were clipped.

It had hit Jo hard, physically and mentally. In a way it was harder for Jeff because he still felt like the same person, but suddenly the woman he'd had so much fun with was constantly exhausted, irritable and tearful. He tried his best, but some days nothing he could do or say would be right.

Jo dragged her mind back to the present.

'I do love you, Jeff. But not in the needy, obsessive way you clearly want.'

She knew that whatever she said or did right now was fruitless. Jeff was going. It was 'hasta-la-bye-bye-wife-and-kids' in pursuit of firm thighs and a soft nature. Well, fine.

It suddenly hit her that she pitied him. He was the bad guy, the one who was leaving his children. And he clearly had no idea how much guilt he was going to have to cope with. He *and* Candy.

But Jo gained no comfort from that, because she knew Thomas and Sophie were going to be devastated. So devastated it pained her even to think about it.

Jeff stood up. 'I'm sorry, Jo.' He made a move as if to hug her, but she shrank away from his touch.

'Don't. Just get out.' She kept her voice calm.

'If that's what you want.'

Jo let out a bitter snort at his transparent effort to turn things round and make it look as though it was her decision he was leaving. 'What other option is there?'

But he had already walked out of the room.

She heard the floorboards upstairs creaking as he crept around, probably packing a bag. Her chest tightened and she felt the telltale pinpricks of imminent tears in her eyes. She was determined not to cry again in front of Jeff, but needn't have worried as the next sound she heard was the front door clicking shut.

One small click, one giant step for her marriage.

Usually, Jo loved the evenings when Jeff went out and the kids were asleep upstairs. She would potter from room to room relishing being alone. But this was a different kind of 'alone'. Jeff wasn't coming back and she felt her chest contract with terror at the silence around her. This was no longer a happy family home. It was a broken home.

She walked into the hallway. Jeff's overcoat had gone, but his green wellingtons were lying where he'd kicked them off after a particularly muddy walk on the local common at the weekend. Thomas and Sophie's discarded boots lay next to them. Jo bent down to tidy them up, God knows why. As she straightened up she caught sight of herself in the hall mirror.

She looked old. Bloody old.

Her hair was scraped back from her face in a rather haphazard ponytail, and her eyes had dark circles under them. Eyes that had once seduced Jeff, and a few others, were now dulled by the misery of the past few hours.

'She's twenty-three.' Jeff's words rang in her head. Jo was thirty-three, and right now felt twenty years older than that. No wonder he left.

Hot tears of self-pity began to run down her cheeks, falling onto her old college sweatshirt. Everything she knew and trusted had suddenly been ripped from under her.

She wanted to curl up in a corner and stay there for ever, but she couldn't even do that. She *had* to hold things, herself, together. Because in a few hours' time the children would be up, sublimely ignorant of how their lives were about to change.

Trudging back into the sitting room, she stared at the clock. One a.m. and all's hell, she thought ruefully. Would Jeff call tomorrow and say he'd changed his mind? Unlikely, at least in the short term. The prospect of regular blow jobs would render him incapable of making any rational decision. Nope. This was it for now. Jo Miles, single mother of two. Back on life's overcrowded shelf of thirty-something women.

This time, there was no one to hold back for, so she let it all out. Great, racking sobs engulfed her and she fell to her knees on the carpet, head bowed like a prisoner awaiting execution. She had never felt emotional pain like it, a mixture of hurt, anger, frustration and the feeling of total, utter failure.

Ten minutes later, her eyes swollen with crying, the sobbing subsided into an exhausted whimpering. Mustering what little strength she had left, she pulled herself to her feet and found herself face to face with a graduation photograph of Jeff looking remarkably like Forrest Gump.

Picking it up, she hurled it at the far wall, where it made a loud splintering noise as the frame separated from the Perspex front. Walking over to where Jeff smiled up at her from the carpet, she ground her foot into his smug face until his features were unrecognisable.

'Now you know what it feels like to be walked over,' she said, flicking off the sitting-room light.

3

Jo felt a light tapping on the end of her nose. She opened her eyes to find Bridal Barbie dancing on the duvet.

For one wonderful moment, life was normal. Then last night's showdown snapped into the present and a blanket of depression enveloped her, as though someone had turned her body power switch to 'off'.

'Where's Daddy?' asked Sophie, doing a forward roll across the end of the bed.

Jo wanted to scream, 'He's dumped us to go and shag some gymslip bimbo,' but instead she just lay there and watched her six-year-old daughter as she bounced up and down on the vast brass bed Jeff's parents had bought them as a wedding present. Oh, for the years when nothing mattered except whether Scooby Doo would catch the villain or what was for tea, that blissful time when all responsibility and major disappointments were still years ahead.

'He had an early meeting at work,' said Jo, dodging a head-on collision as Sophie bounced towards her.

It was amazing how easy it was to lie. Sophie, with her bobbed white-blonde hair and almond-shaped brown eyes, was innocence personified. She still believed in Father

Christmas and the Tooth Fairy. The older, more cynical Thomas had been forbidden from telling her the truth.

Now here was Jo telling her daughter a blatant lie. But *that* conversation was something she just couldn't face right now.

The doorbell rang. It was the cavalry, otherwise known as her best friend, Rosie. Jo had called her an hour ago at 6 a.m., in a terrible state of panic.

'Jeff's gone. He's left me,' she'd sobbed into the receiver. 'I don't think I can cope with the kids.'

There had been no need to say any more. She knew Rosie would rally round and there would be plenty of time for them to talk details later on.

'That's your Aunty Rosie at the door.'

'Aunty Roseeeeee!' shrieked Sophie, and hurtled out of the room.

Jo's head thudded back onto the pillow and she stared at the ceiling. There was a little brown patch right above the bed from when she and Jeff had opened a particularly explosive bottle of champagne on her birthday a couple of years ago. I wonder if he was unhappy then, she thought miserably. Her eyes were raw from yet another crying session in the small hours and her head ached from lack of sleep. She had eventually managed to drop off after taking a couple of Melatonins, but a damn car alarm had gone off at 3 a.m. and that was that. It was the same one that had disturbed her and Jeff on numerous occasions and they had left several snotty notes on the windscreen.

'I don't know about you, but they clearly want to know if someone is walking past their car,' Jeff once said. It had made her laugh, and while the alarm shrieked in the background, they had made love in a flurry of duvet and giggles. The memory of it brought her emotional nausea flooding back. The thought of getting dressed, eating, or even moving from the cocoon of the king-size duvet felt impossible. She wanted to ignore the nightmare her life was about to become.

Rosie popped her head round the door. 'I'm here. I'll sort the kids out and take them to school, and we'll talk later. You OK?'

'Better now you're here.' Jo managed a weak smile before Rosie headed back downstairs.

She turned her head and stared at Jeff's side of the bed. He'd always bagged the right-hand side, even on holidays. Her bedside table was cluttered with old tissues, a dust-covered glass of water, earplugs, books, and various half-empty jars of 'miracle' creams. She could do with a miracle in her life right now. By contrast, Jeff's side housed just two items: a framed photograph of him and the kids at Alton Towers, and Jack Kerouac's novel *On the Road*, a nostalgic look at the author's carefree years as a young man. Another clue to the mid-life crisis Jeff was clearly going through. I wonder if The Cliché recommended he read this, Jo thought, reaching over to pick it up. Tucked inside was a bookmark Sophie had made at school with 'I love you daddy' scribbled on it. Tears pricked at the corner of her eyes and she threw it on the floor. 'Bastard!'

'Don't swear, Mummy.'

She sat bolt upright to find Thomas standing in the doorway clutching a mini-box of Coco Pops. He had a milk moustache and his Batman pyjama top was unbuttoned.

'I've told Aunty Rosie that I'm allowed to have these for breakfast, but she still says I have to come and ask you first.' He raised his eyes heavenwards.

Jo smiled and swung her feet onto the floor. She reached for her slippers and put on the first dressing gown that came to hand on the back of the door. It was Jeff's. The smell of him enveloped her as she put it on. Well, not him exactly. More that Fahrenheit aftershave he always insisted on wearing despite her protestations. She had always hated it, but now it seemed like the most precious scent in the world, evoking memories as swiftly as a favourite record.

Thomas had run back to the kitchen, so she followed the distinctive smell of burning toast down the stairs. Sophie and Thomas were sitting at the kitchen table whilst Rosie rushed around looking flustered.

'I don't know how you do this every morning, I really don't,' said Rosie, as a thin wisp of black smoke rose behind her from the toaster.

Jo raised an eyebrow at it and Rosie swung round in panic. 'Shit! I mean sugar. That's the fourth slice I've burned.' She poked a knife into the charred remains and tried to extract them.

'Don't you have a toaster at home, then?'

'Ha bloody ha. What I don't usually have is two children distracting me with an endless stream of questions. So far this morning, I have been asked why the sky is blue, and what is the difference between perhaps and maybe.'

'Do enlighten me.'

'How the hell would I know? You're the one with the degree. Not to mention the slim figure and the good looks,' said Rosie with a grin. 'Actually, why *am* I friends with you?'

Sophie let out an ear-piercing shriek as Thomas stuck Bridal Barbie's foot in a jar of peanut butter.

'For God's sake, Thomas, grow up,' snapped Rosie, grabbing the doll and wiping it clean.

Jo smiled. It was almost pleasurable to see someone else struggling with the arduous routine she went through every morning. Jeff was no help.

'Thanks, Rosie. I couldn't have faced this morning without you. I don't know what normality is any more,' she said, pouring herself a glass of milk. The fridge smelt like something had died in it.

'What does normilliaty mean?' asked Sophie.

Rosie swiftly changed the subject by handing back her Barbie doll. 'How many of these things have you got now, young lady? There's a Barbie for everything these days. Whatever next? Klaus Barbie?'

'I want Bicycle Barbie. She comes with clothes and a real bicycle,' said Sophie, her eyes wide in wonder.

'Have you heard about Divorced Barbie? She comes with all Ken's stuff,' said Rosie, looking over at Jo and laughing. 'Oh God, sorry. Me and my big mouth. I wasn't thinking.' Tact had never been her friend's strong point.

'Don't worry about it.' Any further conversation would have to wait. Big Ears and his friend Even Bigger Ears were quietly digesting every word. But she was itching to sit down with Rosie and talk. She could think about nothing else. Rosie had always been good at giving relationship advice, even though her own were always disastrous. She had only had one long-term boyfriend, but it ended abruptly after six years when Rosie discovered he had a child he'd never told her about. It wasn't the child that bothered her or even that he'd not told her about it. It was because he'd disowned his daughter, now seven.

'I couldn't be with a man who didn't acknowledge the existence of his child,' she said at the time. 'What kind of person must he be? I've been living with a stranger all these years.'

Jo had first met Rosie at sixth-form college in Oxford. Rosie had been in the area since the age of seven, whereas she was the gauche new girl whose parents had moved there from Worcestershire when she was just sixteen. She remembered feeling terrified as she'd stood at the front of the class while the form teacher asked someone to look after her. No one had put their hand up, so the teacher had instructed Rosie to be her guide. Rosie had made it very clear she wasn't impressed to be saddled with her, but after a couple of weeks they had become firm friends. She studied her friend. Rosie wasn't unattractive, but Jo had found herself in many arguments throughout those all-important teen years, when boys had referred to her pal as 'the ugly friend'. She knew it had taken its toll on Rosie's confidence. They'd spent hours trying to straighten her wiry brown hair and had both supported each other through several emotional disasters too, but Jo knew she'd never needed Rosie more than she did now.

Somehow, with Rosie's help, she managed to go through the morning routine of getting the children washed and into their school uniforms. The state school they attended was just five minutes' walk away, so at least she didn't have to join the morning merry-go-round of mothers double parking their ridiculous four-wheel-drive jeeps with bull bars.

Rosie walked the children to school, and Jo dragged herself upstairs to get dressed. Even the simplest task felt beyond her. She stood staring at the contents of her built-in wardrobes for what seemed like hours. Inside was an impressive collection of clothes ranging from the long silk gown she'd worn to Jeff's last company Christmas party, to a couple of business suits and several casual outfits. She reached inside and grabbed jeans and a T-shirt from one of the shelves. Clipping her hair back with a couple of Sophie's flowery slides, she checked her face again in the mirror. Yep. Still looked 105. Felt it too.

Can I blame him for leaving me for a younger model? she thought, placing both hands on her cheeks and pulling them towards her ears. 'Yes I bloody can,' she said aloud, scowling at her reflection. Her insides felt like they were on a constant spin cycle.

Tea. That's what she needed. The British cure for all ills. She headed downstairs to put the kettle on. Ten minutes later Rosie arrived back to find her staring at the floor. The kettle was empty and cold.

'Coffee?' said Rosie brightly. In her effort to be jolly, Jo's bosom buddy was starting to sound like Mickey Mouse. Another octave higher and only dogs would hear her. Jo knew that Rosie had never seen her in such a state and that she felt at a loss as to how to help.

'Thanks again for helping out this morning, Rosie. I still don't know how I managed to get the kids ready. Habit, I guess.'

'Yes, like anyone who feels they're about to drown in a sewer, you just kick your legs and go through the motions,' said Rosie. Jo had chastised her in the past for making jokes at inappropriate moments, but she still did it when she was nervous.

'I feel like I already have drowned,' said Jo, tears welling in her eyes. 'It's so weird . . . so bloody wretched.' She picked up the corner of the tablecloth and used it to wipe her eyes.

'Tell me everything,' said Rosie quietly.

Twisting a handkerchief round and round her fingers, Jo talked. When she stopped, Rosie held her breath for several seconds then let out a long sigh. 'I know I've always said you can't trust a husband too far or a bachelor too near, but I can't believe what I'm hearing. I mean, you and Jeff were so stable, boring even.'

'Thanks, Rosie. Not so boring now though, are we?' said Jo, not waiting for an answer. 'That's what makes this so impossible to believe. I thought Jeff and I were stable. OK, so it wasn't the most exciting marriage in the world, but we knew where we were. Or at least I thought we did. It would never have crossed my mind he would leave me for someone else, let alone a bloody twenty-three-year-old.' She stopped and stared miserably into the middle distance.

'It's a shame Jeff took those bloody photos with him. We could have stuck pins in them,' said Rosie, absent-mindedly picking cat hairs from a cushion. 'What does The Cliché look like?'

Jo noticed she had already adopted her soubriquet for the enemy. 'She's your average bottle blonde with the thighs of a twenty-three-year-old. Why?'

'Oh, I was just thinking about that famous story of a man who had three women to choose from.' Rosie put her empty cup in the sink. 'He gave them all a thousand pounds and told them to do what they liked with it. The first woman spent the lot on a designer suit. The second woman spent five hundred and invested the rest. The third woman invested the lot. So which one did he marry?'

'Haven't a clue.'

'The one with the biggest tits.' Rosie's face broke into a wicked grin.

43

For the first time in hours, Jo laughed. Genuine, therapeutic laughter. It was a start.

'There you are, you see. Your old mate can still make you laugh, so things can't be that bad, can they?'

But by the time Rosie had finished her sentence, Jo's feeling of leaden misery had returned. 'How does that old saying go? "You never know what you want until it's gone",' she said.

'But *is it* what you want?' asked Rosie tentatively.

'What do you mean?' Jo frowned and took a sip of the weak, over-milky coffee that had been placed in front of her.

'I don't know . . . it's just that I can look at your relationship with Jeff from an outsider's point of view, and it was far from perfect, wasn't it?'

'What relationship isn't?'

'Yes, I know that. But the bottom line of why most people stay together is because, despite the occasional rocky patch, they love each other and enjoy each other's company.' Rosie paused. Jo got the impression she knew she was waffling, so she went straight for the jugular.

'Do you love Jeff?'

Jo's eyes widened in surprise. It was the first time Rosie had ever asked her that. Through their twenties they had talked about little else but sex. Once she and Jeff had married their conversations had turned more to Rosie's sex life, or lack of it, and their jobs.

'How odd, Jeff asked me that too,' said Jo. She had

picked up a piece of scrap paper from the table and was systematically tearing it into tiny pieces.

'And what did you tell him?'

'Of course I love him. I married him and had his kids, didn't I?' She was irritated that first Jeff and now Rosie were making such a big issue out of whether or not she loved her husband. As she saw it, he had left her and any blame lay firmly at his doorstep.

'Come on, Jo. You know that's not an answer.' Rosie paused and looked at her. 'OK, you're probably not going to like this, but I'm going to say it anyway. I have thought it ever since you told me you were going to marry him, but never said anything because I knew your mind was made up.'

'What is it?' Jo was irritated by the big build-up. She also had a nagging feeling she was about to hear the lurid details of another Jeff misdemeanour that she knew nothing about. She fixed Rosie with an obstinate glare.

'Jeff's not the right man for you. Never has been.' Jo watched as Rosie fell back onto the cushion behind her as if she had just delivered a Churchillian speech.

'Is that it?'

'Well, that's enough, isn't it? I mean, it's not every day you're told that the father of your children is the wrong man for you.'

'But that's just your opinion, Rosie. It doesn't mean it's true. There are sides to my relationship with Jeff you never see.'

'Oh, right. So as soon as I walk out the door you become animated and interested in each other, do you? Because from where I've been sitting these last few years you two seem to have little in common other than Thomas and Sophie. I don't mean to sound cruel, but it has to be said.'

Jo retreated into a sullen silence. She knew she had spent years whinging on about Jeff. He was emotionally stunted, inconsiderate, insensitive, often lazy, you name it, she had criticised him for it. But now that he had really done something for her to rant and rave about, she found herself defending him, irritated by her friend's attack on her marriage. She started slightly as Rosie took her hand. Embarrassed by the chipped and bitten nails that had once been fastidiously buffed and painted, she curled her fingers into a tight ball.

'You used to be so much fun, Jo, and I was so proud to be your friend. You had an enthusiasm for life I always envied and a magnetism I could only aspire to. I can't tell you the times I saw a bloke I fancied when we were younger and within minutes he would be totally absorbed in you. It wasn't your fault, you just had something that drew people to you.'

Jo felt a solitary tear run down her face. It scared her how utterly empty and devastated she felt. She knew she was unrecognisable as the girl who had entranced so many over the years. Rosie had always told her she imagined her marrying someone equally mesmerising. A man who adored her and was devastatingly good-looking with a fantastic career. She remembered the countless times they had sat round the kitchen table at Rosie's parents' house and described the man of their dreams. Rosie's criterion was that he had to be breathing, but Jo had always come up with a princely description.

When she met Jeff she knew Rosie dismissed him as someone who wouldn't be around for long. He was fairly good-looking, but he was never going to set the world alight. Yet the relationship went on. And on. Much to Rosie's obvious annoyance. Then, horror of horrors, they got married. Rosie was smiling on the wedding photos, but Jo knew it had taken every ounce of effort in her body. Here we are ten years on and she's been proved right, thought Jo. But she didn't say it. She was stirred from her trance by Rosie's touch as she reached out to tuck a stray piece of hair behind her ear.

'Since you married Jeff I've watched your zest for life slowly drain away. Now you just seem sad and tired all the time, bored even. Bored of life with a man who doesn't inspire you in any way.' She stopped talking and they both sat in silence. The only sound Jo registered was the kitchen clock ticking.

Then Jo straightened her back, rose to her feet and stood looking down at Rosie. 'Have you finished? Because if you *have* finished telling me what a waste of time my ten-year marriage has been, not to mention my children, then I'd like you to go now. I have things to do.'

Rosie looked stunned. 'Jo, I didn't mean to upset you.'

'Oh, don't worry, you couldn't upset me any more than

Jeff has already. It's just that I thought you'd come to give me moral support, not slag off my marriage.'

'But Jeff's left you for another woman. You were calling him all the names under the sun earlier. What's changed all of a sudden?'

'Look, I really don't want to discuss it any further. I'd be grateful if you'd just leave and give me some time to myself.' Jo turned her back and stared out of the window.

'Well, if that's what you want, I'll go.' Rosie's voice was barely audible.

After she'd left, Jo walked through the eerily quiet house and sat on the bottom stair in the hallway. She was still seething over Rosie's remarks about her marriage.

It was alright for *her* to criticise it, but she damn well wasn't going to let anyone else attack it. Was this through loyalty to Jeff, she wondered? If so, why on earth was she still defending him? Jo couldn't work out why she had been so snappy with Rosie. Maybe it was because she didn't like the truth. A lot of Rosie's comments had hit a raw nerve and she hadn't liked the feelings they'd stirred up. When *did* she become miserable? She'd had slight misgivings on her wedding day, but didn't any bride? Once she had taken her vows she remembered feeling relieved that there wasn't a choice to be made any more. Now she just had to get on and make the best of the marriage.

Suddenly, a particular memory drifted into her thoughts and she sat bolt upright. Her father.

As they had circled the church for the second time in

their attempt to be 'fashionably late', he'd leaned over and whispered in her ear, 'It's not too late to change your mind, you know.'

Jo had laughed as he said it, but when he sat back, she saw he wasn't smiling. She'd forgotten that moment until now.

Looping her arm through the banisters, she leaned her forehead against the cool gloss of the wood and wondered whether her father had felt the same as Rosie about her marrying Jeff. Getting to her feet, she walked through to the sitting room and moved a small stool in front of the built-in bookshelves. Stepping up, she reached to the very top shelf and pulled down a dust-covered photograph album. Sitting on the floor, she opened the first page and studied the single photograph on it. Her and Jeff on their wedding day.

There was nothing like wedding photographs for dating quickly and theirs were no exception. The look was pure eighties. Jeff was wearing a shiny suit and his hair, pre bald-patch, was short at the sides and heavy on top. He had a moustache Tom Selleck would envy. Jo's dress looked like an explosion in a doily factory, with huge shoulder pads covered in lace and a drop waist. Wearing sky blue eyeliner and her shoulder-length hair curled backwards, she looked like Farrah Fawcett on acid. But they seemed happy enough. They were both beaming at the camera and the smile was genuine enough to reach their eyes. Jo turned the page.

Here were the bride and groom posing with her parents

and Jeff's mother. His father had died of a heart attack when Jeff was eight. Jo's mother Pam was in her element with a hideous hat the size of Texas, a scarlet suit to match her face, and Minnie Mouse-style shoes with black bows on the front. But Jo was interested in the expression on her father's face. She peered closely at the picture. He did indeed look miserable. She'd never noticed it before. He was standing next to her mother, but there was a good six-inch gap between them. His face was impassive, but his eyes looked sad, defeated somehow. I suppose all daddies think no one is good enough for their little girl, mused Jo as she smoothed out a crease in the page.

On the facing page was Rosie, chief bridesmaid and decked out like the Christmas fairy. Jo hadn't wanted an adult bridesmaid, preferring instead to stick to her cousin's cute little daughter, but she knew Rosie was desperate to have a key role on her big day. So she had walked down the aisle with little Chloe and the rather larger Rosie behind her. Or 'the bat and ball' as Jo's brother Tim had called them.

Tim. I wonder what he thought about me marrying Jeff, she wondered. Not a great deal probably. Thinking wasn't Tim's strong point. He would have regarded the whole day as a chance to get pissed free of charge and maybe grab a snog with one of Jo's old school friends. Tim was four years younger than Jo but acted as though he was twelve most of the time. They had hated each other for much of their childhood but had now settled into a more easygoing relationship. He was also a fantastic uncle to the kids and lived conveniently round the corner.

She closed the wedding album and placed it back on the shelf. On the shelf, just like me, she thought. Her throat tightened. In the photographs she had looked so full of hope for the future.

She closed her eyes and slumped back against the wall, deep in thought. Five minutes later the phone rang. Her heart leapt into her mouth. Could it be Jeff?

'Hello?' Despite making every effort to sound calm, her voice was shaky.

'Are you alright, dear?' It was her mother.

Jo and her mother had always had a strained relationship, but the sound of a friendly voice was too much for her and she made a small choking sound as she tried to suppress a sob.

'Jeff's walked out on me and the kids,' she blurted.

'What . . . do you mean?' her mother faltered.

'For God's sake, Mum, which word don't you understand? He's gone off to shag someone else. Does that make it any clearer?' Jo snapped, angry for telling her mother so soon.

'There's no need to swear, Jo.'

Bloody marvellous. Here she was having a virtual breakdown and her mother still managed to speak to her like she was twelve years old.

'Look, Mum, I'm sorry to drop it on you like this, but you've called at a bad time, you know? It only happened last night.'

'Well, what on earth did you do to make him leave like that? I mean, Jeff's a good man. He wouldn't have left without a reason.'

Jo was momentarily stunned by her mother's hardly veiled attack on her wifely skills. 'That's it Mum, you take his side. I suppose if he'd given me a couple of black eyes that would be my fault too, would it? Look, I really can't listen to this crap right now. I'll call you in a couple of weeks.' She broke into another sob and put the phone down. It rang again seconds later but she ignored it.

Great, she thought, as she plonked herself down on the sofa. First Jeff, then Rosie, now my mother. Who am I going to fall out with next?

She was starting to feel guilty about being so hard on Rosie. After all, she had only said those things out of a mis-guided sense of loyalty. And she had been an absolute rock coming round and cooking breakfast this morning. She picked up the phone and got Rosie's answering machine.

'Hello, I'm not here right now. But if you're good-looking, single and a multi-millionaire, please leave your name and number and I'll marry you as soon as I get back.'

Jo smiled and waited for the beep.

'Hi Rosie, it's me – the worst friend in the world. Listen, I'm really sorry about earlier. I didn't mean to bite your head off like that. It's just that . . . well, you know. Anyway, sorry sorry sorry, and give me a call.'

She felt better after that. Enough to think about food for the first time since lunch yesterday.

52

4

Having walked the children to school, there was a spring in Jo's step as she set off back home. The day was hers until 3.30. She could go shopping, do a few laps of the local pool, or just slop around the house with a packet of chocolate biscuits and a weepy movie. No contest.

Jo quickened her pace towards the Blockbuster video store. She sighed with a degree of contentment as she walked past the market stalls selling spring flowers. Life wasn't so bad.

Three months ago, she couldn't have imagined ever feeling light-hearted again, yet here she was relishing rather than dreading the prospect of a whole day to herself.

Since that cold February night when Jeff had walked out on her and the children, Jo had faced an enormous daily struggle to cope. The hardest part of all had been breaking it to Thomas and Sophie that Daddy was no longer going to be living with them.

It was a week after Jeff had left. Jo had explained his absence in the meantime as a business trip. When she felt she could relay the bad news without crying, she waited for Sophie to go to tea at a friend's house, then sat Thomas down on his own.

'Mummy and Daddy haven't been getting on too well lately, so we've decided it's best if he moves out for a little while,' she said, taking his felt-tip-stained hands in hers.

'Has he gone away for ever?' Thomas looked crestfallen.

'No darling. You'll still see lots of him, he just won't be living with us for a while unless we can sort things out. Mummy and Daddy just need a bit of space from each other that's all, but he still wants to see you.'

'Why won't you let him stay here any more? It's not fair.' His face looked crumpled.

The urge to scream, 'He's left us for some little tart' was overwhelming, but Jo fought to control her emotions. Whatever she felt about Jeff's behaviour, she wasn't going to punish the children for it. Even if it took ten years for the children to make up their own minds that their father had been at fault, then she was prepared to wait.

By contrast, Sophie was remarkably unfazed by the news. Jo waited until Thomas was in the bath, then sat her daughter on her knee and, during the course of a conversation about whether Goofy was a dog, casually mentioned that Daddy wouldn't be living at home anymore.

'Why not?' said Sophie distractedly, her eyes on the television.

'Oh, it's just easier for him to live nearer town because of work. You'll still see a lot of him at weekends and stuff,' said Jo, with all the jollity she could muster.

And that was it. It had been as simple as that. Quite what the long-term effects would turn out to be was another matter. She would just have to wait and see. Today, as she browsed round the new release section of the video store, the future didn't seem too bleak after all.

Stopping in front of the 'Romantic' titles, she was pondering whether to watch *Sleepless in Seattle* for the sixth time when a loud voice boomed out behind her, 'Don't bother with that crap. Lots of shagging, Chuck Norris and a car chase, that's what makes a good movie.'

'Hi, Tim.' Jo swivelled round to find her brother beaming broadly. He was wearing a scruffy T-shirt with the words 'Best before 1989' on the front, and a pair of baggy combat trousers with oil marks from his dilapidated racing bike down the legs.

'Hmm. Romantic video, huh? Could mean she's met someone and is planning to seduce him, or it could mean she's having yet another night alone and making herself feel miserable.' Tim raised one eyebrow quizzically.

Jo smiled indulgently. 'The latter. Except I'm going to watch it this afternoon on my own, rather than this evening.'

Tim had been a godsend since Jeff walked out. Shortly after Jo had slammed the phone down on her mother, Tim had appeared on the doorstep making cavalry-style trumpeting noises through her letterbox. When she opened the door, she was horrified to see his friend Conor standing behind him, a rather sheepish expression on his face.

'So what's going on then? I've just had Mum on the

phone in a right state saying Jeff has left you for another woman. She says you weren't answering your phone and might be trying to harm yourself,' boomed Tim, settling himself into a wicker chair with his feet on the kitchen table.

'The only person I want to harm right now is Mum,' said Jo through gritted teeth. She was less than thrilled that Conor was hearing the raw facts about her private life. She was also painfully aware that her eyes were red and puffy from crying.

'So who's the totty, then?' said Tim, kicking off his well-worn deck shoes.

'Sorry?'

'The one Jeff's taken off with. Who is she?'

'Oh. She's one of the secretaries at work. And she's twenty-three, believe it or not.'

'Twenty-three!'

'I know, ridiculous isn't it?'

'Ridiculous? It's bloody amazing, the crafty git. How's he managed to pull a twenty-three-year-old at his age?'

'Tim, that's hardly the point.' She was irritated by her brother's unsympathetic attitude, but it didn't surprise her.

'Oh, come on, Jo, he'll be back. After all, there aren't many men, married or otherwise, who would say no to a bit of twenty-three-year-old if they thought they could get away with it. Isn't that right, Conor?'

Tim looked questioningly at his friend who was leaning against a worktop studying his CAT boots as if they were the most fascinating thing in the room.

'I would.' As he spoke, Conor lifted his head and ran a hand through his floppy fringe. He looked extremely awkward.

Tim looked momentarily stunned then laughed nervously, unsure of whether he was joking. 'Yeah, right. And Dolly Parton sleeps on her front.'

'I'm serious,' said Conor, picking a fluffball from his rather shapeless sweater. 'If I loved someone enough to marry them, I wouldn't cheat on them. And if they cheated on me, I would leave.'

The finality of his remark rather put an end to the conversation and all three stood in silence for a moment.

'I'll make some tea.' Jo walked over to where Conor was standing and switched on the kettle. She caught a whiff of his aftershave, something expensive she didn't recognize.

'Honestly, Jo, once the novelty of shagging some babe has worn off, he'll come crawling back,' said Tim, digging himself into an even deeper hole.

'I'm not sure I want him back.' Jo was shocked to hear herself say this, but it was true.

'But he's the father of your children—'

'Precisely. But it didn't stop him leaving though, did it?' she snapped before Tim could finish his sentence. 'Sugar?' she asked Conor, firmly indicating the other subject was closed.

'Two, thanks,' he said, then paused and turned to face her. He looked nervous. 'Um look, if you need any help with the children over the coming weeks, just shout. I mean, I'm sure there are lots of things you need to sort out and they know me, so I'm more than happy to take them off your hands for a while.'

Jo resisted the urge to look surprised because she didn't want to make him feel uncomfortable about his offer. 'That would be great, thanks.'

As it happened, both Conor and Tim had proved to be invaluable where the children were concerned. Every time he saw his sister's lower lip start to quiver, Tim would playfully pick up a child under each arm and boom, 'Come on, we're off to the park.' He'd also done a fair amount of babysitting when Rosie dragged Jo out to various wine bars, trying to snap her out of her depression.

'I'm just not ready for this Rosie,' Jo had whined into her wineglass, during a night out, about a month after Jeff had left. 'I don't know if I will ever be ready for it again. I'd forgotten what a hideous cattle market it was.'

'Don't knock it. It's a way of life for some of us,' said Rosie. But, as usual, she acquiesced and, half an hour later, found herself sitting in a curry house while Jo, once again, went over and over what had gone wrong with her marriage.

Jo wasn't quite so absorbed in it now. She was on the road to recovery. Instead of thinking about her problems thousands of times a day, she had reduced it to hundreds. Work helped. Her job as an interior designer had really taken off once spring arrived, and she had three major projects on the go. The routine of taking the children to school, coming home, putting on a suit and going off to various appointments – this had been the glue that had held her together. Now she was recovered enough to begin to relish rather than dread the thought of a day to herself with nothing to do. Like today.

'Conor and I were planning to have a spot of lunch in that little Italian down the road. Why don't you come? You can sit in and watch a video any time,' said Tim, reading the back of the film she'd chosen and wrinkling his nose in disapproval.

Conor and Tim had been at junior school together and were inseparable for many years. When Jo was about sixteen, her twelve-year-old brother and his friend had driven her mad with their juvenile behaviour, putting a dead mouse in her bed, hanging her knickers on the garden gate, and generally making a complete pest of themselves. But as her relationship with Tim had mellowed over the years, so had her attitude to Conor. A year ahead at school, he had left home when he was seventeen to study architecture at London University. Jo hadn't seen him again until her and Jeff's wedding almost two years later.

Conor's late arrival to the reception had caused quite a stir among her friends. Then nineteen, he was six foot two and extremely handsome in an artistic way. He had shoulder-length hair swept back from his face, a permanent five o'clock shadow, and the strong jawline usually associated with Mills & Boon heroes. But the effect had been rather lost on Jo because she was so besotted by Jeff.

'Yes, why not?' she smiled, heading off to pay for the video. 'I fancy a bit of pasta. I might even live a little and have a glass of wine.'

'Great. I'll just take the bike home and collect Conor, and we'll come to the house at twelve-thirty and walk to the restaurant. OK? See you then.'

They arrived at the house at 12.15 and decided to have a quick cuppa before leaving. As Conor sipped his tea and chatted to Tim in her kitchen, Jo took the chance to study him for the first time.

He was clean shaven now, and his hair was shorter, but still sexily unkempt. He was dressed casually in jeans and a sweater, and she remembered that Tim had mentioned something about him being made redundant from his job with a prestigious London architects' firm. He owned a house around the corner from Jo, and had given Tim a 'temporary' place to stay when he came to London two years ago. Her brother was still there.

It suited Jo because it meant Tim often took the children out to the local park, and Conor frequently went with them. Thomas doted on him because he was good at football, and Sophie was constantly badgering him to play aeroplanes and swing her round by her arm and leg.

'Right, let's get going then, Sis.' Tim's voice cut into her thoughts.

'I'll just go and change.'

She rushed upstairs and started rifling through her wardrobe. Jeans? Too tight. Long skirt? Too frumpy. Suit?

60

It's lunch, not a wedding. Pausing, she gave herself a mental shake. What on earth was she doing?

She was going out for lunch with her brother and his friend, who were taking pity on her because her husband had walked out. They wouldn't give a damn what she wore. In fact, they were probably sitting downstairs right now waiting for her to appear in sackcloth and ashes.

Then she acknowledged it. She cared what she wore. Her life was in ruins and here she was worrying about what people thought of her. Good! she thought, grinning at herself in the mirror as she applied some Touche Eclat to the dark circles under her eyes. There's life in the old girl yet.

Five minutes later, she was standing in front of them dressed in beige capri pants, loafers, and a denim shirt. She had freed her hair from its ponytail and her painstaking 'natural look' make-up had worked wonders.

'You look great,' smiled Conor, holding eye contact just a little longer than usual.

'Thanks.'

The Italian restaurant was empty when they arrived, so they were seated in the prime table by the window. With its neatly pressed red gingham tablecloths and Mateus Rosé bottle candle-holders, it reminded Jo of restaurants from her childhood.

When she was young, a meal out was rare. Restaurants were places to celebrate an occasion, and she remembered vividly going to a Berni Inn for the first time on her eighth birthday, her eyes popping out on stalks at the piece of Black Forest gateau placed in front of her. Now people ate out simply because they couldn't be bothered to cook.

The waiters at Numero Uno greeted Jo like a long lost relative, presumably because she had popped in for supper there one night last week with Rosie.

'Do you come here often?' asked Conor.

'Ha! That's what he says to all the girls,' laughed Tim. 'Don't you, mate? The other night we went to this wine bar and within half an hour he had top totty crawling all over him. I don't know how he does it. I always manage to get some bird so ugly she'd make a mule back away from an oatbin.'

'That's complete rubbish.' Conor scowled at Tim before picking up a menu and studying it intently. 'It was you who came away with someone's phone number.'

'True, but it wasn't much use.'

'Was it a wrong number then?' asked Jo, amused by her brother's desperation to find a girlfriend.

'Well yes, but there was a bit more to it than that.' Tim was tearing off a corner of his napkin and writing down a number. He passed it to Jo who frowned in puzzlement as she read it. 770 2219.

'So?'

'Turn it round and hold it up to the light,' Tim said, pouring himself a generous glass of wine.

Jo burst out laughing. 'It says Piss off.'

'Precisely. But I suspect if Conor had asked for her

number it would have been the genuine one. She was all over him.'

'Bit obvious though, wasn't she?' Conor poured wine into Jo's glass.

'That's how I like them, mate,' sighed Tim. 'All this hard-to-get nonsense baffles me. I'm beginning to think that even women on death row would only want me to be their friend.'

'Ah, diddums,' smiled Jo, reaching over and patting his knee. 'Miss Right will turn up one day, you'll see.'

'I thought she had when Gemma came along,' he said wistfully. 'But she turned out to be Miss Always Right, which isn't quite the same. Anyway, I'm off to the loo. I'll have the lasagne. If I'm not back in ten minutes I may have tried to drown myself in the sink.'

As he wandered off and Conor gave their food order to the waiter, Jo chastised herself for worrying about what she wore for lunch. Conor clearly had women falling at his feet, so why on earth would he be even remotely interested in a thirty-three-year-old mother of two with enough emotional baggage to sink a cruise liner? Why would any man for that matter, when there were countless uncomplicated twenty-somethings on the dating scene?

'Chin up, you've gone all glum.' Conor's voice broke into her thoughts.

'Yes, sorry. I was just thinking about . . . things,' she said with an apologetic shrug.

'Well, if you ever want to talk "things" through with

an objective outsider, then feel free to call me. Alternatively, you can tell me to mind my own business.'

'That's a kind offer, thanks, but I think I need to stay in my cave for a while longer and work things out in my own mind.'

'Good God, I leave the table for two minutes and a gloom descends,' boomed Tim, slapping Conor on the back as he squeezed past to his seat. 'Who's died?'

'My marriage,' muttered Jo, now wishing she'd stayed at home.

'A good night out will cheer you up,' said her brother, blowing smoke in her face. 'I was just thinking it would be quite good for us to take you to a bar, because the women won't be quite so suspicious if you're there. It could work a treat.'

'And I thought you had my best interests at heart.'

'Oh, come on, Sis. You never know, you might just enjoy it. How about Friday night? You could get Rosie to babysit, she's got no life.'

'She'd be thrilled to hear you say that. I could ask her, I suppose, but I don't know if I'm up to it really. Let me think about it and I'll call you tomorrow.'

The rest of the meal passed in small talk. As they left the restaurant, Jo started to say her goodbyes to them both. She ached to be alone with her thoughts before the children had to be collected from school.

'Goodbye? Nonsense, we're coming with you,' said Tim, grabbing her elbow.

'No, we're not.' Conor's voice was measured but firm. 'Jo needs some time to herself now. Come on.'

As he dragged Tim away, Jo mouthed 'thanks' at him and set off towards the house. As she waited to cross the road, she considered how sensitive Conor was compared to dear, bumbling Tim. His earlier remark about infidelity had made quite an impression on her, and she wondered why he wasn't involved in a serious relationship. From what Tim had said, he obviously had plenty of offers.

Letting herself into the house, she kicked off her shoes and stood in the cool hallway for a moment, savouring the silence.

Her eyes focused on her old school photograph hanging by the light switch. She and nine hundred other girls at her old grammar school, young and bursting with enthusiasm for the future. None of them knew then of the pain of childbirth, the worry of responsibility and bills, or the highs and lows of adult relationships. It was all to come. If she knew then what she knew now, would she have married Jeff? Yes, because otherwise she wouldn't have had Thomas and Sophie. But taking them out of the equation, maybe not.

Jo walked through to the kitchen and flopped into a chair. Casting her eye over the children's plastic play table at one end of the room, she picked up an old copy of *Hello* magazine and began flicking through the torn pages where Sophie had been gathering pictures for her scrapbook.

Gloria Hunniford's bouquet was missing from the main

picture, but the interview about her wedding to hairdresser Stephen Way was still intact. Jo read every word avidly. Here was a woman who had been through one marriage and had three children, yet managed to fall in love again at an age when society imagines women to be past it. Yet here I am, thirty-three and attractive, thinking I'm on the scrap heap, she thought. Her mind was made up.

She would go out with Tim and Conor on Friday night.

5

By the time Jo had packed the children off to school on Friday morning she had already changed her mind about going out that night.

It was a blustery, slightly chilly day, and the thought of getting dressed up to spend the evening with her brother and his friend seemed too much of an effort. She had already made up her mind she'd have a lousy time, and besides, there was a four-star film on the telly later that night. She picked up the phone and dialled Rosie's work number.

'Hi, it's me. Listen, I don't fancy going out tonight after all. Have you still got to go to that dull leaving do, because otherwise you could just bring a bottle of wine round here. There's a good film on. We could talk all the way through and then say, "Well, what the hell was all that about?"'

But Rosie didn't laugh at her pathetic attempt at a joke. 'Oh, I see. The thought of getting dressed up and mingling with the outside world is too exhausting, is it?'

'Yes, something like that.'

'Well bloody snap out of it, for Christ's sake.'

'Sorry? I thought you were on my side.'

'I am. Which is why I'm forcing you to go out.

Mr Wonderful isn't going to run out of petrol on your doorstep. You've got to get out there and *find* him.'

'Rosie, I have absolutely no intention of meeting anyone. My life is a big enough mess as it is, without complicating matters further.'

'Just go out and have a laugh then. Anything's better than sitting in moping all the time. You're becoming Miss bloody Havisham. I can see I'm going to have to come and open the curtains, blow away the cobwebs and kick you out of the front door myself.'

'No, don't worry. I'll go,' replied Jo wearily. 'I'd rather be bored to death by them than nagged to death by you.'

At 8 p.m. she was sitting alone in her local Pitcher & Piano wine bar, her eyes glued to the door in anticipation of Tim and Conor's arrival.

Ten years ago she wouldn't have batted an eyelid to be sitting alone, but now she felt vulnerable and exposed. She busied herself by rifling through the contents of her handbag and re-reading several old letters and school circulars. Tim had always teased her about her voluminous bag, stuffed to its straps with superfluous rubbish.

'Fuck me, here's the Magna Carta,' said Tim once, pulling out a yellowed piece of paper that fragmented at his touch.

By 8.15 there was still no sign of them. She was just about to drain her glass and leave when a breathless Conor rushed in.

'God, I'm so sorry, that bloody brother of yours held me up. I was waiting for ever for him to come out of the bath, and he was still starkers at eight o'clock wondering what to wear. Not a pretty sight. I've left him to it and he'll meet us here as soon as he's ready.' His face was flushed with the exertion of running.

'No worries. I was quite happy sitting here on my own,' she lied.

As he queued at the bar for their drinks, Jo noticed several women casting an appreciative eye in Conor's direction then glancing back towards her. They probably think I'm his girlfriend, she thought, feeling a warm flush of satisfaction creep up her neck. It was a far cry from their childhood days when Jo spent most of her time trying to get away from Tim and his little chum. She always felt Conor was led astray by Tim's excessive behaviour, but it hadn't made her like him any more at the time.

On one occasion, she had come home from school to the blissfully peaceful sanctuary of her bedroom and was indulging in one of her many fantasy conversations with a poster of Leif Garrett on her bedroom wall. It was a game she often played, where she would pretend he was asking her out and she would flirt back to him.

Halfway through telling him that maybe, just maybe, she would go to the pictures with him, she heard a muffled shriek coming from inside her wardrobe. She opened it to find Tim and Conor with each end of her school scarf stuffed in their mouths to stop themselves laughing. She smiled at the memory now, but at the time she had been mortified about it for at least two years.

'So, how's things with you?' asked Conor when he returned to their table with two large glasses of chilled Chablis.

'Now *there's* a question. Do you want the social nicety answer of "fine", or do you want the truth?'

'Oh, definitely the truth. I've never been one for social niceties.'

'Well, in a nutshell, the kids are missing Jeff like mad but seem to have reconciled themselves to the fact that their parents are no longer together, and I . . .' She trailed off, staring miserably into her glass.

'You what?' said Conor. His brown eyes had softened with concern.

'I'm still not sure what I think about it all, but I do know that I don't feel as desperate as I did. That's a start, isn't it?' She looked at him with a quizzical smile.

Despite boring Rosie into a stupor with the dull minutiae of her shattered marriage over the past few months, Jo genuinely wanted to steer clear of the subject tonight and have a good time. Conor seemed to read her mind.

'May I recommend that we drop the subject that makes you miserable and concentrate on making sure you have a great time, if only for tonight? More drink!' He drained his glass quickly and headed off to the bar again.

Jo was already feeling slightly light-headed from the

first two glasses, and knew she should start to slow down. But the alcohol was numbing her sadness, and the temporary liberation from misery was seductive. While Conor queued at the bar, Jo scanned the room. It was full of the middle-class types who would have been described as Yuppies in the eighties. A group of girls in Alice bands, chinos, and quilted car coats stood huddled in a corner, giggling and glancing at a group of men across the room dressed identically except for the Alice bands. It was obviously only a matter of time before the two groups merged for some collective braying.

It exhausted Jo just to watch them. God, she thought, how I hated being single. Sure, it had its benefits, but most of the time it was a fairly tedious state where you spent your time searching for that special someone to go on regular cinema trips with. If ever she forgot how wearing singledom could sometimes be, she always had Rosie and Tim to remind her, although the latter did nothing to help himself.

'I give up,' he had groaned a few days earlier. 'I just can't seem to win with women.' He had seemed so genuinely glum that Jo had attempted to get to the bottom of his regular rebuttals by the opposite sex.

'Start at the beginning. What do you first say when you see a woman you like?' she asked earnestly.

He thought about her question for a moment. 'Well, I tend to go the humorous route.'

'That's good. Like what?'

'Um, something like, "Does this condom make me look fat?"' he said, showing no discernible trace of embarrassment.

Jo had looked at him in disbelief. 'That's not funny, Tim. It's just offensive, particularly to someone you've never met.'

'So what would you suggest then?' He looked wounded.

'Even the old cliché of, "Haven't we met before?" would be better than that.'

'I tried that another time,' Tim had said disconsolately, 'and she said "Yes, I'm the receptionist at the VD clinic", and walked off.'

Jo was smiling at the memory when Conor returned to the table with two more glasses of wine.

'What's funny?' He placed one in front of her.

'Oh, I was just thinking back to a conversation I had with Tim the other day about his lack of success with women.' She noticed that Conor had pulled his chair slightly closer to hers.

'Funny you should say that,' he said, 'but that reprobate brother of yours has just rung to say some girl he had a meaningful one-night stand with a few weeks ago has called him for a date tonight. He says he hopes we can manage without him.'

Jo felt a brief flutter of butterflies in her stomach, but suspected it was the wine making her feel that way.

'So?' Conor's voice snapped her out of her drink-induced trance. 'Do you think we can manage without him?' A brief smile crossed his lips.

'Oh, absolutely,' she smiled. 'In fact, we'll probably have a much nicer time without Tim flapping around. He doesn't suffer from stress himself, he's just a carrier.' Oh God, she thought. Now I know Tim isn't coming I've suddenly started talking drivel.

'Right, another drink here, then I think we should find a restaurant and have a bite to eat. That sound good? Or do you have to get home for a certain time?'

'No, the kids are at Jeff's, so that's great.' She smiled weakly. 'Better hold the drink, thanks, till we get to the restaurant. Excuse me, I need the loo.' With a rising sense of panic, she walked across the bar. She felt dangerously out of control and needed time to gather herself.

She sat fully clothed on the closed loo seat. Was this now a date between her and Conor? The fairy of self-doubt appeared and whispered in her ear. Of course not, he's just looking after you because your brother is so unreliable. He'll take you out for a meal then get shot of you as soon as he possibly can.

'Look, if you've got something else you'd rather be doing, then please feel free. I'm really not that bothered about going to eat,' she said as she returned to the table.

'No, I want to. Unless of course it's you who'd rather not.'

'No, no. I'd like to.'

'Good. Well, I'm glad we've got that sorted out,' he said, looking at her as if she were barking mad. 'Perhaps we can get on with the rest of the evening now.'

* * *

It was 11.30 by the time they fell out of the Yasmin curry house and into the waiting mini-cab, with pre-requisite stained seats and Magic Tree air freshener.

'Green Road first, please,' slurred Jo, 'then on to Fairfields Avenue.'

'Nonsense,' mumbled Conor to the driver. 'Just go to Fairfields Avenue please.'

He turned to Jo. 'I'll come and have a coffee at your place, then I'll walk home. The fresh air will do me good. Besides, I've had a nice time tonight and I don't want to say goodbye to you just yet.'

Paralysed by a surfeit of wine, Jo found herself agreeing. The stomach butterflies were no longer fluttering, they were swarming. The last time she'd been on the dating scene, cab journeys home had always been awkward affairs where you sat in silence, wondering what would happen when you got to your place. Would they get out too? Or would they stay in the cab and mutter the gut-wrenching statement 'See you around'? Yet Conor had simply taken control of the situation and suggested coffee at her place, as if it were the most natural thing in the world.

She remembered a recent conversation with Tim and Rosie where her brother had informed them both that any man who says, 'Fancy a coffee?' really means 'Fancy a shag?' 'Unless of course, you're sitting in Starbucks at the time,' he had added in all seriousness.

The cab pulled up outside the house and Jo stood on

the pavement while Conor paid the driver. Despite the numbing effect of the alcohol, she was nervous as hell.

'I wonder if Tim's one-night stand has just become two,' said Conor, as Jo fumbled with her front door lock. 'If so, he'll be even more unbearable to live with.'

Her jacket still on, Jo stood in the middle of the hallway, unsure what to do next. Conor's mention of sex, even if it had been someone else's, had momentarily thrown her. Pulling her gently by the elbow, Conor led her into the living room, helped her off with her jacket, and pointed at the sofa.

'Sit down. I'll get us a drink, if that's OK?' He looked at her questioningly.

Jo nodded silently. Comforted by the familiar surroundings, she had relaxed to the extent that she knew she was about to do something completely out of character. But she didn't care.

'Tea, coffee, or something else?' said Conor, throwing his jacket onto the other sofa. He was now staring at her in a blatantly hungry fashion, a coiled spring that would ping in her direction if she gave the nod.

'Something else.' Jo's voice was so low she was in danger of sounding like a cheesy Hollywood voiceover.

'Like what?' His voice cracked slightly. He licked his top lip with a nervous flick of his tongue.

Jo stared at him. Her body was aching for an affectionate, masculine touch, but her boring, sensible mind kept telling her to hold back. The drink-fuelled body won.

'I want *you*,' she whispered. Immediately, her words were followed by the thought: Fuck, did I really just say that?

What she'd said hung between them, waiting for his response. She felt as if her heart was beating in the open air for all to see. She couldn't believe she'd said such a thing. What on earth had she done?

Conor stepped forward and enveloped her in his arms. 'I want you too,' he mumbled, nuzzling her neck. 'I've always wanted you.'

Jo resisted the childish urge to say, 'What? Ever since you were ten?' and tilted her head back into 'take me' mode.

Lifting his head, Conor cupped her face with one hand whilst the fingers of the other traced the outline of her lips. She closed her eyes as his fingers entered her mouth and eased her teeth apart. His tongue flicked into her mouth and her insides went onto spin cycle.

How wonderful everything seems when you first kiss someone, she thought. In a week's time I'd be saying, 'Have a bloody shave, you're cutting me to ribbons.' It crossed her mind to pull away, but the dull, throbbing ache between her legs killed all rational thought.

Conor's hand was inside her blouse now, his fingers pulling her flimsy bra cup to one side. As he started to lower his head, Jo's thoughts briefly turned to what underwear she was wearing. If only she'd known this was going to happen . . . she had on a trusty old faithful she had always referred to as her Sheffield United bra. No cups and no support.

Whether it was the thought of Conor seeing it, or just sheer common sense saying this was not an ideal situation, Jo didn't know. But as Conor stooped to take her aroused nipple in his mouth, she pulled away and started to do up her blouse. She ended up fastening it two buttons higher than it had been all evening.

'No, we mustn't,' she panted. 'We'd only regret it in the morning.'

Conor took a step back, an expression of bemusement on his face. 'I thought you wanted us to do this?'

'I did . . . I do,' stumbled Jo. 'It's just not a good idea. You're my brother's friend.'

'I didn't realise there was a law against it,' said Conor, his tone measured. 'Tell you what, I'll give him a call now and tell him I don't want to be friends any more, OK?' He took a step towards her.

'No!' Jo leapt backwards as if she'd been electrocuted. The spell of alcoholic oblivion combined with lust had been broken, and they stood in the middle of the room like two awkward teenagers. The second rejection had clearly sunk in with Conor. His face had clouded.

'Look, why don't you stay the night in the spare room? It saves you walking home, and it also means we can wake up in the morning and pretend this never happened, get our relationship back on an even keel sort of thing.'

Conor was clearly unimpressed. 'If that's what you want.'

'It is.' Jo's voice was firm, but it took all her willpower

to stop herself from dragging him upstairs to bed and damning the consequences.

At 5 a.m. precisely, her eyes flicked open with all the panic of someone who has to catch an urgent flight and fears they've overslept.

She knew there was something bothering her. Indeed, it was fast asleep in her spare room.

She'd almost had rampant sex with her brother's friend, a man who had known her children all their lives and who regularly visited her home, the home she had now sullied with their sordid, but admittedly enjoyable, little grope. How would she ever look him in the face again?

Creeping down the four stairs leading to the spare room, Jo put her head around the open door. With dark hair falling across his peaceful face and early-morning stubble, she thought she'd never seen a more handsome man. He was emitting tiny snores. God, she thought, he even snores beautifully. Unlike Jeff who sounded like a wounded warthog, especially after a few bitters.

Compared to the sleeping beauty in front of her, she was a complete fright. She turned back to her room. Her mouth was gummed up from dehydration and her pillow resembled the Turin shroud where last night's make-up had rubbed off. Remembering flashbacks of their brief passion, Jo felt the telltale ache of desire pulsating between her legs and tried to block it from her mind.

'Tea,' she muttered under her breath, the elixir to cure all ills.

As she nursed a cuppa in the kitchen, she recalled their conversation in the curry house and winced as she remembered how she'd interrogated Conor about his romantic history.

She only knew snippets of his life, gleaned from what Tim had told her over the years, but last night she'd grilled him about every last detail, until he started to get the worried look of a man expecting to get home and find Thumper boiling on the stove.

'So, have you got a girlfriend?' she'd said, before they'd even eaten the first poppadom. Standing now in the sober daylight of her kitchen, Jo couldn't believe how forward she'd been.

'No, there's no-one special,' he'd replied, spooning a dollop of mango chutney onto his plate.

'A-ha. When men use that expression, it usually means there's a succession of alright-for-nows floating around.'

'Nope, not in my case. I don't see the point in seeing people regularly unless they mean something to you. In the meantime, I practise a lot on my own,' he grinned.

'But how do you know that they might not eventually mean something to you . . . if you don't see them regularly?' Jo stumbled halfway through, trying to work out if she had actually said what she'd set out to say.

'Bloody hell, I'm having a curry with Sigmund Freud.'

Over the next two hours, Jo had established that his

last relationship had been with a girl he met at university. It had lasted five years and he'd not had a long-term relationship since.

'Why did you break up?'

'She went off with one of my colleagues at Offley Architecture. That's why I quit the job, because I couldn't bear to look at him every day.'

'God, I'm so sorry. I thought you were made redundant. Not that I wouldn't be sorry about that too, of course,' she added quickly.

'Nope. That's just what I tell people so I don't have to give them the real story. My family and Tim are about the only people who know all the gory details.'

'Tim's never mentioned it.'

'He wouldn't. Despite being one of the loudest, brashest people I know, your brother is remarkably discreet when it comes to important matters.'

Jo resisted the temptation to look astonished. 'Maybe it's just the people he tells who are indiscreet,' she smiled. 'Do you want to talk about it?'

Conor yawned, revealing an impressive set of old silver fillings on his back teeth. 'Not really, no. I was over it long ago, so it's not something I even think about these days. But if you want to know, I'll tell you.'

'Sorry, it's just that I have a morbid fascination about other people's break-ups at the moment, for obvious reasons.' She attempted a weak smile, hoping it would persuade him to spill the beans.

Conor begged a cigarette from a couple at the next table, gave out a deep where-do-I-start sigh and leaned back in his chair, a cornered man.

'Well, Sally – that's her name, by the way – was on the same course as me at London University. We didn't get together until the final year, because we weren't sure whether it would last and we didn't want to spoil our friendship. But in the end, we couldn't help ourselves and I did fall in love with her. As far as I was concerned, she was the woman I was going to marry, and I thought she felt the same way. When I got the job at Offley's, I bought the house and she moved in with me. It was great for a couple of years, then I started to notice her behaviour towards me was changing. So I confronted her and—'

'Hang on, whoa,' Jo interrupted. 'How did her behaviour change?' It always infuriated her how dreadful men were at relaying the finer detail of any situation. She and Rosie could make the most mundane anecdote stretch for hours.

'Oh, I dunno. Less sex, wanting to go out on her own a lot more, that kind of thing. Anyway, I confronted her and she admitted there was someone else. When I pushed her on the subject, she confessed it was one of my colleagues. We'd even been out for dinner with him and his girlfriend a couple of times, and I couldn't bear the thought he was probably sitting there laughing at me and thinking, "I'm screwing your girlfriend." So I kicked her out immediately and quit my job the next week. I never gave him the satisfaction of punching him.'

Puffing on the last centimetre of his cigarette, Conor ground it into the ashtray with a finality that suggested the subject of his relationships was spent too.

'Wow. I admire your strength of will,' said Jo. 'Although I suppose it's easier to block someone out of your life if you don't have children with them.'

'True. I look back on it as a valuable lesson now, because I know I would never allow myself to cheat on anyone. I wouldn't want them to feel the pain and humiliation I went through.'

Draining the last dregs of her tea and placing the cup in the sink, Jo smiled to herself as she remembered having to grip the edge of her chair to stop herself lunging across the table and enveloping Conor in a bear hug.

The unmistakable creak of the spare bedroom door wiped the smile from her face.

'Shit, shit, shit,' she muttered, scurrying towards the downstairs loo. She ran inside and closed the door, as Conor's footsteps came down the stairs.

'Hello?'

'Hi, I'm just in the loo,' she squeaked through the lock-less door. 'Won't be a moment.'

Turning on the tap for no apparent reason other than something to do, she peered into the minuscule fish-shaped mirror hanging over the sink. Her carefully applied eye-shadow from last night had gone blotchy and her mouth was encircled only in the remnants of a particularly long-lasting lip-liner, giving her the Gothic look of someone who had

82

died in the night. Using damp loo roll, she dabbed at her face in an attempt to clean it. She could have kicked herself for wasting time daydreaming when she could have been repairing her make-up. Though she was adamant she'd done the right thing by stopping their liaison last night, she was vain enough to want to look her best in front of him. But, lacking the tools and the time, it wasn't possible. He would just have to be treated to the real 'natural look' as opposed to the one that took at least an hour to perfect.

Flushing the loo, she dragged her fingers through her hair in a last-minute mirror check, then opened the door and walked through into the kitchen.

Conor was leaning nonchalantly against the draining board dressed only in his boxer shorts, looking utterly edible.

'Good morning. How's your head?' he asked.

'I was just about to call the restaurant. I think I lost it there last night.' She pulled her dressing gown tighter to her body.

'I see. Is that a joke, or a rather loaded statement suggesting you regret what happened between us?' he said quietly.

Jo froze. She wasn't used to a man who was so direct about everything. Usually, they danced around an issue, desperate to avoid any confrontation. She was hoping Conor would act as if nothing had happened, then leave and carry on as usual. But he stayed firmly rooted to the draining board.

'Well?' He looked directly at her.

'Look, I really don't want to talk about it right now. I've got an appalling hangover and I'd rather just go back to bed, on my own, and sleep it off.' She didn't mean her voice to come out sounding so shrill.

He stared at her for a moment, his eyebrows raised. 'In that case, I'll go. And by the way, the "on my own" bit was unnecessary. I would never get into your bed without an invitation.'

As he walked out of the kitchen, Jo slumped onto a chair and let out a sigh. God, what a bloody mess, she thought.

He came down five minutes later, fully dressed with his jacket thrown over his arm. Standing in the kitchen doorway, he looked at her for a few seconds before speaking.

'I know you don't want to talk about it now, but I know after I walk out of that front door I may not get the chance to be alone with you again, so I just want to say something. If you can remember anything of last night, I told you I had always wanted you, and that's true. But you were with Jeff so there was nothing I could do. Now you're not with him, and I would never have forgiven myself if I had let the opportunity pass to tell you what I feel.' He paused and cleared his throat. 'I really like you, Jo, and I would like us to go out on a couple of proper dates to try and get over this brother's friend obsession you seem to have. Have a think about it. I'll leave the ball in your court as to whether you want to do anything about it.'

He waited for Jo's response. There wasn't one.

'Right,' he said, with false brightness. 'I'm off then. I'll see you soon – I hope.'

Jo cleared her throat. 'Yes, of course. Thanks for dinner.'

She knew she should stand up and see him out, but she couldn't face the prospect of an awkward encounter in the hallway, so she remained seated. As she heard the familiar click of the front door closing, she let out a long, slow breath and felt all the tension rushing out of her shoulders.

'Thank God for that,' she said aloud, although she felt curiously deflated. The simple fact was she would have liked nothing more than an evening of uncomplicated sex. But there was no such thing with your brother's friend. There was also no such thing when you were recovering from a marriage break-up and had two children by another man. She felt that life would never be simple again, and it depressed the hell out of her.

Still, she thought, at least I have the whole day to myself to do absolutely nothing. What bliss! Will it be a bath then back to bed? Or back to bed for a while and then a bath?

'Decisions, decisions,' she said to the cat, who had wandered in through the flap.

The phone rang.

6

'Hello?' Her voice sounded nervous, fearful it was Conor calling from his mobile just two minutes down the road.

'Hi, it's Jeff. Listen, Sophie has got really bad tummy pains and wants to come home. I've tried to talk her out of it, but she just keeps crying and saying she wants Mummy.'

Bed then bath? Or bath then bed? Bloody neither, thought Jo, as she saw her child-free weekend vanish into thin air. She immediately felt guilty for such selfish thoughts.

'Poor little thing. How long has she been like that?'

'Since about ten last night. I tried calling you but there was no answer and you hadn't put the machine on. She eventually drifted off to sleep at about midnight, so I thought I'd leave it until this morning. So . . . did you have a good night?' Jeff paused before casually throwing the question at her.

'What's that supposed to mean?' snapped Jo, feeling a warm flush creeping up the back of her neck.

'Er, exactly what it says, Jo. I was merely asking if you'd had a nice evening, as you were clearly out some-where.'

'Yes, fine thanks,' replied Jo, hastily gathering herself. 'Bring her home now. I'll be here.'

Half an hour later he arrived at the door with a tearful Sophie, looking very sorry for herself and clutching a Paddington Bear hot water bottle to her stomach.

'Where's Thomas?' said Jo, looking over Jeff's shoulder as she gathered her listless daughter into her arms.

'He's playing with my next-door neighbour's son in their house. I said I'd only be half an hour and I didn't see any point in dragging him along.' Jeff closed the door behind him.

'He'd better not be with her,' muttered Jo, careful to keep her voice low so Sophie wouldn't hear.

Jeff raised his eyes heavenward. 'He's not. I'd hardly risk your wrath, knowing how unreasonable you are about the children seeing Candy. When you meet someone new all the rules will be different no doubt.'

Jo shot him a deadly look and carried Sophie upstairs.

'I want to sleep in your bed, Mummy,' she murmured, nuzzling into Jo's neck.

'Alright sweetie, of course you can.'

Turning back the duvet with one hand, she laid Sophie on the bed and tucked her in. She heard a creak at the top of the stairs and peered round the door just in time to see Jeff disappearing into the spare room. She followed.

He had often frequented it in the latter months of their marriage, after arriving home late and, the next day, saying, 'I didn't want to disturb you.' Now she knew he'd slept there for selfish reasons after no doubt exhausting himself with rampant young Candy.

'I see all traces of me have been removed,' he said, his eyes scanning the room, absorbing every little detail. He walked towards the bed. 'Ah, but traces of others remain.' He gave a triumphant smile and stared pointedly at the pillow. The two dark brown hairs on it may as well have been highlighted with a large neon sign flashing, 'Gotcha.'

'What are you wittering on about?' snapped Jo. 'They're probably yours.'

'Darling, I think even you might have changed the bedding after three months,' said Jeff sarcastically, lowering his face to the pillow and making an elaborate sniffing noise. 'I also don't remember wearing this particular brand of aftershave.'

Furious, Jo turned on her heel and left the bedroom. If Jeff hadn't become a solicitor, he'd have made a top-rate detective. He was one of those men who was like a dog with a bone if he thought he'd unearthed something suspicious. He also revelled in the discomfort of others. It didn't take Hercule Poirot to know an almighty row was on the way.

'So who is he?' He had followed her into the kitchen.

She knew she should ignore the remark and ask him to leave, but after all these years he knew exactly which buttons to push to infuriate her.

'Look, I've really got no idea what you're talking about. And quite frankly, if I wanted to shag every man within a four-mile radius it would be absolutely no fucking business of yours, alright?' She hated herself for taking the bait.

'Now, now, temper, temper. I was merely asking, and I see you have answered my question by your use of the word "shag",' said Jeff pompously. 'If someone brings up a subject unprompted in court, it always proves it's on their mind.'

Whirr. His verbal fishing line shot across the room and hooked itself straight into the corner of her mouth. He was the prosecuting solicitor. She was the defendant. And he was winning the psychological game.

'It wasn't unprompted. You pointed out what you thought to be evidence of me sleeping with someone, and I have denied it. Now let's drop the bloody subject,' she snapped. But he ploughed on as if he hadn't heard her, taking two steps away then swivelling on his heel as if addressing a witness.

'Quite frankly, I'd be thrilled if you were seeing someone because it might make you a little more understanding of my situation.'

Jo gave an exasperated gasp that came out like a repressed snort. 'Your situation? And what might that be? Now let me see. Ah yes, you walked out on your wife and children to shack up with some twelve-year-old and now you want some understanding, do you? Well, you can just fuck off!' She folded her arms with as much fury as she could muster.

'Oh, very adult. I thought after three months you might

have calmed down about all this, but I can see I was expecting too much of you.'

They sat in stony silence for a few moments, Jo staring out of the French doors, Jeff looking at the ceiling. The next time he spoke, his voice was more conciliatory.

'Look, all I'm saying is that surely it's better for the kids if we can establish some kind of routine when they come to stay with me. It's awkward that Candy has to go and stay with friends simply because you don't want her to meet the children.'

Jo shot him a glance to see whether he was joking, but his expression was deadly serious.

'Frankly Jeff, I don't give a fuck if Candy has to sleep in a cardboard box on the Embankment. She's not my concern and never will be. What I don't want is for the children to meet a succession of "aunties" in your life.' She was fighting hard to keep her voice calm, because she knew it would have more impact.

Jeff let out one of those how-can-you-reason-with-women sighs and stood up. 'I've said it before and I'll say it again. Heck, I might even get a T-shirt with it printed on the front just to hammer home the message once and for all. Candy is not a fling. She's a permanent fixture in my life and you'd better get used to it.'

Jo rubbed her face with the palm of her hand. Suddenly, she felt exceptionally weary and wanted him out. 'Yes, you left your last lot of permanent fixtures behind with this house when you left, didn't you, Jeff?

Which reminds me, you don't live here any more, so would you please leave.'

Here was her husband standing in what was once their family kitchen, defending his mistress to her. It shocked and depressed her to the core.

Jeff started walking down the hallway. 'Fine. I'll bring Thomas home at tea-time tomorrow. I'll let myself out.'

After the familiar click – the second man that day to let himself out of her house – Jo stayed rooted to the spot. She felt overwhelmed with sadness. What on earth was happening to her? One minute she had been a happy-ish married woman with two children, the next she was a single mum who needed only a couple of glasses of wine to make her behave with wanton abandon towards the first slightly interested man that came along.

The empty day ahead that had seemed so attractive an hour ago now felt like an abyss of loneliness in which she would spend her time clock-watching and trying to find something – anything – to fill one hour, never mind several. Jeff was the villain of the piece, and yet he was the one enjoying the best of both worlds. He had the thrill of a new relationship unhindered by the twenty-four-hour responsibility of their children, and could play the doting Daddy on days when it fitted into his golf or football-watching schedule.

Jo, on the other hand, had the twenty-four-hour responsibility of the children with no thrill to look forward to. Just a mundane round of making packed lunches, washing and ironing. Her encounter with Conor no longer felt illicit and exciting. It felt cheap, sordid and meaningless. Now here she was, a thirty-three-year-old mother of two, blowing all her hard-earned self-esteem in one rash evening. The hopelessness of her situation engulfed her, and a small tear ran down her cheek.

'Jo Miles, pull yourself together,' she muttered to herself, but it was no good. She walked across to the kitchen table, sat down, and had a damn good self-pitying weep.

When the phone rang five minutes later, she was already feeling better from the release of her pent-up emotion.

'Hello?' she said tentatively.

'Hi, it's me.' It was Rosie. 'I'm just checking you went on your night out with the chaps and didn't wimp out.'

'Um, yes, sort of.'

'Any good?'

Jo knew if she told Rosie the gory details now they would be on the phone for the next two hours. So she decided to wait.

'It was certainly interesting. Listen, I've got Sophie back with me because she's got tummy ache, so why don't you come round tonight and I'll fill you in then?'

'Great. I'll bring some wine.'

'Bring two bottles. We'll need it.'

By the time Rosie arrived at 7.30, Jo was feeling philosophical about life again. That afternoon, she had crept into bed alongside Sophie and drifted off for a much-needed two-hour sleep. Sophie's temperature had gone down, and she was now upstairs watching a video of *Toy Story 2* for the squillionth time.

'Ta-dah!' Rosie held up the two bottles of wine as she walked through the door. 'A full bottle in front of me leads to a full frontal lobotomy.'

'I feel like I've already had one,' laughed Jo, following her into the living room. She had laid out two glasses, corkscrew, bowl of tortilla chips and a selection of dips in preparation for their natter.

'I was going to put out some Kendal mint cake too, because this is going to be a long one,' she said, while Rosie struggled with the cork, her Titian curls flopping into her eyes.

'Bloody hell, I didn't think a night out with your brother and his friend would be that interesting,' said Rosie, as a satisfying 'pop' indicated a drink was finally on its way.

'Ah, well that's it you see.' Jo decided there was no point beating about the bush. 'Tim didn't show up, so I went out with Conor on my own and we ended up playing a rather exuberant game of tonsil tennis.'

It was unfortunate timing as Rosie had just taken a large slug of red wine. She began to make elaborate choking noises as a small trickle escaped from the side of her mouth and dribbled down her chin.

'Fucking hell, Jo.' She cupped her hand under her jaw

to catch the drips. 'There I was thinking you were enjoying a small sherry in the local wine bar, and all the time
you were shagging your brother's best friend.'

'No, no, it didn't go that far. We did go for a drink
and then dinner, and then it just sort of happened,' said
Jo sheepishly.

'It just sort of happened,' repeated Rosie. 'What, like rain
"just sort of happens" or accidents "just sort of happen"?
Christ, I wish snogging a gorgeous bloke would "just sort
of happen" to me. If it weren't for those people that frisk
you at airports I'd have no sex at all.'

Jo shrugged apologetically. 'I know it sounds ridiculous, but I genuinely didn't mean it to happen. I think it
was the combination of too much alcohol and a craving
for affection.'

'It's called lust,' said Rosie matter-of-factly, 'and all I
can say is, you jammy cow. He's a real catch.'

'There's no way it will happen again, it was a one-off,'
said Jo. 'I've only just started to adjust to Jeff walking
out. No way do I want to start another relationship. You
know what they say? There's so little difference between
husbands, you may as well keep the first.'

'You'd be mad to let that one get away. But never mind
all that. Tell me what happened. I want to know every
little detail.' Rosie plumped up a cushion behind her and
tucked up her legs for maximum comfort.

Cradling her wineglass in both hands, Jo started to
talk about the night before. After so much silent thought

on the matter, it felt odd to hear her own voice speaking about it. It also felt exceptionally therapeutic.

Halfway through describing the way Conor had held her face, she was stopped in her tracks by Rosie letting out a deep sigh. 'God, that's soooo romantic. You are Mrs Lucky living in Lucky House on Lucky Lane in the town of Lucky.' Rosie was prone to exaggeration. 'Honestly, Jo, you have no idea. Most men's idea of romance is grunting, "You scrub up well for an old bird", before lunging at you. Sorry, carry on,' she added as Jo shot her an exasperated look.

Jo completed her story, right up to the point where Conor had quietly let himself out of the house. 'So that's that. I'll never be able to look him in the face again,' she said, with more than a tinge of regret. She looked up to find Rosie staring at her with a strange expression on her face.

'So hang on, let's get this straight. You got passionate with an incredibly handsome man with a great body and a good brain, who, instead of walking out and saying, "See ya", told you that he wanted to take you out on a proper date?'

'Well, if you put it like that, yes.'

'What other way is there to put it? If I was you I'd be round there right now with my painfully blank diary in one hand and an indelible pen in the other.'

'Yes, but that's you. Your life isn't as complicated as mine. Meeting a new man when you already have children is altogether different, because it's not just about great sex and seeing what develops at a later date,' said Jo, taking a small sip of wine. 'Besides, starting a relationship now just isn't an option . . . with anyone.'

'What, ever?' Rosie topped up their glasses.

But Jo wasn't listening. She was staring into the middle distance, various thoughts in her mind.

'The most depressing thing about all of this is that it's brought home to me how complicated it's going to be if and when I start dating again. You never know whether something is going to turn out to be just a fling. At what point do you decide it's something more and introduce them to your children? And what if your kids don't like them?'

'Conor knows them already, so you wouldn't ever face that dilemma,' said Rosie. 'And best of all, you wouldn't have to suffer the indignity of dating lots of unsuitable men. Do you remember that time I took out an ad in the *Sunday Times*?'

Jo burst out laughing. 'I do. It was a nightmare for you, but it kept me entertained for months.'

Desperate to widen her search for a man, Rosie had placed a personal ad two years earlier and received more than fifty replies. So she and Jo had spent a delicious Sunday afternoon sifting and giggling their way through the envelopes, placing them into piles of 'worth a try', 'only if desperate' and 'serial killers'.

Rosie went on dates with all ten of the 'worth a try's'

and even ventured into the 'only if desperate' category a couple of times. But it proved fruitless.

'Bloody hell, they should all be done under the Trade Descriptions Act,' she said one afternoon, after a particularly disastrous date with a man who had described himself as 'huggable' and turned out to have more body hair than Chewbacca.

Bent double with laughter, Jo had spent the next hour reading out descriptions from the personal ads while Rosie gave her slant on what they really meant.

'Distinguished.'

'That means fat, grey and balding.'

'Educated.'

'Means he'll speak to you like you're a moron.'

'Friendship first.'

'As long as it involves nudity.'

'This one's used a lot. Professional.'

'It just means they own a suit.'

'Free spirit.'

'He shags around.'

'Honest.'

'Pathological liar.'

With all these social misfits around, it was little wonder that Rosie thought Jo mad for not giving it a go at least with Conor.

Standing up, Rosie placed her empty wine glass on the mantelpiece and looked at the clock. It was just after midnight.

'It's pumpkin time. I'd better go, because I'm going to force myself to get up early for the gym which I hate. If God had wanted me to touch my toes, he'd have put them on my knees. Maybe I'll just go to the beauty parlour instead, well, for an estimate anyway!'

Jo giggled. 'You always manage to cheer me up with your self-deprecation.'

'Happy to be of service. I'm off. If I stay here, we'll just end up gossiping all morning and not a pot will be emptied, as my grandmother used to say.'

'OK. Thanks for coming over. It's really helped to be able to talk it all through with someone. I thought I was going to burst this afternoon.' Jo stood up and stretched her hands towards the ceiling, letting out a dramatic yawn.

'Anytime.' Rosie yawned too.

As Jo opened the front door, Rosie stepped outside and paused halfway down the mosaic pathway.

'I've just thought of another crucial reason why you should give it a go with Conor.'

'Oh yeah? What's that?' smiled Jo.

'He knows how to handle your mother.' With that remark, Rosie marched off down the street.

Jo closed the door and slumped with her back against the stained-glass window.

'Shit, shit, shit,' she muttered. Just when she thought matters couldn't get any worse, Rosie's comment had reminded her that indeed they could.

Her mother was arriving tomorrow.

7

The sound of a cab door slamming shut snapped Jo out of her trance-like state. She was sitting in the living room with Sophie who, though feeling slightly better, was milking her illness for all it was worth, watching videos with a suffering expression, swathed in her Barbie duvet.

The doorbell rang and Jo felt her insides subside with dread.

'She will not get to me, she will not get to me, she will not get to me,' she chanted under her breath as she walked into the hallway.

'Mother, you made it!' she enthused as she flung open the front door.

'Don't sound so disappointed, dear,' said Pam, thrusting her cheek at her daughter to indicate a kiss was expected. Jo obliged, and as usual her mother turned her head at the last second which meant she got a mouthful of wiry grey hair and mock satin headscarf.

'Now, where's that poorly little granddaughter of mine?' Pam swept past Jo into the house.

'She's in the living room watching *Home Alone* for the umpteenth time.'

Jo stood on the doorstep and looked down at the two large hold-alls her mother had left there. It's going to be a long stay then, she thought wearily, as she bent down to pick them up.

Relations between her and her mother had been strained since the phone call immediately after Jeff had walked out. It had been two weeks before Jo had responded to Pam's many messages, and even then she had made the call under sufferance after much pleading from Tim, who said he was going to commit hara-kiri if he had to play go-between any longer. Her mother had made a stiff apology and they had made an arrangement for Jo and the children to visit in a couple of weeks' time. But the trip had been a disaster. From the moment Jo arrived, her mother had clearly made it her weekend's ambition to make her daughter 'see sense', and try to patch up her marriage.

'Worse things happen at sea, dear,' she'd said.

'Yes, but I'm not at sea. I'm in a semi in South London,' Jo had muttered.

'Don't be facetious, Jo. You know exactly what I mean.'

This kind of conversation happened every time Jo found herself alone with her mother, so she had spent the entire weekend trying to dodge their 'little chats' as Pam called them.

Her father had seemed curiously philosophical about the whole mess, and one of Jo's fondest memories of her visit was a long talk they'd had sitting in the Pam-free sanctity of the garden shed. As he sat and scraped the caked-on mud from his ancient wellingtons, Jo had told him the details of how she'd caught Jeff having an affair and how he said he loved the new woman.

'Mum thinks I should fight for him,' said Jo, raising her eyes from the floor to gauge her father's reaction to the remark.

'Pointless,' he said matter-of-factly. 'If Jeff has gone that far down the line with this woman, he needs to go and get her out of his system. Even if you had persuaded him to stay, you would both have ended up hating each other for it.'

'Why?' Jo was surprised at her father's clear-cut, insightful view. She had always thought him the type to avoid even thinking about emotional matters in any depth, let alone discussing them.

'Because every time he was out of your sight you would be wondering whether he was with her, and it would eat you up. And even if he wasn't with her and trying hard to stay away, he would probably start to resent you for it. Unfair I know, but I think it's the truth.' He paused and looked at Jo apologetically, but she didn't respond. 'The best thing is to let the whole thing burn itself out, because, believe me, it will,' her father continued. 'He'll be missing the children already, and the age gap between them will start to grate once the novelty wears off. The question you need to ask yourself is, when he wants to come back, will you be willing to have him?' He looked directly at Jo, his eyebrows raised.

She stared at the floor for a few seconds, then looked up and gave a half-hearted shrug. 'At this point in time, I really have no idea.'

Her father's face softened. 'You don't need to know it right now,' he said. 'In fact, you shouldn't even think about it until it happens. Easier said than done I know, but just get on with your own life, and the rest will fall into place.'

Jo had felt buoyed up by the conversation, liberated by the fact that at least one of her parents seemed to understand the pain and sense of hopelessness she was experiencing.

She'd never heard her parents argue beyond the odd snappy remark here and there, but on this visit she was startled by a particularly bitter tirade from her father to her mother shortly after they'd scaled the east face of a large Sunday joint.

He had been sitting quietly in the corner of the living room reading the local newspaper, while Jo and her mother remained at the dining table chatting.

Naturally, her mother hadn't been able to resist the chance to drag up the subject of Jeff one more time before Jo and the kids set off back to London.

'You have to work at a marriage, you know,' said Pam, leaning across and picking a minuscule piece of fluff from Jo's sweater.

'I wasn't aware there was anything that needed working at, Mum.' Jo gave a we've-been-here-before sigh.

'Well, they do say a happily married man never strays,

so there *must* have been a reason why he did what he did.'
Her mother's mouth had set into a determined line.

Jo had heard so many variations of Pam's irritating perspective on her marital problems that she couldn't even be bothered to get worked up about it any more. But on this occasion, she didn't need to. Her father did it for her.

'For Christ's sake, woman, will you shut up about the bloody subject! You're like a stuck record. The poor girl has come here to get some support, not to be attacked at every given opportunity.' He was red in the face with undisguised rage.

Pam looked so startled by her husband's outburst that, for a moment, Jo thought she was going to cry. Her bottom lip trembling, her mother looked across at him with the hurt expression of a small child that has been told off and doesn't know why.

It was a defining moment for Jo. She had long ago realised her parents weren't infallible as individuals, but she had never really considered their marriage might be anything but happy. Now it was staring her in the face for the first time that their relationship was far from the perfect picture she and Tim had imagined as children. It finally dawned on her that Jim and Pam had endured their own rocky patches, insecurities and compromises that everyone had to cope with. But they had obviously done a sterling job at shielding their children from the often harsh realities of married life.

Perhaps I didn't put enough effort into my relationship

with Jeff because I thought happy marriages just happened, Jo thought to herself.

In the past, she and Rosie had indulged in endless conversations about how their family backgrounds might have affected their own adult relationships. Rosie's father had been a violent drunk and, as a child, she had witnessed many frightening scenes. At the age of nine, she had threatened her father with a knife to make him stop beating her mother, and the experience had never left her.

'It's not that I don't trust men, I do,' she said once. 'It's just that I keep a sharp eye on how they behave after a drink. Any sign of even the slightest bolshiness and it's all over for me. Been there, seen it, got the bruising.'

The avoidance of violent men was the only hangover Rosie seemed to have from her turbulent past, and this consoled Jo when she thought of the effect her and Jeff's split might have on Thomas and Sophie.

'If I keep things as friendly as possible with Jeff in front of them, then they might just emerge from it all with a re-alistic view of relationships, which is no bad thing,' she told Rosie. 'I had an idealistic view because my parents seemed to have the "perfect" marriage, and look where it got me.'

Her thoughts were sharply interrupted by the un-imaginable sound of her parents embarking on a full-scale row.

'How dare you speak to me like that. I am merely trying to save our daughter's marriage, rather than encourage her to give up on it, which is what you seem to be doing.' Her mother's voice was quivering with emotion.

Jim had thrown his newspaper to the floor and was pacing up and down in front of the fireplace. 'Don't start bloody crying, that's all I need. It may have escaped your attention Pam, but Jeff left Jo, not the other way round. This is the twenty-first century now, women don't need men to survive any more. She can get on with her own life.'

Pam shot him a bitter look, tears welling up behind the large spectacles Tim always described as 'Morris Minor headlamps'. 'With that attitude, why does any woman bother getting married at all? You men are all the same, you always think the grass is greener. But it isn't, it's just different.'

They fell into a stony silence, exchanging hard looks across the soft furnishings.

'Look you two, don't fall out over me,' Jo pleaded. 'Jeff's gone and, for the moment, there's nothing I can do about it. Let's move on.' Her words sounded convincing, but deep down she sensed her parents' argument had nothing whatsoever to do with *her* marital problems.

As far as she knew, from the limited, stiff telephone conversations with her mother since, things seemed to have settled down again after Jo had left. So she was surprised when her mother had called to say she would be making a long visit.

Pam had never left Jim for more than a weekend before. It was just one generation behind, but Jo never ceased to be amazed by how different their marriage was compared to hers. She and Jeff had often taken separate long weekends away with friends to give each other a break from the children.

As a teenager, Jo remembered shaking her head in disbelief as she watched her mother lay out her father's clothes each morning.

'He's not bloody disabled, Mum,' she would snap, furious that her mother was displaying all the signs of a downtrodden serf.

'I know that, dear,' her mother would reply, in a sing-song voice reminiscent of a Stepford wife. 'Don't start all your feminist nonsense with me.'

Her mother had accused her of being a feminist so many times that Jo had enlarged and photocopied an old Rebecca West quote and stuck it to her bedroom door. It read, 'I myself have never been able to find out precisely what feminism is: I only know that people call me a feminist whenever I express sentiments that differentiate me from a doormat.'

With a wry smile at the memory, Jo trudged upstairs with her mother's holdalls and wondered whether her father was now walking around starkers because Pam had gone away. On the way down, she bumped into her mother coming the other way.

'That poor child needs some fresh air rather than sitting around watching videos. I'm going to dress her and take her to the park to get some colour in her cheeks,' she said.

I like long walks, particularly when taken by people who irritate me, thought Jo. Pam always made her feel she was somehow inadequate as a parent, so her way of dealing with it had been to keep her mother at arm's length. She realised that a fortnight of painfully close contact lay ahead, and sat down on the bottom stair with a heavy sigh.

Pam bustled back past her clutching a pink dress and matching cardigan, together with the white frilly ankle socks that Sophie had steadfastly refused to wear since a hopeful Jo had bought them a month ago.

'They're horrid,' she'd moaned. She had also declared virtually overnight that Barbie was 'babyish', thereby rendering her entire bedroom décor obsolete. But Jo noticed she still played with the dolls in the house – it was only in public that the plastic blonde was now persona non grata.

'You'll be lucky,' said Jo to Pam. 'She's gone into her combat trouser phase since you last saw her.'

She was nursing a cup of coffee in the kitchen when Sophie walked in trussed up to the nines in the pink regalia.

'You flatly refused to wear that when I wanted you to.' Jo was open-mouthed with the injustice of it.

Sophie was about to say something when Pam swept into the kitchen and answered for her. 'You just have to be firm, dear. Children will always do as you say if you let them know who's boss.'

As Pam turned to place Sophie's empty juice cup in

the kitchen sink, Jo wrinkled her nose and poked out her tongue at her mother's back.

'Mummy, that's rude,' piped up Sophie, ignoring Jo's murderous glare.

Pam wiped the work surfaces with an air of self-importance. 'I don't know what you did whilst my back was turned, Jo, but I suspect it wasn't a good lesson in manners for your impressionable daughter. Come on, Sophie, let's go to the park.'

The door slammed and the phone rang. It was Tim. 'Hi Sis, have you murdered her yet?'

'No, but I've come pretty bloody close. And there's still thirteen days and twenty-three hours to go,' sighed Jo, idly spelling the word 'bollocks' on the fridge with Sophie's magnetic letters. 'I've decided distant relatives are the best kind, and the further away the better.'

'I know, grim, isn't it?' said Tim, as Jo wondered how it could possibly be that way for him, considering so far he'd done sweet FA in helping to shoulder the burden that was their mother. How did the old saying go? A son is a son until he gets a wife, a daughter's a daughter for life. Tim hadn't got a wife but he'd still managed to offload most of the parental duties on to Jo. This occasion was no different.

'Listen,' he said nervously. 'I know I was supposed to be joining you for Sunday lunch but—'

'Tim, you promised!' interjected Jo. 'You know I can't handle Mum on my own for too long.'

'I know, I know. Look, I'll come round early evening instead, if that's OK. It's just that it's a lovely day and Conor and I want to go fishing.'

Jo marvelled how men have the capacity to feel absolutely no guilt at all in the pursuit of their own selfish desires.

'What you mean is that you and Conor want to stand by the riverbank and drink yourself stupid, while the fish swim by in complete safety.' She felt a little flutter of anxiety as she said his name.

'Damn, you've rumbled us. Anyway, we'll see you later.'

'We? What do you mean, we?' she snapped.

'I thought I might ask Conor. You know how good he is with mother. It'll take the heat off us for a while.'

'No, Tim, what you mean is it will take the heat off *you*. If I'm going to put up with her on my own all day, you can damn well suffer it this evening without help. Come alone.'

Tim let out a long, deep sigh. 'If you insist. I'll be round at about six.'

Jo placed the phone back on the cradle and stood staring at it for a few seconds. She couldn't face the double dilemma of having to deal with her mother as well as the awkward situation with Conor. She hoped her insistence that Tim come alone hadn't alerted him that anything was amiss. Maybe Conor had already told him, but she doubted it. She suspected Tim wouldn't be able to resist having a subtle dig here and there if he was privy to such a hot piece of gossip.

She looked at the clock. It was noon and a table was booked at a local restaurant for 1 p.m. Thomas wasn't coming home until 4 p.m.

Jo was furious with Tim for backing out of lunch, but it had always been the same story. Tim could do what he liked and was clearly Pam's favourite, while Jo felt she was always doing something wrong.

Tim was a struggling actor who had very little work, yet Pam supported him wholeheartedly as well as financially on occasions. Jo earned much more as an interior designer, but her mother was always saying, 'Why don't you get a proper job?'

Jo wished she had the guts to tell her mother, 'If you like Tim so much, why don't you stay with him when you come to London?' but she could never quite manage it. The female guilt gene at work again.

Picking up the phone, she dialled Rosie's number and crossed her fingers in the hope of an answer. When one came, her relief was palpable.

'Oh, thank God you're there,' she said dramatically. 'Look, I'm really sorry to ask you this, but do you fancy coming for Sunday lunch with me, Sophie and my mother? Tim was supposed to come but the git has just pulled out, and I seriously don't think I can handle it on my own.'

Rosie paused. 'Jo, I'm so sorry, but I can't. I'm giving eight pints of blood this afternoon.'

'Oh ha bloody ha. Pretty please?'

'Go on then. But you owe me.'

'Thank you, thank you, thank you. One o'clock at Ashfords, table in the name of Beelzebub. If not, try Miles.'

Jo heaved a sigh of relief. The sound of the key in the door made her sit up and straighten her back in anticipation of the next round of tense exchanges.

'There we go, that's much better for her than sitting in front of the television.' Her mother's wind-whipped face gave her the look of a toby jug.

'Thanks, Mum. By the way, Tim's not coming for lunch, he'll come round early evening instead. But Rosie is going to join us.'

'I see. Couldn't face having lunch with me without some back-up, eh?' Her mother may have old-fashioned views, thought Jo, but she wasn't stupid.

'Don't be ridiculous. I just thought you'd like to see Rosie, that's all.' She knew it sounded unconvincing but she didn't really care.

By 3 p.m. they were back at the house, with Sophie once again firmly planted in front of the television, much to the disapproval of Pam.

Jo's theory that her friend's presence might alleviate matters had proved to be entirely wrong, and lunch had been a rather uptight affair, where Pam had persisted in pressing Rosie to side with her point of view over Jeff's desertion.

'Honestly, these things can be worked out, can't they, Rosie? You should point out to Jo that if she doesn't get back with Jeff she might end up on her own.' She looked at Rosie and realised her remark had been tactless. 'Not that there's anything wrong with being on your own, of course,' she added hastily.

'I'm sure you meant it in a kind way. But I don't think Jo should have to ingratiate herself in any way by trying to make Jeff see sense. He's completely in the wrong and should be here right now begging her to take him back.'

Pam fixed her with a forced smile. 'That's a very quaint view dear, but there are always two sides to every story.'

'Yes, and I know both sides to this sorry tale and *still* think Jeff is in the wrong. In fact, he's so bloody stupid he could throw himself on the ground and miss.'

Jo could see Rosie was close to losing her temper. It happened rarely, but when it did it was memorable. So she spent the rest of the lunch interjecting at tense moments with a string of irrelevancies designed to distract. The wallpaper was lovely. The weather was even lovelier. And as for the food, well it was just *incredibly* lovely. Turning down Jo's invitation to return to the house afterwards, Rosie had muttered something about a Blockbuster video that needed returning and hastily left.

Back at the house, Jo was so desperate to dilute her mother's company that she kept looking at the clock and willing Jeff to arrive back with Thomas. He eventually pitched up at 4.30 p.m. and her mother got to the door first.

'Jeff! Come in and have a cup of tea. I haven't seen you for ages.' Pam's tone was positively gushing.

112

'Shit!' muttered Jo in the kitchen. She could have kicked herself for not getting there first, grabbing Thomas, and preventing Jeff from coming in.

'Hi, how's Sophie?' Jeff asked as he walked into the kitchen and sat down.

'Ask her yourself on your way out. She's in the living room watching telly,' said Jo, desperate to get rid of him.

He returned two minutes later with Pam hot on his heels. 'She's fine. Your mother has worked wonders with her.'

Jo was about to snap back with a sarcastic retort when her mother's booming voice rang out.

'Now then Jeff, I'll bet you've missed my tea, haven't you? You always said no one could make a cuppa like mine,' she said, putting the kettle under the tap.

'That's for sure,' replied Jeff, nervously glancing across at Jo. He was clearly wondering whether she would tell Pam the truth, that Jeff had always loathed her overly strong tea.

She decided not to hang him out to dry completely, but Jo couldn't resist a private dig.

'Seeing as he likes it so much, give him that extra-large mug at the back of the cupboard.'

By now her mother was scurrying around the kitchen opening every cupboard door. 'Have you got any biscuits dear? You know how Jeff likes a biscuit with his tea.'

'No, Mum, I haven't. I don't like the kids eating them, and *as Jeff isn't here any more* there's no need.' She said the words loud and deliberately, but the effect was clearly lost

113

on Pam who was placing a steaming vat of dark orange liquid on the table.

'There we are, Jeff. The next time you pop round, I'll make sure there are some biscuits or a nice piece of cake for you.'

'Thanks, Pam. You certainly know how to look after me.'

Jo knew the remark was made deliberately to wind her up, but the tension between her and Jeff seemed to go straight over her mother's head.

'Now then, isn't this nice and civilised? Honestly, I don't know why you two can't just work out your differences and get back together. You've got two lovely children who would be thrilled to bits if Mummy and—'

'Shut up, Mum.' Jo stood up and paced the floor in front of the sink. 'The reason we can't get back together is because Jeff has chosen to go off with some nubile bimbo rather than stay with me and the children. He has made his choice and there's not a damn thing I can do about it, so spare me the bloody speeches about saving the marriage. It's *him* you should be lecturing.'

Jeff slammed his untouched tea mug down on the table, the contents splashing over the side. 'Right, that's it. I'm off. I'm trying to keep things friendly here, but every time I come round you cause an argument.' He looked at Pam and softened his tone. 'I'm sorry you had to witness this.'

It was enough to tip Jo over the edge. 'Oh, do me a fucking favour with the pleasantries towards my mother,' she snapped. 'You've never bloody liked her and, what's more, you've always hated her tea!'

She pointed triumphantly at the full mug on the table as Jeff marched out of the kitchen and down the hallway.

Jo heard him say goodbye to the children in the living room, then one minute later the front door slammed shut. She turned to look at her mother who was staring into space with a shocked expression.

'Is it true that he never liked me?' she said forlornly, after a few moments.

Jo was desperate to tell her mother the truth about all the rude remarks Jeff had made about her over the years. But even though her mother drove her to distraction, Jo still couldn't bear to hurt her deliberately.

'No, it's not true,' she smiled weakly. 'He does hate your tea though.' She picked up the mug and poured the contents into the sink.

Her mother's mouth reminded her of a rip in a paper bag. With heavy heart, she knew another lecture was on the way.

'Sometimes, Jo, it's better to rise above these things and keep matters pleasant between you. It won't be long before he and this girl start having arguments, and if you provide a sweeter surrounding for him to come to, he will. No man likes to come home to a war zone.'

Jo couldn't even be bothered to reply. The fact that it was Jeff who had started the war and thrown a hand grenade into all their lives seemed to have escaped her mother. She knew that whatever she said, the gulf between her and this woman who laid her husband's clothes out each morning would never narrow. So it was better to say nothing.

'You see, that's the first time you've not answered back. I do believe you're coming round to my way of thinking, dear.'

8

Grabbing the beige cardboard file marked 'Frampton Road', Jo made a quick check of her appearance in the hall mirror before stepping outside into the watery sunshine.

As she fumbled for her car keys, she waved to the small figure of her mother in the distance, walking back up the road after taking Thomas and Sophie to school. Despite being driven to distraction several times a day during the past fortnight, Jo had to admit Pam's presence had freed up valuable time for her to concentrate on work.

She had just started a huge project in Chelsea and was nervous about it because it was the most ambitious project she'd ever taken on. Rosie, who was always wittering on about 'perception', had persuaded her to fork out a fortune for an ad in the back of a glossy property magazine, delivered free to all the classy areas of London.

'If they see your ad in there, they'll think you're really established and used to doing such big projects,' she said. 'If you need it, I can give you a reference letter about your "excellent work" on my flat. They don't need to know it was only the downstairs loo.'

The advertisement had only spawned one call, but it

was a biggy; the restoration of an entire six-storey house. The money was excellent, but more importantly, it would last for months, and meant she had something to focus on other than the breakdown of her marriage, which was even beginning to bore her. Astonishingly, her mother hadn't mentioned it for a couple of days either, but was still in the habit of shaking her head in sorrow on the rare occasions Thomas and Sophie were playing nicely together, as if to say 'poor little mites from a broken home'.

Deep down among the loose tampons, old tissues, discarded sweet wrappers and scrappy pieces of wallpaper samples lurking in her voluminous handbag, she found the keys to her little blue Renault Clio, or 'the rollerskate' as Tim called it.

As she began a nine-point manoeuvre to get out of the tight space she had been sandwiched into by her neighbours' his 'n' hers BMWs, her thoughts turned to the meeting she was about to have with Martin Blake, the owner of Frampton Road. She had only been to the property once, very briefly, but it had been enough time to establish that it was top-to-bottom burgundy flocked fleur-de-lis, like a giant curry house.

'I can't stand it,' said Martin Blake, with masterly understatement, curling his lip and casting a despairing eye around the vast living room. 'I want minimalist.'

Jo's heart had sunk when he'd said this, as minimalism wasn't her forte. But she wasn't about to turn down such a lucrative job.

She worked her way out of the parking space and was about to pull away, when her mother drew level with the car, panting and placing her hand on the wing mirror to steady herself.

'I've been thinking. I'll probably head off back home on Sunday,' she puffed. 'I spoke to your father this morning and I think he's getting fed up of me being away for so long.'

On the contrary, I'll bet he's loving every moment, thought Jo. Instead of escaping to his shed every five minutes, he'll be smoking in the house and watching all his favourite sports programmes in peace and quiet.

'OK, Mum. I must say we'll miss you when you've gone. Your help has been a godsend.' She wasn't sure about the 'miss you' bit, but she meant the last part wholeheartedly.

She had hoped to spend the car journey getting her thoughts straight on exactly how she would articulate her 'vision' of the new-look Frampton Road to its owner, but instead she became distracted by the worry of how she would cope with juggling work and the children without Pam's help.

She toyed with the idea of employing a full-time nanny and making Jeff pay. God knows he deserved to suffer somehow, so why not financially? But she couldn't do it to the children. They'd already had one parent walk out, they needed her to be there for them as much as she could and not hand over responsibility to someone else.

Maybe an au pair was the answer. But then she

remembered the angst suffered by her friends Martha and Rob after they'd employed a Czechoslovakian girl to live in and help with their children. Svetlana had rapidly proved herself to be Dagenham – two stops past Barking – and developed a serious drink problem to the point that even Rob's lighter fuel couldn't be left unattended.

There had been a memorable Christmas Day when Rob's elderly parents were visiting and the family had decided to play a word game. Everyone had to come up with various category words beginning with a certain letter, in this case 'T'. A girl's name? Tabitha. A car? Toyota. A TV show? *Taggart*. Everyone was managing quite well, with the exception of Svetlana who was understandably frustrated by her lack of English.

The next category was four-letter words and Rob started with 'tape', followed by Martha's 'tick' and Rob's mother with 'tank'. Then it was Svetlana's turn.

'Twat,' she said, smiling broadly.

Rob said his ageing parents never really recovered from the incident, and six months later Svetlana came home in tears to announce she was pregnant and the father had 'done a legger', as she put it.

No, I'll just have to find another way, thought Jo, as she slowly pulled to a halt at some traffic lights.

Thwack! The unmistakeable thud of another car hitting hers jolted her out of her thoughts.

'What the . . . ?' She leapt out and swivelled on her heel to glare at the offending car.

The driver was opening his door and stepping out, much to the annoyance of the man behind who was now hooting his horn and trying to steer round them. It was chaos. Jo opened her mouth to give him what for.

'Bloody hell, I'm so sorry,' he said, before she could get a word in. 'It's totally my fault. I wasn't concentrating.'

His profuse and hasty apology threw her, and Jo stood by the side of her car at a loss.

'That's OK,' she said, bending down to inspect the damage. There was a slight dent on the bumper and an even slighter crack in the rear light, neither of which she was sure had been caused by the latest bump.

Straightening up, she looked at the other driver properly for the first time. He was in his mid-thirties, with dark blond hair and hazel eyes. He wasn't conventionally handsome, with a large nose and slightly protruding ears, but he had a devastating smile now being used on her to great effect.

'Well, they do say Volvo drivers are the worst on the road,' he grinned.

Jo found herself thinking how incredibly attractive he was, despite driving a battered, rusting Volvo with a ridiculous bull bar for all those wild animals you find in West London.

'Look, don't worry about it,' she said, tucking her hair behind her ears then immediately pulling it out again. 'My car's not exactly brand new and the damage is really small. Besides, my idea of double parking is to put my car on top of another, so let's just forget it.' She looked anxiously at her watch, fearful she was going to be late for her appointment.

His smile faltered for a moment. 'At least get the rear light fixed. I'll pay for it personally rather than lose my no claims. Let's quickly swap details.'

As he leaned across to the passenger glove box for a pen and paper, Jo glanced at his right hand for any sign of a wedding ring and surreptitiously scanned his car for child seats. Negative on both counts.

As she explained to Rosie later, she hadn't done this because she fancied him. It was because, owing to her newly single status, she had become fascinated by the private lives of other thirty-somethings.

'It's like when I bought the blue Clio, I suddenly noticed all these other blue Clios on the road. Now I'm single, I notice all those who are in the same position,' she had said.

The man re-emerged from his car clutching a piece of paper and rummaged through his inside pockets for a pen. As he scribbled down his name and number, Jo took the opportunity to study him a little closer. He was wearing a faded Ralph Lauren polo shirt, chinos and beige deck shoes. Perched on his head were a pair of Oakley wrap-around sunglasses. He had broad shoulders and the kind of hairy forearms that would have made Rosie swoon with lust.

'It's very nice of you to be so forthcoming about all

this,' she said, making conversation. 'London is usually such an unapologetic, fast-moving place.'

'Every time I think the world is moving too fast, I just go to the Post Office,' he said, flashing another smile.

'My name is Jo Miles. Here are my numbers.' She handed over one of the cards she'd had printed on a machine at her local newsagent. It said, 'Miles Ahead, Interior Design'.

'I'm afraid I'm all out of business cards,' he replied, handing over the piece of paper with his numbers written on. 'I'm Sean Goode. Or Sean Bloody Fantastic to my friends.'

Jo smiled. 'Well, Sean, I have to be on my way now. But thanks again for being so honest.'

He shrugged. 'Don't thank me, thank my mother who drilled it into me. It has its drawbacks though. I started out with nothing, and I've still got most of it, as you can see from my luxury motor.'

Turning to get back into her car, Jo stopped with one leg inside the door. 'There's no point having a nice car in London because of the madmen who drive into you all the time,' she said. 'It was an unconventional introduction, but nice to meet you anyway.'

As she drove off with a cheery wave, she glanced at her clock on the dashboard. Shit! She was already five minutes late to meet Martin Blake, and she was at least ten minutes away.

Tipping the contents of her handbag onto the passenger

seat, she found her ancient mobile phone, reminiscent of a house brick, and switched it on. The pre-programmed words 'I am happy' appeared on the screen to greet her.

'Hello, Martin? It's Jo Miles. I'm really sorry but I'm running about ten minutes late because someone ran into the back of my car. No, no, I'm fine. I'll see you shortly.'

She ended the call and picked up the piece of paper that was lying on the central console on top of all her eighties compilation tapes.

'Sean Goode,' she said aloud. 'Hmmm, I'll bet he is.'

Joining the flow of traffic, she completed her journey to Chelsea deep in thought. It was a balmy summer's day, she was on her way to a lucrative assignment, and she'd just discovered that she could still find men attractive despite her recent trauma. Only yesterday she had grumbled to Tim, 'Life is a shit sandwich and every day you take another bite.'

Today, it didn't seem quite so bad after all.

9

Clasping a selection of swatches under her arm, Jo climbed the steps to the grand, mahogany double doors of Frampton Road and rang the bell.

She heard footsteps echoing down the empty hallway, and the door was flung open to reveal Martin Blake speaking into a cordless phone. He gestured for her to enter.

'Hang on a minute, Bob,' he said briskly into the telephone before placing his hand over the receiver. 'Sorry Jo, I just have to finish this call. If you wouldn't mind waiting in the living room, I'll be through in a moment.'

Jo walked in and sat down on the only sofa in the ornately decorated room. There was a small table beside it, nothing else, presumably because she was about to gut the place and start again.

The entire 20ft by 20ft room was decorated in the aforementioned flocked wallpaper, and the dark red carpet was covered in the stains of ages. There were large misshapen patches on the walls where pictures had prevented the wallpaper from fading. Stacked against one wall were about a dozen paintings bound in bubble wrap. The front one had been ripped open to reveal what looked like a Hockney.

'Sorry about that.' Martin Blake walked in and leaned on the giant grey marble fireplace that dominated the room. 'It was a call from New York and it had to be taken then.'

Jo straightened her back. 'I should be the one apologising. Sorry I was late.'

He made a sweeping 'Forget it' gesture with his arm. 'Is there much damage? Let me know if you need it fixing quickly. I have a great little chap who looks after my cars for me.'

Cars. Little chap. Jo considered these words for a moment. They spoke volumes about the kind of man Martin was. Wealthy and highly organised, for a start. The living, breathing example of her father's favourite old saying: 'If you want something doing, ask a busy man.'

'Thanks, but there's hardly any damage. Besides, you'd hardly notice another dent on my old crate.'

I'll bet Mrs Blake drives around in a little Mercedes Sport or BMW convertible, she thought, clocking the thin band of gold on his wedding finger.

'Now then, what are we going to do with this hellhole?' said Martin, glancing round the room. 'Firstly, I want to show you what will be the main focus of this room.'

His knees clicked as he crouched down and took hold of the Hockney, tearing away the last vestiges of bubble wrap around it.

'I love that,' Jo enthused. 'I've got a smaller version of the same one in my downstairs loo.'

'This is the original.' He said it in such a matter-of-fact

way that it took several seconds for Jo to realise she was now staring at a small fortune.

'Blimey.' She could have kicked herself for such an idiotic response, but he didn't seem to notice that the woman who had advertised in such a classy organ was displaying all the signs of being several floors short of the Penthouse.

'I want it there in the grand scheme of things.' He pointed to the large expanse of wall above the fireplace. 'Before we go over the plans, do you want coffee?'

Jo nodded. 'That would be lovely. Thank you.'

He walked over to the telephone unit on the table next to her. He hit the button marked 'Kitchen', and a disembodied voice crackled through the speaker.

'Yes, sir?'

'One coffee please, Mrs Richards, and I'll have a mint tea.'

'Certainly, sir.'

They spent the next half an hour poring over her suggestions for the basement and ground floor of the house, with Martin chipping in occasionally with specific requests. He wanted mainly cream walls throughout, sunken spotlighting, stripped wood floors, and a stainless-steel kitchen with granite work surfaces. Jo estimated the two floors alone would cost £75,000 in materials and labour.

At first she'd assumed he was making a mint in the City, but the more time she spent with him, the more he didn't seem the Square Mile type. Eventually, her curiosity got the better of her.

'I don't mean to be rude, but I'm probably going to be,' she said. 'What exactly do you do?'

'I wonder that myself sometimes,' he laughed, before telling her he was the owner and chairman of an independent record company that had discovered the hugely successful band Hedonist.

'They must have sold an awful lot of records,' she said, nodding towards the Hockney that was now resting back against the wall.

He followed her gaze. 'It's lucrative, but admittedly not *that* lucrative. I was lucky enough to wise up to the Internet very early on, and I registered the name Music.com. I didn't do anything with it, I just sat on it until the whole dotcom revolution took off, then sold it to Mega Records in the States for the highly publicised amount of $30 million.'

'Now why didn't I think of that?' she said, studying him with renewed respect.

He was about half an inch short of six feet, with neat dark brown hair that had started to turn grey at the temples, and his eyes were dark blue and kind. He had a small, rather endearing gap between his front teeth. Immaculately dressed but very formal, in a dark grey suit, crisp white shirt, silver monogrammed cufflinks and red polka dot tie, he could be described as quite handsome, and he would certainly attract those members of the opposite sex who were turned on by power and money.

'Underneath every successful man, there's usually a woman,' Tim had once said, lamenting his own lack of achievement in both work and love.

But Jo, who liked overtly charming and funny men – or 'dangerous' as Rosie described them – found herself put off by Martin's slightly staid, businesslike manner.

'What about you?' His question punctuated her thoughts.

'Sorry?' She blinked rapidly.

'Is the world of interior design good to you?'

Jo pursed her lips. 'Well, it buys me Athena-style Hockney prints for my downstairs loo and that's about it. But in fairness, I have only recently stepped up my business out of necessity.'

'Oh?' He raised his eyebrows questioningly.

'My marriage broke up recently, so it's a case of wanting to be more independent while also doing something that takes my mind off it all.' She hoped she hadn't said too much.

Silent for a couple of beats, he stared at the carpet then looked straight at her. 'Sorry. I didn't mean to pry like that.'

Jo shrugged her shoulders. 'Don't worry, I'm kind of used to being single again now. It's just a bit tough sometimes, juggling work around school hours.'

'How many children do you have?'

'Two. A boy, eight, and a girl aged six.'

He walked across from the fireplace and placed his empty cup on the table. 'Well, I'm happy for you to come here during hours that suit you, so don't worry about that. I know plenty of people who put in a twelve-hour day and do half the work of a more motivated person who only does a half-day. Provided the work gets done properly, I don't care what hours you put in.'

Jo felt a wave of relief that her honesty hadn't lost her the job. 'Thanks, I appreciate it.' She stood up and started to gather up the swatches scattered around the floor. 'I'll be off now, but I'll be in touch when I've put together a more detailed proposal of what we've discussed today.'

He walked out into the hallway in front of her and opened the door. A spectacular stream of sunlight poured in, forcing them both to shield their eyes.

'If there's any problem, however small, you have all my numbers to call me. Talking about cushion covers will make a pleasant diversion from dealing with temperamental artistes,' he said, smiling and shaking her hand.

Back out on the leafy Chelsea street, Jo stood slightly obscured behind a large oak tree and studied the outside of the house. White and double-fronted, with six storeys and various balconies, it had to be worth at least £3 million, she thought to herself. And that's without the improvements she was about to make. She wondered why it was him, and not Mrs Blake, dealing with her over the interior design plans. Probably she was residing in the country estate until the London pad was suitable to visit, thought Jo ruefully. Mrs Blake, whoever and wherever she was, had the kind of lifestyle Rosie had always aspired to.

'Just think,' she once said. 'If you married someone incredibly wealthy, every day would be a holiday. No more horrible bosses to deal with, lunch every day with your friends, shopping sprees, and probably your own driver to take you there. Oh God, yes pleeeease!'

But Jo had told Rosie she felt differently. Yes, she too would enjoy all those benefits in a marriage, but only if she loved her husband. He could have all the money in the world, but if she didn't love him, she couldn't live the lie simply for the sake of material gain.

'Admirable, I'm sure,' scoffed Rosie. 'But if it was the choice between love and money, I'd take the money every time. Love seems to last about as long as a pair of tights these days.'

Standing outside this rather grand house several years after their conversation, Jo found herself thinking that maybe Rosie was right. After all, she had married Jeff for love and look where it had got her. Single with two young children and facing the daunting task of dating again if she was ever to have the chance of lasting happiness with another partner.

Jo started to walk slowly down the road to where she'd left her car.

10

Her mother's last weekend with them turned out to be the most eventful of all.

At 9 a.m. on Saturday, Jeff arrived to take Thomas and Sophie to Chessington World of Adventure and promised to have them back by teatime. It was fast becoming the routine that Jo was the mundane parent, chivvying the children to school, administering discipline, and forcing them to do their homework; whereas Jeff was the fun one, pitching up at weekends with an action-packed itinerary and bags of sweets. Jo consoled herself that one day the children would understand that although her input had been the most mundane, it had also been the most important.

By 7 p.m. Jo still hadn't heard from him, and was pacing up and down the kitchen floor in a fury.

Where the bloody hell is he? she fumed, hitting redial for the umpteenth time. Yet again, Jeff's mobile went straight to his infuriatingly self-important message which made him sound as if he was the busiest man on the planet.

'Calm down, dear,' said Pam, looking up momentarily from the newspaper crossword she was trying and clearly failing to complete. 'He is their father after all. It's not as if he's fled the country with them or anything. The traffic's probably bad.'

'In which case he should call and let me know,' snapped Jo. 'He's always been like this. He just carries on doing what he wants to do and everyone else has to fit in round him. What if I had planned to go out?'

Pam let out a long, dramatic sigh. 'Well, you haven't, have you? And besides, if you had, I would be here to take care of the children when they arrive.'

Jo marvelled that her mother could seem so reasonable towards others whilst being so irrational towards her most of the time.

The doorbell rang.

'Halle-bloody-lujah,' muttered Jo, stomping down the hallway. 'What the . . . ?'

She stopped in her tracks at the sight of Sophie standing on the doorstep with shocking pink streaks in her hair. Thomas, thankfully, was streak-free.

'Do you like it, Mummy?' asked Sophie, a red Chessington balloon in her hand.

Jo noticed Jeff had shot past her to the sanctuary of the kitchen, and his greatest ally.

'Erm, it's certainly different,' faltered Jo. 'Is this Chessington's Millennium version of face painting? I hope it comes out.'

'Oh, this wasn't done at Chessington,' said Sophie, scratching her head. 'We got back to Daddy's in time for tea, and Candy did it. She's really nice.'

She followed Thomas into the front room, leaving Jo standing in the hallway, the blood draining from her face. It was met by a surge of anger rising up the other way.

She stood for a few more seconds, staring fixedly at a muddy mark on the floor while she gathered her thoughts about what Sophie had just said. Then she was on her way to the kitchen, propelled by sheer rage.

'Mum, could you leave us a minute please, and make sure the children don't come in.' She deliberately made her voice sound clipped so even her mother would grasp that the kitchen was not a good place to be right now.

But no. Henrietta Kissinger hung on in there doing her bit for diplomatic relations. 'Oh, come on, Jo. They were only a little bit late and the children have had a wonderful time. I'm just making Jeff a cup of tea.'

'Mum, get out.'

This time the brutal tone meant her mother got the message and left the room with a huffy expression.

Jeff sighed. 'What is it now? OK, OK, sorry we're late, sorry we had such a great time, and oh yes, I almost forgot . . . sorry for breathing.'

But Jo was in no mood for his childish wind-up. 'What the fuck do you think you're doing, introducing my kids to that little slapper?'

'Sorry?' Jeff's expression told her he was shocked that she'd found out so quickly.

'Cut the crap. I specifically told you that I didn't want

134

her anywhere near them, and the next thing I know my six-year-old daughter has come back with a hooker's hairdo saying how nice Daddy's new girlfriend is.'

Jeff tipped his head back and let out a mock laugh like an opera singer or a bad actor in a pirate movie. 'Ah, we're getting to the crux of the matter now, aren't we? It's because you can't bear the thought that our kids – and they're *ours*, by the way – might like Candy. You're jealous,' he said, with an air of triumph.

Jo snorted. 'Jeff, I haven't murdered anyone today. Please help me keep it that way. I may be upset that you abandoned me and the kids, I may even be furious about it. But I am not so desperate that I feel jealous of some two-bit little nobody who wears the kind of dresses that start late and end early, and who steals other women's husbands.'

They stood in silence for a few moments, glaring at each other across the kitchen that had once been the pivot of their family life.

'Did she go to Chessington with you?' Jo's voice was quieter now.

Jeff sniffed and shook his head. 'No. But she was at my flat when we got back.'

'All pre-arranged behind my back, I presume. I'm not joking, Jeff. I don't want them mixing with her. And if it happens again, I'll stop being quite so flexible about when you see them.'

He stood up and rubbed his face. 'I see. So if I don't dance

135

to your tune, you'll punish me by using the children as your weapon. Except it won't just be me you're punishing, will it? It'll be them too.'

Jo knew he was right, but she wasn't about to admit it. Not under the current circumstances, anyway.

'You might see it like that, but I don't,' she said. 'I'm protecting my children from seeing their father make a complete arse of himself over some young girl. I'm not saying *you* can't see them, I'm saying *she* can't see them. So, if you care as much about your children as you say you do, it won't be a difficult choice for you, will it?'

For once, she felt she had the upper hand in her war of words with Jeff. It didn't happen often and she was rather enjoying it. It didn't last long.

'Well, I'd like to think you're acting in the best interests of the children, but somehow I don't think you are,' said Jeff. 'They got on perfectly well with Candy.'

'Of course they did, they're a similar age.' Jo knew this comment simply qualified Jeff's view that she was bitter, but she couldn't help herself.

'Oh, ha bloody ha, you're such a comedian. It's clear we're not able to have an adult conversation about our children, but let me tell you this. I won't make arrangements to do things with them and Candy, but I won't ban her from my flat when they're around either. So there will be other meetings.' He paused and looked at Jo who was silently shaking her head but saying nothing. He continued, 'If you start playing silly buggers over when I can see them, I shall have no hesitation in telling them that it's your doing and not mine.'

Jo looked across at Jeff as he sat defiantly staring at her, and felt nothing but pure hatred. Sitting there now, in her kitchen, the man she had shared ten years of her life with seemed like a complete stranger. Spanning a hand across her forehead, she rubbed her throbbing temples as she spoke.

'Jeff, do you have any idea how many times I have wanted to tell the children the real reason why Mummy and Daddy aren't together any more? God, it would be so easy to do and it would feel so bloody good. But, even though it would make me feel better and give you what you deserve, I don't do it. Purely because it would hurt *them* to know the truth about what a lying, cheating weasel their father is. I'm protecting them from knowing that, yet just because I don't want them mixing with your girlfriend, you would quite happily paint a bleak picture to them about me.'

'Yep. You got it.'

A Tom and Jerry vision flashed into Jo's mind, of her burying a frying pan in his face while he hopped around the room. She knew there was a destructive game of Call My Emotional Bluff going on here, and she suddenly felt weary.

'Get out, Jeff. You're not an adult, you're just a child that owes money. Come back when you've grown up.'

Taking his jacket from the back of the chair and

137

walking towards the door, Jeff made a last parting shot. 'The words "pot" and "kettle" spring to mind, Jo. When I've gone, just think about what you've said today and in retrospect you'll see how unreasonable you've been.'

She didn't answer, preferring to stare out of the window with her back turned to him. His last remark had reminded her how controlling Jeff had been to live with. Used to planting auto-suggestive remarks into the minds of juries, he would often use the tactic on Jo, to great effect.

She remembered one occasion, about six months after Sophie was born, when Tim had offered to look after the children at his place so she and Jeff could have the day to themselves. Jeff said he wanted to 'chill out' around the house, savouring having it to themselves for a change. But Jo had wanted to do what she missed most in the world since having children: a day of shopping, punctuated by lunch in a trendy café and maybe an early film showing. Under sufferance, Jeff had agreed. But instead of relishing their valuable, undiluted time together, they'd had an almighty row within the first hour.

'You seemed to take a shine to him,' he said, almost conversationally, as they emerged from a shop.

'Who?' replied Jo, looking back over her shoulder.

'That shop assistant. You couldn't take your eyes off him.' Jeff looked straight at her, clearly trying to gauge the reaction.

'What? I don't even remember seeing a shop assistant. I was looking at the clothes.'

His face clouded. 'Oh, for God's sake, Jo. Why do you always have to deny everything? It's not as if I *care* that you fancy some other bloke anyway. Just bloody admit it. It infuriates me when you play dumb.'

Jo was not about to admit to an incident that had never happened, so a huge row ensued that resulted in Jeff stomping off home.

'Don't you see?' Rosie had said later. 'He didn't want to come shopping anyway, so he simply caused a row so he could go and do what he wanted to do in the first place – sit at home and watch telly.'

In those days, Jo used to spend a lot of time defending her husband's moods out of a misguided sense of loyalty. 'Oh, that's a bit harsh, Rosie. I mean, maybe I *did* look at the shop assistant in a certain way. It's just that I don't remember doing it.'

Rosie raised her eyes heavenward. 'That's because you didn't. It's just Jeff controlling the situation as usual.'

At the time, Jo had pooh-poohed it. But now she was no longer in his thrall she could see her friend had been right. Thinking about it now, this small but significant slice of objectivity empowered Jo and lifted her spirits immensely. I'm finally seeing him for what he is, she thought. Maybe it's not such a loss after all. She heard Jeff saying goodbye to the children and letting himself out, then the unmistakably brisk footsteps of Pam walking down the hallway. Without even looking at her, Jo raised her hand to gesture for silence.

'Whatever it is you're going to say, Mum, I don't want to hear it, OK?'

'I was merely going to ask if you wanted a gin and tonic, dear,' said Pam with uncharacteristic sweetness.

Jo did, and she took it with her upstairs where she had an indulgently long bath and mulled over how she was going to deal with the Candy scenario.

Tim arrived for Sunday lunch at precisely two minutes to 1 p.m.

'I see you have timed your arrival perfectly to make sure you wouldn't get dragged into any preparation,' said Jo, turning her cheek for him to kiss.

'Sis, you know me so well,' he said cheerily, pushing a rather haphazard bunch of flowers into her hand.

'Ah, I see the neighbours are missing some of their prize blooms,' she said, tweaking one of the sagging rose petals. 'Wouldn't it be more diplomatic to give them to Mother? You haven't seen her in almost a week.'

'You're absolutely right,' he said, grabbing them back again. 'Where is she?'

'Donning her sackcloth and ashes for your arrival, no doubt. And by the way, don't even *think* about leaving early.' She tapped her forefinger on his chest. 'You're on mother duty today, as well as washing up.'

Tim took a deep breath and made the sign of the cross. 'Ah yes, some days you're the dog, some days you're the tree . . . right, here we go.'

Ten minutes later, everyone was sitting round the dining table surveying the spread Jo had placed before them.

'Giant's bogey anyone?' said Tim, holding up the dish of sprouts.

'Uuuurrrhhhh!' spluttered Sophie before collapsing into fits of giggles.

'Or how about a glazed hamster poo?' Tim lifted the bowl of kidney beans and both of the children went into paroxysms of laughter.

'Tim dear, *must* you? It's hard enough to get the children to eat vegetables as it is.' Jo noticed her mother's admonishment of Tim was done with a soft voice and a twinkle in her eye, unlike the harsh tone she often used with her. But she couldn't hate her affable brother for it.

'So Bruv, how's life, love and the universe?' she said, squeezing his arm.

'Well, life is pretty much the same, really. No work equals no money, that sort of thing. Love is pretty shitty – sorry, terrible,' he glanced at Sophie who was clearly oblivious to the remark and trying to insert part of a sprout up Thomas's nose. 'And as for the universe, well I was thinking of going out and saving it sometime next week.'

Jo smiled indulgently. 'So what happened to the girl you went out with when you were supposed to be seeing me and Conor?' There was that name again. Me and *Conor*. She rolled it around in her thoughts for a moment.

'Oh, Bernice Winters she was called.' Tim yawned,

revealing a mouthful of partially chewed sprouts. 'Can you believe that? Her name was Bernie Winters, as in the comedian. Trouble is, she looked more like Schnorbitz.'

'As you're being so rude about her, can I assume she's dumped you?' said Jo, passing him the gravy.

'Yes, you can. Honestly, I will never understand women. They're such hard work because they don't know what they want.'

'Girls don't either,' said Thomas, wrinkling his nose in disapproval of the fairer sex.

'Some of us do,' said Jo, laughing and tweaking her son's nose.

'No, Sis, you *think* you do, then when you get it you try and change it. I read this brilliant thing on the Internet the other day that summed it up, really,' said Tim, leaning over and stealing one of Jo's crispier roast potatoes.

'Go on, enlighten me,' she said, ignoring the pinched expression of her mother who was clearly expecting a rude anecdote.

'It was entitled, "How to Impress a Woman", and listed things like kiss her, cuddle her, caress her, love her, wine and dine her, spend money on her and go to the ends of the earth for her.'

'And?'

'And "How to Impress a Man" was to show up naked and bring pizza,' he said, taking a bite of his stolen potato. 'That sums it up really. We are simple creatures, and you lot are infuriatingly complex and difficult.'

Jo shook her head. 'Excuse me, but when I want an opinion from you, I'll tell you. You're right that you're simple, but that's because you only think about one thing.' Tim was nodding his head slowly with an expression that said: What's wrong with that? 'A man on a date wonders if he'll get lucky,' Jo continued, 'whereas the woman already knows. So in which criterion did you fail by Schnorbitz's standards?'

'God knows.' Tim let out a heavy sigh. 'She started wittering on about our mismatched karmas and how her clairvoyant had said that now was not a good time for her to start a relationship. I only wanted a till-dawn-do-us-part relationship, you know, the occasional shag.'

'Timothy, watch your language.' Their mother always used their full names when she was telling them off.

Jo was keen to steer the conversation round to Conor, but her guilt stopped her from doing something that, otherwise, would have seemed entirely natural. In the end, she didn't have to.

'By the way, Mum, Conor sends his regards,' said Tim, looking hungrily at the apple crumble Jo had just put on the table.

Pam's face visibly softened. 'How is the dear boy?'

Conor had been like a second son to Pam and Jim because of the amount of time he spent at their house with Tim as a child. Jo had lost count of the times she had come home to find the two young boys tucking into crisps or a chocolate bar that had originally been bought for her, while an indulgent Pam stood by smiling at them. It had crossed her mind on several occasions that her mother would much rather have had two sons.

'He's fine,' said Tim, tickling Sophie under the arm. 'He was a bit down for a while, but he's picked up again now. Probably because he's got some new bird in tow.'

'Oh?' said Jo, attempting to sound nonchalant. 'Who is she? Anyone we know?'

'Dunno,' Tim shrugged. 'He never talks about that sort of thing. He'd been with the last one for a whole century before I even met her.'

Jo's mind went into overdrive, editing her next remark before she spoke. 'Yes, he mentioned something about her on the night you didn't turn up,' she said carefully. 'He was pretty cut up about it at the time.'

Tim pulled a face of surprise. 'He told you the full story, did he? Blimey, you're honoured. I thought no one knew except me, him and Sally.'

'No, no, not the whole story. Just a bit, and that was only because I pestered him to tell me,' said Jo, feeling anxious. The last thing she wanted was for Tim to go home and make Conor think she'd been bragging about knowing his secrets.

They finished eating the apple crumble, and Tim stood up and started clearing the plates. Jo was wondering how she could return to the subject of Conor's new woman without looking too interested, when her mother came to the rescue.

144

'So, do you think we'll get to meet this new girl?' said Pam, looking questioningly at Tim.

He stopped wiping the table and looked at her as if she'd just asked him to explain the theory of relativity. 'God knows, Mother, but I doubt it,' he said, lifting Thomas's arm to wipe under. 'I only know he's seeing someone because I saw her drop him off the other night. He'd told me he was going out on a work-related matter, the crafty old bugger. Yes, yes, Mother, I know it's a swear word,' he added, before Pam could admonish him.

'What does bugger mean?' said Sophie, the remains of her apple crumble and ice cream smeared around her mouth.

Tim winced and took a sneaky sideways glance at Pam who had a sanctimonious expression on her face.

'Come on, let's play Charades,' he said, in a transparent attempt to change the subject, scooping up a child under each arm. 'You two are on my team against Mum and Grandma.'

Half an hour later, Thomas and Sophie were doubled up with laughter watching their grandmother trying to mime the second syllable of the film *Zulu*.

'I won't forgive you for this, Tim,' said Pam, as she squatted and pulled a strained expression.

Jo knew the answer because Tim had used it on her once before, but she wasn't going to let her mother off lightly. 'Something to do with skiing?' she said.

By now, her mother was pulling an imaginary chain.

'I know, Casey Jones!' Jo sneaked a look at Tim, who had tears of laughter pouring down his face.

Jo hadn't had such fun in a long time and, bizarrely, her mother's interpretation of *Zulu* become a pivotal point on her daughter's road to emotional recovery. Sitting there, laughing with her mother, brother and children, Jo understood that a sexual relationship wasn't the only source of happiness. It was so long since she'd been single, she'd forgotten that.

It comforted her to remember it now.

11

One week later, and Jo was fast realising that the relief of her mother's departure was tainted by the sheer inconvenience of no longer having anyone to collect the children from school. Despite Martin Blake being so reasonable over her working hours, there had been a couple of occasions when she'd had immovable meetings with workmen, and both times she had called Jeff to see if he could take the afternoon off work to help out with the children.

'Jo, I'm trying to do a job here,' he'd puffed self-importantly.

Not that this attitude had come as any surprise to Jo. It had always been Jeff's view that as he earned most of the family income, it absolved him from having to do much else. So if ever Jo had planned to do something while the children were at school, and one of them fell ill, it was her problem. So the likelihood he would have been much help after the split was a faint one. Instead, good old Tim had come to the rescue, thanks to the erratic nature of the acting profession. Today she was about to call on him for a third time, having given up on even bothering to ask Jeff.

'Hello, my dear, sweet brother.'

'Yes, of course I'll pick them up.'

'Oh God, am I really that transparent?'

'Yep, but never mind. I love spending time with the children anyway. What time are you stuck till?'

'It shouldn't be too bad. I have a meeting with a flooring designer and it might run over slightly, but I should easily be back by, oh, let's see, four-thirty?'

'OK, I'll collect them from school then take them up to the park and wear them out a bit. We'll come back about five for one of your slap-up teas because I'm getting sick of the thespian diet of Pot Noodle and baked beans. Deal?'

'Deal. And thank you. I honestly don't know what I'd do without you.'

As it happened, her meeting finished at 3.30 on the dot, so Jo took the opportunity to pop into Marks & Spencer to buy the promised feast. She got back to the house at 4.30, kicked off her shoes, and let out a long, contented sigh as she sat down with a cup of tea. Not long afterwards, the doorbell rang and Jo walked back down the hallway, smiling at the sight of two small shapes silhouetted through the stained glass of the front door.

'Hurry up, Mummy,' said Thomas through the letter-box.

She flung open the door with a wide smile.

'Hell . . . o,' she faltered. Standing behind the children was Conor.

'Hi.' He looked sheepish. 'Tim's agent called for the

first time since the *Bismarck* sank and said there was an audition this afternoon. Rather than bother you with the problem, he asked me to collect Thomas and Sophie. I hope you don't mind.'

'Of course not, don't be silly. You're helping *me* out for goodness' sake,' she babbled, wondering anxiously whether to invite him in, or say thanks and goodbye there and then.

Thomas solved the dilemma. 'Can he come in and see my science project? Pleeeease, Mummy!'

'Yes, of course. Unless he has to rush off.' Jo smiled at Conor, who was now being dragged into the house by an enthusiastic Thomas.

'Coffee?' asked Jo, feeling a faint flush creep up her face as she remembered the last time that particular beverage had been offered.

'Thanks,' he said, with a quick smile. 'I'll just nip upstairs to Thomas's room and look at his project, then I'll be down.'

As Jo fussed around the kitchen making coffee, she took a few deep breaths to calm herself. It wasn't that his presence excited her in *that* way, merely that she realised the way she behaved with Conor now was crucial to their future friendship. If any awkwardness between them could be dispensed with, then no-one would be any the wiser and things would return to the comfortable and convenient way they once were, with him popping round with Tim and joining in with family life.

Thomas walked into the kitchen and plonked his science project on the table. He had changed from his school uniform into his beloved Arsenal kit which, despite being only three months old, was probably already out of date. Conor, looking as deliciously casual as ever in black T-shirt and faded jeans, was two steps behind him.

As Jo stirred the coffee, she surreptitiously watched the two of them flicking through the project. Thomas was leaning against Conor's leg and had one arm thrown casually round his shoulder.

Jo remembered what Rosie had said about Conor already knowing the children. It was the main reason she wanted things to be restored to how they once were. Now that their father had left, she felt it much more important for Thomas and Sophie to maintain contact with male role models such as Tim and Conor. That was her sole motive, she told herself. It wasn't that she didn't find Conor attractive. She did. But that and his great relationship with the children still weren't enough for her to consider him as a future partner.

'I have to feel that buzz,' she'd said to Rosie recently, when they were talking about relationships in general.

'Oh, puh-lease,' Rosie had scoffed. 'That "buzz", as you call it, is probably just a feeling of danger because you're attracted to men who are difficult. You mistake difficult for interesting.'

Jo pursed her lips. 'But that doesn't mean I have to settle for someone boring.'

'See? There you go again. Automatically assuming that a bloke is boring just because he isn't a complete tosser. There is a middle ground, you know.'

'Maybe you're right,' said Jo grudgingly. 'But I have yet to find it.'

'No, what you mean is, you have yet to give it a try.'

Maybe she's right, thought Jo. But I'm not ready to give up on the 'buzz' just yet.

'Thomas! *The Simpsons* are on.' Sophie's shriek from the living room startled her.

'I'll show you the rest another time,' said Thomas, closing up his project file and heading for the door.

Normally, Jo might have lectured them both about letting television dictate their lives and made them do some schoolwork, but she wanted time alone with Conor to get their friendship on an equal footing again.

'Children really brighten up a household, don't they?' she smiled.

'So, how have you been?' asked Conor, ignoring her remark.

'Fine, thanks. I managed to survive mother's visit, but only just. When there's nothing more to be said, she'll still be saying it.' Jo was determined to keep the conversation neutral.

Conor laughed. 'Ah yes, the State Visit. Tim invited me round for Sunday lunch a couple of weeks ago then mysteriously uninvited me. I hope it didn't have anything to do with what happened between us?'

Again, Jo was completely taken aback by his direct-ness. So much for avoiding sensitive issues, she thought. Feigning indignation, she replied, 'Of course not. I just didn't want to inflict mother on anyone outside the family, that's all.'

She could tell by his expression that he knew she was lying, but he let it pass without further comment.

'So what's the audition Tim's got then? *Hamlet*? *Macbeth*?' she said brightly. She was dying to ask Conor about the new girlfriend Tim had mentioned, but she decided to stay on safer territory.

Conor shook his head. 'He wishes. No, he's gone to audition for a part that was absolutely made for him. It's something in a Pot Noodle ad.'

Jo burst out laughing. 'Knowing him, he'll negotiate a year's free supply instead of a fee.'

Conor nodded slowly in agreement, then drained his coffee cup. 'Right, I'll be off then. Thanks for the drink.'

His abrupt termination of the conversation slightly wrong-footed her. 'Oh right, no, thank *you* for looking after the children. You saved me a lot of hassle.'

'No problem, they're very special kids. You've done a good job. They seem remarkably unfazed by the break-up.' He was standing in the middle of the kitchen looking straight at her.

She felt she should simply say, 'Thanks' and show him out, but something made her want to carry on the conversation.

'I'll admit it's been difficult,' she said hesitatingly. 'There have been so many times when I've wanted to sit them down and tell them the truth rather than the "Mummy and Daddy just don't love each other any more" rubbish, but it would break their little hearts and I can't do that.' She felt the telltale pinprick of a tear, and blinked furiously to stop it.

'That's commendable,' said Conor. 'There are a lot of people who don't put the feelings of children first. They make it all about what adults want.'

Jo studied him for a moment, an expression of slight puzzlement on her face. 'If you don't mind me saying, you seem fairly switched on about all this for someone who doesn't have children.'

He had taken a couple of steps towards the kitchen door, but turned to reply. 'You don't have to be a parent to know. Sometimes, you can be a child who was in such a situation.'

'God, sorry,' she said, kicking herself for forgetting that Conor's father had walked out of the family home when his son was twelve and had never returned. In truth, Jo had been an extremely self-obsessed sixteen-year-old when it happened, and had paid little attention to the plight of her brother's friend.

'Forget it, it was all a long time ago.'

'So how did your mother cope with it?' asked Jo, assuming from his earlier comment that the situation wasn't handled well.

'Let's put it this way. It happened when I was twelve and my mother spent the next six years until I moved away to college telling me what a terrible person my father was. I can't blame her for saying it, but it was tough for me to deal with at that age. For the next couple of years I thought my name was Shut Up.'

He looked forlorn. Jo's instinct was to cross the room and give him a big hug, something she would undoubtedly have done before their recent sexual encounter. Instead she stayed where she was.

'What's your relationship with your father like now?' she asked, vaguely remembering Tim once saying that there was contact.

'Patchy. My mother had told me so many times that he'd left because he didn't love *me*, that I spent my formative years cutting him out of my mind. By the time I had suffered a couple of my own relationship knocks and realised there are always two sides to every story, there were too many years lost for us to ever be really close.'

'So what was his side of the story?' It was a dreadfully personal question, but Jo had to ask it.

'A long one,' he said with a sigh. 'But basically he left because he couldn't stand my mother's moods any more, then spent years trying to get access to me. He hung on to all the legal letters and court documentation so he could prove it to me when I got older.' He paused and flipped back the cuff of his jacket to look at his watch. 'And all the time there I was thinking he'd just walked out and forgotten about me.'

'I'm sorry.' Instinctively Jo crossed the room and placed her hand on his shoulder.

'Don't be,' he said, a touch too briskly. 'God, I hate people who bore everyone with their problems, and here I am doing exactly that.' He moved further towards the kitchen door, letting Jo's hand fall back to her side.

'Well, I did ask,' she smiled. 'And it's done me the world of good to hear it, because it makes me determined to carry on saying nice things about Jeff to the kids. So thanks for that.'

'At your service, ma'am,' he smiled, clicking his heels together and tilting his head forward in a semi-bow.

As they walked down the hallway towards the front door, the phone started to ring.

'Don't worry, you get that. I'll talk to you soon, I hope,' he said, stepping onto the doorstep.

'Thanks again!' shouted Jo over her shoulder as she dashed into the living room to pick up the phone that was being steadfastly ignored by her two square-eyed children.

'Hello?'

'Hi, it's Sean Goode.'

'Sorry?' Jo was distracted by the sight of Sophie doing a headstand and putting her grubby feet against the wall.

'The bad driver who crunched your car.'

'Oh yes. Hi.'

155

'You haven't called, so I'm ringing to see what's happened about getting the damage repaired.'

'To be honest, I haven't even thought about it since. As I said, it was only a slight bump, so let's just forget about it.' She was silently gesturing at Sophie to get down, but her strong-willed daughter was ignoring her.

'Oh.' He sounded disappointed.

'But thanks for calling to ask,' she said reassuringly. 'There aren't many people who would be so concerned about someone else's car. You've restored my faith in human nature.'

'Um, well actually, that wasn't the only reason I was calling.'

'Oh?' Jo's attention was now firmly fixed on the voice on the other end of the line.

'I was rather hoping I might be able to persuade you to have a drink with me one night. If I'm honest, I was being cowardly and using the car business as an excuse to call.'

'I see.' She thought back to the day of the minor accident and remembered Sean 'Bloody Fantastic' with a smile. He was certainly cute and surely there was no harm meeting him in a public place. It was only a drink after all. 'Yes, why not?' she said, thinking how proud Rosie would be of her decisiveness.

'Great! How about one night next week?'

'As my diary consists of blank pages for the rest of the year, I'm sure that'll be fine.' Jo winced as she said it,

156

realising that if she was going to get back into the dating game, she would have to play harder to get.

'Sounds exactly like mine,' he said. 'What a pair of Billy No Mates we are.'

She wondered if that were true, because she couldn't imagine for one moment that such a wickedly charming man would be short of social engagements. He'd probably just said it to make her feel reassured. In which case, she liked him better already.

12

The date for 'The Date', as Rosie was insisting on calling it, was Thursday night.

'It's only a drink, for God's sake, don't get too excited,' said Jo, as her friend rifled through her wardrobe the night before like a deranged makeover consultant.

'Bloody hell, love, has anyone told you the war's over?' Rosie was holding up a peach twinset.

'That was Jeff's favourite,' said Jo, a raft of memories flooding her mind as she stared at the familiar outfit from the early days of their marriage. The days when he had often still removed her clothing for her.

'Right. Charity shop,' said Rosie dismissively, chucking it on to the ever-growing pile behind her.

'What?' said Jo, in an aggrieved tone. 'I like that. I'll probably wear it again.' She retrieved it from the pile.

'No you won't.' Rosie snatched it back. 'Not unless you want to die a lonely old spinster. It's hideous and ageing and that's precisely why Jeff liked it, because it meant that while you were wearing it no other man except Roy Orbison would look at you.'

Jo folded her arms in exasperation. 'Well, on that basis,

I suspect most of my wardrobe will be empty in an hour's time. I've always based my style on comfort.'

'Precisely,' said Rosie, tut-tutting at some drainpipe jeans she'd found buried under a pile of old shoes. 'You have to find your own style again now. I'm not saying you should walk around like mule dressed as lamb, but you're only thirty-three for Chrissakes. Lighten up.'

Rosie's malapropisms had always been a source of amusement to Jo. 'It's mutton, not mule, you daft cow.'

'Mutton, mule, moose, whatever. It's shit.'

'And you're an expert on fashion, are you?' she said, eyeing Rosie up and down.

'Hey, you'd be surprised how much it costs to look this cheap.'

'Point taken,' said Jo, gathering up an armful of clothes and stuffing them into a binliner. She knew Rosie was right, but her natural urge was to hoard objects from her past as if they were the very glue that held her life together. She had every letter and postcard ever written to her, every school report, and clothes dating back to the heyday of David Cassidy. No wonder minimalism isn't my design speciality, she thought as she watched Rosie shriek with laughter at the discovery of a frayed Doctor Who-style scarf.

Five minutes later they were having a glass of wine in the kitchen, surrounded by three overstuffed binliners.

'Well, all that little exercise has established is that I have absolutely nothing to wear tomorrow night,' said Jo, raising an eyebrow in Rosie's direction.

'Nonsense. It's been an emotional and psychological spring clean that will prove to be a significant turning point in your life.' It never ceased to amaze Jo how Rosie could get psychoanalysis out of any situation. 'But I agree with you on the nothing to wear bit. It's time for a raid on Antebbe, I reckon.'

Antebbe was the curiously named local clothes shop that relentlessly and determinedly went on selling trendy outfits whilst surrounded by a staunchly middle-class clientele that favoured the more matronly look. Or the 'hideous and ageing' look, as Rosie had referred to it.

'New outfit?' scoffed Jo. 'I can't afford to go buying new clothes just for a quick drink with some lousy driver I don't even know. I've got no money of my own until the interior design invoices get paid. Jeff keeps me on a very tight financial rein.'

'Really?' Rosie looked shocked. 'Can't you ask your solicitor to try and get more?'

'Er, what solicitor? Jeff said it would be a waste of money because he could sort it all out for nothing.' She knew what was coming. Rosie didn't disappoint.

'Jesus effing Christ. I sometimes wonder how someone so bright can be so damned *stupid*!' She banged the table as she said the last word. 'He's controlling you again. Of *course* he wants to keep the financial arrangement between you and him, because he's probably getting away with daylight bloody robbery.'

Jo gave a deep sigh. 'I must say, there's barely enough

to get by on. I've had to start eating into my rainy day fund, and it wasn't a significant amount to begin with. It's minuscule now.'

'Right, the raid on Antebbe is postponed. We're off to find a local solicitor.' Rosie picked up her handbag from the floor as if to leave. 'My mother has always said to me, "Trust your husband, but get as much as you can in your own name."'

Jo looked mildly panicked. 'I can't. Jeff will go mad.'

Slapping the palms of her hands over her face, Rosie's next words sounded muffled. 'Jo, let's get one thing straight.' She dropped her hands. 'Jeff walked out on *you*. He introduced the kids to his new girlfriend when you specifically asked him not to, and now it turns out he's probably fiddling you out of what's rightfully yours financially. Why the fuck would you spend even one nano-second worrying about what he thinks of anything? It's about time he faced up to the high cost of leaving.'

'But he's still the father of my children,' said Jo sadly. Even she wasn't convinced by this argument, but it was all she could think of at the moment.

'All the more reason why he should treat you fairly.' Rosie's mouth had set into a firm line. 'You're the one with the fulltime responsibility whilst he swans about playing Lothario. He should be kissing your feet with gratitude, not leaving you short.'

'I know what you mean, but I've never been into demanding equal this and equal that. Provided I can get by and it means the children don't get dragged into any court procedure, I'd rather leave it like that.' She stood up and started brushing crumbs off the breadboard, in the hope her action would indicate an end to the matter. But no.

'This isn't about making demands, Jo, it's about being treated fairly.' Rosie stopped and looked straight at her.

Jo sighed and didn't make any attempt to reply. She stared out of the window onto the back garden and wished all the problems would just go away. She wanted things to be how they once were. Her life might have been mundane perhaps, but at least it had been relatively uncomplicated. Now all the mundane tasks still had to be carried out by Jo Muggins, but on top of that she was dealing with the psychological strain of adultery and desertion, as well as struggling financially. Rosie was right. She had to do something. 'OK then. But just an initial meeting first to see which way the land lies, and that's all. I'm not promising I'll act on anything the solicitor tells me.'

'Fine,' Rosie stood up. 'Anyway, Jeff should be grateful it's only a divorce you're thinking of. In my family, we don't divorce men, we bury them.'

Less than two hours later they were back at the house. As Jo walked into the living room and sat down, she caught sight of her face in the mirror. It was ashen.

'Cup of tea?' said Rosie.

'Thanks.'

The meeting with the solicitor had been emotionally

draining as well as quite distressing. It had felt odd to be telling the most intimate details of her private life to a complete stranger, but it had also felt quite cathartic. She couldn't be sure, but Jo felt that by discussing her separation in such formal circumstances, she had taken another major step towards a full emotional recovery. But she still had a long way to go.

When she and Rosie had first arrived at Stones & Co, a surly receptionist who was better suited to a doctor's surgery had told them there were no appointments that day.

In a dismissive gesture, the woman had returned to her magazine. But Rosie continued to stand stock still in front of her, looking thoughtful.

'What are you doing?' asked the woman, clearly irritated at having to look up yet again from an article entitled: 'Are you hot stuff in bed?'

'Oh nothing, I'm just trying to imagine you with a personality,' said Rosie. 'Look, it's taken me for ever to get her here, and I might never persuade her to return. Isn't there anyone she could speak to who knows about family law, even just for a few minutes?'

In the middle of this impassioned plea, Jo noticed a middle-aged, well-dressed woman step out of a room at the rear of the rather scruffy office, situated above a hardware store in the High Street.

'What's the problem, Leanne?' she said to the receptionist as she walked across the room towards them.

'This lady wants this lady to see a family law specialist,' said Leanne, gesturing listlessly from Rosie to Jo. 'But I've explained they have to make an appointment.'

The woman studied Jo, who was by now wishing she'd never come. Suddenly, this all seemed rather official and scary and she wanted to run home, crawl under the duvet, and pretend that Jeff had never left her. As she was about to make her excuses and leave, she realised the woman was speaking.

'I have a spare fifteen minutes. Come on through,' she said, gesturing back to the door she had just emerged from.

'Mrs Burnett will see you now,' said Leanne, somewhat unnecessarily, fixing them both with a murderous look.

'I'll wait out here,' said Rosie to Jo, nervously shifting her weight from one foot to another. She picked up an ancient copy of *OK!* magazine. 'Ah, I see Noah has invited us into his lovely Ark,' she joked. Jo smiled, Leanne totally ignored her.

Jo followed Mrs Burnett into the rear office. Immediately she felt at home, thanks to the floor-to-ceiling clutter. Bookshelves were stacked haphazardly with legal reference books, box files, dictionaries and even a few novels. The floor was strewn with papers and files, heaped into separate piles, each with a post-it note on top.

'I know where everything is, but no-one else does,' smiled Mrs Burnett, following her gaze.

Jo felt just as she had in the sixth form after being called in to see the headmistress over her poor maths results. 'It's very nice of you to see me at such short notice, Mrs Burnett.'

'Call me Hazel.'

'Well . . . Hazel, I don't really know what I'm doing here. I mean, my situation is really very straightforward compared to some.'

'Your friend seemed very keen for you to see me.'

'She would, because she thinks I'm hard done by.'

'Well, why don't you tell me everything from the beginning and we'll see if the law feels that way,' said Hazel, smiling warmly.

Ten minutes later, Jo had done precisely that. The photos. The showdown. Candy. And how she had let Jeff see the children whenever he liked. 'I should explain that a large part of the reason why I'm here is because he introduced the children to his new girlfriend when I specifically asked him not to. My friend thinks he's taking the piss . . . sorry, I mean mickey.'

'Don't worry, I've heard worse than that in my job.' Hazel fell silent for a moment, turning a Mont Blanc pen over and over in her manicured fingers.

'Let's see,' she said finally, putting down the pen and placing her elbows on her cluttered desk. 'As your estranged husband is a solicitor, I would suggest there could be some level of hidden agenda here.'

'Really?' Jo found it hard to accept that, on top of leaving her for a younger woman, Jeff might also still be shafting her in other ways.

'Yes. Because unless there is a documented separation of some kind, it makes it very easy for him to wander off, check out his new life, and if it doesn't work out, wander back into the marital home again. If you are seen to willingly take him back after an infidelity, it virtually wipes the slate clean until the next one. If there is a next one of course.'

Jo let the words sink in for a moment. 'So what are we talking about here?' she said slowly. 'Are you saying I should be rushing home and changing the locks this afternoon?'

'Hmm. Well, I certainly wouldn't let him wander in and out of the family home as if nothing's changed, so if he's got a key I'd try and take it back without making a big deal about it.' Hazel looked up from her notes. 'You have to decide whether you are fighting a battle to win him back, or to establish a fair deal for you and your children for a future without him.'

Jo had heard variations of this conclusion from Rosie, but to hear it from an impartial source hammered the point home.

Hazel continued, 'The minute you establish the exact grounds on which your relationship is operating from now on, the nearer you'll be to sorting everything out once and for all. It sounds like it's rather in limbo at the moment.' Her words hung in the air.

'So, let's take one thing at a time here,' said Jo. 'Financially, do you think I'm being ripped off?'

'Speaking with my legal hat on, yes I do. But there are other factors to be taken into consideration here. If you decide to take him to court over this, it will be on record for your children to learn about at a later date, and you may only emerge from it with a fairly insignificant extra amount.'

'So what do you suggest I do?' said Jo, feeling unable to grasp all the emotional and circumstantial implications of what was being laid before her.

'I suggest you go away, focus your thoughts on exactly where you stand with your estranged husband, then come back and see me for another chat. This one has been for free,' said Hazel, smiling at Jo then glancing at the clock on the wall.

Jo gave the best humble smile she could muster. 'Thanks. I'd like to say it's made things a lot clearer, but as I'm sure you know, these matters are never simple.' She stood up and headed for the door.

Hazel shook her hand. 'Well, you know what they say? Life is something that happens to you while you're making other plans.'

As Jo and Rosie walked out, Leanne looked up from that night's TV schedules. 'I hope you realise how lucky you were that Mrs Burnett was able to see you at such short notice.'

Jo ignored her and kept walking.

'If I want any more shit from you, I'll squeeze your head, OK?' said Rosie, before sprinting down the stairs two at a time.

'Well?' she said as they fell into step with the throng on the street.

'It seems you may be right,' said Jo, peering up at the cloudy sky and wondering if it was going to rain.

'I knew it!' Rosie sounded triumphant and looked it too. 'I *knew* that crafty git was pulling a fast one on you.'

Jo stopped in her tracks and held up a hand. 'Hang on, hang on. It's not that simple. First of all, I have to go home and do some serious thinking.' She started walking again. 'Talking to Hazel – that's Mrs Burnett's name, by the way – has made me realise I've been burying my head in the sand, hoping all the problems will go away. I have to address them.'

Hurrying to keep up with her, Rosie prodded her in the arm. 'Er, isn't that what I've been saying since time began?'

'Probably,' said Jo, prodding her back and grinning. 'But you're biased.'

'You're damned right I am,' said Rosie indignantly. 'So what do you think you'll do about Jeff?'

'I'll double-cross that bridge when I come to it,' she said, feeling buoyed by her little spot of Hazel therapy. 'Come on, let's go home for a cuppa.'

13

'Ah, it's the television star. Is this the doorstep challenge?' said Jo, pretending to look for the cameras.

Tim took a bow and stepped into the house, muttering, 'Don't mention TV ads to me. What a bloody farrago!'

'Why?' said Jo in genuine surprise. 'I'd have thought a part in a Pot Noodle ad was everything you'd ever aspired to. God knows, you eat enough of the bloody things.'

Tim was already in the kitchen where he opened the fridge, helped himself to a lager, sat down and put his feet up on the table. 'I know, but it didn't turn out quite how I'd imagined.'

'Go on.' Jo had to get ready for her drink with Sean, but she had a few minutes to spare.

'Well, when I got there it all looked very professional and they started telling me what I had to do. But it didn't take me long to realise I hadn't been given a script. I seemed to have fuck all to say.'

'That's not such a big deal, is it?' Jo shrugged. 'As long as we get to see you.'

'That's just it. They then led me on set and pointed at this fucking huge Pot Noodle outfit made out of foam rubber with holes for my legs and arms. I had to prance about in that. You don't even get to see my bloody face!'

'That's terrible.' Jo clasped a hand over her mouth, trying to hide her sniggers.

'It's alright, I know you're laughing. Conor pissed himself when I told him. At this rate I'm going to have to start selling furniture for a living. My own.' He took a swig of his beer and stood up. 'Anyway, you go and get ready. Where are the kids?'

'One's on PlayStation, the other's bathing, or should I say drowning, her Barbies. They're back in favour – temporarily at least.'

Jo headed upstairs to put the finishing touches to her make-up. Following her lunch with Conor and Tim, she was going for the natural look again tonight. After all, it had worked then. And, as any self-respecting woman knows, it took twice as long to apply as any other kind of make-up.

After much deliberation – although not as much as there would have been before Rosie pared her wardrobe down to the bare essentials – she had laid her chosen outfit on the bed. An old pair of faded Versace jeans, together with a plain white T-shirt and pale-blue pashmina. She was aiming to look casual but classy.

Rosie had rung her three times today to ask what she was wearing, clearly anxious that Jo might have got desperate and torn open one of the charity shop binliners that were still piled in the corner of the kitchen.

'I'll be wearing absolutely bloody nothing if you don't get off the phone and let me decide,' Jo had said.

She walked down the three small steps into Thomas's room to find Tim had taken his place on the PlayStation and was in the middle of decapitating an opponent.

'Right, I'm off. See you later,' she said, scowling at the screen before giving Thomas a hug.

'What are you up to?' said Tim, his eyes firmly fixed on the kick-boxing session now playing out before him.

'Oh, just having a drink with a friend.' She knew Tim wasn't paying attention enough to ask anything more. 'I shouldn't be late.'

By the time she had driven to Fulham, squeezed her car into a parking space, and walked the quarter of a mile back to the bar, Sean was already waiting. She spotted him through a sea of heads, casually flicking through a copy of *Time Out*.

'Sorry I'm a bit late. It's not easy to park round here.'

At the sound of her voice, he looked up with the devastating smile that had made such an impression on her the other day. 'No probs. I was just catching up on some film reviews. I love going to the cinema, but there's nothing worse than wasting your time on a terrible film.'

Jo smiled and sat down in the empty armchair next to him. 'Wait until you have kids. You spend your life learning to sleep through films.'

'I take it you have children, then?'

During one of many conversations about the separation,

171

her mother had rated the chances of Jo finding happiness with another man as very slim. 'You're a complicated date now,' she'd said. 'Most men will run a mile when they find you have children by someone else.'

So Jo was pleased that Sean had remained in his seat. But she had to admit it felt weird to be having a drink with a man who knew absolutely nothing about her. Not even that she had children.

'Yes, two. Boy and a girl,' she said, wondering whether thirty seconds into the evening was a bit early to show him the photographs in her purse.

'More of this in a moment.' He leapt up. 'First of all, what's your favourite drink?'

'The next one,' she laughed. She was pleased to see he got the joke immediately.

'I know what you mean. But I need a bit more of a clue on the first date.'

Date. He'd used the word date. 'A small glass of house white will do nicely thanks.'

He disappeared into the crowd and she sat back to study the clientele in the small, trendy bar with its ochre walls and comfortable furniture. A couple in the far corner were clearly in the middle of a 'deep and meaningful', as Rosie always referred to conversations about relationships. Jo could see the woman was trying desperately not to cry. Bastard, she thought, I'll bet he's dumping her, preferring these days to take the anti-men stance.

In the middle of the room, a twenty-strong group of

men and women had taken over several small tables and were dominating the atmosphere with their loud remarks and raucous laughter. A couple of the men were wearing Hackett shirts with the collars turned up, and all the girls were dressed in sporty-style fashions such as fleeces and tracky bottoms. Rugby players and their girlfriends, thought Jo with a wry smile. She loved people-watching and making snap judgements on their relationships and careers. What would I make of Sean and me if I were studying us? she wondered.

He fought his way back to the table carrying her wine and a pint of draft bitter for himself. 'There's a couple at the bar having the most almighty row,' he said, his eyes shining with the spectacle of it. 'I think she's caught him out being unfaithful.'

Jo's smile withered as he said it, but she made a swift recovery. 'Really? How do you know?'

Sean took a slug of beer. 'I heard her say, "How could you, she's a dog", or something like that. Mind you, I think she's well rid of the greasy sod. He doesn't need a haircut, just an oil change. Anyway, chin chin.' He clinked his glass against hers.

Jo raised her glass to him then took a sip of her wine. 'I love people-watching too,' she said. 'Come on, let's see how good you are. What do you make of that couple over there?'

She laughed as Sean tried to observe the couple in the corner as nonchalantly as he could, pretending to look at the ceiling then working his way round to where they sat.

He turned back to Jo several seconds later.

'Oh, they're definitely splitting up. I reckon he's just told her that he needs some space, that she's far too good for him, and that she should go and find someone who appreciates her more.'

'Very good!' Jo nodded to the boisterous crowd in the centre of the room. 'What about them?'

As Sean studied them, she studied him. He was wearing a pair of beige linen trousers with a white linen shirt that showed off his healthy, golden tan. His shiny, dark blond hair was just long enough to form little kiss curls at the back of his ears, and he had the habit of regularly running his hand through the front to brush it away from his forehead. Jo liked what she saw.

He turned back to her and rubbed his chin in thought. 'Hmmm, I'd say they were a cricket team, or maybe rowing club members, out on a bonding exercise with their wives and girlfriends. How did I do?'

Jo gave him a broad grin. 'Very well indeed. I had them down as rugby players, but same thing really. You're good at this.'

'Oh, I don't know,' he said, wrinkling his nose. 'You can usually always tell sporty types because they have such appalling dress sense.'

'I take it you're not sporty, then?' said Jo, although she thought he looked rather fit.

'No, not at all, I'm horribly lazy,' he said stretching his arms above his head and yawning. 'I went jogging once, but by the time I realised I wasn't fit enough to do it, it was a bloody long walk back.'

Jo felt herself relax. Whatever happened, she found Sean very good company and knew she was in for a fun evening.

'Bloody hell, how long does this live out of water?' said Sean, looking past her towards the door.

Jo shifted her chair slightly and caught sight of the woman Sean was referring to. She was at least 16 stone with more chins than a Chinese phone book, no discernible waist, and wearing a crop top and skin tight, beige lycra leggings that made her look naked from the waist down.

Turning back, Jo buried her face in her hands and started to giggle at Sean's remark. It felt good to be with someone who made her laugh. She and Rosie liked nothing better than to sit and make bitchy comments about passers-by in the safe knowledge that they would never know what had been said.

'So what would you make of us if you were them?' she said, pointing back to the centre of the room where one of the sporty types was now drinking a pint of lager in one go while his friends did the slow hand-clap. She couldn't believe she'd asked such a provocative question, but something told her Sean would rise to the challenge.

'Well,' he said slowly, with a half-smile. 'I'd think, there's a bloke who fancies the woman he's with like mad and would like to see much more of her.'

Jo felt a familiar but delicious sensation inside her stomach. The butterflies of attraction, flirtation and uncertainty – that heady mix of emotions that herald the start of a possible new relationship and you wish you could bottle for ever. 'I see.' She looked straight at him, her eyes flickering with mischief. 'And what would you think I was thinking?'

Sean flopped back in the armchair and let out a short sigh. 'Oooh, now that's a tough one because I don't know anything about her,' he said. 'But at a guess, I'd say she'd recently come out of a long-term relationship and was rather wary of starting something new. She thinks she quite likes his company, but she'd have to go on a few more uncomplicated dates before deciding whether to get more involved.' He stopped suddenly and raised his eyebrows at her, awaiting a response.

'Very good,' she laughed. 'But as I told you I have two children, then it's a fair assumption they might be the result of a long-term relationship. And as I'm here having a drink with you, then it's also a fair assumption to think that the relationship might be over.'

Sean slapped a palm against his forehead. 'Dammit, she's rumbled me. And there I was thinking she'd be overwhelmed by my psychic powers.'

'You'd need to do better than that. Nice try though. Another drink?' Jo was beginning to wish she hadn't brought the car.

'No, no.' He sprang up. 'I invited you out for a drink, so I'm paying for everything.'

Good-looking, funny, and pays for everything. Pinch me, pinch me.

When he returned from the bar, Sean was brandishing a plate of prawns with a little pot of mayonnaise dip on the side. 'I know you said you didn't want to eat, but I thought I'd get these for us to pick at.'

Jo had indeed said she only had time for a quick drink, because she'd wanted the option of escaping early if he'd been a complete bore. But right now she was thinking she'd like nothing more than to enjoy a six-course meal with this entertaining man. As he sat down, he pulled his chair slightly closer to Jo's. It was almost imperceptible, but she noticed it immediately.

'So tell me,' he said, dipping a prawn in the mayonnaise. 'Are you – were you – married?'

The evening had been going so well, but inevitably the subject of Jeff had to come up and ruin it, she thought ruefully. 'I'm separated from my husband, but we're not divorced yet,' she said, taking a prawn. 'We only split up a few months ago.'

Sean looked concerned. 'I'm sorry to hear that, particularly as you've got children. What went wrong?'

'He left me for another woman,' she said matter-of-factly. 'One of the secretaries at his firm, who's ten years younger than me.' Three months ago, she couldn't even have contemplated making such an admission to a total stranger. But each time she said it these days, it bothered her less.

Sean just looked at her for a moment, then sat up straight and arched his back in a stretch. 'Well, more fool him.'

'Have you ever been married, then?' asked Jo.

'No. I almost did once, but we called it off a few months before when we realised we were both a bit half-hearted about it.'

'Would you like to be married?'

'I haven't really thought about it,' he said quickly. 'My job doesn't help when it comes to a permanent commitment.'

'Ah yes, what do you do? I was going to ask you earlier, but it's such a naff question, isn't it? In London, it's always one of the first questions people ask each other and I hate it. Particularly when I first had the children and wasn't working, because you could see them switch off and think "dull nobody".' She waited for him to express shock that anyone could think she was a dull nobody, but he didn't.

'I'm a TV cameraman for *The World Right Now*. It's great because I get to go all over the world covering wars, military coups, geographical stories and so on, but it's lousy for relationships.'

'I suppose it depends on the kind of relationship you have,' she said, straight from the 'what they want to hear' phrase book. 'If you're with someone you trust, I always think long periods apart can sometimes enhance it and keep the spark going.'

'Precisely!' Sean's face lit up at this momentous meeting

of minds. 'I've always thought that. Trouble is, I never found anyone who thought the same.'

Jo decided a change of subject was in order before they held hands and skipped off down the street into the sunset. 'So where are you off to next?'

'No idea. It's all news-based, so things can happen at any moment. That's why I have this.' He lifted his shirt to reveal a small pager attached to his belt. Jo noted it also revealed a fairly taut brown stomach with a thin line of hair leading down.

'So lots of plans can go awry at the last minute?' she said.

'Absolutely. But thankfully no little tin-pot dictator staged a bloody coup and disrupted my plans to meet you tonight.'

'Indeed.' Jo could have kicked herself. Indeed? What kind of a moronic answer was that? It suddenly dawned on her that she really liked this man. If she didn't, she wouldn't be analysing every little remark they both made.

'So would you like to do this again?' He sounded nervous.

The question took her completely by surprise because it had a booby trap element to it. If he'd said, 'I'd like to do this again', she would have known the score, but his ambiguous phrasing meant she was being asked first to nail her colours to the mast. Fifteen years ago, Jo would probably have said something crass like, 'That depends on whether you want to,' but if there was one thing being in her thirties had taught her, it was to be confident enough to say what she felt.

'Sure, why not?' She was trying to sound as casual as possible, but in truth she was very keen to see Sean again. She wasn't thinking about him in terms of a proper relationship. She wasn't thinking *that* about anyone. No, she liked his company and found him attractive. I want to have some uncomplicated fun, she thought, and he's just the right man for it.

'I'd better be off now,' she said. 'I've left the children with my brother, and I'm never quite sure who looks after who.'

She stood up and pushed back her chair. Sean did the same. He picked up her pashmina from the back of the chair and draped it round her shoulders. Out on the street, they stopped and faced each other.

'My car's that way,' she said, pointing towards Putney.

'Mine's that way,' he laughed, pointing in the opposite direction. 'But I'll walk you to yours first.'

'No, really, I'll be fine.' Jo was anxious to end their first meeting now, so she could go away and savour it without any eggy moments.

'Well, if you insist.' Sean stuck out his hand to shake hers.

She took it. His hand was warm, dry and firm. 'I enjoyed tonight immensely, thanks.'

'Ditto. I'll be in touch about organising another get-together.' He leaned forward and kissed her gently on the cheek.

'Great. I'll wait to hear from you. In the meantime, drive carefully.' Jo smiled at him, then turned and walked away down the street.

What kind of a kiss was that? she thought. Was it an 'until-next-time' kiss? Or was it a 'you'll-never-hear-from-me-again' kiss? She had no idea, but she hoped it was the former. She wasn't sure what had happened there tonight, but she did know she'd had a wonderful time and not given Jeff or their problems a passing thought. It felt good. A hundred yards down the road, she couldn't resist any longer and turned round to see whether he was still in sight. He was standing outside the bar exactly where she'd left him, and raised a hand to wave as he saw her turn round.

14

She stirred as the bedroom door creaked open. Sophie was standing by the side of the bed, a Pokemon mug in her hand.

'Mummy, I've made you a cup of tea.'

Jo sat bolt upright. 'Sophie, you know you're not to touch the kettle.'

'I didn't.' She handed Jo a mug with some brownish liquid sloshing around in it.

'What is it then?' Tentatively, Jo sniffed the contents.

'I made it with cold water. The bag's still in there,' said Sophie.

Jo pretended to take a sip, trying not to look at the off-putting contents. 'Hmmm, that's lovely, thank you darling. I'll just put it on the side here and finish it after I've got dressed.'

Sophie walked out of the room. 'See, Thomas! I told you she'd like it,' she shouted.

Closing the door to her en-suite bathroom behind her, Jo hastily tipped the contents of the mug into the basin. She looked up and caught sight of her bloodshot eyes in the overhead mirror, and the memory of her night out with Sean suddenly popped into her head. She smiled.

'I doubt he'd fancy you if he could see you this morning,' she said aloud to her reflection. Sean had *said* he'd call her, but already Jo's new found self-esteem was ebbing away. Last night, she'd been convinced he was interested, then just a few hours later, here she was doubting he'd ever call again.

It wasn't that she envisaged living happily ever after with this man; she was still finding it hard to envisage that with anyone so soon after Jeff's bombshell. But she had found Sean's interest a great tonic, a little boost to her fragile ego. It had felt good and she was keen to see him again for that reason alone. The last time she'd been in the dating arena, the words 'I'll call you' could mean anything from the next day to never. I wonder if people still play those mind games at our age? she mused. I suppose that's something I'm about to find out.

Sloshing cold water onto her face, she picked up a towel and buried her face in it while she sat on the loo. With classic timing, the phone started ringing.

'Sophie! Thomas! Get that. I'm on the loo!'

Just as she was lunging for the out-of-reach loo roll, she heard footsteps pad into her bedroom.

'Hello?' Sophie had picked up the call.

'No, she's on the toilet.' It went quiet, presumably whilst the caller said something.

'OK.' Jo heard the receiver being replaced.

'Who was it?' she said, standing up and pulling down the baggy old T-shirt she'd worn to bed. She went back into the bedroom.

'Don't know,' said Sophie, who was carrying a Barbie by its multi-coloured hair. 'It was a man.'

'What did he say darling?' Jo tried not to sound irritable.

'I said you were on the toilet and he said he would call back later.' Sophie had clearly lost interest in the phone call and was flicking through the channels on the bedroom television.

'Oh well, if it was something urgent, then I'm sure they will,' shrugged Jo. There was a time in her pre-children twenties when, if she had been waiting for a particular man to call, such a vague message from one of her flat-mates would have prompted Gestapo-style questioning to try and establish who it was. What was his voice like? Was it a payphone? Old or young? Eventually, everyone in the all-female house had come to an agreement that if any man called the premises, he was not allowed to ring off until they'd got his name, number and inside leg measurement. It was a sisterly gesture to prevent anyone going through the angst of constantly wondering whether *he* had rung, whoever *he* happened to be at the time.

That's a feeling I don't miss, Jo thought to herself, as she threw on another T-shirt and a pair of cut-off denim jeans. She glanced at her bedside clock. It was 8.15 and the children were still in their pyjamas.

The next half an hour passed in a flurry of break-fast, teeth-cleaning, dressing, and putting the finishing touch to the lunchboxes she'd prepared late the night before, which meant lobbing in a couple of Penguin bars.

By 9.15 she was back at the house having walked the children to school. She was just settling down to read the newspaper with a cup of tea when the phone rang again.

'Hello?'

'Hi, it's me.' It was Rosie.

'Hello me,' said Jo fondly.

'So how was the hot date?'

'It was fun. I thought this might be him calling actually, and I have to confess I feel mildly disappointed that it isn't. Only mildly though.'

'Ooh, sounds promising. So what's the juicy goss then? Was there another bout of tonsil tennis?' Rosie's voice had risen several octaves in excitement.

'Certainly not! And may I remind you that the Conor business was completely out of character and only happened because I drank too much.'

'Yeah, yeah. And the band played believe it if you like, as my old grandma used to say.'

'Your old grandma used to say quite a lot didn't she?' laughed Jo, who had heard thousands of sayings attributed to her over the years.

'So what happened then?'

'Nothing as such, we just got on really well. He makes me laugh, and I find him very attractive. With any luck

185

the feeling's mutual and we'll have some uncomplicated fun for a while.'

'Right, well as this conversation could be holding up the progress of the next Romeo and Juliet, I shall bugger off,' said Rosie. 'Ring me later to let me know what happens.'

Jo settled herself at the kitchen table to read the newspaper. There was an interview with Jerry Hall about her divorce from Mick Jagger. Jo read every word avidly.

'I feel in my prime,' Jerry said. 'I feel more confident and stable than I've ever felt. I had gotten a little depressed last year and it was really tough and I thought I'd given up work completely. But somehow I managed to have a friendly divorce which is a miracle and I'm quite proud of that.'

She's right, thought Jo. It's much harder to keep things civil when all you want to do is throttle the bastard for cheating on you. She went on reading.

'If you manage it, you keep your dignity, and the best irony of all is that it probably makes you more attractive to the man who left you in the first place,' commented the journalist.

'I think also when you have been in a long relationship, especially a dysfunctional one, you need time on your own so as not to, hopefully, attract the same sort of person again. A womaniser,' added Jerry.

Jo sat back in her chair, deep in thought. It's funny, she considered, but I still don't think of Jeff as a womaniser. He has only been unfaithful to me once, but unfortunately it

186

turned out to be a major infidelity that wrecked our marriage. A horrible thought occurred to her. Was Candy the first? Or was she just the one he got caught out with? Maybe there had been others throughout their marriage that Jo had never got wind of. She sat there, her mind rewinding furiously through the last few years leading up to Jeff's walkout. Had there been other occasions when behaviour out of the ordinary might suggest he was having an affair? She couldn't think of any, but that didn't necessarily rule it out.

Often, objective outsiders will notice more in a marriage than someone who's actually part of it, but because they don't want to cause any unnecessary trouble, they never voice their suspicions. Little wonder, thought Jo, remembering the occasion she'd snapped poor Rosie's head off for saying she never thought Jo and Jeff were suited in the first place.

Folding up the Jerry Hall article and tucking it in a drawer for future reference, she made a mental note to ask Tim and Rosie whether they had ever suspected Jeff of having affairs in the past.

The phone rang. Distracted by her dark thoughts of Jeff's possible infidelities, it didn't cross her mind to wonder who it might be calling.

'Hello.'

'Ah, you've finished waving your prawns off to the coast, have you?' It was Sean.

Jo couldn't help laughing at his rather base observation. 'Actually, I was doing a wee, thank you very much.' She couldn't believe she was having this conversation with a man she barely knew.

'Glad to hear it. I wouldn't like to think I'd poisoned you on our first date.'

'No, you didn't.' Date. He'd used the word again.

'Look, the reason I'm calling, apart from the fact that I like talking to you anyway, is that thanks to the ever-volatile Middle Eastern situation, I'm being sent to Kuwait to do a special,' he said. 'It should only take a week or so, but things can get pretty hectic and it would probably be difficult to call from there. I didn't want you to think I'd forgotten you.'

'Don't worry, you don't have to check in with me.' She was unsure why she'd felt the need to make such a defensive remark.

He didn't seem fazed by it. 'I know that. But I want to see you again when I get back, so I thought I'd call and arrange it now. It'll give me something to look forward to when I've only got hairy-arsed blokes and camels for company.'

She laughed. 'Well, we both know my diary is completely blank, so it's no use me flicking through pages and pretending otherwise. You name the date and I'll be free.' It felt quite liberating to be so honest.

'Right, Friday week it is then. If there's any problem, I'll call you beforehand. But as it's a special and not an on-going news story, there shouldn't be.'

'Great. I'll leave my car at home this time.'

'Yes, let's get bladdered,' he said enthusiastically. 'I'll need it after a week without alcohol.'

Jo couldn't help a small triumphant smile as she replaced the receiver. She had a date. A proper, bona fide date with a man she found very attractive and good company. It gave her a buoyant feeling she thought she might never experience again in the early days after Jeff's departure.

At 12.45 p.m. she edged her car into a parking meter bay about fifty yards from Martin Blake's house. Today, instead of staying in and discussing the plans, they had agreed to relocate to a local restaurant for a change of scene.

It was a warm June day and Jo was wearing a white strappy top tucked into a bias-cut, calf-length floral skirt, a cotton jacket thrown over her handbag. The brown Gucci sunglasses Jeff had bought her three birthdays ago were perched on the top of her head.

She rang the bell and Martin opened the door almost immediately, stepping straight outside. He was more casually dressed than usual in dark blue linen trousers, Gucci loafers, and a crisp white cotton shirt unbuttoned to reveal the top of a hairy chest. His hair was still wet from the shower.

'We'll walk round. It'll only take a few minutes,' he said, relieving her of the heavy project folder she had tucked under her arm.

La Trattoria was an Italian restaurant in the true traditional sense, run by a whole family who cooked, waited tables and served at the bar. It was one of the most popular restaurants in the area and virtually impossible to get a table without six months' notice.

'When did you book this, last Christmas?' said Jo, settling down at the prime table by the window and handing the waiter her jacket.

'No, this morning,' said Martin. 'They keep a few tables back for regulars and I come here all the time.' At that moment, the owner emerged from the back of the restaurant.

'Mr Blaaaaake! A pleasure, as always!' A thin weasly man with Brillo pad hair, he pumped Martin's hand effusively and turned to Jo. 'And who is zees beautiful young lady?'

'You could say we're in business together,' replied Martin, smiling across at her.

'Enjoy your meal. It makes a pleasant change to see you here during the day. He works too hard you know.' The owner directed the last remark at Jo.

'I'm sure,' she smiled, widening her eyes at Martin.

When the owner had wandered off again, she picked up the bread basket and offered it to Martin who patted his flat stomach to indicate he wanted it to remain that way.

'So, are you a workaholic then?' she said, breaking up a bread roll for herself.

'Used to be. But I'm trying very hard not to be now. I've got to that age when you realise there are more important things in life.'

'Like what?'

Martin shrugged. 'Like family, kids, that sort of thing, I suppose.'

'Don't you have any?' Jo knew she was being nosey, but she couldn't help it. Martin Blake fascinated her because he was such a dark horse.

'Not that I know of.' It was clear she was going to have to drag any further information out of him.

'Have you never married?' She took a sip of the glass of chilled Chablis the waiter had placed in front of her. She'd noticed it was Premier Cru.

'What is this, twenty questions?' he laughed.

'Sorry, it's just that relationships fascinate me at the moment because of my own situation, and apart from that you're wearing a wedding ring.' She nodded at his left hand.

'Ah yes, you said the other day that you've just split up from your husband.' He ignored her observation. 'How's that all going?'

'Slowly and painfully. Marriage is great when it's good, but bloody awful when it goes wrong. You're best out of it,' she said, deftly changing the subject back to him.

'I know what you mean, but I like to think that at the age of forty-five I'm better equipped to choose someone I could spend the rest of my life with than I was, say, when I was in my twenties.' He took a small sip of wine. 'Those are the years when you're slogging away trying to make a name for yourself, so it's little wonder relationships get neglected and go wrong. I've got time to give someone now. Trouble is, all the women I would be interested in are probably married with children.'

Jo picked up the other half of her bread roll and started to demolish it. 'With your money, you could land a twenty-something dolly-bird who'd give you the best years of her thighs,' she said.

'Not interested.' He shook his head as he said it. 'Their age invariably matches their IQ. One of my downfalls as a wannabe Jack the Lad was always that I had to respect a woman to find her attractive.'

'My husband left me for a twenty-three-year-old,' she said. Again, she felt absolutely nothing saying it.

'Really?' Martin looked surprised. 'Whatever for?'

'Limitless blow jobs and pert breasts, I suppose,' she shrugged. 'You tell me, you're a man.'

'Well, it's nice of you to notice, thanks.' He looked faintly amused. 'But I wouldn't be the slightest bit interested in a twenty-three-year-old . . . for whatever reason.'

The arrival of the starters punctuated their conversation. Jo had a generously covered bruschetta whilst Martin opted for a Caesar salad without croutons or dressing.

'Bloody hell, that looks like something a rabbit would turn his nose up at,' she said, peering into the salad bowl.

'I try to eat healthily and do as much exercise as I can. You've got to start looking after yourself at my age.' Martin patted his chest at the heart area.

As they tucked into their respective dishes, Jo found

herself feeling slightly irritated by his fussiness over food. She didn't like a man to be overweight, but she also found it a turn-off if he tried a little too hard to stay in shape. Real men order straight off the menu, she reckoned.

'So anyway, *have* you ever been married?' she persisted.

'Dammit, I thought I'd deflected that subject,' he said, clicking his fingers in mock exasperation. 'Yes, I have. Once, when I was very young.'

'And?'

'And it lasted all of eight months. We were both in our twenties and she got bored of waiting for me to finish work all the time. She wanted to go out and have fun, and I wanted to build up a business. So she went and found fun with someone else. Can't say I blame her.'

'Are you still in touch?'

'Good God, no! I haven't heard from her in, ooh, nearly twenty years. Once the quickie divorce was finalised there wasn't really any need to speak again. It wasn't as if we had children.'

'Yes, they certainly keep you in touch with one another,' sighed Jo. 'Jeff and I are still falling out over the kids. I've banned him from letting them socialise with The Cliché.'

'Sorry?'

'That's what I call the twenty-three-year-old because she's one of his secretaries at work.' Martin poured her another generous glass of wine. She noticed he didn't give himself any.

'You should let her mix with the children,' he said. 'They're the greatest weapon you have.'

'How do you figure that out?'

'Well, she's twenty-three and there's no way she'll be ready to take on the responsibility of children. She'll still be into clubbing, drinking, and sleeping off hangovers. Just think how the presence of children will disrupt her routine, not to mention their romantic little lie-ins.'

Jo's eyes narrowed whilst she contemplated what Martin had just said. 'I never thought of it like that.'

Clearly warming to the subject, he carried on. 'Then the arguments will start. She'll want to know why his children are there all the time, and he'll get sensitive and say it's because he loves having them and if she really loved him then she'd make the effort to get on with them.' His eyes were shining at the brilliance of it all. 'Oh yes, it's a classic. If I were you, I'd start the offensive this coming weekend.'

The main courses arrived and the conversation moved on to the next stage of the house refurbishment. As Jo tucked into a gargantuan steak, Martin ate his way through a frugal plate of penne with tomato sauce and listened to her plans. By the time she'd had a coffee, it was 2.45 p.m.

'Crikes, I'd better get going. I've got to pick the children up from school,' she said, tapping the brightly-coloured Swatch she'd won in a *Reader's Digest* giveaway two years ago.

'You head off. I'll sort this,' said Martin, gesturing to

the waiter to bring the bill. 'Oh, by the way, if the children have a favourite band they'd like to see, just ask and I'll get tickets. That goes for you too. Perk of the job.'

'Thanks Martin, that's really kind of you.' She stood up and shook his hand. 'And thanks for lunch too. I feel I should have treated you really, what with all this work you're giving me, not to mention marital advice.'

'Nonsense. Anyway, it's been a pleasant diversion from work. As the owner said, I don't get out much during the day.'

Having said she'd call him when the next round of decisions was needed, Jo left the restaurant and walked briskly to her car, where a traffic warden was lurking in preparation for the meter to go two minutes into penalty time.

She arrived at the school just as children started walking out into the playground where parents gathered to collect them. Sophie was going to tea at a friend's house today, so it was just Thomas she was looking out for. He walked out looking disconsolate and alone behind a group of babbling classmates.

'Hello munchkin,' she said cheerily, using the pet name he'd had since a baby.

'Hiya.' He looked excessively glum.

'Oh dear, bad day?' She ruffled his hair.

'Mummy?' Rather than simply ask his question, Thomas was in the habit of always getting his mother's undivided attention first.

'Yes.'

'Are you and Daddy going to get divorced?' He looked up at her questioningly.

'What makes you ask that?' Jo was momentarily thrown.

'Because Jake says you are. He says Daddy isn't ever coming back and that he's going to marry his girlfriend instead.' Thomas's face had creased with worry.

Jake was the class know-it-all. And what he doesn't know he makes up, thought Jo. It was obvious to her that Jake's parents must have given him the information, then he in turn had blabbed at school. She recalled the little shit had also been the one to tell Thomas there was no Father Christmas.

'Daddy and I haven't decided what's going to happen yet, but you'll be the first to know, darling.' Jo could feel a tear pricking the corner of her eye and surreptitiously poked a finger there to rub it away. 'Whatever happens, you'll still get to see him as much as you like.'

'Will he marry Candy?' Suddenly, Thomas looked a vulnerable, lost little boy.

'I don't know, sweetie. Daddy and Mummy are still married at the moment, and all that matters to us is that you and Sophie are happy.'

His face suddenly lit up. 'If you went and told Daddy that you loved him and want him to come back, he would, I know he would.'

Jo felt her heart lurch. 'No Thomas, he's with Candy

196

now. He doesn't love Mummy any more but it doesn't mean he doesn't love you and Sophie. We all have to try and make the best of the situation.'

Thomas fell silent as they turned the corner into the main parade of shops. Jo couldn't bear to carry on with the conversation, so she practised the ancient art of parental distraction.

'I'll tell you what. As it's just you and me today, why don't we walk down to the toy shop and see if they've got a new batch of Pokemon cards in? Don't tell Sophie though,' she grinned.

'Cool! Thanks Mum.' Thomas's face was transformed by a beaming smile and he ran ahead in excitement.

I wish the thought of some new Pokemon cards would solve all my problems, thought Jo wistfully, as she hurried after him.

15

The children safely ensconced in front of Sunday morning television, Jo luxuriated in a foam bath and enjoyed what she suspected would be her only calm period of the day.

For a few self-indulgent minutes, she lay there and thought about Sean. His face. His smile. His sense of humour. And his seeming straightforwardness. She marvelled that not only had she bumped into a man, or rather he'd bumped into her, who had all these qualities, but also he seemed genuinely interested in getting to know her better. It was a nice, empowering feeling, and one that made her more than ready to take on the curse of Jeff, who was arriving in one hour's time to spend the day with the children.

In a heated phone call not long after the pink hair debacle, Jo had categorically banned him from taking the children anywhere near his new home.

'You can't do this, Jo,' he'd said.

'Yes I can, because you can't be trusted to do as I ask,' she'd replied firmly. 'I'm not stopping you from seeing them, merely saying you have to come here instead. You can take them to the local park.'

'We'll talk about this later,' he'd snapped, so Jo knew today was probably going to be strained.

Twenty minutes later, her bath over and quietly humming to herself, she looked out of the window at the clear blue sky and pulled on a knee-length floral dress she'd bought at the local As New agency for a tenner. It flattered her slim figure. She brushed her hair and reached for a scrunchy, then had second thoughts. The other evening, Sean had remarked that her hair looked nicer loose than it had the day of the collision when it had been tied back.

'Loose I think,' she said to the mirror.

Unusually, she also applied a light touch of mascara and lipstick. Amazing what even the mild interest of a new man can do for your self-image, she thought idly.

The doorbell rang at 9.30 sharp.

'Get that will you, kids?' bellowed Jo. There was no response.

'So much for missing their beloved father,' she muttered, running down the stairs.

As she opened the door, Jeff bent down to pick up the bag at his feet. When he looked up, he seemed taken aback.

'Bloody hell, what's with you?'

'What do you mean?' she frowned.

'You look different. Your hair's down and you're wearing make-up.'

'Well, bugger me, alert the media,' snapped Jo.

As he walked in to the living room to say hello to the

199

children, Jo stayed in the hallway and took a deep breath. He will not get to me, my life is moving on, she silently chanted to herself.

'Tea?' she said cheerily, popping her head round the living-room door to find Jeff being totally ignored by Thomas and Sophie who were staring gormlessly at SMTV.

'Yes please.' He got up and followed her into the kitchen.

'It's a nice day. I thought we could take them up to the park and play frisbee,' she said casually, flicking the kettle switch and reaching for two mugs.

'Yeah, whatever,' replied Jeff, still looking at her curiously. 'So what's with the change of appearance, then? Anything to do with the phantom aftershave wearer?'

Jo stared at him blankly for a moment, then realised he was referring to the night Conor had stayed in the spare bedroom.

'Just because I wear my hair loose and put on some mascara, it doesn't mean I have a new man,' she said. Well not exactly anyway, she thought.

'Bloody hell, don't tell me it's for my benefit, then?' If Jo didn't know better, she could have sworn Jeff looked hopeful.

'Very funny,' she smiled. 'No, it's for me.'

'Oh.' He piled three sugars into his tea. 'Well, you look great anyway.'

'Thanks,' replied Jo, and she meant it.

She rapidly concluded that if she could remain un-affected by Jeff's occasional caustic remarks, it put her in a far more powerful position than being rattled by them. She also realised that her burgeoning flirtation with Sean had given her something else to think about than what a great time Jeff may or may not be having with Candy. Her indifference was a formidable weapon.

'There's something else different about you, apart from your appearance,' he said as they strolled on the common an hour later. The children had been forcibly dragged from the TV, and were now sullenly and half-heartedly throwing a frisbee to each other.

'Really? Like what?' Jo knew full well what it was but was relishing every moment that Jeff remained in the dark.

He frowned. 'I don't know exactly, but you seem more at ease, somehow.'

'That's probably true. Life feels good right now.' She stooped down to pick up Thomas's baseball cap that was lying in the grass.

'So what's changed then?' Jeff had stopped walking and turned to face her.

'If you want the truth, I think I'm almost over you,' she said, waving at Sophie in the distance. 'Still not completely maybe, but as near as dammit. Enough to want to get on with my life, anyway.'

'I see,' he said flatly. 'What does that mean exactly?'

'What does it *mean*?' she shrugged. 'Not much I guess, except that I've been to see a solicitor about starting divorce proceedings.'

Jeff had just taken a swig from a can of Diet Coke, which he proceeded to spit all over the grass. 'Hang on, whoa!' he spluttered. 'What the bloody hell did you do that for?'

'Do what? The solicitor or the divorce?' she said sweetly.

'Both.' He looked shellshocked. 'Why didn't you talk to me about it first?'

'To be honest, I didn't see the point. We've argued so much since you left and I knew the subject of divorce would cause another row. It's so much better to do these things dispassionately through a third party, wouldn't you agree?'

He was looking at her as if she were an alien being who'd lost all contact with the mother ship. 'No, I fucking don't.'

'Oh.' She feigned a disappointed look. 'Well, it's too late now anyway, because I've decided that's what I want to do. I mean, it's not as if this situation could drift on for ever anyway. I'm sure you'd like to make things official with Candy at some point, and you can't do that if you're still married to me, can you?'

She was laughing inside at her own reasonableness, knowing how much it would infuriate him. It worked a treat.

'Marry Candy? Have you gone fucking mad?'

She raised her eyebrows in mock surprise at his vehement outburst. 'Well, it has been a few months now, hasn't

202

it? Believe you me, it won't be long before she's badgering you for an engagement ring. Out with the old, in with the new, eh?'

Jo started walking towards the children who were now some distance away, trying to retrieve their frisbee from a mischievous Jack Russell terrier. Jeff followed.

'She can badger all she bloody likes, she won't be getting one,' he said, lobbing his Coke can into a bin.

'Well, frankly Jeff, that's between you and her. It doesn't concern me any more. All I care about is that the children get to see you as much as they want, so I've been thinking . . .' She tailed off, remembering Martin's thoughts on letting the children pervade Candy and Jeff's life.

'Yes?' muttered Jeff, clearly finding it difficult to take everything in.

She let out a long, laboured sigh. 'I've been thinking that maybe I'm being unreasonable not letting the children see Candy.'

'You are?' Jeff now resembled a man who'd been blind-folded and spun round three times.

'Yes. So why don't you take them home with you tonight and do whatever you want to do. They'd like that.' More to the point, she quite fancied a night at home on her own with just a video and a takeaway for company.

Jeff slowly shook his head. 'Trouble is, Candy's going on a girls' night out to some club in Soho.'

How classy, thought Jo, but resisted the urge to

comment. Her heart swelled with joy at the thought of an extremely tired and hung-over Candy being jumped on by Thomas and Sophie at 8 a.m.

'Have them anyway,' she smiled. 'It's you they want to see after all.'

'No, I'll tell you what.' Jeff had visibly cheered up. 'Why don't I hang around tonight and stay in the spare room? Then I'll be there in the morning when they wake up. They'd like that.'

Jo pretended to give his suggestion some thought. 'No, that would give out confusing messages. It might make them think there's a chance of you moving back in.'

'It's not *completely* out of the question, is it? Who knows what might happen.' He looked pathetic.

Jo marvelled at the duplicity of men, but particularly Jeff. He'd walked out on her and the children, yet here he was, desperately trying to keep a foot in the family camp in case the new squaw turned out to be a bit of a dud. Well, he could fuck right off.

'Yes, Jeff, it is out of the question.' She couldn't believe she was saying this, but the comforting thing was that she felt she truly believed it. Almost.

'So are you saying that's it, our marriage is over?' He looked dejected.

This time, Jo had to struggle to keep her voice calm. 'No, *you* said that loud and clear when you walked out. *I* am saying I have to get on with my life, and I won't do that unless we divorce.'

'I see.' Jeff's voice sounded clipped. He shouted across to the children who had managed to wrestle back their fris-bee, and they started to saunter home across the common.

Back at the house, Jo plonked herself in front of the television in the living room whilst Jeff crashed about in the kitchen making tea for the children. Afterwards, he ran baths for them and laid out their pyjamas ready for bed. Pink-cheeked, with hair and teeth brushed, they presented themselves before her for a goodnight kiss at 8.30 p.m.

Jeff popped his head round the door. 'I'm just going to read Sophie a bedtime story. Thomas wants to read his own.'

'OK.' Jo plumped up the cushions behind her and leaned back on the sofa with a little sigh of pleasure. If only Jeff had been such a hands-on father when they were still together, their marriage might not have suffered quite so badly.

Jeff had always called himself 'the worker', a descrip-tion he clearly thought gave him licence to sit on his back-side watching sport all weekend, while Jo ran herself ragged after him and the children. It would have been me up there now, bathing, dressing, and reading stories, she thought. This new set-up isn't so bad. Better still, I get to go to bed on my own, read my book as long as I like, and not have to dread the moment Jeff rolls over and tweaks my nipple for some perfunctory sex.

He reappeared half an hour later just as the film *The Goodbye Girl* was about to start.

'Great, I love this film,' he said brightly, settling himself down on the other sofa. 'Nineteen seventy-seven. Bloody hell, I was fourteen when this came out.'

'Yes, I love it too,' said Jo, frowning as she watched him undoing his shoelaces. 'And I'm not being funny, but I'd really like to watch it alone.'

He had already removed one shoe, but stopped undoing the other. 'Really?'

'Yes, really. It's nothing to do with you, honestly. It's just that I rarely get any time to myself these days, whereas you have all week and most of the weekends too, if the truth be known. I quite enjoy my own company, so if you don't mind . . .'

His face clouded. 'Well, what a fucking great day this has turned out to be. First you tell me you want a divorce, and now you're throwing me out of my own house.'

There were a million retorts she could have made to his last remark, but Jo decided to let him get away with it because she'd scored enough victories for one day. She had also quietly removed his family house keys from his jacket pocket – just in case he ever felt tempted to use them in the future.

16

Jo looked at the kitchen clock. It was 11 a.m. and, as usual, Tim was late. An hour late, to be precise.

She loved her brother dearly, but despaired that he would ever keep a long-term girlfriend because of his flakiness and poor time-keeping. When he was still living at home and Jo was paying a fleeting visit one weekend, she remembered answering the phone to an irate girl who wanted to know where Tim was.

'He's watching television in the living room,' Jo had said. 'Why?'

'Because he was supposed to be meeting me an hour ago under the town hall clock and I have been standing here like a complete idiot. Tell him the date's off.' The girl had slammed the phone down on Jo, who couldn't really blame her.

'Damn, I was quite keen on her as well,' said Tim when she interrupted his TV viewing to tell him about the call.

'How can you be keen on someone and forget you're supposed to be meeting them?'

Ten years later and he hadn't changed a bit. Little

wonder he exists on a string of one-night stands, thought Jo, grimacing at the clock.

Tim eventually pitched up at midday, full of apologies and muttering something about unreliable public transport, despite the fact he only lived a few roads away.

More like unreliable brother, Jo reckoned, but she said nothing. She'd fought enough battles lately, without taking issue with Tim, who was clearly never going to change.

'Did you manage to book Smollensky's?' she asked, now regretting her decision to leave the lunch arrangements to someone with the time-keeping skills of the White Rabbit.

'Yep. They're expecting us at one.' He glanced at the fake Rolex that was slowly turning his wrist green. 'We'd better get a move on.'

Smollensky's on the Strand was a vast restaurant that catered specifically for families at the weekend. It was a popular haunt for parents desperate to have their children kept amused whilst they tried to eat a meal uninterrupted. There was a large play area for smaller children, a magician who toured the tables to amuse the older ones, and a puppet show. The whole place was geared up to welcome children, unlike many city centre restaurants where they reacted as if you had the AntiChrist in tow.

Seated at a red leatherette booth for four, Jo and Tim forced Thomas and Sophie to sit still while they placed the orders for lunch. Then Sophie raced off to get her face painted and Thomas went to do the thing that, inexplicably, all boys do: skidding across the floor with each other.

'So, how's life?' said Tim, taking a crafty slurp of Sophie's untouched banana milkshake.

'Looking up,' Jo smiled. 'Things have got a bit friendlier with Jeff, namely because I decided it was churlish not to let the children mix with The Cliché.'

'Blimey,' exclaimed Tim, raising his eyebrows in surprise. 'What brought on that sudden attack of reasonableness?'

'I'm not really sure,' sighed Jo. 'I suppose it was partly because I got tired of arguing about it, but also because I listened to some objective advice from that guy, Martin, that I'm doing up the house for. I realised I was against it because of my own insecurity. It just stopped bothering me, I guess.' She waved over at Thomas who had two large patches of floor dust on the knees of his trousers.

'That's a good sign,' said Tim, waving too. 'A good sign for your peace of mind, anyway. Not necessarily a good sign for any reconciliation though.'

'True.' Jo took a deep breath. 'Neither is the fact that I've started divorce proceedings.' She paused and studied Tim's reaction.

'It really is a serious split then.' His voice was low but his face remained impassive.

'Well, Jeff's not showing any signs of leaving Candy and we seem to have settled into this amicable pattern with the children.' She shrugged. 'So there doesn't really seem any need for me to hang around in limbo. I may as well get on with my own life.'

Tim nodded slowly. 'Yes, it makes sense, I suppose.

209

You could always remarry at a later date if things sorted themselves out.'

'Don't hold your breath,' she smiled. 'Anyway, I'm bored rigid of talking about Jeff and me. What's happening in your life?'

Tim's expression changed to glum. 'Nothing. There, that didn't take long, did it? What shall we talk about now?'

'Oh dear,' laughed Jo. 'That good, huh? In that case, how's Conor? Is he still seeing the woman you told me about?'

Since her brief liaison with Sean, she realised she didn't feel so awkward about raising the subject of Conor.

'He's still seeing her, but he seems a little half-hearted about it,' said Tim, stuffing a piece of French bread into his mouth.

'Oh? Conor doesn't strike me as the type who'd date someone on that basis.'

Tim didn't seem fazed by her sudden knowledge of Conor. 'It's not that he doesn't like her, because he does,' he said. 'It's just that he's very taken with someone else who doesn't seem that interested.'

Jo leaned closer, intrigued by this piece of gossip. 'Really? Who?'

Tim looked her straight in the eye. 'You.'

'Me?' Jo slapped the palm of her left hand against her chest, then let out a transparently false laugh. 'Don't be ridiculous.'

'I'm not,' said Tim levelly. 'He told me.'

'He *told* you?' Jo was incredulous that such a dark horse as Conor had said such a thing to her rather loud, insensitive brother. 'What exactly did he tell you?'

Tim shrugged in submission. 'Not a great deal actually, but the mere fact he told me anything made me realise he's got it bad, because he's usually fiercely protective of his private life. He never discusses it unless it's reached crisis point.'

'I see.' Jo knew that her brother was so emotionally inept that she was going to have to drag every last detail of the conversation out of him. 'So how did he broach the subject?'

Tim pursed his lips in thought. 'Well, he's been a bit moody lately. So when we went out for a couple of beers the other night I asked him what was the matter.'

'And?' Jo wished he'd get on with it.

'And he confessed that he'd always had a bit of crush on you, but that it had increased since you split up with Jeff, and particularly since you and he had dinner together when I couldn't make it.'

'And?' Jo was aware her voice was starting to sound shrill.

'And that's it, really.'

'How can that be it? You just said that I wasn't interested in him, so he must have told you that himself.'

'Oh yes,' said Tim, glancing around the room and beginning to tire of the subject. 'He said he had intimated to you that he would like to see more of you, but that you were patently not interested.'

Jo leaned back in her seat, satisfied she had wrung out as much as Tim knew. Conor obviously hadn't told Tim about their passionate necking session, or her brother wouldn't have been able to resist the urge to tease.

'So is that the case, then?' Tim's question interrupted her thoughts.

'What?'

'Is it the case that you're not interested?'

'Well yes, but not quite that . . . bluntly,' she faltered. 'He took me by surprise when he said he liked me. I mean, he's your friend and I've known him for years. I've never really thought about him in *that* way.'

'Perhaps it's time you did,' said Tim, raising an eyebrow.

Jo shook her head. 'No, I don't agree. Because if it went wrong, it would be so complicated. I'd be losing a friend and that's a risk I don't want to take. Besides, I don't really think he's my type,' she added, as an afterthought.

Tim made a small scoffing noise. 'What's your type then? Dull solicitors with a penchant for younger women?'

Jo was shocked. Tim had never expressed a view before about Jeff, and it was particularly out of character for him to say something so snide and barbed about someone he knew well.

'I thought you liked him,' she said, puzzled. 'You always seemed to get on well.'

Tim shrugged his wide shoulders. 'He was your

212

husband so I made an effort, but he was never really my cup of tea.'

'Oh.' Amazing how many truths of the 'I never liked him anyway' variety emerge after the demise of a relationship, she thought.

'I know you went through hell at first, but now you seem much more content without him,' said Tim, looking more placatory.

'You may be right,' she said. 'I do get lonely, though.'

'I'm sure you do. We all do. The question is, what do you plan to do about it?'

Jo considered his question for a moment, alternating between glancing at him and looking down to fiddle with a beer mat on the table. 'Well . . .' She hadn't been planning to say anything, but suddenly felt a cathartic urge to confide in Tim. 'I have been out on a date with someone I really like and we're going to go out again when he gets back from his latest assignment. He's a television cameraman.'

'Very grand. Who for?' But Tim's question remained unanswered as Sophie bounded up to the table, growling.

'Oh, my goodness, it's a scary tiger!' shrieked Jo, recoiling in mock horror from Sophie's painted face. 'Go and get your brother because here's the food.'

It was 2.30 before Jo and Tim could resume their conversation, when the children had finished their lunch and rushed off to secure a front-row place for the puppet show across the room.

As the waitress cleared the table, Tim said, 'I've been thinking . . .'

'Whoa, steady on,' smiled Jo, anxious for them to get back on the more familiar ground of teasing each other.

But his face remained serious. 'If you don't mind, I'll tell Conor that you and I had a brief chat and that you want to keep things as they are between you. That way, he might start to put a bit more effort into making things work with this new woman.'

'OK,' said Jo reluctantly, preferring he didn't say anything. 'I must say it's very unlike you to get so involved in stuff like this. You must be very fond of him.'

'He's the best person I know,' said Tim matter-of-factly. 'And frankly, if you two got it together it would make me very happy indeed, because I know he'd look after you. He'd certainly never behave like Jeff.'

Jo sighed deeply. 'There was a time when I would never have thought Jeff would behave like he has. Still, it's happened and that's that.'

Tim didn't express any further interest in Sean, and to Jo's relief their conversation returned to the safer ground of her brother's beloved Chelsea Football Club and the financial vacuum of his rather static acting career.

Back at the house, when Tim had gone home and the children were tucked up in bed, she finally had time to mull over their conversation. It had felt nice to have such an honest, heartfelt exchange with Tim, because their relationship had always been on a fairly shallow level. He had surprised her with his depth of understanding over her marital problems, and she regretted not talking to him more in the past. But then she'd never really been the confessional type, preferring to stay schtum about any marital problems out of a sense of loyalty to Jeff. But when he'd smashed their loyal little unit, her pain had made her face up to many of the feelings she'd been bottling up for so long. Furthermore, it had put her relationships with others on to an entirely different level because she had leaned on them like never before.

As the news headlines flickered in the background, she found that Sean kept drifting into her thoughts, with his devastatingly attractive grin and sharp sense of humour. It wasn't long before she was lost in the fantasy of what might happen during their second date on Friday night. He had just swept her off her feet and was carrying her upstairs to the bedroom with a wanton look on his face when the phone rang.

'Fuck. I can't even have a fantasy without someone spoiling it,' Jo muttered to herself as she reached for the receiver. 'Hello?'

'Oh dear, you sound cross. Have I rung at a bad time?' It was Martin Blake.

'No, don't worry. That's just my natural grumpiness.'

'Well, it's very effective, so I won't keep you,' he said briskly. 'I was calling because, for my sins, I have to go to a Steps concert at Wembley to link up with one of the European chairmen who's just over for Wednesday night.'

'And you want some counselling?' laughed Jo, who found it impossible to contemplate he'd *ever* sinned.

'No.' Martin either didn't hear her quip or chose to ignore it. 'I can get four tickets, so I was wondering if you'd like to come along and bring your children.'

Jo hesitated, but as Martin was a business associate and there was no romantic interest, she couldn't see the harm in it. More to the point, she didn't want to deprive the children of such a fun night out.

'That sounds great,' she said. 'I'll ask the children in the morning, but I'm sure the answer will be yes. I'll call you tomorrow to confirm.'

17

Before the Steps concert and her big date on Friday night, Jo had an ordeal to get through. A dinner party.

Since her split from Jeff, she'd marvelled at how the dinner invitations had dried up, as if she were now some odd number on the table plan of life. Then, out of the blue, Sally Keen had called her. Sally was 'Very Keen' to have her round for 'a little, impromptu supper'.

As the call had come a week before the actual event, Sally's version of impromptu clearly wasn't the same as Jo's. But she decided to accept anyway in her new-found spirit of getting out there and starting a new life.

When Rosie arrived to babysit, they discussed the peculiarity of the dinner party circuit.

'As soon as Jeff disappeared, so did the dinner party invitations,' said Jo, fighting her way into a lycra top. 'I'm probably making up the numbers with some other social misfit.'

'I don't even get asked to make up the numbers,' said Rosie gloomily. 'I've been single for so long that all my attached friends have forgotten I'm even on the planet.'

'Well, believe me, you haven't missed anything,' said

Jo, her voice muffled as she struggled to find the neck opening. 'They're usually a nightmare, and I can't believe tonight will be any different. I don't even *like* Sally that much so God *knows* why I accepted.'

Rosie wrinkled her nose. 'Remind me who she is again?'

'We met when I was in hospital having Sophie. She was having her daughter at the same time – Jacasta, can you believe that? – and for some reason she has stayed in touch with me.' Jo emerged through the neckhole and squinted into the mirror. 'Christ, I look like the Elephant Man.'

Rosie nodded her head in agreement. 'Well, it's nice of her to invite you anyway. She probably thinks you need cheering up.'

'I doubt it,' said Jo ruefully, pulling out a dress from the wardrobe. 'She probably wants to gloat because her marriage is still intact. But her husband is so boring he makes Alan Shearer look like Billy Connolly. I couldn't spend a day with him, let alone a lifetime.'

'Oh well, have fun,' laughed Rosie. 'You've always got Friday to look forward to.'

Jo smoothed the dress over her thighs. 'Believe me, it's a shining beacon in my life at the moment. That and the Steps concert, of course.'

'Sorry?'

'I'm taking the kids to a Steps concert tomorrow night. Or rather Martin Blake is taking all of us.'

'Hang on, hang on,' said Rosie, waving her arms in

front of her. 'You're going on a date with the mega-wealthy Martin Blake and you forgot to tell me?'

'It is absolutely *not* a date.' She shot Rosie a warning look. 'It's a Steps concert. He didn't know anyone else with children who might want to go.'

'Jo, believe me, in his mind it's a date. He's just being clever because he knows the best way to get you out is to come up with something your children would want to do.' Rosie stopped talking and gave the thumbs up to Jo's dress.

But Jo wasn't paying attention. She was annoyed by her friend's assumption, particularly when she hadn't even met the man involved. 'Even if he saw it that way, and I don't for one moment think he does, it's definitely not a date because I'm not the slightest bit interested in him,' she said defiantly. 'Besides, he's quite nice-looking, rich, and says he wants to settle down. He could get anyone he wanted, so he wouldn't waste his time with me.'

By this time, Rosie had fallen face down on the carpet in a mock sobbing fit, thrashing her feet against the floor.

'I know you think I'm mad,' added Jo, 'but if the spark's not there then there's not a damn thing I can do about it.'

'No, but you're dismissing it before you even try,' said Rosie, sitting up again. 'Instead, you're hankering after some geographically challenged relationship with a cameraman who's probably earning peanuts by comparison.'

'We've had this conversation before,' said Jo wearily. 'I'm not interested in money like you are. I want romance and passion.'

Rosie made a loud snorting noise. 'You want difficult bastards, that's what you want. You think straightforward men are boring.'

'Jeff wasn't a bastard when I married him. He just became one,' she said quietly, suddenly feeling very lacklustre about going to a houseful of strangers for a night of mind-numbing small talk.

Rosie picked up her sudden gloom and hastily changed the subject. 'If you don't want him, introduce that Blake bloke to me. Quite apart from anything else, I could do with the sex.'

Jo smiled and gathered up her house keys to put in her handbag. 'Right, how do I look?'

'Like a woman who's going to a dinner party she doesn't want to go to,' said Rosie.

'Good. That's precisely the look I wanted to achieve. I have specifically chosen an outfit to blend in with Sally's wallpaper.'

After saying goodnight to the children, neither of whom shifted their eyes from the television, she walked outside and got into her car.

'Right Ms Miles, I hope your skill for dinner party repartee hasn't abandoned you,' she said to herself as the engine rumbled into life.

Half an hour later she pulled up outside Sally Keen's rather grand house in Richmond, Surrey. Through the brightly illuminated front bay window, she could see some of the guests already indulging in polite banter over pre-dinner drinks. As the sound of false, tinkling laughter rang out, she suddenly felt very weary. Dinner parties had been water off a duck's back when she'd been with Jeff, but now they seemed a rather daunting experience to face alone.

There would be no one to exchange those 'let's go home soon' glances with, no one to latch on to as a life-raft in the raging ocean of banality that often accompanied such a gathering. With heavy heart, she trudged up the steps to the front door.

'Ah, that must be Jo!' She could hear Sally's irritatingly la-di-da voice through the door and assumed she must be the last guest to arrive.

'Hello darling!' said Sally, enveloping Jo in a bear hug and an overpowering waft of Chanel No. 5. 'I thought you might have got cold feet.'

'I'm only fifteen minutes late,' said Jo, glancing at her watch.

'Yes, dear, whatever. At least you're here now.' Jo could see Sally had lost none of her ability to make her feel she was always a little bit of a disappointment. 'Now then, let's introduce you to everyone,' said Sally, placing a palm in the small of Jo's back and expertly manoeuvring her into the double reception room, stuffed with beautiful antique furniture and paintings.

'This is Sue and Mark.' The simpering woman took Jo's hand for one of those limp handshakes that makes you feel like you've been slimed. By comparison, her husband's grip was vice-like.

'Ouch. Did you used to be in the army by any chance?' teased Jo, rubbing her hand.

'No, but I'm in the Territorials,' he boomed, as she made a mental note not to sit anywhere near him.

'And this is Mandy and Bob,' said Sally, moving round the room to where a couple sat perched together on a two-seater sofa. She was head to foot Aquascutum woman, with an expression which suggested her knickers might be made of the roughest tweed, while he was very much Reform Club, with blazer and cravat. Neither stood up.

'Hello,' said Jo, nodding and smiling. They didn't smile back, and she made a mental note not to sit next to them either. I'm running out of guests, she mused, as Sally moved on to the next couple.

'This is Jack and Tina, they're new friends of ours.'

'Yes, Sally hasn't got to know us properly yet, otherwise I'm sure we wouldn't be here,' smiled Jack, extending his hand to Jo. She liked him immediately.

'Jack has a form of Tourette's Syndrome. He just can't seem to get through a social occasion without insulting at least three people,' laughed his wife Tina. 'So watch out.'

Jo smiled warmly. 'Don't worry, I have a brother like that.' She was determined to remain glued to Jack and Tina's side, but Sally had other ideas.

'And *this* is Graham,' she said, stepping back as if to admire a prized exhibit.

Jo hadn't seen him when she first walked into the room, which gave some idea of how unprepossessing he was.

Graham was about five feet six with a puce face, pot belly and fingers like overstuffed cocktail sausages. Because of Sally's rather loaded introduction, Jo also got the distinct impression he had been earmarked as her date for the night. Her heart, shoulders and stomach all sank simultaneously.

'So how do you know Sally?' said Jo, after the hostess had drifted back to the kitchen.

'I don't, I know Paul,' he said, referring to Sally's husband who was clearly being kept manacled to the kitchen by his domineering wife.

'Oh, so are you a graphic designer too?' Jo couldn't believe she'd resorted to the 'what do you do?' question so early on in the conversation, but she was a desperate woman.

'Good God, no. We just attend the same local golf club, that's all. I'm a money broker.' He delivered the last line with all the self-importance of a man who'd announced he had crash-landed a jumbo jet that very afternoon and saved the lives of everyone on board.

'Oh, that's handy.' Jo scrabbled for something to say. 'Perhaps you could do me a better deal on my mortgage.'

'Hardly. I lend money to countries.' He made an elaborate sniffing noise that made Jo feel quite queasy.

'Right, come along everyone!' Sally had returned and was clapping her hands at them like a nursery teacher. 'Let's sit down.'

Jo hovered close to Jack and Tina in the faint hope it would be a sit anywhere arrangement. But she'd forgotten how irritatingly organised and bossy Sally was.

'Now then. You over there, Jack, and you down here, Tina. Sue there, Bob there, Mandy here and Mark there. Jo, you sit opposite Graham here, and Paul and I will go at the ends.'

Jo sank onto her allotted chair and looked down the table where she noticed Jack was trying to catch her eye. He nodded silently in Graham's direction, then pulled his tie up round his neck in a hanging gesture. Jo got a fit of the giggles.

'What's so funny?' said Graham, now seated and pouring himself a generous measure of red wine.

'Oh nothing, just a private joke,' she muttered.

'I always find private jokes rather rude,' he replied, using his napkin to wipe a line of sweat from his top lip. His beady eyes darted around the room, clearly trying to work out who the joke was with.

If Jo was going to get through this torturous dinner, she knew she would have to make an enormous effort to achieve an even slightly interesting conversation with the odious Graham. So she resorted to the age old charm offensive used at dinner parties across the land. She talked to him about his favourite subject. Himself.

'So how did you get into the money business?' It was a question that heralded the start of an hour long monologue from Graham about his expertise in the field and how no one could touch him for profit margins. Or boredom thresholds, thought Jo.

Slumped over her crème brûlée, she sneaked a peek

down the table and saw Sally nodding in her direction, a triumphant look on her face. As Jo had suspected, it had been a set-up all along. Just because her husband had left her for a younger woman, she had clearly become a figure of pity to others who felt they should introduce her to new men. Men like Graham, a fat, dull, and pompous bore with halitosis, dandruff, and God knows how many hidden neuroses just waiting to be unveiled by some unlucky woman.

Is this what they think of me? she despaired, as she watched Graham launch into yet another anecdote about his financial expertise. Do they really think I'm so desperate I could find this man attractive? I would have to be heavily drugged to even kiss him. She knew she couldn't sit there and listen to him droning on a moment longer. She stood up.

'I'm sorry Sally, but I'm going to have to go. I really don't feel well,' she said, putting on her best queasy expression which wasn't hard considering she'd been sitting opposite Baby Shamu for over an hour.

'Darling, no! And you and Graham were getting on so well.'

'It happens all the time, I'm afraid. It's the stress, I think.' She gave a little grimace at Sally as if to say, 'I know you'll understand.'

'Sweetie, that's terrible, but I do hope you'll come again soon. I have to go and help Paul in the kitchen with the coffee, but I'm sure Graham will see you to the door.'

Sally was clearly not going to be defeated in her bid to match-make.

'No, really I'm fine,' stuttered Jo, feeling her stomach bungee-jumping at the thought of spending one more nanosecond in the ghastly man's company. 'I'll see myself out.'

'Nonsense, nonsense,' puffed Graham, rising from his chair and shuffling round the table.

Jo cast a desperate expression round the room in the vain hope that someone might sense she needed rescuing. But no-one knew her well enough to pick up the signs, so she said a heavy 'Goodnight all' and walked into the hallway with Graham lumbering behind. Whenever I get asked to another couply dinner party as a single woman, and find myself tempted to say 'Yes', I shall remember this painful moment, she told herself.

Taking care to keep her back to him at all times, she opened the door and stepped out into the cool night air, turning briefly to bid him goodnight. It was the fleeting chance he needed to plant a sweaty, fumbling kiss right on her mouth. Suddenly her queasiness wasn't fake any more.

'Would you like to go out for dinner sometime?' he said, his small eyes studying her carefully.

Like all women, Jo had learned a million gentle let-downs over the years. It's not you, it's me. I'm just not ready to date again after the operation. My jealous ex-boyfriend is a psychopath and I wouldn't want to place you in danger. The list was endless. But tonight she felt too weary to bother with any of them.

226

'Thanks, but no I wouldn't,' she said.

He looked stunned. 'Really?'

'Yes, really.' Jo started to descend the steps. She stopped at the bottom and turned to see his small, moist mouth curling into a sneer.

'I was only inviting you out of pity because your friends said your husband dumped you for a younger woman. Frankly, I'm not surprised.'

Jo stood looking at his portly frame silhouetted in the doorway and thought how much he resembled a pig skewered for a barbecue. She considered what he'd said for a moment. Just as she was about to reply, he took a step back and slammed the door. She toyed with the idea of going back in and retaliating, but decided to rise above it and drive home instead.

As she drove home on subconscious automatic pilot, she found herself smirking at the thought of what was being said about her right now at Maison Keen. One of the beneficial things about hitting her thirties was that she no longer bothered what people might be saying about her when she wasn't around. She vowed she would never see Sally again. If there's one thing recent events have taught me, she decided, it's that life's too short to bother with people you don't even like that much.

When she arrived home twenty minutes later, Rosie was in floods of tears as the credits rolled on *Goodbye Mr Chips* starring Peter O'Toole and Petula Clarke.

'She never found out he was made headmaaaaaster,'

227

she wailed, loudly blowing her nose into a pile of scrunched-up loo roll.

'Rosie, it's a film,' sighed Jo. 'I'm the one who should be weeping after the night I've had.' She threw her handbag onto the sofa and plonked herself next to it.

'Crap, was it?'

'I got saddled with one of those terrible bores who, when you ask how they are, tells you. I even thought about jabbing a knife in my eye, just so I could be taken to casualty and get away from him.'

'So you won't be going to any more dinner parties in the foreseeable future then?'

'Quite frankly, there's more chance of the Queen beating Linford Christie over 100 metres. I'm off to bed.'

18

Martin Blake swept up to the house in a sleek, black Mercedes S-class, complete with capped chauffeur.

'Wow!' said Thomas who had been keeping watch in the front bay window for the past twenty minutes. 'He must be stinking rich!'

'Thomas, look at me.' Jo put on a stern voice and forced him to turn round. 'You're not to say things like that, particularly to Martin. It's rude. Now get your camera and come along.'

'OK,' he said sulkily, his arms dropping to his sides as he walked into the hallway.

Jo opened the door to find Martin dressed in an extremely smart suit and tie. 'You look very formal for a Steps concert,' she smiled.

''Fraid so,' he said apologetically. 'I have to look businesslike for my meeting with the European guy, so I've had to abandon my usual gold sequinned halterneck and lycra trousers.'

So he does have a sense of humour, albeit a dry one, Jo thought, as she ushered the children towards the gleaming car that looked rather incongruous next to her humble Clio.

'Thomas, Sophie, this is Martin. I'm working for him at the moment,' she added, keen that the children didn't think he was a boyfriend.

'But, Mummy, you don't have a proper job,' said Sophie, scrambling over the rear leather seat to sit in the far corner.

'Yes I do, love,' said Jo, anxiously rubbing at a scuff mark on the seat. 'I decorate people's houses, and I'm doing Martin's for him.'

Despite Martin's offer to swap, she insisted on sitting in the back with the children, mainly to keep an eye on them. Sophie had a habit of announcing she felt sick, then throwing up less than two seconds later, as the faint whiff of vomit that permeated Jo's car proved. She wanted to catch it in her lap rather than suffer the embarrassment of Martin's expensive car seats being ruined.

It took them just over an hour to get to Wembley, as the traffic near the arena drew to a virtual standstill. The whole way, Martin regaled the children with his tales of the rich and famous.

'Have you met Michael Jackson?' asked Thomas, wide-eyed.

'Yes, many times,' said Martin, swivelling in the front seat to face them. 'He's seems nice enough, but he does seem to lead a rather strange life.'

'What about the Hooplas?' said Sophie, referring to her favourite girl band of the moment.

'Ah, that one's easy because they're on my record label,'

said Martin. 'They all hate each other but they can't split up because they're making too much money.'

Jo sat quietly and watched the enthralled expression on her children's faces as they listened to Martin's stories. Children are such fickle creatures, she thought. You can spend hours doing their homework with them, taking them to the park, or cutting out endless pictures from endless magazines for their scrapbooks. But tell them a couple of stories about famous people and give them some free Steps tickets, and you've won them over instantly.

'What football team do you support, Thomas?' asked Martin, pressing the radio's scan button to find a music station that wasn't playing records of the 'got my girlfriend up the duff' rap variety.

'The Gunners,' said Thomas, punching the air with his fist and making a whooping noise.

Martin smiled. 'I'm an Arsenal supporter too! In fact I've got a season ticket. I'll take you along to a match one Saturday if you like.'

Thomas looked like he was going to pass out with sheer excitement. 'Cool!'

'That's if Mum says it's OK, of course,' said Martin, giving Jo a pensive look.

'How could a Saturday afternoon with boring old Mummy possibly compete with that?' She was irritated that Martin hadn't thought to mention it to her first, out of Thomas's earshot.

'Here we are,' said the driver, sweeping past the queue

of vehicles waiting to get into the public car parks, and heading for a gate marked 'Backstage passes only.'

The gate opened and the car pulled up right outside the backstage door. 'Cool!' said Thomas again, leaping out.

'Good evening, Mr Blake,' said the security guard on the door, standing aside to let them pass.

Bloody hell, thought Jo. Never mind Thomas and Sophie, I could get used to this sort of treatment as well.

They followed Martin through the backstage area, past all the racks of stage clothes that were labelled with the individual names of the band members.

'Man, look at this,' said Sophie to Thomas, and Jo found herself wondering at what point her children had turned into miniature hippies.

As they approached a small door in the far corner, Martin dug in his pocket and pulled out four shiny laminates with the words 'Steps: Access All Areas' written across them.

'We'll just nip into the VIP bar for a quick drink before the concert. I warn you there are seven hundred support bands who all look and sound exactly the same,' said Martin, wincing at Jo. 'I'll be in my meeting, but there's nothing to stop you going and watching them.'

'Thanks. Did you get the seats with a restricted view that I asked for?' Again, her attempt at a joke seemed to fly straight over Martin's head. Either that, or he didn't think it was the slightest bit funny.

They walked into the bar and immediately he was

enveloped by a group of people calling his name and shaking his hand. Anxious not to be a millstone around his neck, Jo steered Thomas and Sophie into a clear corner of the room and told them to wait there while she queued at the free bar for some drinks.

'I didn't realise you'd wandered off.' It was Martin. 'I was going to introduce you to some of my colleagues.'

'You don't have to do that,' said Jo, praying he wouldn't. 'We'll be fine keeping out of the way. It was very nice of you to invite us in the first place. I don't expect you to look after us as well.' She took the two orange juices being handed over by the barman.

'Give those drinks to the children and come and meet them now,' said Martin, clearly not going to be dissuaded.

Jo sighed and followed him across the room to the same group of people who had greeted Martin when he first arrived.

'This is Jo, everyone,' said Martin. 'This is Betty, Frank, Ray and Tony.'

I'll bet they're all thinking, 'Who the bloody hell's this?' thought Jo, as she smiled sweetly and shook hands with them. Their curious expressions certainly suggested that.

A tall grey-haired man called out to Martin, who muttered, 'Excuse me a minute', and left Jo standing alone with the group, who didn't waste any time in interrogating her.

'So how did you meet Martin then?' said Betty, her eyes narrowing suspiciously.

'I work for him.'

'Oh? Doing what?'

'I'm doing the interior design on his new house.' Jo gave a firm smile as if to indicate that was all she wanted to say on the subject, but Betty seemed to be on a roll.

'I see. So how come you're here?'

What a rude woman! Jo suspected Betty's nosiness was rooted in jealousy, either because there was a history between her and Martin or her feelings were unrequited. Either way, she wasn't having it.

'I really don't think that's any of your business, do you?' She gave a quick, thin smile, and walked back to where the children were sitting, uncharacteristically quietly, where she'd left them.

'The support acts are about to start!' boomed a young man through the bar door. Everyone in the room just carried on drinking and talking.

'Come on you two, let's go to our seats,' said Jo, gesturing to Thomas and Sophie to stand up.

As if by magic, Martin appeared at her side. 'Where are you going?'

'To see the bands,' she said with a note of surprise. 'After all, that's what we're here for, isn't it?'

He looked doubtful. 'Well, why don't you get the children settled and then come back here for a drink.'

Jo shook her head. 'No, they're too young to be left in such a crowd on their own. I'll stay with them.'

'Oh, OK.' He looked disappointed. 'I'm still waiting for

the European guy to arrive, so I'll wait here then probably sneak in when Steps are on.'

Jo endured an interminable hour and a quarter of various teenagers wearing wraparound microphones, doing jerky dance routines, and warbling dozens of songs that were indistinguishable from each other. It was parent hell.

Martin materialised about two minutes before the main act. 'Have I missed anything?' he enquired.

'Hardly. They don't write a good tune any more,' Jo shouted above the noise. 'God, it's official. I have turned into my own mother.'

Conversation was impossible, so they sat side by side in silence while Thomas and Sophie leapt up and down, clapping their hands in time with the eternally smiley and energetic Steps. Martin had the running order in his hand, and he and Jo mentally ticked off each song, counting down to the encore when thousands of pieces of silver paper showered down from the ceiling and stuck in everyone's hair.

'Come on! Let's beat the rush,' said Martin, grabbing her elbow.

Jo gestured to Thomas and Sophie to follow, and the four of them headed back to the VIP bar just moments before the crowds started pouring out of the arena.

'That was soooo brilliant!' enthused Thomas, his face pink from excitement.

Martin ruffled his hair. 'Good, I'm glad you liked it. I can get tickets for pretty much anything, so let me know if you want to go to anything else.'

Again, Jo was irritated by him making the offer before checking with her. Her children couldn't be bought, she thought, then changed her mind as she watched Thomas and Sophie crawling all over him.

'Did your meeting go OK?' she asked, changing the subject.

'He didn't show,' said Martin. 'It looks like I might have to fly out to Madrid to see him instead.'

It fleetingly crossed Jo's mind that there had never been a meeting in the first place, but she dismissed it almost instantly. After all, she thought, if he wanted to get me out on a date he would hardly have chosen a Steps concert as the ideal event. If anything, it would break up a relationship. Then she remembered Rosie's suggestion that he was inveigling his way in through the children. That certainly made more sense given his promises of Arsenal matches and other concert tickets. But then again, maybe he was just being kind. Jo decided the only way to really know his intentions would be to see whether he pounced on her at any stage or asked her out on a proper one-on-one date. She hoped he didn't, as her refusal might cause an awkwardness between them and there was still several months' work left to do on the house.

'Ah, here they are.' Martin's voice broke into her thoughts.

'Who?' said Thomas, following Martin's gaze across the room.

'Steps. It's the meet and greet bit now. Come on, I'll introduce you both.'

He grabbed Thomas and Sophie by the hand and headed towards the band. They returned five minutes later, the children clutching signed photographs in their hands.

'They signed this for us and we had our photograph taken with them as well,' babbled Sophie, her eyes shining with pure, unadulterated joy.

'I'll get a copy of the picture over to you on Monday,' smiled Martin. 'Now as it's quite late and we've got a bit of a journey home, I suggest we head off now.'

Within ten minutes of setting off, both Thomas and Sophie had fallen asleep, their heads resting on each of Jo's shoulders.

'Thanks for organising all this, Martin,' she whispered. 'They really did have a fantastic time.'

'It's a pleasure,' he smiled. 'Actually, it's been nice for me to bring someone along who still gets excited by these things. I'm afraid I've become a little jaded about it.'

They lapsed into silence, and for the rest of the journey Jo studied the back of Martin's head and wondered what made him tick. He was certainly powerful and successful in business, but she got the impression his personal life was less than satisfactory and he was now hankering after the family set-up all his contemporaries had developed years ago. She had a few female friends like that too. Unlike Jo who'd had Thomas and Sophie in her twenties and struggled to juggle motherhood with work and marriage, they had opted to be single-minded about their careers throughout their twenties and early thirties. Now suddenly, when they hankered after marriage and children, they were finding it difficult to meet men who weren't already married or had enough emotional problems to keep a convention of therapists going for a week. A couple of them had decided to get pregnant without a man, well without a man after the conception at least, but were struggling to conceive. So whilst there were times when Jo envied them as they jetted off for their child-free Caribbean holidays, there were also many times when she almost felt superior because she'd successfully achieved a family life. Well, until recently anyway.

It was 11.30 p.m. by the time they arrived back at the house. Gently, she nudged the children awake. Martin got out of the car and carried Sophie to the front porch while Jo fumbled for her key. The children murmured a sleepy, 'Thank you, Martin', and trudged inside.

'Yes, thank you,' said Jo, standing on the doorstep. She hoped to God he wasn't going to pounce.

'Anytime.' He took a step forward and her stomach turned with apprehension. 'I'm not going to bite you, Jo.'

She looked down, to see his arm extended for a handshake, and suddenly felt incredibly stupid. She shook it.

'We'll speak soon about the house, no doubt,' he said, turning back towards the gate.

'Indeed,' she said, thinking of Sean. 'And thanks again for a lovely evening.' She closed the door and leaned with her back to it until she heard the car pull away.

'You vain, silly little cow,' she muttered aloud. 'He's not in the slightest bit interested in you.'

238

19

The rest of the week passed quietly between meetings with floor fitters and curtain makers, but on Friday afternoon, Jo had a meeting of a far more personal nature – a second visit to Hazel Burnett to say she wanted to press ahead with the divorce.

'Are you absolutely sure?' asked Hazel, peering over the top of her glasses.

'No, not absolutely,' sighed Jo, nervously picking at the chipped nail varnish on her thumb. 'But I'm pretty sure, and I have to make some sort of decision to enable me to move on with my life. I'm not very good at being in limbo.'

Hazel leaned forward with an earnest look. 'You do realise that putting it all on an official footing might set you back a bit? You know, in terms of the friendly understanding you seem to have with your husband at the moment?'

'That's a risk I'm prepared to take. I rang him last night to say he and his girlfriend could have the children on Saturday, so he certainly can't complain that I'm being unreasonable.'

Hazel tilted her head to one side. 'Why the change of heart about her?'

'I'm just tired of fighting about it, I guess.' She stared out of the window. 'Also, I've stopped caring so much about it. She won't replace me in my children's lives, and that's what matters to me, really.'

'Well, this all sounds very healthy,' said Hazel cheerfully. 'You've clearly gone into the acceptance stage, so it's onwards and upwards from now on.'

'You sound like a therapist!' laughed Jo.

Thinking about it as she waited for Jeff to arrive on Saturday morning, she had to admit she felt bolstered by the meeting. It was nice to know that someone who spent all day dealing with people's divorces felt that she, Jo Miles, was handling her situation in a mature and reasonable way. There had been times when it was bloody hard, she thought, but at least I've managed to hang on to my dignity whilst my husband was behaving like a prize shit.

As usual, at 9.30 on Saturday morning, the doorbell rang. Despite knowing their father was there, both Thomas and Sophie carried on playing their board game Tummy Ache.

'Are they ready to go straight away?' said Jeff, looking slightly flustered. 'Candy's waiting in the car.'

'Come on, you two! Dad's here and wants to go now,' shouted Jo over her shoulder. She turned back and studied the vision on her doorstep. Jeff was dressed in combat trousers, a tight T-shirt, trainers, and an elasticated beaded necklace. The midlife crisis look.

'So what are your plans?' she asked.

'There's a puppet theatre on down at the South Bank, so we thought we'd take them to that, then get some lunch,' said Jeff, checking the Tag Heuer watch that had incriminated him in the photographs all those months ago.

We. Jo mulled over the realisation that while that innocuous little word used to apply to her and Jeff, it now referred to him and Candy. To her surprise, it didn't bother her too much.

'We'll get them back by six,' added Jeff. Though Jo had agreed they could socialise with Candy, she had drawn the line at the children staying the night.

'Hi Dad,' said Sophie, listlessly walking down the hallway with Thomas following closely behind. 'Where are we going?'

'To a puppet theatre,' he smiled.

'We went to see Steps this week with Mummy and Martin,' said Thomas, his face lighting up at the memory. 'And we met them backstage.'

'Mummy and Martin, eh?' said Jeff, looking straight at Jo who laughed nervously. 'And who might Martin be?'

'He's a business client,' she shrugged. 'He's the one I'm doing up that house for in Chelsea.'

'I see.' Jeff didn't look at all convinced. 'Anyway, come on, you two. Candy's waiting.'

Jo kissed the children goodbye and stood on the doorstep smiling benignly until they'd gone through the wooden gate at the end of the path.

She closed the door and sprinted up two stairs at a time with the speed and agility of a mountain goat. She crept up to the bay window in her bedroom and peered out from behind a curtain. Jeff and the children were just crossing the road to his black BMW that was parked a little further down the street. Jo could see Candy was sitting in the front seat. As the children approached, she got out of the car, smiling, and bent down to give each of them a peck on the cheek. She was wearing a fuchsia pink pair of jeans, a black vest top with sequinned neck detail, and black stiletto sandals. Very gangster's moll, thought Jo. Again, she was relieved to find she felt absolutely nothing as she watched Candy lean into the back seat of the car and check the children's seatbelts.

'From now on, you two, you can have the children every weekend if you like,' she said aloud. 'This new arrangement means I get far more time to myself than I ever did when I was married. Talking of which . . .'

She remembered she had a delicious day lined up with Rosie. Shopping along the Kings Road, punctuated by a light lunch and possibly a glass of champagne or seven.

An hour later, she stepped off the bus and walked towards the little coffee house where she'd arranged to meet Rosie. Much as she loved her children, she felt an exhilarating sense of freedom at the thought of a whole day being able to do her own thing. She even toyed with the idea that, if she'd let the children stay the night at Jeff's, she would have had the evening to herself too. Maybe another time.

'You look nice,' said Rosie, who was sitting up at the window bar as she walked in.

'Thanks. I thought I'd surgically remove my ubiquitous T-shirt and jeans and dolly up a bit,' said Jo, who was wearing a floral, capped-sleeve dress she'd bought last summer.

'So how was old tosspot this morning?' said Rosie. She handed Jo an orange juice she'd bought her earlier.

'Quite bearable, actually.' She removed her coat. 'The Cliché was in the car so I ran upstairs and peeped out of the window.'

Rosie smirked. 'And how was the vacuum with nipples?'

'Looking frightfully sequinned but annoyingly slim, actually,' sighed Jo. 'But in all honesty, I didn't give a shit.'

'Attagirl,' said Rosie, clinking her glass against Jo's. 'Now, let's spend some money.'

For once, Jo actually had some to spend thanks to the first payment from Martin arriving two days earlier. She had no intention of spending it all, but she did want to get something special for her date the following Friday.

'So what look do you think I should go for with Sean?' she said. 'Virginal maybe? Sluttish?'

'No, we both know you're a total slut,' teased Rosie, 'but we don't want him to know that just yet. I suggest we start at the basics.'

She grabbed Jo's arm and dragged her into a rather expensive-looking underwear shop.

'Why are we in here?' hissed Jo, shooting a nervous glance at the rather snooty assistant behind the counter.

'Because I've seen your underwear drawer and it's a disgrace,' replied Rosie, flicking through hangers of bra and knicker sets. She shook her head as the assistant descended and asked if she required help.

Jo looked horrified. 'Believe me, it won't go that far.'

'Believe me, the heady combination of alcohol and the fact that you haven't had sex in nigh on six months means that there's every chance it will,' said Rosie, a touch too loudly. 'So why not be prepared? If you return home with it all untouched by human hand, there's always another time.' She shoved Jo towards the changing room and thrust a selection of underwear into her hand.

'We're fine, thanks,' said Rosie as the assistant hovered into view again. 'Christ, how many times do I have to flush before she goes away?' she hissed to Jo.

Two minutes later she popped her head back round the curtain. 'That is the dog's bollocks,' she enthused. 'God, I wish I had your figure.'

Jo was wearing a black lace balconette bra and matching briefs, and she had to admit it made her look very bulging in all the right places for a change.

'OK, I'll get this,' she said reluctantly. 'But nothing else. You can put all these back.'

By the time they sat down for lunch at 1 p.m., her friend had persuaded her to buy £50 worth of Mac make-up, a clinging pencil skirt and matching top, and an eye-catching, long pink skirt with a frill at the bottom. She had also strong-armed her into making a hairdressing appointment for highlights.

'So have you heard from Mr Wonderful since he went to foreign climes?' said Rosie, tucking into her Caesar salad.

'No,' replied Jo. 'But then I didn't expect to really because he said it might be difficult to call. I assume he'll ring before Friday though, to let me know when and where. You still OK to baby-sit?'

'Oh shit!' Rosie clamped a hand over her mouth and Jo's face fell. 'I'd completely forgotten that a multimillionaire is whisking me off to the Caribbean that night, so I can't, sorry.'

Jo heaved a sigh of relief. 'Very funny. I was a bit worried there for a moment. I could always ask Tim, but I'd feel more comfortable if it was you, just in case I want to creep in during the early hours.'

'Oh, early hours now, is it? A minute ago you were categorically not going to sleep with him.'

'I'm not. What I mean is that we might go to a night-club.'

'Well, if I was you and I got the chance for uncompli-cated sex with a man I found attractive, I'd take it. You'd be mad not to,' said Rosie, leaning over and breaking off a piece of Jo's untouched garlic bread.

'We'll see.' Jo stared wistfully out of the window. 'I'm not very good at that sort of thing, and I don't want him to think I'm a pushover.'

Rosie scoffed. 'Bloody chance would be a fine thing

for me. The last bloke I met seemed to be everything you want in a man, but he turned out to have a heart of gold, nerves of steel, and a knob of butter. If this one turns out to be half decent, I'd grab him with both hands if I were you.'

'As I said, we'll see.'

Clearly bored by the subject, Rosie yawned and asked for the bill. 'So how was the Steps night?' she said, taking a credit card from her purse.

Jo fumbled for hers too. 'Very good actually, and I was right that it wasn't a date. He shook my hand on the doorstep when we got home.'

Rosie made a pooh-poohing noise. 'Nonsense. That's simply the actions of a man who knows he has plenty of other opportunities to see you because of the house. He's biding his time so he doesn't scare you off.'

Jo laughed. 'Rosie, you are such a fantasist!'

'Am I? You mark my words, chum.'

20

Sean eventually called late on Wednesday night, but Jo could barely hear him as the line was so crackly.

'I'll keep this short, I'm just calling about Friday,' he said.

'Yes?' Jo's heart was in her mouth in case he was calling to cancel.

'Let's meet in the same bar as before, around eight. OK?'

'Fine.' She felt a surge of happiness that it was still on.

'Great, see ya.' With that, he was gone.

Jo stood staring at the receiver for a few seconds, before shrugging and placing it back on the cradle. I suppose there are lots of calls like that when you date someone who travels to far-flung places, she thought. Still, at least he'd called and at least he hadn't cancelled. She was determined to think positive.

The day after the call, she had driven over to Martin's place to check on the flooring that had been laid in the kitchen. It was the first time she'd seen him since the concert, but, like her call from Sean, it turned out to be a rather brief experience.

He opened the door while simultaneously putting on his jacket. 'Hi there,' he said briskly. 'I'm afraid I have to go out, but I didn't think you'd need me here anyway. Mrs Richards will make you a cup of tea. We'll speak soon.' He picked up his briefcase from the hallway floor and headed out of the door.

'Bye,' said Jo, as the door slammed. She walked down the steps to the basement kitchen where Mrs Richards was standing by the newly installed, attractively named Smeg oven.

'Hello dear,' she said, nodding at the floor. 'It's looking good, isn't it? Have you come to check it out?'

'Yes, I just need to make sure everything's been done to specification. I won't stop long.' Jo bent down to touch the maple boards.

'Do have a quick cup of tea while you're here. Did you see Mr Blake on his way out?'

Martin had told Jo that, despite his protestations, Mrs Richards insisted on calling him that.

'Yes, he seemed in a dreadful hurry.'

'He always is, dear. I do wish he'd slow down a bit and find himself a nice young woman. Someone like yourself in fact,' she said with a twinkle in her eye.

'Oh, I can assure you it's all business with me,' said Jo quickly, keen to steer away from the subject. 'I don't think I'm exactly his type.'

Mrs Richards raised her excessively bushy eyebrows. 'Oh, I wouldn't be so sure, dear. I've seen all types over the years: tall, short, brown hair, blonde hair. All slim though. He likes a nice figure, does Mr Blake.'

Jo said nothing because she felt rather uncomfortable that Mrs Richards was telling her such things. It also crossed her mind that Martin would be furious if he knew his housekeeper was discussing his private life with someone who was ostensibly a complete stranger.

But Mrs Richards rattled on. 'Mind you, they never last long really because he's such a perfectionist. A lot of them get fed up because he spends so much time working, but then that's why he's so successful, isn't it? A lot of them are attracted to his money, but don't like the hard work he has to do to get it. Having said that, he can afford to slow down since he sold that Internet thingy.'

While she droned on in the background, Jo inspected the floor closely and found the fitter had done an impressive job. She drained the last of her tea, and placed her cup in the sink.

'Thanks for the tea. I must be off now,' she said, heading for the stairs.

'Anytime dear. I've enjoyed our little chat.'

Jo regaled Rosie with the story of Mrs Richards's verbal diarrhoea when she arrived to baby-sit the next night.

'Bloody hell, if you get the housekeeper on your side, you're halfway there,' said Rosie with a serious expression. 'Remember all that trouble Mrs de Winter had with Mrs Danvers?'

'What *are* you on about?'

'You know, the grumpy housekeeper in *Rebecca* by Daphne du Maurier.'

'No, I don't mean that, you idiot. I mean, why would I even *care* whether Mrs Richards likes me or not? I won't see her again after the project finishes.'

Rosie said nothing and fixed her with a knowing look.

Jo gave an exasperated sigh. 'Oh, you're not back on that me and Martin thing again are you? Play another record for God's sake, it's not going to happen. Quite apart from anything else, I am about to go on a date with another man.'

'And you look great,' said Rosie, looking her up and down.

Jo was wearing a pair of tight black trousers, black mules, and a black and white polka dot halter-neck top that showed off her slim shoulders. She had kept the hairdressing appointment Rosie had forced her into, and her dark blonde hair was now scattered with a few flattering highlights that softened her face.

'What a transformation!' smiled Rosie, looking at her watch. 'Come on, you'd better get going.'

This time, Jo was leaving her car at home and had ordered a local mini-cab. Unusually, it arrived on time without half an hour's worth of phone calls, where the control room told her it was either 'two minutes away' or 'outside your house now', when patently neither were true.

Twenty minutes later, it pulled up outside the bar. She felt self-conscious as she paid the driver, wondering whether Sean was watching her through the window. But she needn't have worried as there was no sign of him when she walked around the bar.

'Been stood up? You can come and sit with us if you like, darling,' leered a Neanderthal-looking man sitting near the women's toilets.

'Er, no thanks.' Jo scuttled back across the room and squeezed herself into a gap at the packed bar counter. She only had a small handbag with her, so she prayed she wouldn't have to wait long or there'd be no scrap paper to rifle through. She jumped out of her skin as she felt someone's fingers squeeze her waist.

'Hello gorgeous.' It was Sean.

Jo clasped a hand to her chest. 'Gosh, you shocked me. For a minute, I thought it was that amoeba-brained yob who tried to chat me up earlier.'

'Sounds like a bright guy to me. I'd certainly try to chat you up if I saw you standing alone.'

Jo wasn't quite sure how she felt about this statement, but didn't have time to think about it before he'd swept her away.

'You go find a seat. I'll get the drinks,' he said, pointing to a hatchet-faced couple just vacating a table.

He returned clutching two brightly coloured drinks with straws and umbrellas. 'A couple of comedy cocktails to get us going,' he said, sitting down next to her and planting a quick, light kiss on her mouth. 'By the way, have I mentioned how gorgeous you look?'

251

'Yes, you have,' smiled Jo, uncertain how to handle his flattery after years in the compliment-free wilderness of Jeff.

Sean drained his cocktail glass in two or three glugs and slammed it down on the low-level pine table. 'Sorry, I'm not usually like this,' he smiled apologetically. 'It's just that I'm starved of alcohol. I'll go and get us a more sensible drink now.'

He returned a few minutes later with a bottle of house white wine and two glasses.

Jo pulled a face as he filled one of them to the brim. 'Before we get too drunk, I want to know more about you,' she said.

He picked up his glass and leaned back in his chair. 'I was born in South London, I have one sister, and both my parents are unfortunately dead. Right, that's got that out of the way. What shall we talk about now?'

'Whoa!' she laughed. 'First of all, how old are you? I forgot to ask before.'

'I'm twelve,' he said, flinching as Jo gave him a stern look. 'OK, OK. I'm thirty-five.'

'And what does your sister do?'

'What? Um . . . not sure.' He looked slightly irritated. 'I don't hear from her much, but the last I knew she was working as a croupier on cruise ships.'

Jo could sense he was uncomfortable with her questions, so she decided to leave the sensitive subject of his parents' deaths until another time. 'Well, you certainly seem to love your job,' she said in an attempt to be placatory. It seemed to work.

'Yes, I do.' He visibly brightened. 'It suits me perfectly, although lately I've found I'd like to stay put a bit more. I used to think of myself as a bit of a maverick, but the trouble is that mavericks can turn into sad old fucks when they get older.'

When he said this, a vision of Jeff flashed into Jo's mind. She ignored it. 'So do you think you might change jobs?'

'No, I'll always be a cameraman because I love it. But I might consider leaving *The World Right Now*, because to be honest war zones do tend to blend into one another after a while.'

Jo smiled. 'You should have come and covered the war zone that has been our house for the past few months.'

'That bad, huh?'

She nodded. 'Yes, but we seem to have come to a bit of a truce now. We manage to speak to each other without having an argument, and I've even let the children meet his new girlfriend.' Jo was aware she was drivelling on about personal matters when Sean hadn't asked her to, but she was so nervous she couldn't bear any silences.

'Do you mind if I kiss you?' he said suddenly, cutting right across her babble. Without waiting for an answer, he leaned across the table and slowly placed his lips against hers.

They tasted slightly salty, but the softness of them surprised her. As he started to slowly move his mouth, Jo felt a flutter of nerves as she realised this wasn't going to be a quick peck. There was nothing else for her to do but pull away or respond. She chose the latter. I can't believe I'm having a full-blown snog in a crowded bar, she thought, her insides churning over as the kiss continued. Jeff and I barely held hands in public. As Sean pulled away and smiled at her, Jo sat bolt upright and quickly cast an anxious glance around the bar. She'd anticipated a small crowd gathered round, but not a single soul was looking in their direction.

Sean nonchalantly took a cigarette out of its packet and lit it. 'I've been wanting to do that since the day I hit your car.'

'Have you?' Jo couldn't think of anything else to say.

'Yep. In fact, before I hit your car,' he said, shaking the match to extinguish it.

'Sorry?'

'I wasn't going to tell you this, but what the hell,' he said, taking a drag on his cigarette and puffing the smoke to one side. 'I had pulled alongside you earlier and really fancied you, so when you were in front of me at the traffic lights, I deliberately nudged the back of your car.'

For a few moments, she thought he was joking. But his straight face told her he was serious.

'What a strange thing to do.' She was unsure what she felt about this little confession.

'I know,' he shrugged. 'But hey, you've got to take chances in life when you see them. If I hadn't done that, we wouldn't be sitting here now.'

He seemed remarkably laid back about his actions, so for now Jo decided to follow suit and worry about it later. She poked him in the arm. 'In that case, you *can* bloody well pay for my cracked light.'

'A pleasure,' he grinned. 'In the meantime, let me pay for more drinks. Come on, let's go to another bar with a bit more atmosphere.' He stood up.

Five minutes later they were in a bar twice as dark and noisy as the last one.

'I'll get the drinks!' he bellowed. 'You find a square inch to stand in.'

Jo positioned herself in a tight, dark corner at the end of the long bar, and leaned against the wall. As she watched Sean fighting his way through the throng and grabbing the attention of the barmaid, she marvelled at what a determined man he was. She wasn't sure whether to be flattered by his rather drastic method of meeting her, or to run a mile. But after years of Jeff's indecisiveness, she found it sexually exciting to be with a man who knew what he wanted in life and grabbed it.

Sean returned clutching another bottle of white wine and two glasses which he promptly placed on the bar, leaving his hands free to place around Jo's waist. Pressing his body against hers, his mouth bore down for a passionate kiss that left her feeling light-headed with a pounding desire she'd not felt since the early days with Jeff. For a moment, she forgot about her problems, she forgot about her mother, Rosie, Tim, and even her children. She was lost in the deliciously carefree feeling of physical contact with a man she found extremely attractive. God, it's like being a teenager again, she thought. When you don't have a care in the world and a kiss is of monumental importance. They spent the next hour tucked away in the corner, their kissing sessions punctuated by conversation shouted into each other's ear.

'I find you very attractive, Jo,' he said, idly caressing the back of her neck with one hand.

'The feeling's mutual,' she bellowed back. The music stopped just as she said the last word, making conversation a little easier.

'I'm a bit of a tricky bugger to have a relationship with because of my job and stuff, but I think we could be good together,' he said.

'I agree.' She deliberately kept her answer short in the hope he would elaborate, and it worked a treat.

'I know you have commitments and things to sort out, but I'll never be a burden on your time because I'm away so much. So what do you say?'

How delicious to have the ball back in my court, she thought, after so many emotionally strained months of being messed around by Jeff. It felt good.

'Why not? Let's give it a go,' she smiled. Her calm exterior belied the fact that her stomach was doing euphoric somersaults.

'Fantastic,' said Sean, planting a smacker on her lips. 'This calls for a celebration. Come on, I have a bottle of champagne at home.'

21

Sean's flat was part of an unprepossessing modern block in the less chic part of Fulham. It had a gloomy communal hallway with eighties-style red and grey stripey wallpaper and a faint odour that suggested it hadn't been cleaned since its opening. Kicked to one side was the ubiquitous pile of unclaimed post found in every block of flats, addressed to people who had moved away long ago. Jo followed him up one flight of stairs to a door marked 24 in plastic letters.

''Scuse the mess,' he said, fumbling to get the key in the lock. 'But I haven't been around much to tidy up.'

She walked in expecting to find a complete tip, but found that, compared to her house, it wasn't the slightest bit messy. In fact, it resembled a hotel room or show home with everything neatly in its place.

'On the contrary, it's very tidy,' she said loudly to Sean as he crashed about in the kitchen, presumably getting the champagne.

She was standing in his living room, which rather contradicted its name and looked distinctly unoccupied. There were a couple of arty-farty photographic books on the coffee table, a pair of greying hotel slippers by the side of the black leather sofa, a mini-stereo, and an answering machine flickering in the corner. There were a few books on one of the shelves, but not a single picture or personal photograph in the room.

'It's very sparse,' she said, as Sean walked in clutching two full glasses of champagne and a bowl of tortilla chips.

'I know, I love miniman . . . minmila . . . I like it like this,' he grinned, handing her a glass.

'You love minimalism, is what you're trying to say,' laughed Jo. 'Funnily enough, I'm trying to achieve that look on a house in Chelsea at the moment.' She was making polite conversation, but Sean clearly wasn't listening. He was fumbling in his CD rack in the corner, and a few seconds later the strains of Moby filled the room.

Perched on the edge of the sofa, Jo suddenly felt awkward and rather wished she hadn't come back to this rather soulless flat. It was so long since she'd been with anyone except Jeff that she was unsure what to do next. She was also unsure of whether she even wanted anything to happen next. Staring at the floor, she had just decided this was all moving rather too quickly for a second date when Sean sat down next to her and gently took the champagne glass from her hand. He placed it on the coffee table and murmured, 'Now, where were we?'

He started kissing her tenderly at first, then building up the pressure until Jo lost her balance and fell back against the sofa cushions. The idea of stopping their passionate embrace right then crossed her mind, but the bad fairy perched on her shoulder and whispered, 'Why the hell not?' After that, unstoppable feelings of pure lust blocked out all rational thought and she gave in.

His hand reached through the armhole of her halter-neck top and pulled it to one side to expose her breast. She let out an involuntary gasp as his tongue flicked the aroused nipple and his left hand caressed the other through the flimsy material. The double breast stroke had always been a winner for Jo, and within seconds they were tearing at each other's clothes in a drink-induced frenzy. Anxious not to break the sexual spell, they continued to kiss mercilessly. As Jo made the final tug on Sean's Calvins, his penis sprang out in an admirably erect state.

'Gosh, he does look cross,' she giggled, unable to take her eyes off it.

'He's bloody furious,' murmured Sean, guiding her hand to the base of the shaft.

As she slowly ran her hand up and down, Jo couldn't help comparing it to Jeff's. It felt so strange to have a different penis in her hand after so many years of the same old one.

'That's why I'm not sure if I could be faithful for years on end,' Rosie had said once. 'It would be like eating in the same restaurant every night. You always know what you're going to get.'

But the special on offer tonight suited Jo very nicely. It was long, but not too long, with an admirable width.

She sat up and started to lean her face towards his penis, but Sean gently pushed her back and slowly removed her pants. She closed her eyes, then opened them as she heard a rustling noise. It was Sean opening a condom.

'Are you small, medium, or liar?' she smiled, reaching forward to assist. As she continued to caress him, he started to push two fingers inside her whilst using his thumb to gently stimulate her clitoris. She closed her eyes again as a small wave of sheer, unadulterated ecstasy rippled through her body.

Just when she thought it couldn't get any better, she felt Sean's hair brush the soft underskin of her thighs. He planted dozens of small kisses between her legs, avoiding the clitoris until she thought she might die from the expectation.

'Is that good?' he murmured, as his tongue finally made contact.

'Really good,' she whispered.

His tongue got to work and his fingers slid their way in and out. Jo abandoned any sense of dignity and began to moan loudly. Within two minutes she felt the familiar surge of warmth begin, followed by a sheer rush of ecstasy to all her nerve endings. She came in glorious shudders, her own fingers pressing her clitoris as Sean's mouth moved away. Spreadeagled on the sofa with him knelt in front of her, she finally opened her eyes. Staring straight at him, she said, 'Now fuck me.'

As Sean lowered himself into position, she grabbed his

penis and guided it towards her. She buried her head into the side of his neck and inhaled the musky smell of new masculine sweat. There was nothing like it.

Straightening his muscular arms, Sean studied her face as he slowly pushed himself into her. As he started to move in and out, Jo let out a small gasp of pleasure. God, she'd missed this.

His thrusts becoming more urgent, he moved his head down to her neck again and began to murmur quietly in her ear. 'Is that good? Do you feel wet? Tell me how it feels . . .'

'It . . . feels . . . great.' She'd never been very good at talking dirty. If there were night classes in it, she vowed to sign up the next day.

'Tell me how wet you are.'

'I'm really wet,' she whispered.

'Tell me what you want.'

'I want you to fuck me harder,' she said, and he duly obliged until he came in a tense, blissfully silent shudder.

'Can you stay the night?' he murmured in her ear.

'Not all of it, but some,' she said.

She woke up with a start at 4 a.m. in a strange room with an unidentified arm thrown across her chest. A wave of nausea swept through her body. For once, it had nothing to do with the amount of alcohol she'd consumed, and everything to do with the fact she'd had sex with a virtual stranger who had all but ram-raided her car to get a date.

It doesn't get much lower than this, she thought. Desperate to extricate herself from Sean's arms, she wanted to escape, to gather her thoughts over a cup of coffee at home. But would he wake up?

A faint smile crossed her lips as she remembered Tim telling her and Rosie about a disastrous one-night stand he'd had.

'I had the bloody beer goggles on,' he said. 'I left the bar with Cindy Crawford and woke up with Michael Crawford. It was a real dingo gnaw, I can tell you.'

'A what?' Jo frowned.

'A dingo gnaw. When dingos get caught in traps in the wild, they sometimes eat through their own leg to escape. That's what us chaps call it when you wake up next to some ugly bird and your arm is trapped under her. You'd rather eat through it to escape than risk waking her up.'

Now here was Jo experiencing her very own dingo gnaw, except the creature involved was far from unattractive. But she knew he'd be dangerous to wake up.

Slowly rolling over onto her side, she waited for his arm to drop onto the bed. Her heart thumping against her chest wall, she lay motionless as the gentle snoring stopped and he started to make rapid breathing noises. As she waited for him to start snoring again, she studied the room she had paid so little attention to four hours previously. After getting into bed, they'd had slow but passionate sex again, then cuddled up and fallen asleep.

The bedroom was most definitely minimalist again,

with cream walls, beige carpet and slim, fitted ash wardrobes along one wall. The kingsize bed dominated the room, flanked by two bedside cabinets that housed just one office-style lamp each. There was a small alarm clock on Sean's side of the bed and a copy of last month's *GQ* magazine.

It seemed an eternity, but after a few minutes, his breathing became deeper again and she decided to risk an exit manoeuvre. Grabbing a towelling gown from the back of the door, she tiptoed out of the room and went in search of her clothes that were scattered all over the living-room floor. After a panicked search, she found her newly bought knickers tucked down the back of the same sofa on which she'd been willingly ravaged just hours before.

She looked around for some paper, but there wasn't a scrap to be found nor any sign of a pen. She was reluctant to start opening drawers in case he woke up and thought she was snooping. Rummaging in her handbag, she tore a piece from the bottom of an old school newsletter and found a pen nestled among the old toffee papers and tissues.

She wrote, 'It's 4 a.m. and I have to sneak back to my own bed before the children wake up. Thanks for a lovely evening. Jo xx'. She sat staring at the note for a moment, then hastily added, 'PS. Give me a call soon.'

Leaving it on the coffee table, she picked up her shoes and tiptoed along the wood floored hallway to the front door, closing it gently behind her. In the corridor, she put on her shoes and sprinted down the stairs and out of the communal door. It was still dark. Someone must be looking out for me, she thought, as a vacant black cab suddenly came into view. The driver looked at her suspiciously, and it crossed her mind he might think she was a prostitute, sneaking out of a client's house at such an unearthly hour. But she didn't care. It was a safe lift home, the place she wanted to be more than anywhere else in the world right now.

Creeping up the stairs to bed, she paused only to look in on Thomas and Sophie's rooms to check they were fast asleep. If you knew what Mummy had been up to, you'd be horrified, she thought.

By the time she'd folded her clothes and laid her head on the pillow, it was 5 a.m. and a particularly persistent bird was starting to sing noisily outside her bedroom window. Jo drifted off into a deep, pleasant sleep, her head full of thoughts about her re-acquaintance with passion.

Part Two

22

One year later

A cup of tea in her hand, Jo stood in the large bay window of the living room, watching the road outside with a look of apprehension. Jeff was due back with the children any minute and she was looking forward to seeing them for the first time in a week.

He and Candy had taken them to an apartment in Tenerife on the previous Thursday and, for the first time since becoming a mother, Jo had enjoyed a blissful week of pleasing herself. She'd toyed with the idea of escaping somewhere with Sean, but in the end he'd been unable to get away from work. So instead, they'd spent the weekend at Forest Mere health farm in Hampshire, being pampered with massages, mud wraps and Thalasso water therapy. They were also going out this evening, something she felt an acute pang of guilt about, not having seen the children for a week.

'Listen, they've had a great holiday and probably barely given you a thought, so don't worry about it. Enjoy yourself,' said Rosie, when Jo had mentioned it.

That's easy for you to say, Jo thought, you don't have children. She couldn't remember the guilt-free, selfish days of no offspring, and wished she could be more like some aristocratic women who palm their children off to boarding school at six, allowing them to occasionally visit home until they are eighteen, at which point they go off to university. Unfortunately, she had inherited her mother's worry gene when it came to parenting. She fretted about absolutely everything, more so now that the children no longer had the traditional set-up of Mummy and Daddy under the same roof. It had taken her six months to introduce Thomas and Sophie to Sean, and even then she'd worried herself sick that it was too soon.

'The trouble is,' she told Rosie, 'you find yourself having to categorise new relationships very quickly when you already have children. All that playing it cool stuff goes out of the window, because you need to know whether it's just going to be a fling or turn into something more meaningful.'

Spontaneity was also a thing of the past, with every night out having to be planned with military precision.

She thought back to the first couple of months with Sean, when it would have been so much easier if she had simply introduced him to the children. But she wasn't sure of the longevity of the relationship and didn't want them to meet every passing fancy in her life, so she had taken the harder option of having to see Sean away from the house and organising babysitters.

As ever, Rosie had been a godsend. But a month ago, she'd started seeing a man she met in her local health food shop which, although Jo was thrilled for her, had buggered up a lot of her social plans.

Tim was babysitting tonight. He said he had lines to learn for the soap opera he'd started performing in three months earlier, and that he may as well memorise them here as there.

Jo looked up as she heard the familiar hum of Jeff's engine and saw him reversing into a space across the street. She took a step back from the window, so he and Candy wouldn't think that she was watching them. She was intrigued to know how Candy had coped with someone else's kids for a whole week in such an enclosed space, and knew Thomas would tell her every delicious detail of any holiday tensions that might have arisen. He was her little fly on the wall. Sophie got on very well with Candy, but a mutual interest in gaudy make-up and big hair had a lot to do with that. Thomas was less impressed.

'She puts on this stupid baby voice when she talks to Dad,' he said in disgust one day. 'And she's always wearing ridiculous shoes that hurt her whenever we walk anywhere.'

Sixteen months ago, Jo would have been thrilled to hear all this. But after a while she found herself feeling quite sorry for Candy. It must be tough dealing with someone else's kids when you're that young. She remembered feeling anxious about Sean meeting the children, particularly as he didn't have any of his own. The days when dating was simply about whether two adults liked each other had long gone. Now she had to worry about whether he liked her children, and whether they in turn liked him. It was a minefield.

'It's a lot to take on,' she'd said to Rosie.

'Not really,' Rosie replied. 'He knows the deal. If he wants you, the children are part of that package.'

Rosie had made it clear to Jo on a couple of occasions that she wasn't too keen on Sean. 'He's too smooth for you, and there's something rather insincere about him,' she'd said, wrinkling her nose. But Jo had put it down to a touch of the personal jealousy that often creeps into female friendships when one has a boyfriend and the other doesn't.

The first meeting between Sean and the children had been coffee followed by a walk in Battersea Park at 9.30 one morning.

'Where are we going?' said a sullen Thomas, furious at being torn away from his PlayStation.

'We're going to meet a friend of mine in the park, where we're all going to get some *fresh air*,' said Jo, wrestling him into his puffa jacket.

'What friend?' he said suspiciously.

'You don't know him.'

'Well he can't be much of a friend then, can he?' Thomas was in a phase of testing every boundary and was often incredibly rude to her. So much so, she had recently administered a couple of sharp smacks to the back of his legs.

But today she decided to ignore it, because she didn't want to meet Sean with a red-faced, weeping child in tow, who then proceeded to sulk for two hours.

A minute or two of silence passed, then Thomas said with a tone of undisguised disgust, 'He's your boyfriend, isn't he?'

'Don't be silly, darling.' Jo felt well and truly skewered by her young son.

'Why are we going to meet him on a Saturday then? We *never* go to the park on a Saturday because you always say it's too crowded.'

He was absolutely right and Jo wished he'd just shut up about the subject and return to being the blissfully ignorant toddler he once was. Nine-year-olds were getting too mature and astute for their own good. Mind you, so was seven-year-old Sophie who, the week before, had suddenly said, 'Mummy, do you know what gay means?'

Jo had always vowed that whenever her children showed an interest in the subject of sex, she would always talk to them about it. So she took a deep breath and started to tell Sophie that being 'gay' was when two members of the same sex loved each other.

Her daughter raised her eyes heavenwards. 'I know that, Mummy. I just wanted to check that *you* knew.'

Arriving at the park, Jo manoeuvred the car into one of the hundreds of empty spaces. 'Here we are,' she said with false brightness, turning round to look at her sullen children.

'Where are we meeting your *friend*?' said Thomas, the last word dripping with sarcasm.

'In the little café by the boating lake,' she said, setting off briskly in that direction with Kevin the teenager and Perry – as she and Rosie had recently named them – trailing behind her. Sophie had wanted to watch Steps on SMTV, so she too was less than pleased about having her hair ferociously brushed and being forced out of the house.

They arrived at the café ten minutes later, but there was no sign of Sean yet, for which Jo felt grateful. Like all desperate parents, she hoped she could buy a better mood out of them by settling them down with a drink and an ice-cream first. Her mother would have balked at such blatant bribery, but she didn't care. Needs must.

They found a bench table outside in the watery sunshine and watched listlessly as one of the café staff hosed down the tarmac. There were only two customers at this painfully early hour; an old man sipping a cup of tea and reading *The Racing Post*, and a surly middle-aged woman having a cigarette while her long-haired greyhound crapped and peed its way around all the tables.

Another ten minutes passed. Still no sign of Sean.

'Does your friend have a watch?' said Thomas.

The combination of his sarcasm and her general stress about Sean's impending arrival finally made Jo snap.

'Look, you little shit. If you can be nice to the little bimbo your father left us for, you can damn well lift your

272

attitude and be nice to my friend for five bloody minutes,' she hissed, scowling at him.

Thomas looked startled at first, then his bottom lip jutted out and he started to blink back tears before storming off inside the café and sitting alone in a far corner.

Jo felt awful for having sworn at him, and particularly for being nasty about Candy. She'd always vowed she wouldn't do that in front of the children. But she stopped herself from following Thomas because she didn't want to pander to his truculent moods.

Another five minutes passed with her and Sophie sitting in silence, watching the Canada geese squabbling greedily over the fragments of bread being thrown their way by an elderly woman who'd arrived with a carrier bag full of stale offerings. Where the hell is he? thought Jo, glancing anxiously at her watch for the umpteenth time. As this was such an important occasion, the least he could do was arrive on time. A hand touched her shoulder from behind and she spun round with palpable relief on her face. It was Thomas.

'I'm sorry, Mummy,' he sobbed, wrapping his arms around her neck.

'That's alright, sweetie,' she murmured, pulling him close to her. 'Mummy's sorry too. It's all forgotten now.'

Mollified, Thomas sat back down at the bench and started to play I-spy with Sophie. Once 'geese', 'pond', 'café' and 'bird poo' had been dispensed with, it was 10.15 and Jo had given up all hope of Sean materialising.

'Come on, you two. My friend has obviously got caught up somewhere else. Let's go home.' Silently livid, she stood up and started to walk back towards the car park.

'Mummy, look!' said Sophie, pointing back the other way. In the distance, a man was running towards them and waving his hands in the air. It was Sean.

'Sorry, sorry, sorry, sorry,' he puffed as he drew near. Bending over and placing his hands on his knees, he stood still for a few seconds trying to regain his composure.

'Do you have a watch?' Jo asked him, sneaking a little wink at Thomas.

'I have absolutely no defence except to say I overslept,' said Sean, raising his hands in surrender above his head. 'Shoot me.'

Thomas made a gun shape with his fingers, pointed it at Sean, and made a firing noise.

'All . . . my . . . money . . . is . . . in . . . the . . . urrrgh,' said Sean, clutching his chest and falling to the slightly wet ground.

Thomas and Sophie both burst out laughing, and any hostile feelings Jo felt towards Sean for being late suddenly evaporated.

'He was amazingly good with them,' she told Rosie, the day after she and Sean had enjoyed a long walk and snack lunch with the children.

'Probably got the same mental age,' her friend had replied dismissively.

Snapping out of her retrospective daydream, Jo cleared her throat and focused on the little spectacle unfolding outside.

Jeff was huffing and puffing as he pulled suitcases out of the boot of the car, while Candy held both of the children by the hand ready to march them across the road. She was wearing a microscopic denim skirt. Jo had to admit she had bloody good legs. Halfway across and certain that the road was clear, she let go of their hands and gestured for them to walk alone up to the front door. Although Jo had mellowed considerably towards the Jeff and Candy situation, she had made it quite clear she didn't want to meet her in any circumstances.

'Hello!' she shrieked, flinging open the door and enveloping Thomas and Sophie in a huge bear hug. 'Did you have a lovely time?'

'It was brilliant. And look, I got my hair braided,' said Sophie, pointing to four brightly coloured plaits in her hair.

'Hope you don't mind. They come out very easily,' said Jeff, walking up the garden path with a conciliatory smile.

'Not at all. It looks great,' she said, actually meaning it. 'Was it a good holiday?'

'Very nice, but very tiring.' Jeff suddenly looked older than his thirty-seven years. 'I think I need another holiday to get over this one.'

'Well, at least you've got the weekend to recover before you go back to work,' she smiled, secretly marvelling to herself how Jeff could be so easily worn out by his own children. She looked after them twenty-four hours a day, seven days a week, with little help or thanks from him.

'I'm afraid Sophie may have picked up a little tummy bug,' he said, turning to open the gate. 'She was sick this morning and was still complaining of stomach pains half an hour ago, so keep an eye on her.'

An hour later, Jo was holding back Sophie's hair while her seven-year-old daughter retched over the bathroom sink, sobbing in distress.

One thing was for sure. Her night out with Sean would have to be cancelled.

With Sophie tucked up in bed, exhausted from so much vomiting, Jo phoned Tim to say he wasn't needed. Now all she had to do was track down Sean.

She dialled his mobile number and waited. There was no answer and, unusually, it failed to divert to the message system. Next she dialled the flat and got his answering machine.

'Hi, it's me,' she sighed. 'Look, Sophie is poorly, so I wanted either to cancel tonight, or suggest you come round here instead. I'm not sure if you'll come home first to get this message and I can't get through on your mobile, but I'll keep trying.'

She put the phone down and sucked the end of her biro, deep in thought. She'd never needed a number for Sean at work because he'd always been contactable on his mobile, but she remembered he'd said that, before coming to meet her, he had to edit his latest piece of film about life in Berlin after the collapse of the wall. She dialled directory inquiries, got a number for GoWorld Television and punched the numbers into the handset.

'Hello, could I speak to Sean Goode in *The World Right Now* office please.' Jo stood and watched two sparrows fighting on the bird table outside as she waited for the switchboard operator to find the right number.

'I don't have anyone of that name on my list. What does he do?' said the woman, adopting the sing-song tone often used by stewardesses and make-up saleswomen.

'He's a cameraman.' Jo cleaned her nails with a safety pin while she waited.

'Ah, that explains it. They don't really have their own extensions because they're rarely in the office. I'll put you through to production and maybe someone there can help you. Hold on.'

'Thanks.' Jo was left hanging on the line listening to Vivaldi's *Four Seasons* being murdered by computerised sound.

'Hello?' The female voice had that I'm-very-busy tone to it.

'Oh hi, sorry to bother you,' said Jo. 'I'm trying to get a message to Sean Goode.'

'He was here this morning, but I can't see him now. Have you tried his mobile?' The disembodied voice was slightly less edgy now.

'Yes,' said Jo. 'But it doesn't seem to be working properly. It's just that I'm meant to be meeting him for a drink later on and one of my kids is a bit ill.'

'Hang on,' said the woman. There was the familiar clunk of the phone being put down, then Jo heard her

278

shout across the room to one of her colleagues. 'Bob, you seen Sean?'

She came back to the phone. 'Sorry, he seems to have gone on the missing list, but I'll tell him you called and give him the message. It's Anne, isn't it?'

'No, my name's Jo,' said Jo, making a mental note to visit Sean in the office one day so his colleagues would remember her name.

There was a small pause. 'Oh sorry, I thought it was his wife calling. So it's not one of Sean's kids who's ill then?'

A fist of nausea punched itself straight into Jo's diaphragm, winding her momentarily.

'His wife?' She heard herself say the words, but felt as if they were being uttered by someone else at the far end of a long, dark tunnel she was now staring down.

'Yeah, his wife Anne. I thought you were her.' The woman was starting to sound slightly curious as to who was on the other end of the phone.

Somehow, Jo managed to gather herself. 'Sorry, yes, an easy mistake,' she said. 'No, I'm not Anne, I'm an old friend of theirs. Our oldest children are the same age in fact. I was supposed to be meeting Sean for a quick drink, but it's *my* daughter who's got a tummy bug.'

'Oh, I see.' The woman was clearly bored with the conversation by now. 'So I'll tell him Jo called and she can't make it tonight, right?'

'Perfect. Thanks.' Jo replaced the receiver and started

to shake, the naked flesh of her arms covered in goose pimples of shock.

Leaning on the work surface, she stared fixedly at the breadboard, trying to analyse and absorb the consequences of the conversation she'd just had.

There were no misunderstandings or mistaken identities, try as she might to find them. The undisputed fact was that Sean was a married man with two, maybe more, children. Jo felt like the most gullible, naïve person on the planet. Armed with this fact, everything suddenly and effortlessly fell into place. The unreliability, the trips abroad that could cover a multitude of sins, the pristine flat with absolutely no personal effects in it.

That was his London pied-à-terre, and somewhere else was his family home, complete with unsuspecting wife and blissfully ignorant children. Children just like Thomas and Sophie, innocent little creatures who deserved better from their father.

Her elbows propped either side of the washing-up bowl, she leaned over the kitchen sink and started to retch at the thought of it. Unwittingly, she had been doing to another woman what Candy had done to her. It made Jo flush with shame even to think about it. Worse, she had spent a year of her life getting to know this man, sharing his bed and – Jo let out an involuntary sob at the thought of it – introducing him to her children.

'You conniving, fucking bastard,' she muttered under her breath. 'You low-life, duplicitous worm.' She knew what had to be done. The question was, how was she going to do it and where?

A flush-faced Tim arrived at 7.30, clutching his script in one hand and a carrier bag full of Boddington's Bitter cans in the other.

'First she wants me to babysit, then she doesn't, then she does,' he chanted with a grin as Jo opened the door. As soon as he saw her blanched face, he stopped.

'Ooops. Has Jeff been winding you up again?'

'Right gender, wrong name. It's Sean,' she said in a clipped voice, trying desperately not to cry.

'Oh dear, had our first tiff, have we?' said Tim, raising an eyebrow. 'Well, it has been a year now. You'd be unnatural if you hadn't.'

Jo bit her lip as her eyes filled with tears. 'He's married.'

The vacant smile on Tim's face vanished quicker than snow on a radiator. 'Married?'

'That's right, married.' Jo gestured for him to follow her into the child-free sanctity of the kitchen. 'I found out today when I tried to track him down at the office. A woman there thought it was his wife calling.'

'Fucking hell, the wanker,' said Tim.

'Can't argue with you on that one,' she fumed. 'Anyway, I need you here after all because I have to deal with this. He doesn't know I know, yet.'

'Shit, I wouldn't like to be in his shoes.'

'He rang earlier having got the message I left at his flat

281

about Sophie being poorly,' she said, her voice tight. 'I managed to convince him she was feeling better, and said I would pop round to his place later on. I want to make sure I end it in private and well away from the children.'

'So you're going to end it, then?' asked Tim.

He flinched as Jo exploded in response. 'Tim, you've said some pretty stupid fucking things in your time, but that one is the Daddy of them all! Of *course* I'm going to bloody end it! Do you seriously think I'm just going to go round there and give him a little telling off?'

Tim sank further into his chair and raised his hands in surrender. 'Well it's just that you seemed so keen on him. It's such a shame to lose it.'

Jo gave a heavy sigh and plopped into the chair next to him. 'I was keen. Very keen. But he's married, which means he has been lying to me and the children all this time. Which makes him scum, in my book. You can't have a relationship with someone who consistently lies to you.'

'I see your point.' Tim stretched his legs out in front of him and yawned. 'Well, don't worry about anything here. I'll kip in the spare room tonight so stay out as late as you like. Just don't kill him, because there's the drawback of a life sentence.'

'Hmm, well maybe just a bit of torture then,' said Jo, picking up her car keys from the top of the microwave.

She pulled up outside Sean's flat at 8.15 and sat in the car for ten minutes to gather her thoughts and do some deep, meditative breathing.

The plan was to deliver her speech in a menacingly low tone before leaving immediately afterwards with her dignity intact. The last thing she wanted to do was lose her temper and show him how much she cared about his emotional treachery.

With a heavy feeling of dread in the pit of her stomach, she rang the bell and waited for his voice to boom through the entry-phone.

'Hi darling, I'm just in the shower and I'm dripping all over the floor. I'll leave the door open for you,' said a disembodied voice. The door buzzed and she pushed it open.

As Jo slowly but steadily walked up the stairs, a brief flash came into her mind of the last time she'd arrived here when Sean was in the shower. As she'd been rummaging in the fridge for some ice to put in a gin and tonic, he'd crept up behind her, naked and soaking wet. Grabbing her hand, he'd led her to the bathroom and dragged her into the shower as she screamed with giggling hysteria.

Her white cotton blouse and T-shirt bra were rendered instantly transparent by the water, and the dark pink shade of her nipples had aroused Sean to the point of no return. Saturated and with sprays of water jetting into her face, Jo had leaned back against the tiled wall whilst he lifted her floral skirt and pulled her newly acquired La Perla's to one side.

Within seconds he was inside her, pumping away, while his hands roamed up her top to caress her erect nipples.

It all lasted approximately five minutes, but it was the most urgent, passionate sex she'd ever had.

'Another fifty-five minutes and that would have been our finest hour,' laughed Sean as he helped her out of her wet clothes and draped them across the radiator.

Remembering it now, Jo felt a terrible sense of loss as she pushed open the door to his now familiar flat and walked inside. She really thought she'd found someone she trusted, someone she could have fun with but also feel secure with. But it turns out he's just another wanker, she thought, walking into the spotless living room and sitting down.

'Won't be a tick,' shouted Sean from the bathroom, and seconds later the sound of the shower ceased.

Jo sat motionless, her eyes darting around the once seemingly innocuous room that now held so many obvious clues to Sean's secret life. No photographs, the hotel slippers, a couple of untouched coffee table books. How could she have been so blind? No-one lives like this, not unless it's merely the occasional stop-over. Even the most slovenly bachelor has family pictures and old books scattered around.

'Hello, gorgeous,' said Sean, towelling his hair as he walked across the room and planted a kiss on her lips.

Just twenty-four hours ago, the 'gorgeous' and the kiss would have made her knees buckle with lust, but now she felt nothing but cold contempt for the man she had shared so much with over the past few months. Or thought she had. She resisted the overwhelmingly childish urge to wipe his kiss from her mouth, preferring instead to fix him with a cold, hard stare.

'I know, Sean.' Her voice was low and measured.

'Oooh, you *know*, do you? Er, what do you know?' he smiled, looking for all the world like an innocent man who had absolutely no idea what was coming.

For a fleeting moment, she thought there may have been some terrible mistake. A misunderstanding. Crossed wires. *Anything* that meant her personal life wasn't about to be turned upside down yet again. But she knew it was hopeless, the evidence was all too obvious.

'I know about Anne,' she said, not taking her eyes away from his face, desperate to see, and judge, his reaction.

'Anne? Sorry, you've lost me.' He didn't flinch. Not even a blink.

Irritated in the extreme, Jo stood up and walked across the room in a bid to disguise her agitation. She was determined to remain in control of the situation.

'In that case, Sean, let me refresh your memory,' she said icily. 'She's your wife, the mother of your children. The woman you conveniently forgot to mention to me.'

This time, guilt was written all over his face as he started to blink repeatedly and breathe heavily. Jo wanted to walk out there and then, but she was desperate to stay and hear his explanation, if he had any. Slowly, he raised his head to look at her, his eyes narrowed as if deep in thought. Finally, he spoke.

'Have you been snooping, Jo? I would have thought

your experiences with Jeff would have taught you not to do that by now.' His face was impassive.

It took a few moments for his remark to sink in. At best she'd been expecting a profuse apology, at worst a further denial. But this? This was even worse. He was attempting to make *her* the villain of the piece.

When she discussed it later with Rosie, she acknowledged she should have walked out in total disgust at this point. But the injustice of his remark kept her rooted to the spot in cold anger.

'I rang you at the office and the woman who answered thought I was your wife. It's as simple as that,' she said dully. 'I had no reason to snoop, as you put it, because I trusted you.'

Like a fly in aspic, she stood there, wanting to leave yet trapped by her desire for the whole sorry mess to be explained away as some terrible misunderstanding.

Sean patted the sofa cushion next to him. 'Sit down,' he said quietly.

Jo sat on the armchair opposite, hunched forward with her arms drawn protectively across her abdomen.

'Look,' he continued. 'I'll admit that when I first started seeing you, all I wanted was a bit of a fling. My marriage has been stale for a long time, and I suppose I was looking for a bit of uncomplicated excitement.' He paused and started wiping his finger across a small coffee stain on the table in front of him. After a few seconds, he looked up to gauge her reaction, but Jo flatly refused to show any emotion at all. 'But then I started to really care for you and got more embroiled than I ever planned to,' he continued. 'It got to the stage where I wanted to tell you I was married, but knew that if I did you would stop seeing me. So I took the selfish option and carried on . . .' He tailed off.

Struggling to fight back tears, Jo felt her face contort. 'You agreed to meet my children. How could you do that when you knew the score?'

He slowly shook his head from side to side. 'I know, I know, it was unforgivable. Again, I was just being selfish. You seemed really keen for me to get to know them, and I knew if I hesitated you might become suspicious or doubt my intentions.'

'Intentions? What fucking intentions?'

Sean stood up and walked across to the armchair, kneeling on the floor beside her. He tried to take her hands in his, but Jo jerked them away.

'Don't let this split us up Jo. I'll leave her, I promise. We'll become a proper family, you, me, Thomas and Sophie,' he said in a pleading tone.

Jo had heard enough. She leapt to her feet, picked up her handbag, and headed for the living-room door.

'Do you seriously think I could play happy families with a man who had destroyed one family to be with another? Christ, you must be a complete fuckwit to even *think* that I could. Which also makes me wonder what I ever saw in you in the first place.'

She ran out of the flat, slammed the door and flew down the stairs without daring to look back. After driving for about half a mile, she turned into a side road and pulled over, her eyes blinded by a wall of tears.

She felt an unmitigated failure. Not just because she was facing the ignominy of Sean's blatant betrayal, but because she'd exposed her children to yet another relationship that now lay in tatters. Her protection of them was paramount. Elbows lodged on the steering wheel, she sat and sobbed relentlessly for about ten minutes, not caring what spectacle she presented to any passers-by.

24

It took Jo a week to tell Rosie what had happened, for two reasons. Firstly, her friend was absorbed in her new relationship, and secondly, Jo felt so ashamed by her naivety that she'd been too embarrassed to broach the subject even to the friend she normally shared everything with.

'It's strange though,' added Jo after she'd told everything to a wide-eyed Rosie as they enjoyed a cool drink in the back garden. 'If I think about it, I don't feel anything like the same devastation I felt when it all went wrong with Jeff.'

'Well, he was your husband and the father of your children, so it's not surprising,' said Rosie, slurping her Diet Coke through a straw.

'Yes, but it's not just that.' Jo gazed up at the sunlight filtering through the old oak tree at the bottom of the garden. 'I genuinely think I will never let anyone close enough again to hurt me as much as Jeff did. Sure, I feel a little wistful that I'm single again, but the worst thing I feel about my break-up with Sean is wounded pride that I could have been so damned stupid.'

Rosie made no attempt to disagree with her on the last point. 'Have you heard from the slimeball since?'

'Yes,' sighed Jo. 'A hand-delivered letter was shoved through the door a couple of days ago in which he declares his undying love for me, says he can't contemplate life without me, and that he is going to leave his wife so we can be together.' She recited the contents as if reading a shopping list.

Rosie gasped. 'Bloody hell. What are you going to do?'

'I've already done it. I sent it back to his London address with a note that said something along the lines of "fuck off and die".' She gave a quick smile, but inside she was feeling decidedly flat.

'Wow, pretty definite then.' Rosie let out a sigh. 'Can't say I'm surprised though.'

'If you are about to say "I never liked him anyway," bloody well don't,' grinned Jo. 'You always said there was something insincere about him and I wished I'd listened to you.'

'Yes, but even I didn't realise how spectacularly insincere he'd turn out to be,' laughed Rosie. 'I just couldn't understand why you opted for him when you had Conor and Martin to choose from as well.'

Jo narrowed her eyes. 'Hmm, well Martin's interest was clearly a figment of your imagination because he's never made a move on me to this day, and as for Conor . . .' She paused and Rosie finished her sentence.

'He's now ensconced with someone else and you've missed your chance.'

'Yes, that's it, rub it in,' said Jo good-naturedly, moving her legs so Rosie could get past and go inside to the loo. 'Everyone's happy except Jo Miles, emotional cripple and spinster of this parish.'

She sat and reflected on this statement for a moment. Despite meaning it as a joke, it was true to a certain extent. She was alone again, thirty-something with two children, an ever-present former husband, and an overbearing mother. Damaged goods, some might say, and certainly not an easy package to take on. No wonder so many men opt for uncomplicated twenty-somethings, she thought. I'm destined to be on my own for ever.

Jeff had Candy, Rosie had Jim, her mother had her father, Conor had Emma, and even feckless Tim had recently seen the same girl more than once.

Conor and Emma. She allowed her thoughts to drift back to the first time she'd met the girl a couple of months ago. It was the Easter weekend, and Conor and Tim had an impromptu early barbecue in their back garden, the April weather being surprisingly warm.

Jo had taken Sean and, while he was playing a partic-ularly energetic game of rough and tumble with Thomas and Sophie at the bottom of the garden, Conor had sidled up to her for a chat.

'Seems a nice bloke,' he said, jerking his head towards

291

Sean. 'Happy?' He was looking particularly delicious in a white T-shirt and beige combat shorts.

'Yes, very,' smiled Jo. 'Emma seems nice too, not to mention horribly pretty.' In her pre-Sean days, she probably wouldn't have mentioned it, but it was amazing what a new relationship could do for your magnanimity.

'Very true,' murmured Conor, glancing over to where Emma was clearly making a valiant effort to listen to one of Tim's excessively long-winded jokes devoid of a punchline. 'She's a lovely person, too.'

They stood in silence for a few moments, both nursing their Budweiser lagers and staring into the middle distance.

'So is it serious?' asked Conor. 'It's been almost a year now, hasn't it?'

Jo noticed a small muscle twitching in his cheek. 'Yes . . . I mean, yes it's been almost a year, not, yes it's serious,' she stumbled. She wasn't quite sure why she'd felt the need to say that. 'What about you?'

He wiped a small line of perspiration from his top lip. 'The signs are all good. I'm a very lucky man.'

Yes, thought Jo, snapping back to the present day as she saw Rosie returning from the loo, everyone seems capable of maintaining a normal, healthy relationship except me.

Of course if, God forbid, her mother knew about her daughter's latest relationship debacle, she would say it was all Jo's fault and that she simply attracted the wrong kind of men. But Jo didn't believe that. After all, she and Jeff had

292

been together for ten years and, even after he'd abandoned her for younger thighs, she still didn't think that deep down he was a bad man. She'd long ago reached the decision that his adultery had been partly her fault for failing to put more effort into the marriage. There was no doubt she'd become complacent, as had he. Better communication and more effort might have saved it. But now they'd never know. At a recent wedding she'd attended, the words of the vicar had stuck in her mind. 'Love is a decision, not just a feeling,' he had droned.

Jo hadn't heard the rest of the speech, becoming lost in consideration. He's so right, she thought. In this day and age of endless temptations and easy get-outs, you have to make the decision to stick with someone and work at making it a good relationship that neither of you want to give up on. Otherwise, it's the rocky road of chasing the chase all the time, never settling down and putting effort into what you've already got.

It struck her that Conor was probably the sort of man who practised what the vicar had preached. 'Lucky old Emma,' she thought.

'Anyway, enough of my sad old life,' she said as Rosie sat back down next to her. 'How are things in the well-balanced world of Rosie and Jim?'

It had been just over a month since Rosie started her new relationship, but Jo still couldn't help smiling when she said their names together. She had already handed over one of Sophie's old Rosie and Jim videos as a joke present.

'Well, I hate to gloat, but it's amazing,' said Rosie, her eyes shining. 'He's funny, kind, considerate, has his own place, and seems to adore me.'

'Please tell me he's got a willy the size of a bell-push or I'm going to throw up with the perfection of it all,' said Jo, pretending to stick a finger down her throat.

Rosie pulled an apologetic face. 'Sorry, but the sex is great too.'

Jo made a choking noise and fell off her chair onto the grass, scrunched up into the foetal position.

'Well, it's about bloody time I had some good luck in love,' Rosie laughed. 'You've hogged it all up to now.'

'Now let me see . . .' Jo had sat up and placed her finger under her chin in mock thoughtfulness. 'My husband walks out on me and the children, and the next man I date turns out to be married. Yep, I can see why you think I have good luck.'

Rosie raised her eyes heavenwards. 'You know exactly what I mean. Admittedly, Sean was bad luck, but if you'd chosen Martin you'd probably be wearing a vast sparkler by now and preparing to become accustomed to a life of untold luxury.'

Jo clambered back onto her chair. 'Look, I've already told you a squillion times. I'm not interested in him and he's certainly not interested in me.'

Jo's anxiety that Martin was one day going to pounce on her had all but vanished in the previous few months. Since the Steps concert, she had spent several meetings

294

and dinners alone with him, poring over the plans for the house that was now nearing completion after a series of unforeseen building delays. She had eventually mentioned she was dating Sean, just in case Martin was harbouring any lascivious thoughts about her, but not once had he even so much as hinted his designs on her were anything but interior and decor-related.

'In fact I'm so convinced he's not interested that I've agreed to fly to Nice with him next weekend to view a house he's thinking of buying,' she said, pulling a flying ant from Rosie's unruly mass of hair. 'He wants an estimate from me on doing it up.'

'Really?' Rosie raised an eyebrow. 'Where are you staying?'

'The Byblos in St Tropez. We fly into Nice, then he's hired some boat for the whole weekend to get us there and back. We fly back to London on the Sunday morning.' Jo lobbed a stone in the direction of a pigeon that was pecking at her wisteria. 'Jeff is having the kids so I don't have to worry about anything. I'm quite looking forward to it actually.'

'I should think you bloody well are! The furthest anyone has taken me is a package holiday in Spain, and Martin isn't even getting a shag out of it.'

'That's for sure. Anyway, the way my love life is going, I'm never going to risk having sex with anyone again.'

* * *

'Cheers.' Martin held his cut crystal champagne glass aloft and clinked it against Jo's.

They were sitting at a table in the legendary Club 55 on St Tropez beach, with its distinctive blue and white stripey seating and abundance of the painfully chic in-crowd.

'Look, it's Joan Collins!' hissed Jo, making it completely obvious she was staring.

Martin looked nonplussed. 'I know, she comes here a lot,' he said. 'Jack Nicholson was in here the last time I came.'

Two bottles of champagne later, Jo never wanted to leave this wonderful place. The sun was shining, the atmosphere was electric, and the numbing effect of the alcohol meant she could have quite happily sat there and people-watched all day.

'Jesus, how long does that live out of water?' she said, emulating one of Sean's remarks and gesturing towards a gargantuan woman stuffing her face with lobster.

'Oooh, miaouw,' said Martin, pulling a face.

They sat in silence for a couple of minutes, Jo brooding about what a laugh she and Sean would have had sitting there and commenting on some of the plastic surgery frights walking past.

'So how are things going with Sean?' asked Martin nonchalantly, as if reading her thoughts.

She had vowed to herself that if the subject came up, she was simply going to pretend everything was fine. But the combination of heat and alcohol had made her brain woozy to the point that she said the first thing that came into her head.

'They went considerably downhill after I found out he was married,' she muttered, taking another swig of champagne.

Martin's eyebrows lifted almost imperceptibly and she found herself irritated by his lack of response.

'That's quite a big thing in a girl's life,' she said sarcastically.

'Indeed,' he replied levelly. 'Want to talk about it?'

She didn't, but she couldn't help herself because the whole farrago was still quite raw and it felt good to get it off her chest with someone so objective. For the next half hour she told Martin everything about the phone call to Sean's office, the showdown, and how he'd offered to leave his wife.

'So the whole thing is one, big fucking mess,' she finished, flopping back in her chair and wiping a bead of sweat from her forehead.

'What do you think you'll do?' asked Martin, gesturing to the waiter to bring the bill.

'Start again I suppose,' she said, her face clouding over at the thought. 'Brush myself off and step right back into that dating bear-pit again. Not just yet though.'

Martin gave a half-smile. 'Are you really so scared of being single? It's not that bad, you know. God knows I've got used to it over the years.'

Jo thought about what he'd said for a moment, then flipped her sunglasses back onto her head and let out a deep sigh. 'I just have this thing about not growing old alone. I want someone to sit on the porch with, so to speak.'

Martin remained silent, a curious expression on his face. He signed the credit card voucher that had been placed before him, then stood up. 'A woman like you will never have to spend life alone,' he said. 'Now come on, this is all getting far too gloomy. I'm going to cheer you up.'

'Where are we going?' She was reluctant to leave the vibrant atmosphere of Club 55.

'To see the house I'm interested in, then back to the hotel to prepare for a wild night out where you are going to forget all your troubles.'

Through the haze of alcohol, Jo managed a quick glance at her watch. It was midnight.

She and Martin had wormed their way into a quiet corner of the Caves Du Roi nightclub under the Byblos hotel, and were both slumped against some cushions watching the action on the dancefloor. It was a heaving, sweaty hotbed of nubile girls, well-off thirty-somethings, and excessively wealthy businessmen in the full throes of their mid-life crisis.

Locked in a quiet stupor, Jo was enjoying watching the men and the different ways they danced. It took her back to her youth, when being asked to dance by a stranger was tantamount to a legal mugging, because of flailing arms and legs.

There was the phantom cigarette extinguisher, constantly grinding his left foot into the dancefloor and swinging his arms like a novice skier, then Casey Jones the train driver, choo-chooing from one side of the dancefloor to the other, occasionally ringing an imaginary bell. There were always a couple of John Travoltas, arms aloft (handy when you needed a cab hailing later), and several Chubby Checkers who twisted to every record regardless of decade or tempo.

Again, Jo found her thoughts drifting back to Sean and what fun they would have taking the piss out of the spectacles now before them.

A half-full bottle of champagne sat in front of her and Martin, at £160 a time. The expensive quirk of Caves Du Roi was that all drinks had to be bought by the bottle, including vodka and gin.

'Come on,' said Martin, leaping to his feet and grabbing her hand. 'Let's show them how it's done.'

As he led her onto the dance floor, the unmistakable beat of 'Night Fever' thumped through the speakers, and Jo felt her spirits soar. There was nothing like a favourite piece of music from your youth to pep you up.

She was surprised to see Martin was an excellent dancer, gyrating his hips in time to the music without looking a fool. Jeff had always been an embarrassment on the dancefloor, like a puppet whose strings had been cut. She'd never seen Sean dance, and now she doubted she ever would.

Martin suddenly moved towards her, grabbed her hand, and spun her round. As the room shot past her eyes, Jo realised she was very drunk indeed, potentially out of control. She was relieved when the next record turned out to be a slow one, and she started to walk back to their seats.

'Hey, hey, hey, where are you going?' shouted Martin above the strains of Frankie Goes To Hollywood's version of 'The Power of Love'. 'Come here.'

He held one of her hands and placed the other around her waist, drawing her towards him. Jo rested her chin on his shoulder and it felt like the most perfect place in the world. Gently swaying from side to side, she became lost in the moment, comforted by the feeling of being in a man's arms again, intoxicated by his smell.

Such was the headiness of it all, she barely noticed when Martin buried his face in her neck and started to nuzzle it. It had always been one of her most responsive erogenous zones, and tonight was no exception.

Gently pulling away, the room still hazy around her, she moved her head until her face was directly in front of his, their noses touching. Suddenly they were kissing, tentatively at first, then becoming more urgent.

To Jo, the man she was kissing at that moment was fairly irrelevant. It just felt delicious to be away from home and responsibilities, and once again to be propelled back to those heady days of youth when a few drinks led to the gay abandon of necking with a virtual stranger in some disco.

The record changed to the repetitive beat of some modern dance track and they were suddenly snapped out of their trance.

'Come on, let's sit down,' said Martin quietly, hanging onto her hand and leading her off the floor.

They flopped back onto the sofa Martin had tipped a waiter to keep free, and he poured them two more glasses of champagne. As he handed her one, his empty hand went behind her head and started to idly play with her hair. Without the heady spell of the music and her head resting on his shoulder, Jo was unsure how to respond.

Martin leaned forward and gently kissed her on the lips, and she smiled nervously. She had an idea what was coming and she wished now that they could just leave and forget all about what had just happened.

'Jo?'

Here we go, she thought. 'That's my name, don't wear it out,' she said brightly, practising her usual habit of saying something completely fatuous at awkward moments.

'Listen, I've been thinking.' Martin's face was worryingly serious.

'Ooh, steady on.' There she was doing it again, but he didn't seem to notice.

'We've known each other for a while now, and I like to think it's as friends rather than just business associates . . .' He paused, as though seeking corroboration of this statement.

'Friends, yes,' said Jo, taking another swig of champagne as fortitude. She had a horrible feeling Rosie's prophecy was about to come true.

'I have grown very fond of you.' He sounded stilted. 'And a few times I've wondered whether there could be more between us.'

'More?' Jo parroted. She knew she sounded gormless, but couldn't think of anything else to say.

'Yes, more. You know, maybe a relationship.' He emphasised the last word as if it were revelatory.

'I see.' Except Jo didn't see. She didn't see at all. Was Martin suggesting something serious here or was he just after a fling? She was too drunk to make any distinction.

'There have been a couple of times before when I thought about saying something to you, but you never gave out any signals that you were interested,' he said, still stroking her hair.

Jo said absolutely nothing, because she didn't trust herself to speak. She hadn't given out any signals because she wasn't interested, it was as simple as that. But alcohol and the excitement of being away from home in such glamorous surroundings had fuelled her libido. She was quite happy to drag Martin upstairs for some uncomplicated sex then forget all about it, but she knew it wouldn't be like that with him. He was an intense man who had obviously thought long and hard before declaring his feelings.

She took a deep breath and tried to regain control of her faculties. 'Look, we're both a little drunk right now,' she smiled, stroking the side of his face as if he were a child. 'Let's sleep on it . . . separately,' she added hastily in case of misunderstanding.

Martin nodded slowly in agreement, but his expression left little doubt he felt crushed by her cautious response. 'OK,' he said quietly, picking up the bill and trying to focus on it in the dark club.

As Jo watched him sign for the extortionate amount without so much as a flinch, her mind went into rapid fast forward.

Here was a man who was nice-looking, successful, and extremely wealthy, a man who had whisked her away for the weekend of a lifetime and paid for absolutely everything. He represented everything she could want in life, someone mature and caring, who would probably treat her brilliantly and never let her down. Was she being a fool for not even considering his proposition?

They walked from the club into the hotel foyer and stood waiting for the lift in total silence, both staring fixedly ahead. As they stepped inside and Martin pressed the button for their floor, Jo studied the back of his head and considered the consequences of dragging him by his tie into her bedroom.

But she just couldn't do it. The passion she always banged on about to Rosie just wasn't there.

Martin walked her to her room and paused outside the door as she swiped the plastic card to enter.

'Goodnight, sleep well.' He lowered his head and kissed her tenderly full on the mouth.

If he'd kissed her passionately, professed to find her irresistible, and bellowed something like, 'Sod the serious stuff, let's just have a shag and talk about it in the morning,' Jo knew it was highly likely she would have slept with him. But he was too much of a gentleman, and she wasn't sure how she felt about that.

'The trouble with women,' Tim had once said, 'is that you love it when a man bosses you around and behaves like a bit of a rogue. You whinge about it, but you love it. Some bird wouldn't shag me last week because she said I was "too nice" and wanted us to be just friends. So I called her an ugly cow, but she still wouldn't.'

He's got a point, thought Jo, as she watched Martin walk down the corridor and disappear round the corner. I really should be mature enough by now not to dismiss a man for being nice and straightforward. She stood there for a while, resting her head against the doorframe and waiting to see if Martin had a change of heart and came rushing back dressed only in a bedsheet.

Five minutes later, she was tucked up in bed. Alone.

25

'I knew it!' said Rosie triumphantly as they sat in the kitchen with a large gin and tonic each. 'What did I tell you?'

'Yes, yes, you were right,' laughed Jo, 'but it really came out of left field. I had no idea it had even crossed his mind before that.'

It was five days since Jo had returned from her St Tropez jaunt, and Rosie had come round to help her prepare a dinner party for that night. But as yet, all they'd done was gossip about Martin.

'Just think,' said Rosie, 'a no-holds-barred Harvey Nicks account, probably some convertible limo thingy, and more designer clothes than Ivana Trump. How can a girl possibly say no?'

Jo tweaked her friend's nose with affection. 'You've always been easily bought,' she smiled. 'Now come on or it will be doner kebabs all round if we don't get cooking.'

It was Tim's thirtieth birthday and Jo had offered to hold a dinner party in his honour, a rash suggestion she had made only yesterday and was now rather regretting.

Those invited were Tim and his new girlfriend Anna,

an extra in the desperately dreary daytime soap he starred in, Conor and Emma, Rosie and Jim, and her, Jo, the big, green gooseberry.

'Why didn't you invite me?' said a disgruntled-looking Jeff when he'd come to collect the children earlier that morning.

'Er, possibly because you have your own life?' said Jo with friendly sarcasm. 'Besides, I don't think Candy would be too thrilled at the thought of you having a cosy dinner with your ex-wife and mutual old friends.'

'She wouldn't know or care,' he said disconsolately. 'She's gone on some hen weekend to Brighton.'

She seems to be doing more and more on her own, Jo thought, but didn't bring the subject up because it might be mistaken for her giving a shit and she quite honestly didn't.

Before last weekend, she would have invited Martin to make up the numbers. But since their little necking session in Caves Du Roi, she'd deliberately avoided any contact with him. As a teenager she'd been amazed to find how a small kiss changed things between her and the opposite sex, and it was exactly the same now. Someone you would happily have called a couple of times a week or whenever you felt like it, suddenly became someone you played it cool with – leaving days between calls and endlessly mulling over when would be the right time to ring. And all because of a kiss. She also knew that contact with Martin might mean having to address the tricky subject of them starting a relationship, and she didn't feel up to making a decision on that at the moment. The ball had been left in her court, and it was staying there untouched for now. If she was honest, she was still completely hung up on the whole Sean business and unable to make any rational decision about the future.

When she'd got back late Sunday from St Tropez, there had been a message on the answering machine from him. Her body had broken out in goose bumps at the mere sound of his voice.

'Jo, it's Sean, are you there?' His voice sounded tentative, obviously knowing she was in the habit of screening her calls. 'Um, well you're obviously out. Look, please call me, we have a lot of talking to do.'

It had taken every last vestige of her willpower to stop herself from calling him there and then. She was desperate to tell him about her weekend and the weird and wonderful people she'd seen, to share her experience and hear him laugh, to say how much she'd missed him.

But she didn't.

By 10 p.m. the dinner party was in full, raucous swing, with Rosie balancing a dessert spoon on the end of her nose and Jim trying fruitlessly to do the same.

'Shit, that's a bad coke problem you've got there,' laughed Tim as he watched. 'Talking of which, did I tell you about Dave Keating's wife?'

'No,' everyone chorused, desperate to hear a piece of

307

gossip about the soap's biggest star, a man who, if he were a cake, would eat himself.

'Well!' said Tim dramatically, warming to the theme. 'It's well known he's got a big coke problem, and she's been trying to get him off it for years. Last year he went into the Priory for a bit of a rest and came out telling her he was clean. But he wasn't.'

'Don't they have baths at the Priory then?'

The remark was so acutely stupid that at first Jo thought it had to be a joke. But no. Emma's face was completely straight, and there was a questioning look in her eyes.

'Darling, what an utterly spazzy thing to say,' said Tim, making absolutely no attempt to explain to a clearly bewildered and embarrassed Emma what the expression 'clean' meant. 'Anyway, where was I?'

Jo noticed that Conor had placed a comforting hand on Emma's leg and was giving her a reassuring smile. It reminded her what a nice man he was, but in an interesting way, rather than the faintly irritating, patronising way that made most women want to run a mile.

'Ah yes,' Tim continued. 'So Dave had told Freda, his wife, that he was clean, and she believed him. So imagine her shock when she found a small bag of cocaine in one of his pockets when she was putting his suit in for dry cleaning.'

'No!' Rosie's eyes were shining at such grade one gossip. 'So what did she do?'

'That's precisely what I asked her when she told me

about it.' Tim took out a cigarette from the packet in front of him. 'She said she decided to take some and see what all the fuss was about.'

There was a collective intake of breath around the table.

'I said, "Oh my God Freda, what happened?"' continued Tim, 'and she replied, "I don't really know, dear, but I got an awful lot of ironing done!"'

Everyone fell about laughing except Anna, who was smiling indulgently, clearly having heard the story before. Only Emma didn't react, surveying the others with a puzzled expression on her face.

'She's not the sharpest pencil in the box, is she?' said Jo to Conor as he helped her carry dirty plates into the kitchen later that evening. A shadow crossed his face and she instantly regretted her unkind remark. 'I know.' She held her hands up in a surrender gesture. 'Sorry, I shouldn't have said that. She's very sweet.'

Conor ignored her and started to pile the coffee cups onto a tray with the sugar bowl and milk jug. He's been here so many times he knows where things are better than Jeff ever did, she thought to herself.

'Tim told me about Sean,' he said, his back to her as he organised the tray. 'I'm sorry. He seemed a good bloke.'

Jo felt a pang as she heard his name. 'Yes, well things aren't always what they seem, are they?' she said with a sigh. 'I really liked him as well, but yet again I've been proven to be a crappy judge of character.'

Conor turned round suddenly, an earnest look on his face. 'And I really liked Sally,' he said. 'But life goes on. I'm proof of that.'

Jo was struck by how handsome he looked in his simple black T-shirt and faded jeans. He really was a striking man. 'That's true,' she said with false brightness. 'I must say, being in love suits you.'

Conor picked up the heavily laden tray and started walking towards the kitchen door. 'Thanks,' he said, his back to her.

When they returned to the table, Tim was regaling everyone with some ancient anecdote Jo had heard a million times before. Rosie was leaning against Jim, absentmindedly caressing his forearm with her thumb, her face glowing with happiness. They complement each other brilliantly, thought Jo. Jim was no oil painting, with his wiry brown hair, round face and ruddy cheeks, but he had a wonderfully calm nature that tempered Rosie's wacky side. He also adored her, which had worked wonders for her friend's cripplingly low self-esteem.

Anna was listening to Tim's story with an admiring expression. She was young, probably about 26, with short, brown hair cut in a gamine style, and a plainish face that improved greatly when she wore make-up. Jo could tell she was slightly awe-struck to be dating such a senior member of the *Winds of Life* cast, a title that had provided hours of amusement for Tim and his puerile farting jokes. Anna was a regular extra who had popped up in scenes

310

as a beautician, traffic warden, and nurse. It was in the latter costume that Tim had fallen for her.

'I'm a sucker for uniforms,' he'd said. 'But even I draw the line at traffic wardens.'

Emma, her red-varnished fingernails stroking Conor's hair, was supermodel gorgeous. She had wide-set china-blue eyes, an elfin chin and button nose, and a Meg Ryan hair-cut that accentuated her innocent look. She was wearing knee-length black boots with kitten heels, a tight, mid-thigh skirt, and a diaphanous blouse that gave just a tantalising glimpse of her small but shapely breasts.

No wonder Conor thinks he's a lucky man, Jo thought. So what if she can barely string a sentence together when she looks that good. Jo let out a heavy sigh, unwrapped another Amaretto biscuit, and stuffed it whole into her mouth.

At 2 a.m. she waved an extremely drunk Tim and stone-cold-sober Anna off into the night and leaned against the hallway wall. Peace at last.

The dinner party had been great fun, but it had felt really strange to be the only singleton in a roomful of couples. Jo had felt encased in her own private bubble, viewing the proceedings as an outsider. Kicking off her shoes and putting the kettle on for a habitual bedtime cup of tea, she once again mulled over her plight as not just a thirty-something singleton, but one who has two young children. A singleton with knobs on, so to speak.

She and Rosie referred to dating in your thirties as

311

'The Pyramid Effect'. Early in life, you are at the bottom of the pyramid, with a wide choice of men. But as you go on, it gets narrower and narrower until hundreds of women are vying for the attentions of a minuscule number of men. Uncomplicated, sane men, that is.

Jo had always thought herself lucky to have met someone in her twenties that she could last the course with. Or so she thought. Instead, here she was back on the market again. The cattle market that was packed with beasts and very few prize specimens.

To her mind, it was incredible that any marriage lasted through the emotionally stressful obstacle course of the twenties and thirties, that time when couples are striving to make it in their chosen careers and be good parents at the same time. It was little wonder so many relationships collapsed under the strain. Maybe, like prison sentences, 'for life' in marriage means about ten years, she thought ruefully. That's all I managed. My husband has gone, and I'm left with Sean, the married man who wants to leave his wife for me, or Martin, the older man who'll offer me security for life.

She thought back to her conversation with Conor earlier that night. He seemed uncomplicated, was good fun, and she found him attractive. But she'd missed her chance there and he was now in love with Emma. He'd said as much himself and he certainly hadn't denied it when she'd said it for him.

'There's only one thing for it, Joanne,' she said aloud. 'Stay single.'

26

Jo placed the phone back on its cradle and put her head in her hands. 'Shit, fuck, damnation,' she said, slapping a chastising palm against her forehead. She had called Sean.

She hadn't meant to. Her plan had been to spend Sunday in blissful isolation, doing odd jobs around the house and pampering herself with all those deliciously indulgent beauty treatments you never get round to once you have children.

But sheer loneliness had got to her. Dozens of times, she'd stood staring at the phone, willing herself to walk away from it, forcing herself to find something – anything – to do that would stop her from making the call. But in the end, the pull was too great and she caved in. Even as she was dialling his number, she hoped the sound of his voice on the answering machine would bring her to her senses.

'Hello?' He picked up the phone after the first ring.

Jo froze. She briefly contemplated slamming the phone down, but she hadn't blocked her number so a simple 1471 on his part would brand her as the weak-willed creature she was. Besides, she wanted answers.

She didn't bother introducing herself. 'What a surprise to get you. I thought you might be having a cosy Sunday lunch with your wife and children.'

'Jo!' He sounded genuinely relieved to hear from her. 'I wasn't sure if you'd call.'

'Don't get too excited.' She deliberately kept her voice flat, but she had to admit it felt wonderful to hear his voice again.

'So how are you?' He coughed nervously.

'Been better.' She wasn't interested in small talk, she wanted to sate her curiosity about Sean's secret life. 'Where is *home* by the way?'

'It's up in Derbyshire,' he said quietly. 'Look Jo, I'm so sorry about all of this. Why don't we meet up and I'll tell you everything you want to know.'

'Forget it,' she snapped, her heart thumping against her chest at the mere thought of seeing him. She was desperate to make an arrangement, but self-preservation kicked in. 'Let's get it out of the way now. So how many times were you in Derbyshire while giving me some old bollocks about working abroad?'

There was a long pause on the other end of the line. 'Not that much,' he said eventually. 'Just a few times. As I said, although I know you don't believe me, things haven't been good at home for some time.'

Jo made a loud scoffing noise. 'Hardly surprising if you go around deliberately driving your car into strange women because you fancy them. How many other affairs have you

314

had, Sean?' The question had just popped into her head right at that moment. Oddly, she had never thought of it before.

'None at all, honestly,' said Sean earnestly. 'I'm not like that, really I'm not. I just couldn't help it with you. At first I thought it wouldn't hurt to meet for a drink, but then I became embroiled and was scared to tell you the truth in case I lost you.'

'Which you have,' she said quietly, letting out a long, hopeless sigh.

'Have I?' His tone was subdued. 'Is there really no way forward for us? I miss you terribly, Jo.'

Up to that point, she had been fine. But as soon as the bastard said something nice she lost her composure and felt her throat begin to tighten in distress. She had mythically played this conversation over in her mind a million times, how he would say this, and she would say that, and how under no circumstances would she show any vulnerability whatsoever. Fat chance.

'I miss you too.' She tried desperately to keep her voice measured, but it cracked halfway through the sentence as she muffled a sob.

'I can't stop thinking about you,' he said urgently. 'Everywhere I go I see something that makes me laugh, except that it doesn't because you're not there to appreciate it with me.'

'I know what you mean,' she said, half laughing, half crying. 'I feel that all the time too.'

He let out a long sigh, and they fell into silence. Jo resisted the temptation to fill the void, preferring to leave the ball in Sean's court.

He cleared his throat. 'It would be difficult for us to start again, I know, but if you *could* find it in your heart to forgive me, I'm fully prepared to leave Anne for us to be together.' His tone sounded really hopeful now.

'What does she look like?' Damn, damn, damn, she thought. She had been adamant she wouldn't ask such a shallow, fatuous question. But she had to know.

'Who?' He sounded confused, but Jo knew he was probably just stalling for time.

'The woman who serves the cheese in your local Sainsbury's. Who the fuck do you think I mean?' She had regained control of her emotions now.

'Sorry,' he muttered. 'Um, she's tallish with brown hair.'

'So's Michael Barrymore,' she snapped. 'Thank God you're not a main witness in a murder trial with those underwhelming powers of description. How tall? Long or short hair? Plain or pretty?' She reeled off the questions as if she were reading a shopping list.

'She's about five foot eight with long hair, sort of layered.' He paused. 'And yes, I suppose she's quite pretty.'

Jo instantly hated her, then instantly hated herself for hating her. She was *not* going to become one of those women who blamed the other woman for her misery. That lay firmly at Sean the Snake's door.

There was too much about this whole sorry tale that

316

was a cliché already. She'd always vowed she would never get involved with a married man, even more so once Jeff had trotted off with his floozy. Yet here she was, madly in lust, love or whatever, with a married man. OK, she didn't *know* he was married when she dated him, but now she did know and here she was still speaking to him when she should just leave well alone.

But, cliché cliché, she found herself being drawn back to him and listening to his stereotypical explanations. They were taken straight from the script used by married men the world over, yet here she was wanting to believe him. Wanting to feel that, somehow, *this* affair had been different, that *this* man wasn't like all the others who had simply been trying to have their cake and eat it.

Sean loved her, *that's* why he had cheated on his wife. The chemistry between them had been too powerful to ignore, she told herself, trying to forget the rather obvious fact that they hadn't even met or spoken before he deliberately drove his car into hers. The simple fact was, she *had* to believe that what had happened between her and Sean was different. Because to think otherwise meant she had to acknowledge she was just another mistress to just another married man who got his leg over someone else whenever he could, and the mere thought made her flush with shame.

'But it's over, Jo, honestly.' Sean's voice interrupted her thoughts. 'I would have left long ago if it hadn't been for the children.'

Another cliché straight from the married men script. The children. Living, breathing, innocent beings, and she hadn't even bothered to ask about them, so consumed was she with the other woman who had been sharing Sean's bed.

'How old are they?'

'A girl of five and a boy of three. Ellie and Max.'

'Nice names,' she said. A boy and a girl, another Thomas and Sophie whose lives could so easily be shattered by their daddy leaving to pursue his own selfish wants and needs. Little human beings that so many people treated as objects to be shuffled around between separate homes, passed backwards and forwards like a Christmas box of chocolates to be shared equally between the adults. And all because one or other of their parents has decided that this particular family is surplus to their requirements and they're moving on.

'I could start the process as soon as you say you'd like to give it a go,' said Sean tentatively.

'Sorry?' This time, it was Jo's turn to stall for time.

'The process of leaving, of starting a new life with you.'

She fleetingly considered what he'd said, then let out a weary sigh. 'I'm not sure I want to be with a man who'd walk out on his wife and children. After all, I've had one of those before, haven't I?' she said, glancing at the clock and realising the devil of whom she was speaking was due back with the children at any minute.

Sean said nothing.

318

'Look,' she added. 'I'll think about everything that's been said, OK? In the meantime, you just get on with your life and I'll get on with mine.'

She replaced the receiver and took a deep breath. Initially, she was angry with herself for making the call. But when she thought about it later, she decided it had been fortuitous, because she had finally put names and vague faces to those whose lives were in her hands. Humanising them had helped enormously in strengthening her resolve to try and stay away from Sean. It wasn't going to be easy, but she just hoped she could hold out.

The doorbell rang.

'Hi. I won't come in, just dropping them off.' Jeff looked distinctly gloomy, not to mention scruffy, in a stained T-shirt and crumpled cords. The drawbacks of living with a young woman, mused Jo. You don't get your washing and ironing done for you. It reminded her of yet another of Tim's classics about older women. 'Lousy shag, but at least you get a great fry-up in the morning.'

Later on, while Sophie read to herself in bed, Jo sat on the closed loo seat and chatted to Thomas who was in the bath. He'd got over his recent embarrassment about nudity and had started letting her back in again.

'So did you have a fun time at Daddy's?' she said casually, rubbing a soggy flannel across his back.

'It was alright,' said Thomas, making 'whoosh' noises and dropping his naked Action Man from a great height into the water.

'That good, huh?' smiled Jo, scrubbing at a particularly grubby area of his neck. 'What did you do?'

'Not much,' he shrugged. 'Dad and Candy had a row.'

'Oh dear. Poor Dad.' Jo had learned over the past year or so that she gleaned far more about Jeff's new life from Thomas if she kept her responses very low key and didn't look too interested.

'We were all going to have Sunday lunch together,' he said. 'But Candy got back too late so Dad shouted at her.'

'Well, I suppose that's understandable.' Jo had also learned to be very pro-Jeff in her observations or Thomas quickly became defensive. 'So what happened after that?'

'They had a big fight and she said he was really boring. She walked out and said she wasn't coming back.' Clearly bored of the subject, Thomas ducked under the water and lay there like a modern-day Ophelia, glassy-eyed and staring at the ceiling.

Jo left him to it and walked into her bedroom where she allowed herself a secret smile. It seemed Jeff's brave new world was beginning to fray badly at the edges.

27

The noise was deafening, a high-pitched collective scream that filled the room and bounced off the walls.

Jo was sitting in the open-plan cafe of the local swimming baths, on a table that overlooked the pool area where Thomas and Sophie were about to start a lesson. Rosie was queuing at the counter for their lunch.

'Sorry, this was all they had left,' she said, placing two plates of dinosaur-shaped chicken nuggets and sad-looking chips on the table. 'They were found in ancient grease, so to speak.'

Tucking in regardless, they reminisced about their school days and how poor their diet had been.

'I used to eat at least two Mars Bars a day. No wonder my backside needs planning permission,' grumbled Rosie, stuffing six chips into her mouth.

Jo laughed. 'Not to mention the two packets of pickled onion flavour Monster Munch a day. God, we loved those. We were always saying we were going to get into shape, but never did.'

'Oh, I did,' said Rosie. 'Trouble is, the shape was round. I'm resigned to that now.'

'I wouldn't worry,' said Jo. 'I'm sure Jim loves every ounce of you, just as you are.'

Rosie scoffed and reached across to steal one of Jo's discarded chicken nuggets. 'Normally I'd poke you in the eye with my fork for saying such crap, but on this particular occasion you're absolutely right. He's such a sweetie pie and, for once, I don't hate him for it.'

'That's because he makes you laugh as well as being nice,' said Jo with a sigh. 'It's the lovely but boring ones we can't tolerate.'

'True.' Rosie stood up and removed her canary yellow fleece. She never wore quiet clothing. 'But I must say it's a huge relief to find I can be happy with a nice man. For years I thought I could only sustain interest in bastards. To me, drama meant passion.'

'God, yes. Do you remember Steve?' Jo pretended to stick her fingers down her throat and made a choking noise.

Steve had been Rosie's distraction through sixth-form college, a time when she should have been concentrating on her A levels but was instead being led a merry dance by a man with the IQ and energy level of a three-toed sloth. He worked as a mechanic in a motorbike shop, and because he earned £75 a week and owned a Yamaha 100 Rosie clearly thought she was dating Steve McQueen.

'I always thought he was the strong silent type, but then one day I realised he just had fuck all to say.' Rosie opened a bag of crisps. 'Relationships were such an effort in those days, weren't they? The greatest thing about going out with Jim is that I don't think too deeply or worry about it. It just seems to work. I now realise that relationships shouldn't be hard, they should tick along nicely with the occasional hiccup.'

Jo sucked her coffee spoon and considered what her friend had said for a moment. 'True, but there's a fine line between being easygoing with each other and becoming complacent. The more I think about it, the more I realise Jeff and I fell apart because we had started taking each other for granted.'

'Er, no,' said Rosie in a staccato voice. 'I think you'll find it fell apart because he ran off with a Barbie doll in human form.'

'No, that was the symptom, not the cause,' said Jo. 'Sure, at first I blamed him entirely, and it still stands that he's the one who walked out. But the run-up to the breakdown? I came to the conclusion recently that I was as much to blame for it as him.'

Rosie didn't look convinced. 'How do you work that out?'

Jo wasn't too sure herself, but she knew that recently she was starting to feel a lot more compassionate towards Jeff. Maybe it was the shock of her experience with Sean, or simply because there were other fish in the sea, whether she was interested in them or not. Whatever, it had made her more understanding towards her errant husband and the routine weaknesses of human behaviour.

'I don't know who stopped making the effort first,' she said, refusing Rosie's offer of a crisp. 'But the other responded and stopped trying too. Before we knew it, we were two strangers living under the same roof. Just existing really . . .' She trailed off and leaned over the balcony to check on Thomas and Sophie.

It was true that her relationship with Jeff had gradually crumbled to nothing. But, like many couples, they were entrenched in the everyday burdens and responsibilities of daily life, and never took time to address the problems. So it had slowly built up, until it became a mountain and even the *thought* of conquering it was too exhausting to contemplate.

Towards the end, their longest conversations had been about the children. They even sometimes spoke to each other through them, using them as a filter for their own verbal inadequacy. When Jeff came home, Jo found herself with nothing to say, resentful even of his time in the office, away from the drudgery of running a home as well as trying to hold a small job together.

'Funnily enough,' she said, turning back to face Rosie, 'I think Jeff's adultery ultimately did me some good. It was the kick up the backside I needed to start working seriously again instead of just playing at it.'

Rosie's eyes widened. 'Wow. That's quite a diversion from the early days when you wanted to roast his chestnuts over an open fire.'

'I know. I do still feel a bit angry with him though,

324

because he took the Candy route rather than sitting me down and telling me he was unhappy. That way, we might have stood some chance of sorting it all out.'

'Trouble is, I don't think many men actually give much thought to whether they're happy or not,' said Rosie, spooning the froth from the top of her cappuccino. 'Some totty comes along in a short skirt, they shag it, then tell themselves later that they only did it because they were unhappy.'

For someone who had minimal experience of long-term relationships, Jo was struck by how intuitive Rosie could be. There was an element of truth in what she'd said. Jeff had never alluded to being unhappy until *after* he'd bolted, making it a rather convenient justification of his bad behaviour. Suddenly, Jo didn't feel quite so magnanimous towards him.

'Speaking of which, it seems young Candy isn't such a sweetie after all. Thomas says she and Jeff had a barney at the weekend and she said he was boring and walked out.'

'Ha! If I remember correctly, I predicted that would happen eventually,' smiled Rosie, waving her paper napkin in Jo's direction. 'Bloody well serves him right.'

Jo sat staring at her for a moment or two, then took in a long, slow breath before speaking again. 'I actually feel a bit sorry for him,' she said sheepishly, silently cursing the return of her magnanimity. She couldn't help herself, she'd always been a very fair person.

'Sorry?!' Rosie spluttered, sending small specks of coffee froth flying across the table. 'For him? What on earth for?'

Jo could hear a faint, reedy cry of 'Mummy'. She looked over the edge of the balcony to see Thomas standing below, waving up at her. She waved back and blew him a kiss.

'There's more pressure on him because he's the one carrying all the guilt of leaving me and the kids,' she said. 'He's the enemy in everyone's eyes, and if things go wrong with Candy it will seem as though it was all for nothing.' She yawned her way through the last part of the sentence. There was something very soporific about swimming baths.

'That's because it was,' scoffed Rosie. 'I mean, how could he ever think a young girl like that would stay interested in *him*?'

Jo started to clear up their plates and place them back on the tray. 'You never know, it might be a mini midlife crisis,' she said. 'He's probably trying to hang onto his youth.'

'In which case, he'd better not introduce her to other men,' retorted Rosie, and they both burst out laughing.

'You never know, it might work out yet,' said Jo.

'Yeah right, and Emma is a secret member of Mensa,' said Rosie.

They'd already had several catty conversations about Conor's girlfriend, and Jo had felt horribly mean doing so. But she had to admit there was nothing more satisfying than a good old bitch with a trusted girlfriend, as long as you knew your comments would never be passed on.

She looked up to find Rosie staring at her with narrowed eyes. 'Would you have the cheating toad back if he asked?' she said.

'Which cheating toad? Don't forget I have two in my life now.' Jo smiled, tucked her hair behind her ears, and began tracing a figure of eight in the sugar bowl with the handle of a teaspoon. 'If you mean Jeff then, truthfully, I really don't know. I'm not the same person I was when we split up, and I'm not even sure we would fit together any more. But he is still the father of my children, so for that reason alone I'd feel it deserves serious consideration.'

28

'Can you believe it? A fucking bus, I ask you! It's soooo unglamorous, I'll never live it down.' Tim slapped a hand against the dashboard to emphasise his distress.

Jo jerked her head to the back of the car where Thomas and Sophie were engrossed in their Gameboys. 'Tim, language!' she hissed.

It was late August, still the school holidays, and the four of them were driving, very slowly indeed thanks to erratic toilet breaks, to Ty Celyn in Wales for a week's holiday on a caravan site. The same site, in fact, where Jo and Tim had spent many bored, soggy days as children.

She had originally planned to take just Thomas and Sophie, and was rather looking forward to evenings spent in simplicity, listening to the inevitable sound of rain on the roof. She saw it as valuable downtime in which to get her thoughts in order about life, love and the universe – in no particular order.

But at the last minute, Tim had discovered he was being written out of *Winds of Life* and had decided to join them in a fit of luvvie pique.

'Of all the deaths the bloody scriptwriters could come up with, being flattened by a number thirty-seven bus isn't exactly up there with the greats, is it?' he moaned, puffing his cigarette out of the window and getting blasted in the face by rain. 'You know what? If I bought a cemetery right now, people would stop dying.'

They were two and a half hours into their journey and he hadn't yet drawn breath over the tiresome subject of his untimely demise from the show, recently described by one critic as 'televisual flatulence'.

Jo took her eyes off the road for two seconds to give him her best scowl. 'If you don't shut up about that bloody show, I'm going to drive deliberately into the central reservation just to provide a diversion.'

'So-rreeee,' he replied, with the tone of wounded indignation she was used to hearing from Thomas.

To make matters worse, Tim's girlfriend Anna had dumped him the day after he'd received the script containing his death by public transport.

'She was obviously in love with the idea of Dimitri and not me,' sniffed Tim, who had been rather dubiously cast as a Greek waiter whose accent had unintentionally veered wildly between Greek, Pakistani and Italian. 'Oh well, she was a moany old cow anyway. If I didn't have bad luck with women, I wouldn't have any luck at all.'

Unable to take much more, Jo pulled into a motorway service station for a spot of light relief. She parked in a disabled space and limped to the main entrance, where she shoved the children into the video games area while she and Tim queued for coffees.

'Excuse me, dear.' An old woman had approached Tim. 'Aren't you on the telly?'

'I certainly am,' he beamed. His chest had visibly puffed out by several inches.

'Thought so. Don't like it much meself, but I have it on in the background because my little budgie Joey gets lonely otherwise. He likes the noise the telly makes.'

She shuffled off as Tim's torso deflated. 'Jesus,' he hissed. 'Just as I thought things couldn't get any worse, I find out a fucking budgie is my greatest fan.'

Thankfully for Jo, the little incident took the wind out of Tim's sails and he shut up about his ailing acting career for the rest of the journey.

Two hours and several rounds of I-spy later, the car pulled onto the bleak seafront that had dominated so many of their childhood holidays. Tim let out a deep sigh of contentment and visibly relaxed.

'Ah for those old days when all we worried about was where the next ice-cream was coming from, eh Sis?' he smiled, rubbing the condensation from the window for a better view.

The heart of Ty Celyn could at best be described as one road of rather bleak houses and several boarded-up shops, overlooking a cracked promenade and a grey pebbled beach. A couple of derelict boarding houses stood at one end, and a rundown amusement arcade provided shelter to several

330

sulky teenagers puffing away at fags just inside the doorway. The Tudor-style pub that had been called The Red Lion in Jo and Tim's youth had clearly been taken over by one of those ubiquitous chains and renamed The Legless Ladder.

Jo edged the car into one of the countless spaces along the front and switched off the engine. Thomas and Sophie didn't look up from their Gameboys for even one second, but Jo and Tim sat quietly for a moment, soaking up the view and all its memories of forced walks along the beach, struggling against the biting wind and mouthing silent protestations at their parents' backs.

Fifty yards in front of them, a family of two adults and three children sat huddled alongside their multi-coloured, stripy windbreaker, mutely passing around sandwiches from a plastic container. They were all wearing cardigans and tracksuit bottoms. Beleaguered was the only word to describe them.

'Ah, the great British spirit,' said Tim. 'Come hell, high water, or torrential winds they will sally forth and sit on the beach, huddled together like characters in a Wilfred Owen poem.'

Jo laughed. 'Do you remember that – ahem – summer, for want of a better word, when Dad insisted we were all going to have a marvellous time despite the fact that we couldn't walk at a forty-five degree-angle to the pavement without falling over?'

'Certainly do,' Tim nodded. 'Do you think we endured those holidays because Dad thought they were character-forming, or simply because we couldn't afford anything else?'

Jo shrugged. 'Bit of both, I suppose. But whatever the reason, something stuck, because here we are reliving the nightmare when we could probably have afforded a package holiday on the Costa del Sol instead. Come on, let's go and check out the caravan.'

They drove down the remainder of the deserted promenade to the Sea View Caravan Park positioned at the far end.

'Abandon hope all ye who enter here,' chanted Tim, as they drove under the dilapidated sign with one end flapping in the breeze.

'Folk don't come round here much, not since that young couple disappeared,' said Jo in her best Deep South drawl.

It was a site of permanent caravans, some owned, some rented out. Jo's parents' caravan had been the former; Jo and Tim's was the latter.

After driving round for a few minutes, dodging small children and slow-moving pensioners, they pulled up outside plot 124, a brown and cream caravan that was indistinguishable from the hundreds of others.

It had frosted windows, rusting sills, and those unspeakable plastic strip curtains that flapped hysterically in the wind every time you opened the door.

'Honey, we're home!' shouted Tim, opening the car door and bouncing out on to the grass. 'And it looks just like the one we inhabited all those centuries ago.'

'No, I think that was plot six six six,' laughed Jo, as her face was slapped by a north-westerly wind of a strength never encountered in the confines of south-west London.

'Bloody hell, time has clearly stood still in Sea View,' said Tim as they climbed inside for a look round.

The seat cushions were covered in the stains of ages; the curtains looked like a particularly ferocious cat had climbed up them, and patches of the carpet were mildewed.

Jo pursed her lips. 'Thank goodness we brought our own bedding or God knows what we'd catch.'

By 9 p.m. the children were in bed, knocked out by the sea air, and the small gas fire was emanating more fumes than warmth. Jo and Tim were locked into an extremely competitive game of canasta, a regular fixture on all the Ty Celyn holidays of their youth.

'Do you think Mum and Dad actually enjoyed these holidays, or were they just a ritual they got locked into and couldn't get out of?' said Tim, as Jo was taking a particularly long time to take her go.

She placed her cards face down on the table. 'Funnily enough, I was thinking about that the other day,' she said. 'There's nothing like a marriage failure of your own to make you put everyone else's under the microscope.'

'The conclusion being?' said Tim, leaning back against the foam rubber sofa present in just about every rented caravan in the British Isles.

Jo frowned. 'Not sure really. Do you remember any rows? Because I don't.'

'Nope, can't think of any. But when I look back it wasn't the kind of marriage that would have lasted in this day and age. It was a bit Terry and June, if you get my drift.' He poured out two more generous glasses of white wine for them both.

Jo laughed at this observation, then sank back onto her sofa with her glass of wine. It surprised her that Tim could be so perceptive about their parents' marriage, at any time, let alone from the perspective of his early teens. She'd underestimated him.

'But I don't suppose divorce was an option in those days,' he added, gathering up all the playing cards and putting them in a neat pile in the middle of the mock-wood Formica table.

'Why? Do you think they even thought about it?' She was shocked.

'Doesn't everyone at some time or another?' said Tim, casually blowing a smoke ring into the air.

'Maybe. But you never really think your mum and dad do. When you're parents, your children always think your marriage is infallible. Well, they used to anyway . . .' She faltered, her thoughts suddenly turning to Thomas and Sophie tucked up in the next room. The wine was beginning to take effect and she felt she might cry at any moment.

'It's different these days,' said Tim, as if sensing her discomfort. 'Children are far more fatalistic about such matters.'

'That's a terrible shame though, isn't it?' she said, tears pricking her eyes. 'Everyone should be entitled to a childhood where they're protected from that sort of thing.'

Tim looked at her with undisguised derision. 'And what good did that do us?' he said, grinding his cigarette into the ashtray. 'We experienced a supposedly stable and happy childhood with two parents who stuck together through thick and thin, yet here we are sitting in a caravan in Ty Celyn on a grim August night. You nearly divorced with two wonderful children, and me . . . well, me without even so much as a steady girlfriend at the grand old age of thirty.'

He had a point, thought Jo. We all beat ourselves up about the psychological effect our actions have on our children, but there are countless examples of those who have triumphed against all odds, and plenty of those who have fucked up despite having the Stepford childhood – a Daddy who trundles off to work and a Mommy who bakes cookies all day. There was no rhyme or reason to it.

It seemed to her that, rather than reacting to a situation, children simply react to the mood or emotions that situation invokes in their parents. If you succeed in shielding them from your emotional excesses, they have every chance of emerging fairly unscathed.

Tim's voice broke into her thoughts. 'And you're so emotionally stunted you even turned down a straightforward, honest, and – let's face it – fucking good-looking bloke who was interested in you.'

'Sorry?' The wine had rendered Jo incapable of interpreting who he was on about. Sean? Martin? She'd forgotten he didn't even know about the latter.

'Conor. Con-*or*!' he said, emphasising the last syllable

as if she were a total moron. He took a swig of his wine and glared at her over the rim of the glass.

'Yes, yes, yes, I know. Maybe I fucked up!' she said, slumping back against the cushions in a mini-alcoholic stupor. 'But it was too soon after Jeff left and I couldn't even think about seeing anyone else. Gimme a break!' Boy, could she feel the wine taking hold now.

'Hello! Hell-oooooo!' slurred Tim, who was clearly three sheets to the wind as well. 'You started dating Sean *moments* afterwards.'

'Not moments, a few weeks,' said Jo, knowing she was arguing on a technicality. 'And it was different with him because I didn't know him. It felt easier somehow.'

She established eye contact with Tim to try and assess his reaction to this insightful remark. All he did was make the raspberry noises of someone who thought what she'd just said was total cobblers.

'I just wanted to be made to feel attractive again, but to have got that feeling from Conor would have been so much more complicated,' she sighed, noting that a small fly had landed in her wine.

Tim watched as she attempted to remove the struggling creature from her glass, then leaned forward and said, 'Why?', an earnest look on his face.

'Why? Effing why?' said Jo. She rolled her eyes and lay back, staring at the ceiling. 'Probably because I've known him for ever, because he's your best friend, because he knows our parents.' She held up a finger for each reason.

'I mean, if it had gone wrong it would have fucked up everything.'

Tim pretended to pick up an imaginary telephone. 'Hello, is that Pinewood Studios? Yes, my sister would like to audition for *any* Bette Davis remake you might be planning.'

'Oh, ha bloody ha.' Jo sat up again. 'It's true though. To me, Sean was just going to be a little bit of harmless fun, no strings attached,' she said, glancing at the clock and noting it was 1.30 a.m. She was about to continue when Tim butted in.

'Sis, *sis*, SIS! Relationships are like tampons. They *always* have strings attached.'

'I don't agree. That's only the case if you fall in love with someone. Unfortunately, that's exactly what happened with Sean before I realised what a duplic . . . dupluc . . . two-faced shit he was.'

She stopped talking and stared out of the caravan window, lost in the melancholy of recent events. Outside, the rain was lashing against the window and she watched as someone's washing line flew past with several items still attached to it.

'But were you?' said Tim gently. 'In love with him, I mean? I'm not so sure. It strikes me that your strength of feeling is there because the relationship never ran its course.'

Jo shrugged, and suddenly felt very tired. 'The trouble is, I'll never know now, will I?' she said wistfully. 'All I do know is that it's over and I feel like shit.'

They sat in silence for a few moments, the only noise coming from the spluttering gas fire and drizzle outside.

What Tim said was true, but Jo could only base her feelings on the fact that after a year with Sean she had still felt passionate about him. Perhaps a year of dating when you have children is different to a year when you are a single woman. Everything has to be planned meticulously in advance, and you simply don't see each other as much because time doesn't allow. So whether her strong feelings for him ran deep enough to sustain a together for ever scenario, she simply didn't know and now never would.

'Have you spoken to him since finding out?' said Tim, taking their empty glasses over to the small metal sink in the corner.

'Regrettably, yes,' sighed Jo. 'I didn't want to, but I couldn't help myself. I wanted some answers.'

'And?'

'And I found out he has a pretty wife and two young children living in Derbyshire.' She stood up and stretched her arms towards the low ceiling. 'I also found out he would leave them if I gave him the nod.'

Tim raised an eyebrow. 'I see. And how do you feel about that?'

Jo walked across to where he was standing and stopped just inches from his face. 'God knows. Torn between hating him even more for saying it, and running off into the sunset with him in pursuit of my own happiness and bugger everyone else's.'

29

Martin reached inside his black leather briefcase and pushed a distinctive red Cartier box across the table to her. 'Happy birthday, Jo.'

She immediately had two thoughts. Shit, because she hadn't bought him anything for his birthday the month before. And fuck, because she'd suggested dinner so she could finally broach the subject she had been avoiding for months: his suggestion in Nice that they might start dating.

'Martin, it's absolutely beautiful!' she gasped, holding the silver tank watch against her wrist in an unashamedly admiring fashion. 'But I absolutely cannot accept it.'

Martin raised his eyebrows questioningly. 'Why on earth not?'

'Because this is the type of present you give to a loved one,' she said, placing the watch back in the box with more than a tinge of regret, and closing the lid. 'We're just friends.'

'Ah,' he said with finality, placing the palms of his hands on the table. 'I get the feeling you're about to give me what is known in polite circles as the brush-off.'

Jo gave him a weak smile and silently toyed with the

avocado and mozzarella salad that had been placed in front of her by a rather flustered waitress. Inwardly, she was cursing Martin for giving her such an expensive present. She'd wanted to edge her way gently into the subject of letting him down lightly, not this way.

She took a deep breath and looked straight at him. 'What you said back in Nice, I have been giving it some serious thought,' she said, popping a piece of mozzarella into her mouth. 'And you are a marvellous man and absolutely someone who would be fantastic to go out with, but . . .'

'Ah yes, here comes the But,' he interrupted with a stiff smile.

'But I just don't think I'm ready to launch back into another relationship yet. When I think about it now, I started seeing Sean far too soon after my marriage broke up, and I really think I need to spend some time on my own and get a sense of who I am . . . if that doesn't sound too wanky,' she added apologetically.

A fleeting expression of mock shock crossed Martin's face. 'No, it doesn't sound too . . . wanky, as you so inimitably put it.' He was doing his usual trick of pushing his food around the plate and eating very little. 'I'm quite happy for us to carry on as friends for as long as you like.'

They ate in silence for a while and Jo marvelled at how reasonable he was. Here was a remarkably mature, kind and, let's face it, wealthy and generous man, who was willing to stand back and wait until she might be ready for a relationship. And yet here she was, arsing him around because she was still hankering after some fly-by-night television cameraman with a crappy car and a secret family up north.

'Thanks,' she said quietly, reaching over and squeezing his hand. 'And thanks for this, too.' She pushed the red box back across the table towards him.

'You're welcome,' he said, pushing it back again. 'From one friend to another. Besides, I can't take it back to the shop and it wouldn't suit me.'

For the rest of the meal, they avoided the subject of Jo's turn-down and talked about everything from how she was progressing with her plans for his property in Nice, to Martin's upbringing in deepest, darkest Kent.

He was the youngest of two sons and a daughter and his parents had run their own grocery business until it had gone bust in 1975, the victim of a supermarket chain setting up nearby.

'All their valued customers abandoned them,' said Martin. 'But they then had the cheek to moan when they closed down because it meant getting in the car for the odd pint of milk here and there. Hypocrites!'

He said his father had become ill with the stress of trying to find another job, and both his brother and sister left school straight after O Levels to get jobs and help keep the family afloat.

'Because I was that bit younger, I stayed at school,' he added. 'And by the time I left, things were much easier at home so I was able to follow my dream of going into the music business.'

He told Jo he was so grateful to his siblings for all they'd done, he had given them £2 million each when he'd sold music.com.

'They both gave up work immediately,' he smiled. 'And it was an absolute pleasure to see it.'

Jo was warming to this marvellous man with each passing minute. 'What about your parents?'

'Both dead, I'm afraid.' His face clouded. 'My father died when I was twenty-five. He had a sudden heart attack, probably brought on by stress. My mother died of breast cancer five years ago.'

'I'm so sorry,' she whispered, making a mental note to call her parents in the morning and be nice to them.

'Don't be,' he sighed. 'It was all a long time ago now, but I just wish they'd lived long enough for me to be able to lavish some luxuries on them. God knows they forfeited enough for me over the years.'

Outside in the cool October evening air, Jo stepped forward and held Martin in a lingering hug. 'You're a lovely man,' she murmured in his ear, noticing how comfortable and safe she felt in his arms.

'But not for you,' he said with a wistful smile, as he pulled away from her.

Jo looked at him, her head on one side. 'Just friends for now, but never say never,' she smiled.

It was 11 p.m. by the time she arrived home and put

her key in the lock, admiring her expensive new watch as it glistened in the street light. Jeff was dozing on the sofa, his mouth wide open and emitting tiny, intermittent snores. A couple of years ago, it was a sight that would have depressed Jo no end, but now she could just wake it up and get rid of it.

Placing a hand on his arm, she shook him gently.

He shot upright, blinking furiously. 'What? what?' he muttered.

'It's me. I'm back . . . you can go now,' she whispered.

Bunching a fist into each eye, he rubbed vigorously and stood up, one leg of his creased cords still wedged halfway up his calf. He had a gaping hole in one of his socks, from which his big toe was protruding.

'I think I'd better have a cup of coffee before I go . . . wake me up a bit,' he said, heading off towards the kitchen.

Jo's heart sank, her hope of a fairly early night and one chapter of her latest bonkbuster rapidly disappearing. She had a sneaking and depressing suspicion that Jeff wanted to talk. She followed him into the kitchen to make herself a cup of tea.

Five minutes later, armed with a cup of coffee and an expectant look, he finally got round to it.

'So what are your plans for Christmas? Are the tribes of Israel coming here?' He made it sound casual but Jo knew it was a loaded question.

'It's only October for heaven's sake! But if you mean my parents and Tim, yes. The plan is for them to come here.' She gave a heavy sigh, to indicate that this was quite enough people thank you.

'I was thinking . . .' he said.

Here we go, she thought.

'I could join you.' He looked at her with the hopeful expression of an abandoned puppy wanting a home for Christmas.

She could almost feel the cranks of her resolve tightening. 'No, I don't think so.'

'Why on earth not?'

'Because we're divorced?'

'That's hardly the point. The children would love it and it *is* Christmas, after all.' He spun the dregs of his coffee round the mug and knocked it back.

Jo sat down adjacent to him at the table. She had hoped to dodge the tricky subject of Christmas and keep things friendly. Still over two months away, the wretched festival was causing friction already.

'You didn't worry about the children last year,' she said quietly.

She was referring to the previous year's festivities, when she'd asked – no, in fact she'd begged – Jeff to spend it with her and the children. It had been many months since he'd left and she was over the emotional worst, but there had still been the faint hope that such a family-orientated time of year would have made him come to his senses.

But no. Jeff had calmly informed her, without any trace

344

of discomfort or shame, that he and Candy wanted to spend a quiet Christmas together on their own.

'I deeply regret that now.' He shuffled uncomfortably in his chair. 'It was really selfish of me, that's why I want to put matters right this year.'

It was a nice try, but Jo wasn't buying it. 'Thanks, but we'll be fine. Really,' she said, standing up and placing her cup in the sink.

She turned round and was shocked by the snapshot image that bore into her mind as she looked at Jeff's face.

He looked old, defeated even, his eyes slightly blood-shot and lifeless. His usually shining hair looked dull and stringy, and he seemed to have lost weight around his girth. In short, he looked a mess.

Sighing, he glanced up at her. 'It's over.'

'Sorry?' She was confused.

'Me and Candy. It's over. Well, she actually said she wants some space, but it amounts to the same thing, doesn't it?' he said with sudden bitterness.

Jo walked across and sat down at the cluttered table. She reached over and placed a reassuring hand on Jeff's forearm. 'I'm so sorry.'

And she meant it. Eighteen months ago, she would have been ecstatic to hear him say Candy had dumped him, but now the revelation simply left her cold.

'I thought something was upsetting you,' she said, removing her hand and leaning back in her chair.

Jeff stood up and strolled over to the French windows,

gazing out into the darkness of the garden, the same garden that a few years ago was the centre of many happy summer days for them and the children.

'It's not losing Candy that's upsetting me,' he said, slowly drawing a nonsensical squiggle in the condensation on the glass.

'Oh?'

He turned round to face her. 'It's my stupidity for leaving you and the children for something so bloody shallow.'

So there it was. With depressing inevitability, the validation of everything Jo had first thought about the foolish, transient little affair Jeff had disrupted so many lives for. And with great irony, it had come in the very room where the devastation had first begun.

But she didn't feel euphoric at the news she had once been so desperate to hear. She merely felt sad that she and Jeff had come to this. Two estranged people, huddled together in the kitchen of what had once been *their* home, lamenting his mistake that had cost them their marriage.

He made an attempt at a smile. 'So – to paraphrase Mud – it's going to be bloody lonely this Christmas.'

That's the real reason he's anxious to come here, thought Jo. It had little or nothing to do with any consideration for her or the children. He just felt sorry for himself and didn't want to spend it alone in his grim little flat. She'd never actually visited his flat, but in her mind it had always been grim. She felt her jawbone clench involuntarily.

'Oh nonsense,' she said with false brightness. 'You can

346

go to your mum's. She'll be thrilled at the chance to spoil you rotten for a couple of days.'

'I suppose I could do that . . . if there's no other option,' he said glumly.

'I'll tell you what,' she said, determined not to cave in.

'What?' His face lit up with hope.

'Why don't you come and get the children on the day after Boxing Day and have them for longer?' she said with a winning smile. 'You can bring them back New Year's Day if you like.'

Jeff's eyes dulled again as he realised that, despite his sterling efforts, a Christmas lunch invitation wasn't going to be forthcoming. 'Yeah, that would be great,' he said flatly.

Five minutes later, Jo waved him off to his car across the street and dead-bolted the front door for the night. She switched off the hall lights and climbed the stairs to bed, a small smile on her face. She had to admit that despite her initial feeling of sympathy for Jeff it had felt wonderful to be in control of him for once, to watch him dance to her tune instead of the other way round.

Better still, her babysitting problems were solved for New Year's Eve.

30

On Christmas Day morning, the house resembled a teenage summer camp with bags, bodies, and strange clothes strewn everywhere.

Her mother and father were crammed into the small spare bedroom that, somewhere along the line, had also become a storage area for all the children's old toys, spare pieces of furniture *you might just need one day*, and bin-liners stuffed full of old photographs. Not to mention the miles of videotape of Thomas doing little more than gurgling in the days when having a new baby was a novelty for Jo and Jeff. Poor old Sophie had been virtually neglected on the video front.

Tim occupied a temperamental put-you-up in the dining room that collapsed every time he so much as glanced in its direction.

'I don't know why you didn't take the spare bed settee from us when I offered it you years ago,' said Pam to Jo as they watched Tim struggling with his temporary resting place.

Jo scowled. 'Because, Mother, it's brown and cream, has no springs, stinks of Ratty, and should have been thrown on a skip years ago. That's why!'

Her parents had only arrived the previous afternoon and already her mother was driving her to complete distraction. It had taken all her power not to lunge at her on several occasions.

'Don't talk about poor old Ratty like that,' sniffed Pam. 'He didn't smell.'

Ratty was her mother's now deceased Jack Russell, and never had a dog so lived up to its name.

'He's bloody Albert Tatlock reincarnated,' said Tim after Ratty had once tried to bite him for walking too near his dog bowl.

Overfed by his indulgent owner, Ratty resembled a butter barrel on legs. Once, he had disgraced himself terribly when he 'got at' a neighbour's female King Charles Spaniel whose owner was hoping to breed pedigree puppies. Instead, she got a batch of equally belligerent Ratty-esque mongrels and never spoke to any of Jo's family again. Ratty had finally slipped this mortal coil three years ago and Pam still hadn't quite got over it. She was the only one he'd never snapped at and, similarly, he was the only living creature she'd never criticised.

'Mum?' It was Thomas bellowing from upstairs.

'Yes?' Jo walked out into the hallway, more to detach herself from Pam than from any maternal consideration.

'Can we open our stockings now?' he shouted. It was 8 a.m.

Jo smiled indulgently. 'Yes, of course you can sweetie. Bring them down to the living room.'

When she and Tim were children, their mother had always planned and run Christmas Day like a military operation. The kitchen was her HQ and the rest of the family were her subordinates to be given orders at her behest.

It was breakfast at nine, then stockings at ten. Well, more a pop sock each really, with two small gifts and the inevitable, ageing satsuma stuffed in the end. Her mother always said she didn't like to 'go over the top' at Christmas, and no one dared point out that when you have children, it's no longer about what you want any more.

Then it was lunch at two, the Queen's speech at three, and finally, main presents could be opened at three-thirty and not a moment before. Pam didn't quite synchronise watches over it, but probably only because she didn't actually think of it.

Up to that point, the presents had sat there under the tree, like cold drinks in the desert, untouchable until Commandant Pam said so.

Many times over the years, Jo vowed to herself that when she had children, they would never have to go through the same regimented torment. So Christmas in the Miles household had always been an entirely different affair where the usual house rules went out of the window.

Red-faced with the exertion, the children dragged in their stockings – well, tights to be precise, each leg stuffed with presents.

'Now that's what I call varicose veins,' said Tim, jabbing a finger into one of them.

'Wow, Father Christmas has been sooooo generous,' said a wide-eyed Thomas with Oscar-winning dramatic zeal.

A streetwise ten-year-old now, he knew damn well Santa was a myth, but he was under pain of death from Jo if he enlightened Sophie, who was still very much a believer.

'I just don't know how he carries everything,' said Sophie, settling herself down in front of the roaring gas fireplace. 'And, Mummy, guess what? He drank the glass of sherry we left him!'

Tim sneaked a quick wink at Jo and licked his lips. His eyes resembled rips in a paper bag and his hair was vertical with the shock of being up so early. Jo figured this was the one day of the year he actually saw the morning before 9 a.m.

Their parents sat on the sofa opposite, together but strangely apart, their very own invisible Berlin wall between them. Jim was looking very Cary Grant in his well-pressed cotton pyjamas, paisley dressing gown and leather slippers, and Pam was fully dressed in cashmere rollneck and tweed skirt, a prim expression on her face. Jo wondered if her father had ever seen Pam naked. She probably had the top button of her winceyette nightie done up for sex.

The children started to rip through their stocking presents at breakneck speed, delight etched on their faces. Most of the gifts were from the local 'everything for a pound' shop, which might just as well be called 'everything falls

351

apart after two days' shop. But Jo knew that, regardless of content and its longevity, it was the simple act of unwrapping a surprise that made Christmas such an unbridled joy to children.

Two pairs of tights emptied and discarded, they shrieked with excitement as they opened their main presents. Thomas had a colour Gameboy and blue Pokémon game, and Sophie had a Barbie jeep and the elusive Barbie bathroom set they had been endlessly seeking for her dolls' house.

'Thank you Mummy!' they said simultaneously, both lunging towards her for hugs and kisses.

'You're welcome. You deserve it,' she said, beaming at them. She was secretly thrilled that they seemed to be enjoying Christmas without pining for Jeff, as they had done the previous year. To Jo, it was the sign she was looking for that her children had come to accept the split and didn't seem irrevocably damaged by it.

It was as if Thomas had read her mind. 'The best thing about you and Daddy splitting up is that we get two lots of presents from you!' he said cheerfully.

'I suppose you can look at it that way,' laughed Jo. Out of the corner of her eye, she could see her mother's disapproving expression at such blatant opportunism from her grandson. Pam was clearly brewing up to some critical comment.

'So what are they going to do for the rest of the day?' she grumbled, frowning at the vast pile of discarded wrapping paper in the middle of the room.

Jo was about to respond, but was beaten to it by her father.

'They'll probably play with their bloody Christmas presents. Isn't that the whole point?' he snapped with an irritable expression. 'I could never understand why we had to stick to that rigid timetable of yours every flaming year. It strangled any enjoyment.'

Jo gave Tim a quick, uncomfortable glance, then looked across at her mother who looked like she'd been slapped in the face. She was sitting bolt upright, as still as a statue.

'Well, why didn't you say something if you hated it so much?' she whispered with a mortally wounded expression.

Jim let out an exasperated sigh. 'I doubt you'd have listened. You never did, still don't in fact,' he replied.

The adults lapsed into silence whilst an oblivious Thomas and Sophie carried on playing with their new toys. Pam's mouth set in a firm line and she began smoothing out the lap of her tweed skirt.

'Right, I'd better get going on our splendid Christmas feast,' said Jo with false brightness. Her father rose to his feet and followed her into the kitchen.

'Sorry about that,' he said sheepishly, placing his used tea mug on the draining board.

'Don't apologise to me. I wasn't the one you snapped at,' said Jo gently. 'It's Mum you should be saying sorry to.'

His face clouded. 'Don't hold your breath,' he muttered. 'I'm just sorry it happened in front of you, that's all.'

Jo looked at him. 'Dad? Is everything alright with you and Mum?' She was dreading his reply. One divorce in the family was quite enough.

Jim let out a long sigh and placed a reassuring hand on her forearm. 'It's fine, love,' he said, brushing a stray piece of hair from her eyes. 'We're just going through a bit of a rough patch and getting on each other's nerves, that's all. Your mother and I often have words, it's just that I rarely get to use mine.'

'Are you sure?' Jo wasn't convinced and it was written all over her face.

He gave her a slow smile and studied her for a moment, a melancholy look on his face. 'As sure as any of us ever are about anything. Now then, do you want a hand with lunch?'

Jo shooed him out of the kitchen and started to peel the potatoes. She realised she'd just been fobbed off with a classic hedging tactic, but decided to let her father get away with it. After all, it was Christmas.

At 3.15 – after her mother had insisted on watching the speech of 'the baked bean', as Tim called her – they sat down for the rather splendid lunch Jo had single-handedly laid out on the beautifully decorated dining-room table.

Tim raised his glass of bubbly in a toast. 'To the family . . . and all who fail in her,' he beamed.

Jo laughed as she raised her glass to her lips and

drank. There's many a true word spoken in jest, she thought. There she was, to all intents and purposes a failed wife, and Tim, a failed actor with a personal life equivalent to a Siberian winter. And her parents? Well, she knew they'd suffered their fair share of failures, though she'd never really been privy to them, only surmised what she could over the years.

Only Thomas and Sophie were failure free, those days yet to come. Jo would have given anything to protect them from that, but knew that everyone has to make their own mistakes.

It was the same story with people the world over, Jo thought. We all witnessed, discussed, and made a mental note of our friends' so-called 'failures' through life, particularly in relationships. Yet when it came to making our own choices, we always thought that, somehow, it would be different for us. That the man *we* met would never cheat on us, that we in turn would never cheat on them. We *had* to have that eternal optimism, Jo reckoned, or none of us would ever get married or make any level of commitment in life.

Looking around the table, she suddenly felt a warm glow to be in the bosom of her immediate family.

'These carrots could have done with a couple more minutes.'

'Sorry, mother?' Jo's warm glow evaporated.

'I said these carrots are a bit hard,' repeated Pam, holding one on her fork as if it were an exhibit in court.

The sound of cutlery clattering onto a plate made everyone jump. 'For Chrissakes, woman, can't we even eat a bloody meal without you making some negative, nit-picking remark?' exploded Jim, his face flushed puce. 'That poor girl's been slaving away to make this, and all you can do is criticise.'

Tim had turned pale and Thomas and Sophie were staring open-mouthed at their usually mild-mannered Grampy, as they called him.

'It's alright, Dad,' Jo muttered, wanting the unfolding scene to stop right there before her home became the setting for yet another marital breakdown.

'No, it isn't alright, Jo, it isn't alright at all,' said Jim firmly. 'These carrots are perfect, far better in fact than the over-boiled mushy monstrosities your mother serves up.' To illustrate the point, he jabbed his fork into a carrot and popped it into his mouth making dramatic noises of ecstasy as he chewed.

The entire table fell into silence, suddenly deeply absorbed in their food. Such was his obvious distraction, Thomas inadvertently popped a sprout into his mouth.

'Gamby's crying,' said Sophie matter-of-factly, using her pet name for Pam.

Jo looked across at her mother who had glutinous tears welling up behind her glasses. One rolled down her flushed cheek and plopped onto her plate as she stared at it.

'Gamby's not crying, Sophie darling,' sniffed Pam, wiping her eyes with her holly-edged napkin. 'That potato

I ate was too hot and it's made my eyes water, that's all. Now come on, eat all your vegetables if you want to grow big and strong.' The rest of the meal passed in uncommonly polite conversation.

'Do I get the impression that at the frankly laughable age of thirty, I am about to become the product of a broken home?' said Tim quietly, as he flicked through the terrestrial TV channels.

It was 11 p.m. and he and Jo were sitting in the living room having just said goodnight to their parents after a particularly low-key Christmas evening of watching television. The rest of the day had passed without incident, but the atmosphere between Pam and Jim had been distinctly frosty, with everyone else tiptoeing round it.

'I doubt it,' said Jo, sipping a mug of hot chocolate, her legs tucked under her. 'I asked Dad earlier if everything was OK and he said they were just going through a rough patch.'

Tim looked horrified. 'A rough patch, at their age? I thought relationships were supposed to get easier as you got older. You know, companionship and all that. Christ, if they get harder then I'm seriously not going to bother.'

'It's nature's cruel joke, I think,' smiled Jo, grabbing the remote and pressing the mute button. 'You meet, get married, have children, then the prime part of your life is spent trying to be all things to everyone. A good employee, a good husband or wife, a good mother or father. Then

357

your children leave home, you retire, and you're left together alone again. If you're lucky, you lift your head above the marital parapet to find you still have something in common and get on.'

Tim's face had suddenly turned serious. 'Do you think there's a chance they'll split up?'

Jo made a scoffing noise. 'God, I hope not. Can you imagine dealing with mother on her own? She'd be visiting us all the time and driving us even more mad than she already does.'

She was trying to make light of what they'd witnessed that day, but secretly it had worried her too. This was an age when her parents should have been enjoying each other's company, free of the stresses and strains of working life and parenthood. Yet here they were doing all the immature bickering of a young couple heading for the divorce courts.

Tim's concerned voice broke into her thoughts. 'Seriously though, Jo, that looked like more than just a rough patch today. Dad looked like he hates her. He couldn't even contain his loathing in front of the kids.'

Jo put her mug on the table beside the sofa, stood up, and stretched. 'Nah, it's Christmas that's all,' she said nonchalantly, hoping it convinced her anxious brother. 'It does that to you. Right now, there are people all over the country having arguments because they have spent the entire day cooped up together in a hothouse of children, chaos, in-laws and so on. It's not a natural state.'

Tim nodded. 'True,' he said. 'I read a magazine article

the other day that said more people instigate divorce at Christmas than at any other time of year.'

They lapsed into silence, Tim channel-hopping again while Jo flicked idly through *Cosmopolitan*. She came across an article entitled 'How to Get Through Christmas'.

'See?' she said, holding it up for Tim to glance at. 'That's what it is, a bloody obstacle course. Santa has the right idea, he only visits people once a year.'

He smiled and pointed at the TV listings page laid out in front of him. 'Look, *Survival* is on. Shall we see if we're on it?'

Rosie had called earlier that day to wish them all a merry Christmas and had Jo in stitches describing the festive scene at her mother's house.

Her ancient grandparents were staying, which tapped a rich, comedic vein. Grandma Violet had snored her way through *Bridge on the River Kwai*, stirring only once to mutter, 'Cruel race, them Japs', before nodding off again. Rosie's 'Granpa Jack' had the beginnings of senile dementia and had read out the joke from his cracker at least six times over lunch.

'We indulged him the first few times and kept laughing,' said Rosie. 'But he got really cross when we didn't react to the last couple of repeats and called us all "humourless tossers".'

Jo smiled now at the thought of her friend's festive experiences and suddenly didn't feel quite so depressed about Christmas Chez Miles.

'Mum and Dad won't get divorced,' she reassured Tim. 'They're just getting on each other's nerves a bit, that's all. They'll be fine.'

Tim yawned. 'I suppose you're right.' He stood up and stretched in front of the mantelpiece mirror, then smoothed an eyebrow. 'Now then, as a resting actor I need some rest.'

'Off you pop, then. And seriously, don't worry. Mum and Dad will be back to their stultifyingly normal selves by the New Year, you'll see.'

As she climbed the stairs to bed, she crossed her fingers behind her back and hoped for the best.

31

The party was raging by the time she arrived at 9.30 p.m. In the otherwise dark, silent street, Conor and Tim's abode stood out, a brightly lit beacon pulsating to the sound of 'London's Burning' by The Clash.

Jo was an hour later than she'd planned to be, held up by her own infuriating indecision about what to wear. After trying on every item in her wardrobe, she'd opted for the trusty old faithful of women everywhere, the little black dress. With its ribbon straps and slightly plunging neckline, it accentuated her slim but shapely shoulders, and the knee-length style flattered her long legs. For fear of looking a bit too Rose Kennedy, she'd draped a cerise pashmina around her shoulders and a matching clutch bag under her arm. Thanks to a newly acquired ringlet machine that resembled a torture implement, her hair hung in loose curls around her face.

'Fuck me, you look fantastic!' yelled Tim, bearing down the open-plan hallway towards her. 'Well obviously, don't fuck me because we're brother and sister and the authorities would frown on it.' He was playing to the gallery, a small crowd of his friends standing in the living room who were now smiling indulgently at Jo.

Tim removed her pashmina and chucked it over the banisters. 'As ever, most of the guests are crammed into the kitchen, frightened shitless of leaving the booze table for even one moment,' he said, raising his eyes heavenwards.

He ushered her into the long, narrow kitchen, where a deafening wall of noise hit them as he opened the door. There were about forty people crammed in, spilling out through the French doors and into the garden where Tim and Conor had placed a few outdoor candles.

'I'm insisting everyone has a vodka and Red Bull when they arrive, just to get them on the road to oblivion,' shouted Tim, pouring her a glass of pale orange-coloured liquid from a jug.

'Thanks!' she shrieked above the din. The drink was way too sweet for her, so she held her breath and knocked it back in one.

'Attagirl!' Tim slapped her on the back, prompting her to have a coughing fit and dribble some down her chin.

As she silently cursed him and searched around for some kitchen roll, Jo looked up and saw Conor across the room. He was standing with Emma, his arm thrown casually around her shoulder, chatting animatedly to another couple. Wiping her mouth, she stood there, looking across the room until he caught her eye. When he did, he raised his glass in her direction with a small smile, but made no attempt to come over.

It's so different going to a party with someone, thought Jo miserably. Even if you don't stick by them all night, they are always there as a security blanket to snuggle up to occasionally in moments of social ineptitude. Jo felt extremely inept right now. Standing in the midst of this heaving, laughing crowd, she had never felt more alone.

Just as she was considering the sudden development of a migraine and sloping off home, there was Rosie walking down the hallway with Jim in close pursuit.

Jo felt herself relax. 'It's the social cavalry,' she said, giving her friend a hug. 'Say hello to your very own gooseberry for the night.'

For the next two hours, she didn't leave their side once, except to join the queue for the one and only loo which, inevitably, didn't lock. Sitting there with one foot pressed against the door, her head leaning against the cool wall to her side and ignoring someone's repeated attempts to get in, it dawned on Jo that she was hopelessly drunk. She'd had two more swift vodka and Red Bulls before moving on to white wine, but instead of feeling nauseous and over-emotional, she felt euphoric. She also felt one hundred per cent sexually rampant.

'Bloody hell, I don't know what's in that Red Bull, but I feel bloody great,' she shouted to Rosie back in the kitchen.

'It's full of caffeine,' laughed Rosie, who was drinking her usual Bacardi and Diet Coke. 'I doubt you'll sleep much tonight.'

Jo suspected it was probably a false feeling, but for the first time in ten years, she felt like her old self again. Devilish Jo, flirtatious Jo, wicked, funny, out-of-control Jo with absolutely no worries in life except where her next kick was coming from. It felt fantastic.

She was stirred from her inebriated reverie by the deafening sound of Big Ben chiming.

'Here we go!' bellowed Tim, turning up the ghetto-blaster he'd tuned in to the radio station covering the event.

Jo found herself being shunted into position by two bit-part actor friends of Tim's, who crossed their arms and grabbed one of her hands each. As the strains of 'Auld Lang Syne' filled the room, they pumped her arms in time to the beat.

She was dreading the end of the music, that time when everyone worked their way around the room kissing complete strangers and saying, 'Happy New Year!' with false brightness.

'Happy New Year!' chorused the bit-part actors, and each turned to give her a peck on the cheek before dis-appearing into the throng to find other, more willing victims who didn't resemble Edna the Inebriate Woman.

Jo found Rosie and Jim and gave them a huge bear hug each before they lost themselves in a drunken neck-ing session of their own. She stood next to them feeling like a spare part and wondering what to do next, when a man she hadn't seen before emerged from the throng.

'Well, just look what Santa's left for me,' he said, a

broad grin on his ruddy face. 'Happy New Year, whoever you are.'

He enveloped Jo in a clumsy embrace and his un-attractive loose, wet mouth bore down on hers. He stank of whisky and stale cigarette smoke, and Jo felt an over-whelming wave of nausea. She tried to push him away but he was too strong. Suddenly, Jo felt him pulling away from her and looked up to see Conor standing there, his hand firmly gripping the back of her assailant's collar.

'Fuck off, Roger,' he scowled. 'Can't you see she's not interested?'

Looking suitably humbled, Roger muttered a barely audible apology and skulked off into the living room.

'Thanks,' said Jo, aware her voice was slightly slurred.

Conor shrugged. 'Forget it. He's always been a las-civious bastard. Happy New Year, by the way.'

'Happy New Year back,' she smiled. It was as if every-one else in the room had shrivelled to microscopic pro-portions. There was no incessant chatter, no music, no noise of any kind. Just her and Conor facing each other in an empty room, or at least that's what it felt like.

He stepped forward and placed the crook of his fore-finger under her chin, gently tilting it towards him. His warm mouth placed a soft kiss on her lips.

As she felt him pull away, Jo moved forward in a drunken attempt to prolong their fleeting contact, but he resisted and took a step back. He looked at her curiously.

'Emma's over there,' he said, jerking his head to one side.

Jo wished the ground would open and swallow her up. 'Yes, of course. I'm so sorry. It's that bloody Red Bull stuff. I'm not used to it,' she muttered.

'Are you alright?' He looked concerned.

'Fine, fine,' she said, a little too enthusiastically. 'You go and see Emma.'

Ten minutes later, she allowed herself a surreptitious sideways glance and saw Conor joking with one of the bit-part actors while Emma lovingly caressed the back of his neck and occasionally blew in his ear.

Perhaps that's what all men want, she thought miserably. A piece of arm candy – the irony of the phrase didn't escape her – who looks good but doesn't interfere with any thoughts or opinions of her own while you're chatting to your mates. Someone who never argues with you, who has sex whenever you want it, who never moans, whinges or expresses any other feelings than sheer bloody joy all the time.

Trouble is, she knew from the experiences of her friends that, although men say that's what they want, the truth was somewhat different. The husband of one of her old school friends had insisted his wife give up her career to be a mother and run the home. He had repaid her by having an affair with a dynamic businesswoman who, he said, excited him, 'Because there was more to her life than just being a housewife.' Such are the anomalies of life, mused Jo, as she wandered into the living room where two couples were locked in an embrace on the sofa, the television flickering in the corner. Apart from them, the room was empty. Jo dialled a cab and sat on Tim's Britney Spears beanbag to wait. She was told it would take half an hour.

Quietly, five minutes before it was due to arrive, she let herself out of the house without saying goodbye to anyone. Anyway, she hated the drawn-out rigmarole of trying to leave somewhere while everyone protested, 'Don't be so boring, stay.'

She was still slightly drunk, but the euphoria had turned into a miserable feeling of loneliness, a sense of desperation that she was returning home to her empty house at the start of a brave new year. A year that, a few weeks ago, she had hoped would mark a new beginning. Ha bloody ha.

'Sorry, instead of Fairfields Avenue, go to Wellington Road please,' she said to the driver.

The words just popped out unexpectedly, and she had no idea why she was going there, or even whether he'd be in. He's bound to be up north, celebrating the New Year with his loved ones. After all, isn't everyone? Everyone but me.

The car pulled up outside Sean's flat and Jo noticed a faint light through the living-room window. She suspected it was merely a burglar deterrent. Well, at least that's what your average householder thought. To burglars, it was probably just a light left on by someone who had gone away but was trying to pretend they hadn't.

She handed the driver a £10 note. 'Wait here, and if I go into the building and am not back out in five minutes, you can go,' she said, aware she was sounding like some bit-part in a gangster movie.

She rang the bell and waited, glancing round at the pathway and flowerbeds that had become so familiar to her over the past year. She felt absolutely nothing, numbed by alcohol. Ringing the bell again, this time more urgently, she was just about to turn away when a voice came through the intercom. 'Hello?'

'It's me. You alone?' Jo's voice was low and non-committal.

'Yes.' His voice sounded expectant. 'Come up.' The door buzzed and she walked inside the unprepossessing hallway, the familiar stale smell filling her nostrils. As she climbed the stairs and heard Sean open his front door, she briefly stopped halfway to try to gather her thoughts.

Had she come for an argument or to make up? Neither, she decided. She was drunk and lonely, and she'd come for some physical contact with a man she'd once loved, probably still loved.

As she walked around the corner, he was standing in the doorway, his hair dishevelled, a bathrobe tied loosely at his waist.

He looked pensive 'Jo . . . I . . .'

'Save it, Sean. I haven't come to talk.' She stepped forward and wrapped her arms around his neck, inclining her head to find his mouth. He responded instantly, kissing her with such passion they stumbled and fell against the hallway wall.

Booting the door closed with his bare foot, Sean tugged her dress up over her hips, revealing the black lace stay-up stockings that, for once, had lived up to their name. He slipped his hand inside her g-string and, with one swift movement, he snapped one of the delicate lace sides. Jo felt them fall to her left ankle.

Pushing his body against hers, he carried on kissing her passionately and lifted his hands to the ribbon straps of her dress. He tugged them both down to reveal her breasts. 'God I've missed this,' he muttered, before taking one erect nipple in his mouth and caressing the other.

'So have I,' she whispered, feeling her insides turn to mush as his fingers moved in and out of her.

She pushed on his shoulders to move him away, and lowered herself to the floor, pulling him down by her side. Her dress bunched up around her middle, she straddled him on the hallway carpet and guided his penis into her, letting out an audible gasp as it entered.

Almost violently, she writhed backwards and forwards on top of him, caring only for her own pleasure. Eyes closed to block out the face of the man who had caused her so much pain, she lost herself in a fantasy world of anonymous sex, greedily taking what she wanted and damn the consequences. Head thrown back, she came in a violent shudder then collapsed, spent, on Sean's chest.

They lay there for a minute or two, catching their

breath whilst the feelings of passion and ecstasy gradually subsided into ones of sobriety and reality. The lethal combination of alcohol and New Year loneliness had brought her to Sean's door, and now Jo felt horribly awkward.

Sean cleared his throat to speak. 'I knew you'd see sense in the end,' he murmured, gently stroking her bare thigh. 'The feeling between us is just too strong to throw away.'

Rolling away from his touch, Jo slowly stood up and pulled her dress down. She said nothing, simply staring at him coldly as she pulled each shoulder strap back up and stuffed her broken, discarded g-string into her handbag. When she was absolutely sure everything was back in its rightful place, she spoke.

'To be honest, I was surprised to find you here,' she said with ice-queen calm. 'Why aren't you playing happy families?'

He rubbed his eyes, apparently disconcerted by the sudden change of mood. 'She thinks I'm away working. I couldn't face spending New Year with someone I no longer want to be with,' he said quietly.

'I see.' Her voice was clipped, but inside she could feel her iron resolve starting to buckle under the strain of desperately wanting everything to work itself out between them.

Here was the emotional bank account she had invested in for a year, only to find it suddenly closed and with no interest payments at the end of it. It all felt like such a waste of time, and the thought of starting to invest some-where else all over again was just exhausting. The burst of passion had heightened her senses again and she suddenly felt distinctly vulnerable. It would have been the easiest thing in the world to fall asleep in Sean's arms and worry about the future in the morning. But she couldn't do it to herself, knowing that if she took him back now, it would endorse his behaviour and set a pattern she didn't want to be part of. Before long, she would be just like any other long-suffering mistress, issuing endless ultimatums about him leaving his wife, threatening to finish it, then taking him back when he made the next set of promises. The mere thought of it snapped her back to her senses.

'I haven't come back, Sean,' she said, looking down at him where he lay on the floor. 'Far from it. I just hated the fact that it had been left in limbo with no proper ending. That fuck was our grand finale.'

'But I thought . . .' He frowned and lifted himself up onto one elbow, looking perplexed. The devilish grin that always floored her was nowhere to be seen.

'What *did* you think, Sean?' Her face hardened. 'That we'd have a shag and everything would be alright? I don't think so. I came here tonight because I was drunk and I wanted sex. It's not my style to seek it with a stranger, so I came to you. I used you like you used me. Feels shit, doesn't it?'

Not waiting for him to answer, she walked towards the door then turned back to face him.

'I also wanted the chance to say goodbye properly,' she said lightly. 'So . . . goodbye.' Blowing him a kiss, she walked out of the door and down the stairs, not daring to glance back.

Euphoric from her feisty exit, she immediately sobered up as she hit the cold night air and wondered how on earth she was going to get home. It had felt good to be so strong to his face, but now she was alone again she felt utterly desolate. Worse, she hated herself.

It's funny, she thought. When you're lonely and drunk, you always go for the quick fix that you think is going to make you feel better. But in the cold light of day it never does and you wish you'd stayed away.

She waited in the shadows across the road, to see if he would come after her. But he didn't. He didn't even look out of his living-room window. After five minutes she began the long walk to the nearest mini-cab office, feeling cheap, and crying all the way.

32

A car alarm shrieked into life, waking Jo with a start. She rolled over and opened one eye, to see the clock registering 9.30 a.m.

Nine and a half hours into the brand new year and she'd already made two major mistakes, she thought, groaning and burying her face in the pillow at her blatant bad behaviour. First, she'd tried to snog Conor while his girlfriend was in the same room. Secondly, she'd slept with Sean. Thirdly, and probably deservedly, she had a Grade A bitch of a hangover. Thank goodness I have no life, she decided. I'm not sure I could cope with an action-packed day.

She lay staring at the ceiling for a while, unable to sleep because of the small man with an exceptionally large hammer who was currently trying to break through her skull. There was a time when an empty day stretching ahead of her would have been a glorious treat. Now it just seemed empty.

She tortured herself for a while with thoughts of what everyone was doing right now as she lay there feeling bilious and alone at the start of another year. She pictured Rosie and Jim laughing together over coffee and warm pain au chocolat, her parents pottering around each other at home, Jeff making breakfast for the children, Conor and Emma snuggled up in bed. She wrinkled her nose at the thought of the latter and changed it to them walking hand in hand in the park. Her only consolation was that Sean was probably alone at this very moment too, though without the hangover or the sense of indignity that she had. Why was it that a meaningless sex session never seemed to trouble men?

After teaching herself to walk again and edging her way slowly downstairs, she made coffee and a vast stack of toast, then crept back into bed again. She took a couple of Nurofen and spent most of the morning drifting in and out of a troubled sleep punctuated by a vivid dream, where she was marrying Martin with Sean, Jeff and Conor as bridesmaids. They were just posing for pictures outside the picturesque church when the phone rang and snapped her awake. It was 1 p.m.

'You're still in bed, you slut! I can tell by your voice.' It was Rosie.

Jo groaned and rubbed her eyes, her finger black with last night's mascara. 'So would you be if you had my hangover. I'm never drinking again.'

'Until next time,' said Rosie who sounded hideously jolly. 'Yes, you were completely blotto on that Red Bull stuff. You never said goodbye, so I thought I'd better check you'd made it home.'

'Good old you.' Jo sniffed dramatically. 'At least you'd bother to look for me if I ended up face down in the gutter.'

Her friend tutted. 'Oh God, you're not having one of your nobody-loves-me days, are you? You always get maudlin with a hangover. Call me when you're better.'

The phone receiver went down and Jo stared at hers for a few seconds before placing it back on the cradle. Having a silent chuckle to herself, she swung her aching legs out of bed. Rosie was absolutely right. She did get boringly maudlin the morning after the night before, and always had done. But today of all days she felt she had more cause than most.

Jeff arrived back with the children at 4 p.m, rather conveniently timed to coincide with the end of a Bette Davis film Jo had sniffled her way through.

'Mummy, your nose is red,' said Sophie disapprovingly, prodding it with a podgy forefinger.

'I know sweetie,' smiled Jo, stuffing a soggy tissue back up her sleeve. 'I've just watched a sad film.' She looked up to find Jeff standing in the doorway, smiling at her in a whimsical sort of way.

'You always were a big softie,' he said gently. 'Do you remember that car advert with the red balloons that always made you cry?'

Before she could answer in the affirmative, Thomas bowled into the room brandishing a page ripped out from the local newspaper.

'It's on! It's on!'

Jeff grimaced. 'I said we might take them to see the new Disney film if it was on,' he said apologetically.

'Oh, did you?' Jo raised her eyebrows in mock disapproval, but secretly she quite fancied the idea after a day spent alone. A bit of mindless Disney moralising would probably do her good.

'Mummy, puh-leeeeease!' said Thomas, clasping his hands together in mock prayer and falling to his knees in front of her.

'I'll think about it,' she said, lifting him to his feet.

The cinema was crammed with those trying to escape the nullifyingly boring prospect of another day housebound, and watching New Year's Day television. So they'd come to watch an even bigger screen instead.

While Jo and the children joined the snaking line for popcorn, Jeff queued for the non-bookable tickets, waiting patiently behind two foreigners who weren't sure what film they wanted to see or what time it was on.

'This is just like old times, isn't it?' he said warmly, settling himself down into the aisle seat and dipping his hand into Jo's salty popcorn.

'Er, no actually,' she murmured out of the corner of her mouth so the children wouldn't hear. 'You would never do this before, always banging on about having time to yourself after such a busy week.'

He had just opened his mouth to answer her when

the opening credits of the film started and Thomas leaned across with an urgent 'Sssssshhhh.'

When they came out of the cinema ninety minutes later, it was a crisp but clear winter's night.

'Look, I'm smoking!' said Sophie, holding two fingers to her mouth and blowing her breath into the icy air.

'Shall we walk back across the Common?' said Jeff, looking questioningly at Jo. 'What about you kids, are you up to it?'

Thomas and Sophie ran on ahead to indicate that indeed they were.

Jo tugged her overcoat closer round her body and fell into step beside Jeff. They followed the children along the dark road leading to the Common.

'Look, there's that high wall,' he said, pointing into the gloom. 'I threw your glove over it once and you were absolutely furious.'

'Don't remind me. As I recall it was early on in our relationship and I very nearly dumped you because of it. What an arse.'

Jeff jutted out his bottom lip, pretending hurt. 'I was just trying to impress you in that rather curious and immature way that men do,' he said. 'I bought you a new pair.'

'Yes, half the price, the wrong colour, and too bloody small,' she scoffed. 'But apart from that, they were perfect.'

Jeff laughed. 'That's the relaxing thing about spending the evening with your ex-wife . . . she already knows what an idiot you are.'

They were on the Common now, striding towards home with the bright lights of a fairground in front of them. As Thomas and Sophie started running back towards them, she and Jeff looked at each other with a weary sense of inevitability.

'OK, but just two rides and that's it!' said Jo, as the children whooped with joy in front of them.

Five minutes later, as her over-excited offspring shrieked with delight on the spinning teacups ride, Jo started to feel exceptionally weary. The cold night air was seeping through her overcoat and into the very marrow of her bones, and she wanted desperately to go home.

She had just endured a long monologue from Jeff about all the inter-departmental problems he was experiencing at work. It had been on the tip of her tongue to say, 'Hey, I listened to all this shit when I was married to you, but I sure as hell don't see why I have to listen to it now.' Instead, she simply let it wash over her while she considered the virtue of rarely having to suffer such tedious minutiae any more. Eventually, they retreated into an exhausted silence. When he next spoke, it took her completely by surprise.

'I'm sorry.'

'What?' She thought she'd heard him correctly but she wasn't too sure.

'I said, I'm sorry,' he repeated, staring fixedly ahead at the teacups ride. 'It struck me that I'd never actually said that to you before.'

Jo felt awkward at his sudden change of tack. 'Sorry for what?' she said, although she knew perfectly well.

'For leaving you and the children,' he said quietly. 'For fucking up all of our lives.'

There was a time when she would have agreed whole-heartedly with this statement, but she wasn't going to allow him to accord himself such importance now, not when so much water had passed under the bridge.

'Oh, I don't know. In a way, you did me a favour,' she said, waving at the children as they spun past.

He looked stunned, then turned to face her. 'What do you mean?'

She didn't get a chance to answer him because the teacups ride had slowed to a halt and the children were hurtling towards them shouting, 'Carousel! Carousel!'

As they made their way over to the brightly coloured horses, Thomas and Sophie ran on ahead and threw them-selves onto the stationary platform, desperate to get the garish mounts of their choice.

'It's really over, you know. Me and Candy,' said Jeff, smiling at the children as the ride started to move and they began to bob up and down, holding on tight.

'Really? I thought she just wanted some space,' said Jo, deliberately keeping her tone nonchalant.

He plunged his hands deep into his jacket pocket. 'She did, but it turns out the space she wanted was infinite and finite,' he sighed. 'She has decided I'm too old and set in my ways.'

'Aren't we all.' Jo gave him a sympathetic smile.

Staring ahead, Jeff remained serious faced. 'She's gone and I feel absolutely nothing except what an old fool I've been to throw away a good marriage for *that*.' He spat the last word out with such ferocity that Jo flinched.

They stood in silence for a few moments, staring ahead at the cosy scene of their two excited children flashing past under the bright, warm lights of a fairground ride.

With a deep sigh, Jo stretched out her left foot and began absent-mindedly pressing down on a lump of soil in front of her. 'It wasn't that good though, was it? Not towards the end, anyway.' After all the months of thinking it, she'd finally said it.

Jeff looked puzzled. 'Is that what you meant earlier, when you said I'd done you a favour?'

'Sort of, yes. I think we'd both stopped making an effort, really. It wasn't just your fault, although of course you were the one who chose to look elsewhere rather than sort out the problems with me.' Jo gave him a quick glance, then started to walk towards the exit of the ride, now virtually at a standstill.

She could tell Jeff was desperate to continue their conversation, but Thomas and Sophie had dismounted and were running towards them.

'Right, you two,' he said, rummaging in his trouser pocket. 'Here's two pounds each to spend in the arcade over there. Once it's gone, that's it.'

'Commonly known as buying time,' said Jo. She

380

watched them sprint towards the arcade and started to follow them. She was about to step inside when Jeff put his hand on her arm and gently pulled her back.

'Do you really think I did you a favour?' He looked hurt.

'Yes, but not because my life is better without you,' she said kindly, not sure whether she meant it or not. 'Simply because I think I had become bogged down by trying to be a good wife, good mother, good daughter, good interior designer, whatever. And I'm sure it was the same for you too.'

He looked at her curiously for a moment, then shrugged. 'Sort of, I suppose.'

This, of course, was ludicrous. Jeff had never become particularly bogged down by anything unless it was work. He avoided his mother most of the time, just making the occasional phone call to check she wasn't dead, and if there was ever any problem with the children, he had always automatically assumed it was up to Jo to sort it out. After all, he had work to do. And as for being a good husband, well that clearly came pretty low down on his list of priorities. But Jo didn't feel the need to bring all that up tonight. It was all done and dusted anyway, and these days she preferred to keep things non-confrontational.

'When you left me, I had to face up to failure,' she said, picking at a piece of chipped paintwork. 'It taught me that you can't be all things to all people. More importantly, it taught me that you have to take time for

381

yourself occasionally, be a little selfish maybe. The way we were going, something had to give. It turns out it was our marriage.'

Jeff frowned, considering what she'd said. Then he turned back to face her. 'It's not irretrievable though, is it?' He looked and sounded pathetically hopeful.

'Our divorce papers said it was,' said Jo quickly, unsure of how to respond to his question.

He placed a hand on her forearm, and she felt a gentle squeeze through the thick layers of her overcoat and sweater. 'Why don't we put all this behind us and start again?' he said softly, his eyes boring into her, looking for a reaction.

'Jeff, I . . .' But before she could carry on he had launched into an impassioned speech, his words spilling over each other.

'I know it won't be easy for you to trust me again, and I deserve that. But I'm a different person from who I was. My time away from you all has made me look at things objectively and realise what I had. I've become a better father and I have learned to appreciate you again.'

He placed both hands on her shoulders and pulled her round to face him, his face just inches from hers. 'You're beautiful Jo, and you're honest and bright and a fantastic mother. I haven't said those things to you in a long time, and I damn well should have . . .'

Tears pricked Jo's eyes, and one ran down the side of her nose and into the corner of her mouth. She raised a gloved hand to wipe it away. She couldn't believe that, even after all this time, Jeff and the thought of their once happy marriage could still prompt such strong feelings.

'Mummy, that machine ate my last twenty pence,' said Thomas crossly, pointing at the offending object.

'Never mind, love,' she sniffed, hoping her son would put her red eyes down to the cold. 'It's time to go home now, anyway.'

When Jeff returned with an irate and indecisive Sophie still clutching her untouched £2 coin, they set off on the short walk home.

'We'll talk about it another time,' she whispered, thankful that Thomas's timely interruption had given her time to regain her composure. Jeff simply nodded in silent agreement.

By the time they reached home ten minutes later, Sophie was fast asleep in the piggy back position on Jeff's shoulder and Thomas was whinging for Britain with sheer bloody-minded exhaustion. While Jeff traipsed upstairs to put Sophie to bed and ordered Thomas to follow him, Jo wandered into the living room to check the answering machine.

There was one message. It crossed her mind that it might be Sean calling after their impromptu sex session, so quietly she closed the living-room door for privacy and pressed the 'play' button.

As she stood and listened to the disembodied voice crackling into the room, the blood drained from her face and she dropped Thomas's anorak to the floor in disbelief.

'Please God, no,' she whispered.

33

By the time she reached Oxford, in a state of great distress, her father was already dead. A massive heart attack, they said. Nothing they could do, sorry. So sudden and all that.

Jo simply couldn't comprehend that the man who had rarely suffered any ill health in his life, give or take the odd cold or two, had had this time bomb ticking away inside him undetected.

'There must have been something you could do,' she said, staring in unblinking shock at the young consultant who informed her that he had tried several times to jump-start her father's heart.

'We tried everything, Mrs Miles,' he said gently. 'There are still tests to be done, but I suspect it was the end result of a problem that had been building up for some time. It's remarkable he didn't have any symptoms before it happened.'

He probably did, thought Jo. But knowing Dad he would have ignored them, fought against them as a sign of weakness. He hated to show any trace of vulnerability, but he'd always been very indulgent to his children whenever they did.

She found her mother sitting in the hospital canteen,

staring into a cup of cold, untouched tea. Without a trace of make-up, she suddenly looked very old and frail.

Jo sat down, unfurled one of her mother's hands from the cup, and held it. Her touch seemed to stir Pam from her trance.

'Hello, dear, good journey?' she said.

Jo decided to ignore the trivial question and put it down to the denial some people suffer from after the sudden death of a loved one. Keeping her voice soft, she squeezed Pam's hand. 'What happened Mum?'

Pam pulled her hand away and placed it in her lap out of reach. Theirs had never been a tactile relationship.

'I don't really know, dear,' she said, picking up a napkin and mopping up a patch of spilt tea. 'One minute he was there, the next he was gone.'

'Talk me through it,' said Jo patiently. She felt curiously calm, strong even. Perhaps because she knew her mother needed her to be. 'Start with New Year's Eve.'

Pam launched into a laborious description of every cough and spit of their New Year's Eve. How Aunty Beryl and Uncle Bill had invited them round, how they'd decided not to go, how they'd watched repeats of *Only Fools and Horses*, then *The Best of Morecambe and Wise*, no, tell a lie, it was the other way round. Jo sighed and waited patiently for her to get to the point. She knew it was probably important for her mother to run through the day with precision.

'Your father had a couple of whiskies I think, and he

got very snappy when I said he shouldn't drink so much,' said Pam, her brow furrowing at the memory.

Unsurprising, thought Jo wearily. Christ, the poor bloke couldn't even have a New Year drink in his own home without being nagged about it.

'Then you called New Year's Day,' her mother continued, 'and we just pottered really. At about four, your father said he was going to his shed to clean his tools. It wasn't unusual for him to disappear in there for a couple of hours at a time.'

His blessed bolthole, thought Jo.

'Go on,' she said.

'At about six, I kept calling out of the back door to see if he wanted a cup of tea, but he didn't answer. So I put on my slippers – or was it my gardening shoes?'

'Mum, hardly relevant.'

But her mother wasn't listening. Her eyes hazy with tears, she had tilted her head back and was staring at the ceiling. 'He was still sitting on his stool,' she murmured, her voice cracked with emotion. 'He had slumped against the workbench and his eyes were half-open. He was still warm . . .'

'It's OK, Mum,' said Jo, moving round to sit next to her. She placed a comforting arm around her mother's shoulders, and this time Pam didn't pull away.

'I called the ambulance first, and then I rang you but you weren't there,' she said, blinking back tears.

Jo gave her a little squeeze. 'I was at the cinema with the children. I got here as soon as I could.'

'I thought there was still hope when I found him. But

now they tell me he had died instantly from a massive heart attack.' Pam stopped, seemingly distracted by a sullen woman clearing tables. 'I couldn't get hold of Tim either and he doesn't have a machine like you.'

Jo had taken her rarely used mobile with her on the fraught, torturous journey through road works to Oxford and called Tim's house at five-minute intervals. She finally got an answer at 10 p.m.

'Hello?' It was Conor.

'Hi, it's Jo.' Her voice was desperate. 'Is Tim there?'

'No, he's not. What is it?' Conor sounded scared.

'It's Dad,' she sobbed, taking care to watch the road ahead. 'He's had a heart attack.'

'Oh God . . . is he . . . is he . . . ?'

'That's the worst thing, I don't really know. I got home to find a message from Mum saying they were on their way to the hospital. I'm on my way there now.'

'Listen,' said Conor, taking control of the situation. 'You just get there safely and I'll worry about Tim. He's in the local having a pint. I'll go and get him.'

Jo had given him the hospital details, then driven the rest of the journey on automatic pilot, unaware that her father was already dead.

'Come on, Mum,' she said, lifting her listless mother by the arm. 'Let's go back up and find out what happens next.'

Five minutes after they'd asked to see the consultant again, and settled themselves down in the characterless waiting room of the Accident and Emergency department, Tim barged in through the doors.

'How is he?' His face was white.

Feeling sick, Jo calmly took his hand and pulled him onto the rigid plastic seat next to her.

'He's gone, love. Mum thought he was still alive when she found him, but it turns out he had died instantly. He didn't suffer.'

It was one of those knee-jerk, irrelevant things you say at such times, like 'At least he had a good innings', and it was probably true that he hadn't suffered. That was reserved for the loved ones left behind.

Neither Jo nor her mother had yet broken down, both frozen in shock, emotionally numbed by the suddenness of it all.

But Tim caved in instantly, huge, violent sobs racking his body. Jo stared at him wordlessly for a moment, unable to equate her flippant, carefree brother with the shaking creature that sat before her now.

Snapping out of her limbo-like state, she reached across and pulled him towards her, wrapping her slim arms around his bulky frame. With her chin resting on his shoulder, she rocked him gently backwards and forwards, murmuring, 'Ssssshhh', as she would to Thomas or Sophie if they'd hurt themselves.

After a few minutes, Tim seemed to calm down slightly. He stopped sobbing, but continued to cling on to his sister as if his own life depended on it. There were just the three of them in the room. Jo looked up when she heard the door creak open, expecting to see the consultant. It was Conor, concern etched on his face. To Jo, it seemed the most natural thing in the world that he should be there.

'Any news?' he mouthed at her.

'He's dead,' she whispered, feeling the first telltale prick of a tear. She hastily blinked it away, wanting to remain strong for Tim and her mother, who was sitting as still as a statue in the corner of the room.

'I'm so sorry.' Conor clearly felt uncomfortable to be encroaching on such a private family moment, and gestured he was going to get a cup of tea.

Half an hour later, Jo found him in the canteen, flicking aimlessly through some abandoned magazine about Country and Western music.

'How's Tim?' he asked, his face ghostly pale.

'I've left him and Mum comforting each other,' she said wearily. 'Well, they're holding hands and staring into space anyway. We've never been a very demonstrative family.'

'He was dreading the thought your father might die before we got here,' said Conor, closing the magazine and throwing it onto the seat behind him.

Jo let out a deep sigh. 'He died instantly. No one got the chance to say goodbye, not even Mum.' She felt numb, as if she were talking about someone else's father. 'Thanks for driving Tim here, by the way. I doubt he was in any fit state to make the journey alone.'

Conor wrinkled his forehead in the manner she'd seen

him do a thousand times before when he was anxious about something. He'd even done it as a little boy. 'It's the least I could do,' he said. 'I was immensely fond of Jim too.'

A small expression of surprise flickered across Jo's face. It had never struck her that Conor harboured any feelings for her parents, other than the minor acknowledgement that they had spawned his best friend. But when she thought about it, it made perfect sense because Conor had spent so much time with them through his troubled, formative years after his father had left home.

'I spent more time with your dad than my own,' he said, as if reading her mind. 'He was everything I wanted my father to be but, as you know, he never was.' His eyes looked watery.

'He was a great dad,' said Jo, nodding and smiling. 'I just can't work out why I haven't fallen to pieces like Tim. I just feel numb really.'

Conor reached across the table and placed a hand over hers. 'They say that sometimes deep shock can be a very dear friend at times like these,' he said softly.

His simple, physical gesture of kindness and concern made Jo's stomach turn over with the sheer stress of pent-up emotion. She didn't want this conversation to go any further now, or she knew she'd lose it completely, right here in this cold, soulless hospital building full of complete strangers.

'Come on,' she said, pulling him up and linking her arm through his. 'There are two people up there who need us to be strong.'

34

She knew it had sounded odd when she'd told Jeff about it on the phone later that day, but it had been a very uplifting funeral.

Despite being January, it was a crisp winter's day with a Tiffany-blue sky and watery sunshine. Everyone had made the effort to come. Conor, minus Emma, Rosie, Jim, lots of her father's former work colleagues, and an impressive turnout of his friends from the local Rotary club where he'd been a member for the past twenty years. Her mother remained remarkably calm, even throughout the moving speeches; one by Jim's old boss Reg Green, and another by Conor.

Tim was supposed to make one but at the last minute he just couldn't go through with it and had passed the emotional baton to his friend.

Struggling to keep his composure, Conor had cleared his throat and nervously informed the congregation that, as he'd had no time to prepare, his words were going to be straight from the heart.

'For various reasons I won't bore you with, I was never really close to my father as a young adult.' His voice was clear and concise and filled the tiny church without the need for a microphone. 'So, at that formative time of my life when I needed a father's guidance in the ways of the world, it was Jim who gave it to me.' He paused and gave a small smile. 'Jo and Tim probably have no idea, but that's because I never told them. I didn't want them to feel I was trying to take their father away from them. I wasn't, of course, and anyway, Jim was such an amazing man he would have had enough kindness to accommodate hundreds of children. He would often take me to one side and say, "Everything alright son?" Sometimes it was, sometimes it wasn't, and if it was the latter he always took the time to talk through any problems with me . . .' Conor faltered slightly and gave a little cough to clear his throat. 'He even called me for a confidential chat when he heard my long-term relationship had broken up.'

Jo raised her head and looked at him in surprise. She had no idea her father had done that.

'We all have a chocolate-box image of what a dad should be like,' Conor continued, 'and Jim was mine. I always felt very envious of Tim and Jo for that reason. He will be a terrible loss to us all, but particularly to his family. But I urge them to look at it from the perspective that they got many fantastic years of happiness with the kind of special man that others never even get to meet in their entire lifetime. Thank you.' He bowed his head and stepped down from the pulpit.

Jo had to use every ounce of willpower to stop the

tight knot of emotion in her chest from enveloping her. Blinking furiously to stop the tears, she stared at the central stained-glass window of the church and steered her thoughts to the practicalities of the wake. She looked sideways to see her mother sitting rigid, staring at the floor and wringing a small white handkerchief round and round her shaking hands.

'Come on, Mum,' she said gently. 'It's time to go home.'

Back at the house, her mother had put on a 'lovely spread', as she called it. The living room was spotless, every surface gleaming and emanating the unmistakable whiff of Pledge. A photograph of Jim, resplendent in dinner suit at his company's Christmas party, took pride of place in the centre of the highly polished wooden mantelpiece.

The noise level started off low, but soon became deafening as the room began to fill up with people arriving from the church.

'There's that old bat from Dad's accounts department,' whispered Jo to Tim, who had perked up slightly now the funeral was over. 'He always hated her, and now here she is stuffing her fat face with free sandwiches in his house.'

'That frock's bloody awful. She looks like a Mercedes airbag,' said Tim loudly in her direction. 'Fuck, I hate this kind of thing.'

'Well, I suppose you'd be a little odd if you were actually enjoying your father's funeral.' Conor had joined them.

Tim slapped him on the back. 'Thanks for the speech, mate, it was great. I had no idea you were that close to Dad.'

'We weren't close as such. I think he just looked out for me occasionally because he knew I didn't have a male role model in my life.' He smiled at Jo. 'You OK?'

'Fine.' She let out a long sigh. 'I hate these things too. I'm just going for a little wander.'

She walked through to the kitchen, away from the noise, unlocked the back door and went down the steps leading to her parents' long and blissfully quiet garden. Halfway down was her father's shed, its door still padlocked.

Jo stooped down and ran her fingers under the bottom lip of the door. There, buried in the soft earth where it had always been kept, was the key. Fumbling with nerves, she unlocked the weather-beaten door and stepped inside. The first thing that hit her was the familiar smell that had assailed her senses as a child, a mix of grass, 3-in-1 oil, and old cigarette smoke.

Everything was as it had always been. Her father's stool was placed against the wall he used as a backrest, and the tools he so lovingly kept pristine were laid out in lines on the gnarled workbench. It was a scene of such tranquillity that Jo found it hard to imagine her father had actually died there.

Tucked under the workbench, she spotted a smaller stool, the one her father had always pulled out when she or Tim came in to chat to him. She'd spent hours there, asking him what that tool was for, why did grass stain so badly, why was the sky blue. Endless questions that he had always answered patiently and in meticulous detail.

She wondered whether he missed those days when he was sitting alone in his shed in later life. It must have felt odd for them both when she and Tim left home and they were left with only each other for company.

Some parents breathe a sigh of relief and relish their time alone together, some are left wondering whatever they had in common. Jo reluctantly suspected her parents were in the latter category.

As she turned to leave, she caught sight of her father's old cardigan hanging on the back of the shed door and her breath caught in her throat. Reaching out, she took it from the peg, pressed it to her face and inhaled. It smelt over-poweringly of him. Stumbling backwards, she crouched on the floor and let out a small, whimpering noise. Within seconds, her body was shaking with violent sobs and she buried her face in the cardigan to muffle the sound. She sat there for at least half an hour, rocking backwards and forwards and letting out all the pent-up anguish of the past few days. She didn't hear the door open, but jumped as a shadow fell across the floor.

'I wondered where you'd got to.' It was Conor.

'I came down here for a spot of reflection and seem to have got myself into a bit of a state,' she said, standing up and wiping her face with the back of her sleeve.

'Come here.' Conor held his arms out and took a step towards her.

Burying her face in his chest, Jo took a deep breath and let it out slowly, feeling safe and secure. She was utterly comfortable, just standing there, being held by the man who was proving to be one of her dearest friends.

'Life is going to feel so strange without him.' Her chin pressed against the rough wool of Conor's sweater, her voice sounded muffled.

'More so for your mum. You and Tim will have to keep a close eye on her for a while. She's going to need you.'

'For the first time ever . . .' She trailed off and straightened her back to face him. 'Thanks for the hug. You go back and I'll follow in a minute. I just need to let my face calm down a bit.'

'Oh, I don't know. I'm told the piggy-eyed look is very in this year.' Conor smiled and tweaked the end of her nose. 'See you in a minute.'

When Jo got back to the house, red-eyed but composed, her mother was in whirling dervish mode, running around with trays of canapés and vast pitchers of orange juice.

She had been baking, marinading, buttering and chopping for two days, and Jo was powerless to stop her, despite trying to help out on a number of occasions. She soon realised that the job in hand – however trivial – was keeping her mother from falling apart. Jo knew it would be the time after the funeral that would be the hardest of all, when there was nothing else for her mother to do other than accept that the man she'd been married to for thirty-seven years had gone forever.

Many people had told her that there might be some small thing that would trigger the grieving process, and

Jo felt she had just experienced her own example of that in her father's shed. She was determined to be there for her mother whenever her trigger moment happened.

So Jeff took the week off work to stay with the children in London, and Jo stayed with her mother waiting for the first sign of emotional meltdown. She didn't have to wait long – it happened the morning after the funeral.

Jo was resting in the spare bedroom, staring at the Colgate-white net curtains and thinking about her father, when she heard a low-pitched wailing noise like that of a wounded animal. At first, she thought it was cats fighting, but then it rose to such a crescendo that she was on her feet in two seconds and running for the door.

Her mother lay across the yellow candlewick counterpane of her bed, her face buried in the folds. In her clenched fist there was a hairbrush.

'Mum, what is it?' said Jo, placing a hand on her back. Of course, she knew what it was, but she was frightened she'd be unable to deal with it.

She wasn't sure at what point she'd realised her parents weren't the infallible, invincible beings she'd spent her childhood thinking they were, but she'd certainly never seen such visible proof of it as she was witnessing right now.

'It's his brush. It was in his side drawer and it still has his hair in it,' wept her mother, her words barely distinguishable through the sobbing.

'Come here.' Jo sat on the edge of the bed and pulled her mother's shaking body towards her. 'Let it all out,

Mum. I had a good old sob yesterday when I found his cardigan in the shed, and I felt so much better afterwards.'

Wrapping her arms tighter, Jo squeezed and rocked with Pam in a reassuring motion. It was the first prolonged hug they had ever shared.

35

Through her mother's grief, Jo learned more about her father in the few days after his death than she had ever known during his life. She sat fascinated for hours as her mother relayed detailed anecdotes of their life together, and of how they'd first met.

'I had gone alone to this do and was placed next to him,' said Pam, her pale, tired eyes shining at the memory. 'When I sat down, I remember thinking, "He looks a bit of a bore," but by the end of the night I was completely in love with him. He made me laugh like no one else.'

'So did he ask you out that night?' said Jo, avid to hear the beginnings of the relationship that spawned her.

'No, he didn't. In fact, he didn't even attempt to flirt with me which I was a little put out by, I remember. But I found out later that he had a girlfriend at the time, so consequently I liked him even more for not pursuing me.'

'So how did you get together?' frowned Jo. She had only ever heard the shortened version that they had met at a dinner dance.

'Oooh, it was at least six months later, and he came into the sweet shop I was working in at the time. It turned out the girlfriend had found someone else, but he said he was secretly quite pleased because he had been very taken with me when we first met but had been too much of a gentleman to do anything about it.'

On another occasion, while rummaging through a box of old photographs, her mother's eyes had misted over when she came across a picture of Jo at a few days old.

'Your father took this on a camera he borrowed from a friend. We didn't have much money in those days,' she said. 'He was besotted by you, cried his eyes out, he did, when you were born. He was mortified that the doctor saw him break down, but he couldn't stop himself.'

Jo smiled. 'I always knew he was a big softie under that composed exterior.'

There had been many more reminiscences about her parents' past that Jo had never been privy to. Then, one overcast morning, they were sitting together in silence in her mother's small kitchen.

'So, how are things in your life?' said Pam, seemingly apropos of nothing.

The question took Jo by surprise, a non sequitur after two days in the emotional hothouse of her mother's devastation and sense of loss.

'How are things with me?' she parroted, letting out a long breath. 'Well, where do I start?'

If her mother had asked her the question two weeks ago, she would have batted it aside with the answer 'Fine', fearing a deluge of self-righteous remarks and lectures would come her way if she told the absolute truth. But in the past few days they had shared so much, and become far closer than before, that Jo felt totally comfortable telling all. In fact, she *wanted* to.

'Are you ready for this?' she smiled, then took a deep breath and launched into a meandering monologue that brought her mother entirely up to date on the disaster zone that was her daughter's personal life. Her relationship with Sean, finding out he was married, how he said he would leave his wife for her, and how she was still all mixed up about it. It was the first time she had admitted the last bit to anyone, even herself.

'Do you love him?' Her mother looked at her unblinkingly, through red-rimmed eyes swollen from prolonged crying.

'I don't know,' said Jo, and it was the truth. She knew she had very strong feelings towards Sean, but she didn't know whether they were caused by genuine emotion or merely the roller-coaster drama of the relationship. 'But I do know I would find it very hard to cause the same devastation to another family that was done to mine.'

Pam stretched her arms up in the air and turned to look out of the window. 'Except that it would be Sean doing the real damage, not you. They're his family and no one forced him to start his affair with you. It's the same story with Jeff.'

Jo stared at the back of her mother's head for a few moments, blinking with incomprehension at what she'd just heard. No lecture, not even a sanctimonious remark. Just an observation that, uncharacteristically for Pam, sounded like support.

Jo resisted the overwhelming urge to say, 'Bloody hell, you've changed your tune', and carried on with her revelations. 'Jeff's affair is over and he wants us to get back together,' she said matter-of-factly, waiting for her mother to start doing cartwheels around the room.

Instead, Pam turned to face her and slowly raised her eyebrows. 'Really? And how do you feel about that?'

Jo sighed. 'No idea. Ten minutes after he suggested it I found out about Dad and I've hardly given it another thought since.'

'I see.' Her mother went back to staring out of the window. A slight drizzle had begun to fall.

Jo felt anxious at her mother's lack of response. 'I know I should give it serious consideration because of the children,' she said, 'but I think I would find it very hard to get things back on track with Jeff after everything that's happened.'

Her mother stood up to open the kitchen window a couple of inches, then returned to her chair and pulled it closer to Jo. She sat and looked at her daughter for a moment or two, something clearly on her mind. After a while, she cleared her throat.

'Your father had an affair.'

Jo felt like she'd been punched in the centre of her forehead, and reeled slightly on her chair. There was no mistaking her mother's clearly spoken words. She stared in disbelief and whispered, 'Sorry?'

'Hard to believe, isn't it?' said Pam, with a thin smile. 'I had no idea of it and I was his wife living under the same roof.'

Jo's brain was pounding with questions she wanted answered, but she couldn't get a proper train of thought together. 'So . . . when?'

Her mother took a sharp intake of breath. 'Oh, years ago. You were about twelve so Tim must have been, oh, seven I suppose.'

'How did you find out?'

'I was told by a local woman who had always disliked me,' said Pam, absent-mindedly scraping her nail backwards and forwards over a mark on the table. 'Do you remember Betty Mayhew? She worked in the corner shop.'

'Um, vaguely.'

'Anyway,' said Pam briskly, 'we had a little disagreement about something and she blurted it out. She said something like, "No wonder your husband needs another woman to keep him happy."'

Jo gasped and placed a hand over her mouth at the thought of such nastiness, but her mother ignored her and carried on.

'So when Jim got home that night, I recounted the incident to him and he broke down and confessed everything.'

Fearful that her mother was going to wear a hole in the table with her persistent scraping, Jo leaned across and gently took her hand. She squeezed it softly as she listened to the whole story.

It turned out the woman was a forty-five-year-old widow from the Rotary Club who was known to both Pam and Jim. She had lost her husband to cancer the previous year, and Pam had given Jim her blessing to help the woman with the occasional odd job that needed a man's touch.

'Trouble is, he ended up touching *her* and the odd jobs became rather more frequent as a cover for their grubby little activities,' said her mother bitterly. 'I still didn't suspect because Jim was such a moral man. I never dreamed he would behave like that.'

'So when you confronted him he ended it?' said Jo, leaping to an understandable assumption considering her parents had stayed together.

'God no. He said he was going to leave us for her. Can you believe that? I begged, I raged, I wept, I tried absolutely everything to persuade him to stay.'

'Well, it obviously worked.' Jo gave a small smile, but inside she felt her heart had been wrenched in two. She felt sorry for her mother, but in truth her pain was for herself in having to face the cold, harsh reality that perhaps her father hadn't been a whiter than white hero after all.

'He stayed, yes,' said her mother in a small voice. 'But not because of me. He stayed purely because he couldn't bear to leave you and Tim. It was "For the sake of the children," as they say.'

Jo squeezed her mother's hand tighter and they sat in silence, united by the curious bond of both being cheated on by their husbands. After a couple of minutes, Jo stood up and filled the kettle for a restorative cup of tea.

'He never forgave me for it,' said Pam, looking up at her. 'I always felt he hated me for not being her. He gave her up, but it was like living with a ghost after that. I always felt he was thinking about her.'

'I'm sure he wasn't really,' said Jo reassuringly. 'After all, you stayed together long after Tim and I left home, so it can't have been for our sake then, can it?'

'No, but she wasn't an option for him by then, anyway. A couple of years after he ended their affair she married someone else from the Rotary Club. I suspect it broke Jim's heart.' A small tear ran down the side of Pam's nose. She wiped her face quickly with the back of her hand. 'I loved him dearly,' she sniffed. 'But I think I've cried enough for him now, not least in the years when he was still alive. I tried hard to be the perfect wife after he'd decided to stay, because I felt so pathetically grateful.' She stopped for a moment and stared into space. 'I would cook, clean, iron, keep myself looking nice, never disagree with him, whatever it took to make him feel he'd made the right decision by staying. But he had all the power after that, and whatever I did wasn't enough. It wasn't a marriage, we just existed under the same roof.'

Placing two piping hot mugs of tea on the table, Jo sat down again. 'I must say Tim and I noticed you were very tense with each other over Christmas,' she said, taking a tentative sip and feeling the piping hot liquid slip down her throat.

'Christmas, Easter, Shrove Tuesday, a Thursday, whatever,' recited Pam flatly. 'We were tense with each other most of the time but usually did a good job of disguising it whenever you or Tim were around. After you two left home we didn't have to bother any more and the atmosphere in the house was at worst bloody awful, at best bearable. Your father retreated to his shed most of the time, and I turned into this nagging, bitter old woman. I was the monster he made me.' She stopped speaking and took a mouthful of tea.

'You're not a monster, Mum,' said Jo quietly. 'You were obviously dreadfully unhappy, and now I know why. I'm so sorry.'

Her mother smiled, a genuine, warm smile. 'What are you apologising for, you daft thing,' she said, ruffling Jo's hair. 'Little Jo, apologist extraordinaire. You've always been too caring for your own good, do you know that?'

'I've toughened up a bit lately.'

'Good. So what is the new tough Jo going to do about her marriage?' said Pam, straightening her back and smoothing down her voluminous Fair Isle sweater.

'Oh Gawd,' she groaned, staring up at the ceiling. 'I thought it was over for good and had kind of reconciled myself to that, and now my mind is in turmoil again.'

'Want my advice?' Her mother raised her eyebrows questioningly.

'Yes, particularly after the conversation we've just had,' smiled Jo.

'Make the decision based purely on your feelings for Jeff and don't muddy it with thoughts of what's best for the children,' said Pam firmly. 'They have already got used to the idea that you've split up, so whatever damage may have been done – and I doubt there's much – has been done already.' She stopped speaking and stared at Jo for a few moments before continuing. 'If you're going to get back with Jeff, you have to be damned sure *he* is what you want, because you mustn't put the kids through a second break-up. If you're unsure, it's best to leave it as it is.'

'What, stay single for the rest of my life?' said Jo forlornly.

'No, that's not what I mean.' Her mother gave an exasperated sigh. 'I'm saying that from this standpoint, you should choose the man you think *you* can happily spend the rest of your life with.'

'I thought that when I married Jeff.'

'Yes, but we all think that in our idealistic twenties. Then the reality of having children and struggling to make ends meet kicks in and it's a miracle any marriage survives.' She took a mouthful of tea. 'You're more mature and realistic now. You've had the children and suffered the knocks and you know better what you want from a man. I'm sure whatever decision you make will be the right one for your long-term happiness.'

Jo was momentarily stunned by her mother's rational,

common sense outlook. She's right, she thought. I'm a different person now. I'm not even the same woman I was a couple of years ago, never mind ten years back when I married Jeff.

Fortified by this revelation, she decided to bite the bullet. 'There's someone else too,' she said, wincing as she said it.

Her mother laughed and shook her head. 'What, apart from Jeff and Sean?'

'Yes, but nothing's happened. It's not sexual or anything,' said Jo hastily, suddenly reverting to a young girl again, fearful of her mother's disapproval.

Pam looked slightly bemused. 'So what is it then? A flirtation?'

'Sort of, but a bit more than that really. It's the man I've been working for as an interior decorator. I've known him for eighteen months and we've become good friends,' said Jo, rummaging in her handbag for Martin's business card. She found it and placed it on the table in front of her mother, who picked it up.

'Chairman eh?' A shadow of doubt suddenly crossed Pam's face. 'He's not married as well, is he?'

'No,' laughed Jo. 'He's very much single and the perfect gentleman. It was all very businesslike for a while, then a few months ago he said he'd like us to start dating.'

'And?'

'And I said I would think about it, but that I'd like us to continue as friends for a while, which he accepted,' said Jo with finality.

'Hmm, sounds like you're not that keen,' said Pam.

Jo shook her head. 'No, that's not true. I just know he's the kind of man I couldn't mess about with. If I started to see him in that way, I suspect it would get very serious very quickly, so I would want to be absolutely sure he was the one I wanted.'

'What's he like?'

Jo's face lit up. 'Incredible. It's hard to describe, but he just sorts everything out. There never seem to be any problems when he's around. You feel that if you suddenly fell backwards, he'd be there to catch you. When I rang to tell him about Dad's death, he was amazing. He said he would get his lawyers to deal with any legal matters for us, free of charge, and he organised that beautiful flower arrangement from the children, you know, the one on Dad's coffin.'

'Goodness me, you *are* spoilt for choice,' said Pam, raising her eyebrows. 'Jeff, Sean, and now . . .' she paused to look at the business card '. . . Martin Blake. Anyone else I should know about?'

Jo smiled and shook her head slowly. 'No, that's it.'

Conor's face popped into her mind as she said it. He had been occupying her thoughts quite a bit lately, but she put it down to his involvement with the family after her father's death. A few hours after comforting her in the shed, he had driven a dishevelled, over-emotional Tim back to London, then called Jo to reassure her that he was OK.

'I've just tucked him up in bed with a hot water bottle and he's out for the count. He's completely drained,' he said.

409

'Poor love,' said Jo. 'Look, at the risk of being tediously repetitive, thanks for everything.'

Conor made a snoring noise down the phone. 'If you say that one more time I'm going to put you across my knee and spank you,' he growled.

'Ooh . . . thanks, thanks, thanks,' she laughed.

After a couple more minutes of idle chitchat about the weather and how her mother was bearing up, Jo couldn't help herself.

'So, how's Emma?' she asked casually. 'I hope she didn't mind you disappearing up here at such short notice.'

'She's fine. It was no problem,' he said quickly. 'So when are you coming back home?'

'The end of the week I think,' she said. 'Mum seems okayish now and I think Jeff has gone into shock at having to deal with the children on his own for a few days. Still, at least he knows what I deal with every day now, so it's no bad thing.'

'Oh, I'm sure Candy has been helping him out,' said Conor sarcastically. 'You know, baking home cookies and stuff.'

'God, I completely forgot to tell you in all the trauma of the past few days, they've split up. She dumped him for being too old.' Jo giggled nervously as she said the last bit, but there was a palpable pause on the other end of the line.

'So what happens now?' said Conor in a measured tone.

410

'Not much,' she hedged. 'He says he wants us to get back together, but I'm not sure that's such a good idea.'

Conor cleared his throat. 'Well, never say never. Maybe you can give it some serious thought when you're back home. Thomas and Sophie would love it, so I suppose that's a major consideration.'

Jo found herself feeling curiously disappointed that he was being so objective about her situation. It wasn't that she expected him to profess undying love for her, but she had rather thought he might express a trace of agitation over her news about Jeff.

'You may be right,' she sighed. 'Either way, there's no rush. It won't hurt to let him stew for a while.'

As Jo sat in silence remembering their conversation, her mother's voice broke into her thoughts.

'Well, love,' she sighed. 'All I can say is you're going to have to be a teensy weensy bit selfish on this one and choose for yourself. Otherwise you might end up like me, sharing your later years with a man you no longer have anything in common with.'

Jo smiled, a broad, warm grin. 'Thanks Mum. You have absolutely no idea how much this little chat has helped me.'

Her mother smiled back, tears in her eyes. 'I'm just so sorry it has taken me this long to be a proper mum to you.'

'Bollocks.' Jo winced for fear of a ticking off, but none was forthcoming. 'I hadn't told you any of this before, so you couldn't have advised me, could you?'

'Yes, but why hadn't you told me?' said Pam. Then, not waiting for an answer, 'Because you felt you couldn't, that's why. You felt I might not be on your side, and it's unforgivable that you were probably right. I was in denial about everything, including your unhappiness.'

Jo tutted her disapproving rejection of this remark and shook her head. 'That's not true. I was in denial myself for a while, but oddly Dad's death has made things a lot clearer for me. Corny I know, but it's taught me to seize the day, as they say. You never know when it might be too late.'

'Precisely!' said her mother triumphantly. 'I'm the classic example of that, but it's not too late for you.'

They chinked their tea mugs together in a toast to Jo's bright new future, whatever it might be.

36

Jeff was already at the restaurant when she arrived, a half-empty bottle of wine on the table.

'Hi, sorry I'm late. Surprise, surprise, Tim was late getting to the house, so I had to hang around.'

'That's alright. Drink?' He looked nervous.

'Thanks.' She watched as he poured her a glass of Pinot Grigio. 'So how was your day?'

'How was my day?' He looked amused. 'How very formal. It was fine, thanks. Much like any other day in fact.'

There was an awkwardness between them, something Jo put down to what they both knew was coming, rather than a genuine inability to converse any more.

When she had called to say she was returning home from her mother's, Jeff had suggested this dinner for two nights later. 'We need to talk,' he'd said.

Jo knew he wanted to continue the conversation they'd started on the Common, the night she learned of her father's death. She also knew he wanted an answer.

'So.' He poured himself more wine. Obviously, he had one thing on his mind. Jo's glass was untouched.

So. Such a small word, but on this occasion so loaded with meaning, she thought. She straightened her back in anticipation.

'So have you thought any more about what I said on New Year's Day?' he asked, looking directly at her.

'Of course I have,' said Jo carefully. 'In between fretting about Dad, of course. I've been doing a lot of thinking about all sorts of things actually.'

'And?'

'And what?'

He gave an exasperated sigh. 'I can see you're going to make this difficult. Still, can't say I blame you. *And what* . . . did you decide about us?'

Jo stayed quiet for a moment, inwardly weary at the thought of the conversation about to follow. 'I decided it won't work between us.' She took a small sip of wine. 'Sorry, but that's how I feel.'

'I see.' A small muscle was twitching in the side of his cheek and he started to blink rapidly. 'And why's that?'

She'd rehearsed the answer to this over and over in her head, but now she was sitting opposite him, her mind went blank.

'I don't know.'

'I don't know,' he parroted. 'And that's a good basis on which to end this marriage, is it?'

'This marriage ended when we got our divorce papers, Jeff. And it ended because *you* went off with someone else.

What we're here to discuss is whether I can forgive you enough for us to start all over again.'

'And from what you've said, you clearly can't.' His eyes were dull.

'No, actually I *can* forgive you. In fact, I did a long time ago. But I don't feel I can trust you, and that's my problem with getting back together.'

They fell into silence for a few moments. Jeff stared at her through narrowed eyes. 'Couldn't I earn your trust back?' he said eventually.

'Maybe, maybe not. I'm not prepared to take that risk. The children seem to have got used to us being apart now. I couldn't bear for them to go through it all a second time, so I'd rather keep things as they are.' She started to eat her usual spaghetti Bolognese, desperate for the meal to be over now she'd had her say. But Jeff clearly wasn't going to take no for an answer.

'Jo, I *promise* you I won't be unfaithful.'

'Didn't you pledge that during our wedding vows as well?' She knew it was a cheap shot, but she was determined not to be talked out of her decision.

He raised his eyebrows. 'Yes, one-nil to you, I did. But I was younger then. Now I know what pain and disruption infidelity can cause, and for what? I'm on my own, away from my kids, and away from you. It's unbearable.' His eyes started to well with tears.

'I know it's unbearable Jeff. I've been through it myself, remember? But I feel stronger now and I also like myself a lot more. I couldn't go back to how we were.'

'We don't have to.' He sat up straight, looking excited at the thought. 'We could start from scratch and lay out new ground rules. We could get a nanny, and you could work full-time if you like.'

'Whoopee. Thanks,' she said flatly.

'We could do whatever *you* want. You at least owe it to the children to give it some consideration.' He stood up. 'I need the loo.'

So there it was. Jo's carte blanche to write her own marital guidelines, to finally call the shots with the errant husband who had caused her so much suffering. He wanted to pick up the pieces of the marriage *he'd* smashed and start all over again, playing happy families. It was neat and tidy, that's for sure. The children would love it, and they wouldn't suffer the stigma of coming from a 'broken home', if there was such a stigma these days. But could she ever get over the reality that it was Jeff who had broken it in the first place? Would every argument or rough patch they ever had make her think he could walk out of the door again at any moment? She had already given a lot of thought to whether she could overcome that fear.

Jeff arrived back at the table.

'It wouldn't work,' she said.

'Why? *Why* wouldn't it work?'

Jo took a deep breath and let it out slowly. 'Because whenever you said you were going to be late home from

416

work, I'd think you were seeing someone else. Because every time we made love, I'd think about all the times you did it with her. Because every time we had an argument about the slightest thing, I'd throw the Candy business back in your face, time and time and time again, and I'd hate myself for it.' She paused and looked at Jeff who was staring at the tablecloth. 'No relationship could survive all that.'

Pushing his untouched plate of food to one side, Jeff looked up. 'Some people get over it.'

'I know they do. But I'm not capable of being one of them. I need to trust someone one hundred per cent to have a relationship with them.'

'Like you trusted Sean?' His tone was sarcastic.

'I trusted him because I had no reason not to. Just like I trusted you enough to get married and have two children. But starting a relationship with someone you *know* has already abused your trust, is not something I can do.'

Jeff brushed away a tear with the back of his hand. His expression hardened. 'So that's it then, is it? The kids will spend the rest of their lives in a separate home to their father.'

'Don't throw that one at me Jeff. You walked out, not me. If you hadn't, we'd still be married.'

'But instead you want to die a lonely old woman, do you? Just like your mother.'

'Leave my mother out of this.' She could see the conversation was taking a nasty turn. 'Let's get the bill.'

They sat in sullen silence whilst Jo silently willed the waiter to hurry up. Now Jeff had finally got the message, she couldn't wait to leave.

After a few moments, he started to rummage in his pocket. 'I'll get this. You go home. I can see you're dying to.' His tone was icy, but Jo almost preferred it that way. It made it easier for her. She stood up and pulled her coat from the back of the chair.

'Thanks.' She leaned down and gave him a peck on the cheek. 'And I'm really sorry, I just can't do it.'

Jeff didn't answer, he just continued staring at his wine glass.

'I'll see you in the morning then. The kids are looking forward to seeing you.'

Still no answer. She managed to reach the pavement outside before the tears flowed. Fumbling for her car keys, she hastily started the engine and drove off before Jeff followed. If he followed.

A few streets away, she pulled over again and leaned back against the headrest. They weren't the racking sobs of the early days of the break-up, just tears of sadness for a lost marriage that had once been so rewarding.

'Wotcha.' Tim peered at her as she walked in the living-room door. 'Oh dear, you look a bit raw around the eyeballs.'

'I am, but I'm OK.' She walked out and headed for the kitchen. Tim followed.

'So how'd it go?' he said, filling the kettle.

'It was awful.' She started to cry again.

'It can't have been worse than when he left you.' He rubbed her arm and pulled out a chair for her.

'Oh, it's not about him and me any more. It's more that he's the father of my children and they'd be ecstatic if we got back together. Their faces kept popping into my head as I was telling him we have no future together.'

Tim sat down at the table. 'Ah, that answers my next question. So you've definitely decided there's no going back?'

'Definitely. Believe me, I've changed my mind a million times over the past couple of days, weighing up every option and getting sentimental about the good times. But as soon as I saw him tonight in the restaurant, I knew it was over. I'd never trust him again.'

'People can get over those things,' said Tim quietly.

'Maybe. But I can't. Mum and Dad didn't either.' She had told Tim about their father's affair as soon as she returned from Pam's. He had seemed unsurprised and said it explained a lot.

'True, but they were a different generation. We're supposed to be all modern and liberated.' He gave her a small smile.

'Sorry, but when it comes to infidelity I'm very old-fashioned.' Jo took a sip of her tea and eased herself out of her jacket. 'Anyway, love rekindled, like a cigar relit, is never the same, they say. So it's the single life for me for a while.'

'Well, at least that's your choice. Some of us don't bloody have one. Singledom chooses us,' said Tim, pulling a gloomy face. 'Pardon the expression, but you've got men coming out of your ears.'

'Not quite. But anyway, none of them are right for me.'

'I still can't believe you didn't even give it a go with that Martin bloke. All that money . . .' Tim winced in mock pain.

Jo smiled. 'You're as bad as Rosie, trying to sell me off to the highest bidder. You know what they say, marrying for money is the hardest way to get it.'

'But I thought you said he was really nice.'

'He was. He still is. But "really nice" isn't enough for me to give it a go. There has to be more than that. Anyway, he was . . . er . . . really nice about it when I told him.'

'Poor bloke. He waited in the wings all that time, only to have you say it wasn't going to happen.'

'I know, I did feel awful about that. But I felt I owed it to him to give his suggestion some proper thought. Because I didn't know he was interested in me in *that* way, I'd never mulled it over.'

Tim looked thoughtful. 'Do you think you'll stay friends?'

'Oh, yes. In fact, when I went round there and told him the other night, he was a complete gentleman about it and said he hoped I would still carry on doing his French home and that, sometimes, we could still go out for dinner as friends. He's a man in a million.'

'Not to mention a man *with* a million, and more besides.' Tim stood up and placed their empty cups in the sink. 'Right, I'm off. What are you up to tomorrow?'

Jo sighed. 'Laughing boy is coming round in the morning to take the kids out, so no doubt that will be a frosty start to the day. Apart from that, nothing. Just sitting around here being morose, I suspect.'

'Sounds unmissable!' Tim gave her a peck on the cheek and started to walk towards the door. 'I'll give you a call and see how you are. Ciao.'

After he'd gone, Jo sat in the kitchen for a few more minutes, relishing the silence and mulling over their conversation. She did indeed want someone kind and trustworthy like Martin. He'd been such a pillar of practical strength to her recently, and she also knew that if she chose him she would be made for life. Not just financially, but for emotional security as well. Martin was the kind of man who made decisions in life and stuck to them. He would never walk out on his wife and two children. It was a tempting package, she thought, but there also had to be that vital spark that everyone always talks about but so rarely finds.

Suddenly, whilst staring at the oven, a flashback popped into her mind and a realisation smacked her straight in the face.

37

Jo stood on the doorstep and kissed each of the children on their cold, pink cheeks.

'Bye you two. Be good.'

Jeff stood on the pavement looking sullen, having refused her offer to step inside the house.

'No thanks. We'd better get off. I've got a busy day planned for them.' His voice had been cold.

Closing the door, Jo leaned her back against it for a moment. The thought occurred to her that she should grab her coat, run outside, and suggest a nice, family day out. But she dismissed it as quickly as it had arrived. It wasn't a precedent she wanted to set now she'd made her point about the future.

It was 10 a.m., and she decided to run herself a long bath, then worry about what to do with the rest of the day after that. As she was pouring in a generous measure of her 'special occasions' Jo Malone lime and mandarin bath oil, she heard the faint sound of the doorbell downstairs.

'God, what now!' she muttered aloud. 'You can't even have the kids for five minutes without forgetting something.'

She opened the door and felt her heart leap violently. It was Conor.

'Hi. A little bird told me you'd be sitting at home feeling sorry for yourself, so I thought I'd come and cheer you up.' He held up an overflowing Marks & Spencer carrier bag. 'I'm going to cook you lunch . . . or rather, I'm going to heat you up some lunch.'

Jo was so pleased to see him, it almost hurt. There is a God, she thought.

'I was going to have a bath, but how could a girl refuse such a kind offer?' she smiled, stepping to one side to let him past. She followed him into the kitchen, her insides churning with nerves.

'Put this in the fridge for later.' He handed her a bottle of champagne.

Jo did as he asked, but felt like she was on automatic pilot, going through mundane motions when all she wanted to do was blurt out what had been playing through her mind constantly since Tim had left the previous night. Jo was a big believer in fate, and she felt it had delivered Conor to her doorstep this morning for a reason.

He started to unpack the carrier bag, placing items in the fridge whilst chatting away about how they might venture out after lunch if the weather stayed nice.

'Conor. I want to talk to you.'

Despite the whole day stretching ahead of them, Jo wanted to tell Conor right now. It had been there, staring her in the face the entire time, and she'd been too damn stupid to see it. Too side-tracked by the reptilian Sean to realise that everything she wanted in a man was here in Conor Davies, mate of her brother and now close friend of hers too.

She knew it was a risk to broach the subject, because since his initial suggestion they try dating, he'd shown no further interest. And of course, there was still Emma to consider. But it was a gamble Jo wanted to take . . . *had* to take for her own peace of mind.

Nervously, she gestured to one of the rattan chairs. 'Sit down.'

'Sounds like bad news.'

'No, it isn't. Although, it could be for me.'

'Okay, now you really *have* lost me.'

She got the strange feeling he was slightly relishing her discomfort. 'Right . . . well . . . um . . . let's see,' she blathered.

'Would you like to phone a friend?' he smiled.

'That's just it Conor. *You're* my friend, but you're also much more than that. You've been such a support to me over Dad's death and everything and I . . .' The words stuck in her throat.

'And you want to thank me from the bottom of your heart?' His eyes had a mocking glint.

She ignored him. 'And I was wondering,' she took a deep breath, 'whether you still had any feelings for me?'

There was a long silence as he looked at her, a thoughtful expression on his face. 'What kind of feelings?'

'The kind you said you had . . . before,' she said, faltering.

He looked puzzled, then slightly irritated. 'Jo, what exactly is it you'd like to know?'

It crossed her mind to just leave the subject and get on with her life. But she *had* to know, even if it meant rejection. So she took another deep breath and closed her eyes. 'I want to know whether there's still a chance for you and me.' She opened her eyes and looked straight at him, waiting for a response.

There wasn't one. Almost thirty seconds passed and he was still staring fixedly at the table. The wait was interminable.

'Well?' she said hopefully, tilting her head to try and see his expression. Her heart was hammering with the anxiety that he was about to say no.

Eventually, he cleared his throat and looked at her. 'On what basis? There's a lot at stake here.'

He didn't specify what, but she presumed he was referring to Emma, as well as possibly Thomas and Sophie. Either way, he hadn't dismissed her completely, and that gave her the confidence to go on.

She dragged her chair closer to his and took hold of his hand. 'Look, I know I have been a total pain in the arse, knocking you back for something shallow with a man who turned out to be married. And I know I have a failed marriage behind me and two children to consider. Let's face it, I'm a nightmare date,' she paused and tried to smile.

'But I've been doing a lot of thinking lately, particularly since Dad died, and it cleared my head in many ways. I realise now that I've always had a bit of a thing for you on the quiet, but when we got together so soon after the Jeff business it terrified me. I didn't want it to go wrong, because there was so much to lose. So I went the other way and shunned you.' She stopped and squeezed his hand.

He gave her a weak smile. 'That's for sure. You made the Ice Queen seem warm and cuddly.'

'Well, I want to make up for that now. I'm in love with you Conor, and I think I have probably been in love with you for a long time. I was just too all over the place to notice. I just wanted to tell you how I felt . . . I needed you to know. I could kick myself for not working it all out earlier, before you met Emma and everything became more complicated.'

He sighed and sat back in his chair. 'Ah yes, Emma.'

'Do you still . . . you know . . . love her and everything?' It felt like her tongue had swollen to three times its natural size.

'And everything?' he said, a twinkle in his eye. 'Oh yes, definitely and everything.'

The mere thought of Conor doing *anything* with Emma, never mind everything, was enough to make Jo want to throw up.

'Oh, I see.' She said it with as much brightness as she could muster, but inside she was fighting sweeping waves of nausea at the thought she might have lost her chance with this wonderful, gorgeous man. 'Well, look, I've said my piece and I fully understand that my timing is absolutely appalling and that you're in love with someone else now, but I wanted you to know how I felt anyway and . . .'

'Shut up.'

'Sorry?'

'I said shut up.'

'Oh, sorry.'

'Stop saying bloody sorry.' He stood up and turned to face her.

'You look angry,' she said, looking up at him.

'I am angry.'

'Why?'

'Because you're a selfish pain in the arse who has been so wrapped up in herself she hasn't been able to see the nose on the end of her face.'

'What do you mean?'

Conor let out a long sigh. Kneeling in front of her, he took her hands in his. 'Emma and I split up on New Year's Day. I never told you because we all got swept away by Jim's death. After that, you never bothered to ask, so I didn't bother to tell you because I thought you didn't care.' He paused and started to stroke the side of her face. 'Jo, I was very fond of your father, but I came to the hospital because of you. I came to the funeral because of you too. It was hell for me to see you so miserable and not be able to openly touch and comfort you.'

He paused, but Jo was incapable of answering. A tight

427

knot had paralysed her throat and tears of relief had started to run down her face.

'And why the bloody hell do you think I'm here today?' he said, brushing them away.

'To cook me lunch,' she sobbed, half laughing, half crying.

'Yeah, right. I came because Tim told me about your conversations with Jeff and Martin, and said you were going to be on your own today. I was convinced you were going to go back to Jeff, so when I heard you hadn't, I dared to hope there might be a chance for you and me. I had to find out, once and for all. *That's* why I came.

'Ever since I first told you my feelings and you knocked me back, I have still felt the same but tried to bury it. I dated Emma, but I couldn't get you out of my mind. In the end, I felt it wasn't fair on her and ended it.'

'So is that a yes then?' she smiled, dabbing her eyes with the sleeve of her cardigan. 'Do you truly want to get involved with a woman as idiotic, short-sighted and baggage-laden as me?'

Lowering his hand from her face, he started to slowly unbutton her shirt. 'I'll think about it,' he said. As it fell from her shoulders and exposed her bra-less nipples standing to attention, he let out another slow, heavy sigh. 'I've thought about it, and the answer's yes.'

Standing up, he yanked his T-shirt over his head to reveal the taut, hairy chest that had mesmerised her during their first, all too brief encounter. With one swipe of his forearm he sent the fruit bowl and various books and news-papers clattering to the floor in a messy heap.

Pulling Jo to her feet and grabbing her hips, he lifted her onto the kitchen table and leaned forward to kiss her, slowly and tenderly at first, becoming more urgent within seconds.

'I'm really sorry, but this is going to be a quickie,' he murmured, pushing her back onto the table and running his hand up her skirt. 'I've waited so bloody long for you I don't think I'll be able to control myself.'

'Ooh, very *Postman Always Rings Twice*,' she giggled, pulling him on top of her.

Three minutes later, they lay on the floor in an exhausted heap, side by side, so closely entwined she could feel his hot breath on her face.

'Conor?'

'Uh-huh?'

'I love you.'

'I love you too, Jo.'

'It's funny, but do you know what made me realise it?'

'What?' He carried on idly caressing her breast.

'The oven.'

He turned to face her. 'You're certifiable, do you know that?'

'I know it sounds daft, but I was sitting here last night, just thinking about everything, and I suddenly remem-bered the day you came round with Tim, just after Jeff had walked out. Do you remember?'

'Yep. I wanted to give you a big cuddle then too.'

'Well, you leaned against the oven, and when Tim was wittering on about how every man would sleep with a twenty-three-year-old if he thought he could get away with it, you said you wouldn't.'

'Did I?' He raised his eyebrows in mock surprise. 'It must have been a tactic to make you like me.'

She gave him a playful punch. 'Very funny. Seriously though, that has always stuck in my mind. Trust is important to me, particularly now.'

'Well, you got it. I'm not going anywhere. I love you, and to show you how much, I'm going to take you upstairs and make love to you properly. Then we'll have that bath of yours.'

'Ooh, a sequel. *The Architect Always Shags Twice*,' she laughed, gathering her clothes and letting him lead her by the hand upstairs.

38

One year later

Jo scooped Sophie into her arms and planted a wet kiss on the side of her peachy, blemish-free face.

'Darling, you look absolutely edible,' she said, glowing with pride. 'A real princess.'

Sophie was wearing a peach taffeta bridesmaid's dress with matching shoes and a garland of cream roses in her hair. Because it was such a special day, she'd been allowed to wear a tiny bit of mascara that accentuated her huge blue eyes.

'And here is the prince!' exclaimed Jo, as Thomas walked into the room in full pageboy outfit. His hair was slicked into a side parting and he was scowling.

'Grandma has made me look a right arse,' he grumbled, ruffling his hair back into his favoured unkempt style.

'Thomas! Watch your language,' chided Jo. 'Best behaviour for the wedding please.'

The living-room door flung open and Pam blustered into the room wearing a cerise wool suit with a vast, circular hat that looked like it had made a forced landing on her head.

'Can you get Channel Five on that?' quipped Jo, but her mother wasn't listening. She had positioned herself in front of the mantelpiece mirror and was trying to fix her brooch so it didn't make her lapel droop.

'Come on, you two, the car's outside. We don't want to be late.' She turned round to look at Thomas and Sophie. 'You look utterly gorgeous, my darlings.'

Jo stood on the doorstep and waved them off, then turned back into the house to put the finishing touches to her own outfit for the big day.

'I now pronounce you man and wife.'

Jo looked at Thomas and Sophie and beamed with maternal pride. They looked like two angels standing there, and neither had put a foot wrong throughout the entire ceremony.

As the bride and groom walked back down the aisle to be showered with rose petals, the guests fell in behind and followed them outside the tiny village church in the heart of Oxfordshire.

It was a crisp winter's day, and everyone stood around stamping their feet, trying to keep warm while the photographer decided who he wanted first. Jo took the opportunity to whisper in Conor's ear.

'Weren't the children fantastic? Thomas looked so handsome in his pageboy outfit,' she smiled, affectionately linking her arm through his. 'I'm so proud.'

'So you should be. They're great kids.' He waved at Pam

who started walking towards them across the picturesque churchyard.

'That was such a beautiful ceremony,' she said, dabbing an eye and smudging her Paint By Numbers make-up. 'She looks stunning.'

'She does indeed,' said Jo, smiling across to where Rosie and Jim were posing for the photographer. 'I can't believe it, Rosie finally married. She always thought hell would freeze over before it would happen.'

Conor gave Jo a swift peck on the cheek and wandered off with Pam across the churchyard, where a crowd of guests stood chatting.

Jo stood alone for a few moments, and was just about to join them when she felt a small squeeze on her arm. It was Jeff.

'That was you and me thirteen years ago,' he said, nodding towards the bride and groom. 'Except that you married an arsehole.'

Jo raised her eyes heavenward and tweaked his cheek. 'Don't be so hard on yourself. It all turned out OK in the end. Come on.'

She placed her hand in the small of his back and steered him over to where Conor was deep in conversation with an attractive brunette woman in her early thirties.

'Ah, I see you two have finally met,' said Jeff, giving the woman a swift peck on the cheek and shaking Conor's hand.

'Yes,' said Conor with a swift smile. 'Angela was just telling me how she beat the pants off you in court last week.'

Jeff frowned, but there was a twinkle in his eye. 'Bloody women. All they have to do is bat their eyelids at the magistrate and they win every case.'

'I think you'll find it was because my summing up was better than yours, and that my client made a far more reliable witness,' said Angela, poking her tongue out at him.

Jo laughed, turning her face from one to the other as if at a tennis tournament. 'Well all I can say is, it's nice to see he's finally met his match,' she said, smiling at Angela. 'He used to drive me mad with his "I put it to you" attitude in arguments.'

Conor stepped forward and casually threw his arm round Jo's shoulders. 'Whereas you and I haven't shared a cross word in a whole year,' he said with a grin.

'Yeah right,' drawled Jo sarcastically. 'And Dolly Parton sleeps on her front.'

The four of them stood there silently for a moment, staring across to where Rosie was posing with Thomas and Sophie who were being uncharacteristically well-behaved. Pam had clearly re-combed Thomas's hair, and this time he'd left it as it was. When the photographer had finished, Rosie scooped up her train, planted a swift kiss on Jim's rosy cheek, and walked over to them with the children in hot pursuit.

'I have to say these two have been absolutely fantastic,' she said, patting their heads. 'Now it's time to go and get drunk!'

Jo took hold of her arm and walked her away from

the group to a quiet corner of the churchyard. 'You look so beautiful. I'm so happy for you,' she said, tears welling in her eyes. She enveloped her in a hug and the two old friends stood there for a few moments just clinging to each other.

'Thanks honey,' sniffed Rosie, dabbing her eye with a lace glove. 'Who'd have thought it, eh? Me married.'

'I would,' said Jo with a warm smile. 'I'm just surprised someone didn't snap you up earlier.'

Rosie gave the thumbs-up to the photographer who was gesturing for her to return. 'I'm going to lob the bouquet in a minute,' she said. 'Shall I make sure it comes in your direction? You know, give Conor a big hint.'

'He doesn't need one.' Jo rummaged in her handbag for her camera. 'He's already talked about us getting married. I'm the reticent one because I've been there, done that, got the divorce.'

'You shouldn't let that put you off. You've got a real gem there, and I've always said it.' Rosie looked across to where Conor was laughing at something Jeff was saying.

'I know. I still can't get over how amazing he is, not just with me but the children also. And to think I spent so long farting about with Sean when I could have been with Conor right from the start.'

'True, but maybe the timing wasn't right then. Maybe you had to experience yet another frog before you realised the handsome prince was the one for you,' said Rosie, blowing a kiss to Jim who was walking towards them.

'Come on, wifey,' he said with a grin. 'You're wanted for some more photographs.' He took her by the hand and led her away.

Jo suddenly wanted a couple of minutes alone, and wandered off down the side of the church to stroll through the small cemetery at the rear. She stopped in front of a tiny gravestone, inscribed with the words, 'Gemma Price, aged three, taken early from this world but never forgotten. All our love, Mummy and Daddy.'

That puts any problems I've had into sharp perspective, she thought. Again, she felt tears welling. She was uncommonly weepy today, but weddings always made her feel like that. She noticed a small, wooden bench bathed in watery sunshine against the rear church wall. Smoothing her dress beneath her, she sat down and stared up at the trees, transfixed by the dappled light through the leaves.

It struck her that she was truly happy; a state of mind that had eluded her for years, possibly even before the break-up with Jeff. The children seemed happy and settled, they had a better relationship with their father than when he was still living at home, and they seemed to have taken a shine to his new girlfriend, Angela. And as for Conor, they totally adored him, as they always had done. He played rough and tumble with Thomas, as well as endless games of football, and he was forever tickling Sophie and playing Ken to her Barbie.

Once she'd made the decision it was to be Conor, Jo saw little point in spending months hiding it from the children.

She had taken so long to wake up to their compatibility, that she just *knew* everything would be alright. When they'd sat the children down to tell them, they had wrinkled their noses and tittered.

'Does that mean you're going to kiss?' said Sophie, pulling a face.

Conor had leaned over and planted a smacker on Jo's lips, and the children had dissolved into peals of embarrassed laughter.

Smiling now at the memory, Jo was stirred from her thoughts by the sound of crunching from the gravel path.

'Ah, here you are. I wondered where you'd got to. You OK?' Conor sat down next to her on the bench and held her hand.

'Fine, thanks. Just having a quiet moment.'

'Shall I leave you alone?'

'No, I like having you around. That's what I love about you, I can have quiet moments even when you're with me.'

They lapsed into silence and, for several minutes, just sat there lost in their separate thoughts.

'Jo?'

'Yes?' Somehow, she knew what was coming.

He carried on looking straight ahead. 'I know you're wary and everything, and I can understand that. But I'm not Jeff and—'

'Yes, Conor. I will.'

'Will what?'

'Marry you.'

'But I was only going to ask if you'd mind me watching *Match of the Day* at your place tonight.'

Momentarily thrown, she turned to look at him. He was grinning from ear to ear. 'Only joking.'

'You shit!' As she gave him a playful punch on the arm, he grabbed her hand.

'So, is that a proper "yes" then?'

'What other kind of "yes" is there?'

'Well, there's the "yes", but I might change my mind in the morning. There's the "yes", but the next time we have a row it's all off. Or there's the "yes", and I mean it enough to go and tell the kids right now.'

She leapt up. 'Race you!'

ALSO AVAILABLE IN ARROW

The Ex-Files
Jane Moore

Take one wedding, add several exes, and stir . . .

Fay Parker is beautiful, successful – and worried she'll never
find her perfect match. So when she meets a caring, good-
looking man who adores her, she casts aside any niggling
doubts and accepts his proposal. In a bid to be modern and
grown-up, the bride and groom invite a potentially explosive
mix of ex-boyfriends and girlfriends and Fay is determined to
enjoy her special day. But there's one person present who
has other ideas . . .

'A witty study of modern manners . . . cracking yarn, told
with pace and humour' *Sunday Express*

'Moore's take on relationships is contemporary and
complex . . . full of blistering one-liners' *Glamour*

'A witty, provocative tale about modern relationships' *OK!*

'A brilliant bridal bun-fight' *heat*

arrow books